5/02

DATE DUE		MAR 03
MAY 16 03		
9-2-03		
9.11.03		
OCT 27 03		
JAN		
AUG 09 03		
GAYLORD		PRINTED IN U.S.A.

THE HOLY BOOK
OF THE BEARD

BY DUFF BRENNA

Waking in Wisconsin (Poems)
The Book of Mamie
The Holy Book of the Beard

NAN A. TALESE
Doubleday
New York London Toronto Sydney Auckland

THE HOLY BOOK
OF THE BEARD

DUFF BRENNA

PUBLISHED BY NAN A. TALESE
an imprint of Doubleday
a division of Bantam Doubleday Dell Publishing Group, Inc.
1540 Broadway, New York, New York 10036

DOUBLEDAY is a trademark of Doubleday, a division of
Bantam Doubleday Dell Publishing Group, Inc.

Book design by Gretchen Achilles

Library of Congress Cataloging-in-Publication Data
Brenna, Duff.
The holy book of the beard / Duff Brenna. — 1st ed.
p.   cm.
I. Title.
PS3552.R377H65   1996
813'.54—dc20   95-35516
CIP

ISBN 0-385-47962-X
Printed in the United States of America
March 1996
First Edition

1   3   5   7   9   10   8   6   4   2

FOR CHRISTINE AND FOR DEAN
OUT OF THE WHIRLWIND WITH INFINITE LOVE

The author wishes to express his appreciation to the National Endowment for the Arts for their generous support, and to Nan A. Talese and Jesse Cohen for believing in *Beard*. And a special, heartfelt expression of gratitude to my agent, Sandra Dijkstra, who said it would be, and it was.

Therefore I have uttered what I did not understand,
things too wonderful for me,
which I did not know.

—JOB 42:3

1.   IN OUR OWN IMAGE

◉   ✚   ♡

This is no wing for an unripe wit. If these feathers flutter too swiftly for you, put this page away, readeth thou Sports or Obits, or the gluttony of Heloise, Section E, p. 5. To such-a-one who lingers over these antique sounds, I offer clydesdales of affection, truth, honor, and courtesy. Answer soon, dear heart. Be virtuous of mind, no more than forty, no fatter than fat, no uglier than doves mourning. To you, dreamed-of love, I pledge my troth. I am SWM, 42, fading knight-errant of Lancelot gentilesse; I am a medieval scholar questing for one last bout of Courtly Love. Write Wolfram, in care of Adam and Eve Possibilities.

Jasper John reads the first ad on the board, smiles his appreciation. Better than usual, this one, this knight-errant. Classy stuff *Lancelot gentilesse*. Fat Stanley could take a lesson there. Girls see knights in shining armor, white horses, rescue. Fat Stanley could call himself Perceval—Perceval the Pure. Or better yet—Quixote. Hi-ho, Rocinante!

"Jasper! Ho, boy, over here." The fat man beckons with his finger. Beside him is a woman in white blouse and blue skirt. Apron over abdomen. Jasper is introduced to her. "This is Mary Quick. She's going to work for us now," says Fat Stanley.

Tired aging eyes, Irish setter eyes. She extends a hand, holds on to Jasper just a second too long for comfort. "Nice to meet you," she says, her voice deep, almost baritone. She's looking at him as if she knows him.

Jasper wanted Fat Stanley to hire a younger waitress this time. One that would wear a miniskirt, chew gum, joke, flirt, liven the place a little. All Fat Stanley ever hires are women over forty. The last one was sixty-six, a real hustler, steady as could be. But she dropped dead in the middle of prime time. Place full of diners. They were so upset, Fat Stanley had to close down for the night.

Helga comes by and gives Jasper's bum a spank. "That table's ready for your expertise," she says, pointing. She goes off mumbling about her feet. Her feet hurt her. Everything hurts her. Helga has had organs removed. She has had radiation treatments. Her remaining organs get biweekly doses of chemotherapy. She is dying of cancer. It really pisses her off. She's got three kids and no husband. She holds down two jobs, works mornings at the pancake house, then comes to Fat Stanley's from noon till nine. Her feet swell while the rest of her withers. She has chronic cystitis and lives on Pyridium. She eats blender food, whizzed vegies with protein powder, soft white bread with Butter Bud sprinkles. On her biceps is a fading tattoo that says PROPERTY OF MIKE. She uses the f-word a lot. "Fuck, fuck, fuck," she says, banging through the double doors, into the kitchen. "Fuck, fuck, fuck," she says, coming back with drinks on a tray. A medicinal smell trails behind her like an old scarf.

Mary Quick is older and rounder than Helga, who is all angles, very geometric, very theorem. Mary Quick has big hips swishing inside a hugging skirt. Heavy braless breasts list port and starboard and leave a hollow of freckled skin in the middle down which a silver chain and a bloated cross hang. The cross is Celtic, with the circle of eternity connecting its hub. It laps the border of her blouse. Her best feature is her hair, thickly Nordic blond, pulled back into a single braid that is knotted Swedish style, like a bull's-eye on the back of her head.

She smells of lavender powder puff and cigarettes. Jasper thinks he likes her. He sees a certain sexiness in shy smiles, moist hands clinging a second too long, breasts leaning against white fabric, nipples nudging, hips full of capacity. Marilyn Monroe was like that, a real woman once upon a time. His love-flame Didi Godunov has that same capacious Monroe body, but not so luscious a mouth. An image of Didi Godunov with bouncy blond hair, pouty lips, and blue polka-dot dress flashes before his eyes, an icon, an Andy Warhol silk screen.

Didi yum, thinks Jasper, still looking at Mary.

"Dishes," says Fat Stanley, pointing toward an unbussed table.

Fat Stanley starts thumbing steaks again, his large left buttock perched on a stool in front of the flaming grill as he monitors a pair of sizzling T-bones and hums a tune from some opera. Occasionally he breaks into song, something Italian, high tenor and awful good. His voice fills the air, arrests the heart for a moment, surrounds them all with a sense of suspension. It has the brown color of a deeper voice at first, then it rises an octave. It keeps rising. Pure as a celestial sphere, his heavenly voice rises, like a flute or a piccolo soaring, until it picks off a high C as if the note itself is a plum at the top of a tree. Then the voice dives down to earth again, settles back humming.

On slow nights Fat Stanley comes out of the kitchen and plays the role of the strolling troubadour, pausing at tables to sing. He is sure he is a hit. He knows his patrons come back again and again just to hear him sing. They want to be entertained. They want to feel special. They want to go home and tell their friends of the tenor chef who sings to them at their table. Pavarotti in a stained apron. The man should be on the stage, or at least he should be recording his voice for posterity. Fat Stanley agrees with their assessment of him. He knows that with a voice like his more should have happened.

Jasper folds his apron and ties it around his waist. He stops by the board again to read the second and third clippings his boss has tacked to the cork. Fat Stanley has been searching for love ever since he came to America as a little boy, a refugee of the war, sent to live with an uncle in New York. He is fifty now (though he tells everyone he is forty-five) and dying for love. He has been putting ads in the lonely hearts column of the *Union* for months: "Bearded Spherical Chef, 45, SWM with Renaissance mind and civilised British background. Opera buff. Golden-throated tenor. Capacity to love deeply. Seeking female for relationship with intent toward commitment."

Woman after woman has answered the Stanley ad, but he has had no luck except with prostitutes who write for a date, do yummy things to him, then charge him a hundred bucks and try to add him to their stable of regulars. To his constant remorse he goes back to them. Whores and personals have become a way of life. He reads the other lovelorn articles every day, and under the heading EEEK!! he pins his favorites to the board.

SWM, 39, one-legged warrior of V-War, purple heart, bronze star with cluster, combat badge, parachute badge, expert rifleman badge, wishes to have searching partnership with wife-minded, nurse-type. Moral Majority background a plus. Be ready to wrap yourself in stars and stripes. Write RA, c/o Adam and Eve Possibilities. No gooks, spiks, or spades need apply.

"Verdict," says Fat Stanley.

"Asshole," says Jasper.

"Did you read them all?"

"Just a sec."

Open-minded SWM, 32, and too much. You won't believe what you're getting. Picture Adonis with shoulder-length hair and witty smile, packerman arms, washboard waist, thighs like oak beams. I work out! I want girl of dreams, 18–25, petite Californian blond. Good teeth a must! Be nubile. I drive a yellow Porsche. Write Spider, c/o Adam and Eve Possibilities. No big feet, no big honkers, no porkers.

"He'll get laid," says Jasper.

"Think so?" says Fat Stanley.

"Oak thighs? Porsche! Oh yeah. Girls go for that."

"Not the good ones."

Jasper shrugs. He heads for the table Helga pointed to, starts sweeping the dishes into a tray. Whistling, hands working deftly, expert busboy fingers doing their thing, he looks up to see a man in black open the door and lumber bowlegged toward the counter. Mary Quick is behind the counter, pad in hand, taking an order from a bearded man in a rumpled white suit. The bowlegged man in black lurches toward Mary, reaches across the counter. Rips her blouse open. Buttons fly like missiles, plink! pe-tew!

"Jesus, son of a—" she says.

She drops the order pad. She wallops the guy with a left hook, followed by a right cross. He steps back blinking. The man in the white suit scurries from harm's way. Mary comes across the counter like a hurdler, her arms in continuous motion, her breasts bubbling over the edges of the torn blouse and into light, nipples jiggling like hot eggs in a pan. Jasper sees brown yolks. A raspberry on top.

"Henry!" she yells. "Henry, you—" she yells.

She pummels him. Her blouse gaps wider. Her breasts are saucy twin devils tempting Jasper to iniquity.

Fat Stanley waddles through the double doors, his monstrous arms pumping. He booms his belly into the *Henry you,* knocking him backwards, causing him to whirl like a novice on roller skates.

"Whoa!" he says. "Hey!"

While Jasper opens the door, Fat Stanley gives the *Henry you* two more staggering belly blows. Sends him reeling outside, onto the sidewalk.

"Flamin legs, fellas!" says the *Henry you.* "Flamin legs!"

He falls. He rolls over on his back, spreads his arms, palms warding off their wrath. "Ease off, boys," he says. "Don't kill the Hank. It was on accident, fellas, I swear by Mama Kabonga's whim-whams!"

"You want bedlam, I'll give you bedlam," Fat Stanley says. He puts his fist right to the man's nose.

"A very unpromisin beginnin," says the man. "I spose this means youz won't gimme a job?"

Fat Stanley's eyes widen. "A job? A job? You hear this blighter, Jasper John?"

The man grins gums and a tooth at Fat Stanley. "Easy now, easy there, boss. The Hank ain't lookin for trouble today. The Hank has a snootful and needs no trouble today. Look here, boss, she knows me. Mary knows her *man.* Tell em, baby. Hey, who loves you, who loves his Punkin?"

5.

Mary stands on the step, one hand gathering the edges of her blouse. She is breathing heavily. She is making little grimaces with her eyes and mouth. "He's drunk," she says, pointing. "This's Henry Hank, fellas. He and me . . . we live together."

"Oh," says Fat Stanley.

She tells Henry Hank he shouldn't come around making scenes during working hours. What's the matter with him, does he want to get her fired?

"I wanna a job too," he bawls.

"You don't want no job, you liar," she says. "Henry Hank with a job —that'll be the day!"

"Awww."

Inside a frame of black hair and a Lincoln beard, Henry Hank has an old face, a face full of lines, deep creases on the brow and around the eyes. His nose is monumentally pitted. One stained tooth thrusts itself over his upper lip. Black sweat trickles down behind his ears and down his neck. His hair and beard look painted on, as if he has soaked them in shoe polish. The sun beats on his head, making it shine like steaming tar.

Mary looks at him with sadness, her eyes drooping like dog eyes, an old Irish setter weary of the chase.

"Some days you tick me off," she tells him. "When are you gonna grow up, Henry? All this endless *stuff,* it's gotta go. We're too damn old, Henry. Too old."

"Awww, Pun*king.*"

Jasper sees a tear dribble from her eye. He slides closer to comfort her. He sucks deep her lavender. He pats her between the shoulder blades, a light, sympathetic gesture that brings a wan smile to her mouth as she glances at him. His eyes keep watch on the freckled, blue-veined bubble of breast peeking out. "Poor Mary," he says, rubbing around her back. Her blouse in back is damp with sweat.

"This is nothing," she tells him. "I seen some things in my day." She rubs her left arm like it is sore.

Henry Hank has rolled forward and risen on his knees. He bows down and kisses Mary's foot, then looks at her. "Forgiven?" he asks, grinning.

"Nut," she replies.

"I need just a little somethin, Punkin. A couple bucks, ten, fifteen. Look here, I'm sweatin like a hairy hawg, Punkin. I'm gettin sunstroked." He looks left, toward the bar across the street. The sign says TEXAS STYLE. "C'mon, gimme your tips, Punkin. I need a foam of beer, mmmwah."

"I haven't gotten any tips yet," she says.

"What? Geez, Punkin, geez. Not a tip one? Flamin legs, Punkin, youz got to be nice to the customers. Am I right there, boss?"

Fat Stanley is calmer. He looks at the man and smiles slightly, a little upper-lip quiver of his mustache. "How long you known him?" he asks Mary.

"Too damn long. I'm sorry about this, Mr. Lipton."

Fat Stanley waves his hand. He takes proud breaths. At his feet Henry Hank sits up, elbows on his knees. He runs his hand through his hair and comes away with black palms, which he wipes on his black trousers. He's wearing cowboy boots with chrome toes.

"I don't mean to bust her blouse," he says, his voice whining at them like he's the victim, the one abused here. "My hand slipped, is all. I mean to give her a kiss, that's all, to pull her up. And then my hand slipped and the buddons go all-flyin. She knows I would'na harm a flea on her head. This is the Hank, ain't it, Punkin? If she lived on Nob Hill, I'd kiss the ground she walks on. That's how I feel about her. Tell the fellas, baby. Who loves his Pun*king?*"

"Go sleep it off," says Fat Stanley. He cracks his knuckles and goes back into the diner, whistling.

A bus goes by, gears clanking, exhaust spraying diesel fumes into the air. Leaning out a window is a greasy-haired punk wearing a baseball cap backwards. "Fuck her, daddy! I did!" he yells. He flips the bone and laughs.

"Ah, the mating call of the sapsucker," says Henry. "Stay out of my garden, youz little fucker!" he shouts at the diminishing, grinning head.

Mary says she is going in and she doesn't want to see Henry's face till quitting time. Her tone of voice is low and whiskey bitter. She nudges him with her toe. Henry salutes her. His eyebrows wiggle like ticklish caterpillars. To Jasper he says, "When the fem kicks youz, it means she's not indifferent. Remember that, kiddy."

"Yessir," says Jasper.

Henry's bottom tooth spars with invisible atoms. "Pee-lite boy."

"Are you going?" Mary asks.

"I'm goin, I'm goin," he answers. "I'll juss crawl into a Dempsey Dumpster and die." He pouts. He holds a stained palm out like a homeless beggar. "Juss two bucks, hey, Punkin? Juss a buck. Fifty cents. Have moicy!"

Her eyes narrow. She puts on a pinched mouth, a slow sick-of-it-all squint, then goes inside.

Mary retreats to the counter, where Helga holds a pair of safety pins. "Lousy skunk," she says as she pins Mary's blouse together. Mary says Henry is basically okay, just too rambunctious, far too much energy for someone his age. "He's fifty-eight, believe it or not," she says.

Helga chuckles. "My Mike used to have gumption like that," she says. "I know his type, oh yeah, them wild ones." She flexes her PROPERTY OF MIKE biceps. "We're shmucks for the wild ones, broads like us."

Behind them, perched on his stool, is the man in the white suit. "Searching for truth in a bottle," says the man, gesturing with his thumb toward the bay window, through which they can see Henry talking to Jasper. "But who can blame a man these days? It's a wonder we don't all go around drunk as dopers."

"Personal experience, Professor?" says Helga.

"You know me."

"Yeah, unfortunately I do."

The man has a patriarchal white beard, stooped shoulders, eyes big as quarters, a forehead rippling with troubles. Pink scalp shows through strands of hair plastered to his head. "Did he hurt you?" he asks Mary. "I notice you rubbing your arm."

"It's nothing," she says.

The professor nods. Mary notices his nose slopes slightly to one side and is semiflattened like a fighter's. "You don't want to hear this," he says, "but you women drive us crazy, yes you do. Take me, for instance. I almost got married once. I thought about it. But she could only speak in trimeters. She'd open her mouth and trimeters would come out, layers of them, one on the other. I couldn't take it. I told myself, Just think of living with a woman speaking trimeters. Agh! The more I thought, the grayer my hair got." He points to his hair, takes a strand, plucks it out, holds it to the light. It dangles from his fingers like toy lightning. "This is the fallout from trimeters," he says. His face pinches up and he snickers.

"Never been married?" says Mary.

"Love the one you're with," he tells her. "I'm Godot." He holds his hand out and they shake. Mary feels large, dry fingers full of strength. "I'm Fat Stanley's resident pundit. You got a question, you ask me."

"I got a question," says Helga.

"Not you—her." Godot points to Mary.

Helga ignores him. "I see two rows of Godots. I see fifty professors talking face to face. Now, what am I looking at?"

"Infinite wisdom," answers Godot.

"A wind tunnel," says Helga.

The pickup bell rings. Helga and Mary head toward the sound, their heads together. "He hates women," says Helga. "All he wants is you know what. Stay away from him."

"He's got an interesting face," says Mary. "Those big eyes."

"Old devil. Don't let him fool you, honey." She holds on to Mary's arm, looks left and right, then whispers. "He's got one *this long*, I swear to God on a stack of Bibles." Helga's hands measure off twelve, thirteen inches. Mary giggles. She wonders how Helga knows the size of Godot's penis, but she doesn't ask.

"Hmmmm," she hums, scanning Godot.

Helga winks. The bell rings again. They can hear Fat Stanley yelling from the back. "Hey," he says, "is this a holiday?"

9.

On the sidewalk Henry reaches out a hand and Jasper helps him to his feet. Henry scratches behind his neck, messing with the leaking shoe polish. "Hot day," he says. "Whew, whew, is this town always so hot in May? Me be sweatin like a hawg." His voice has a gargling-with-gravel roll that Jasper enjoys listening to.

"East winds off the desert," says Jasper, explaining the heat. "They usually come in late summer or fall. Usually this time a year, it's cloudy."

Henry puts his arm around Jasper buddy-buddy. "Gimme twenty, I'll turn it into a fortune, guaranteed definitely."

"How so?"

Henry rubs his fingers. "I got the touch. I'm very good with cards, a real chili pepper. These fingers is hot, kiddy." He wiggles tie-dyed fingers in Jasper's face. "Point me to the underground," he adds.

"Market Street. Market and Tenth," says Jasper. "On the corner is a hardware store. Tell them Arthur MacArthur sent you."

"No shit?"

"Vegas on the coast, they call it. Ask Arthur, the bartender." Jasper points across the street, toward Texas Style.

"Arthur knows?" says Henry. "My boy Arthur?"

"Uh-huh."

Henry gives Jasper a wet kiss on the cheek. "Things is lookin up. Lissen here, kiddy, youz should know me better. I'm one hell of a man, ask Punkin if I ain't. The Hank has done it all." He holds Jasper in a grip and talks fast. "Once upon a time I was a bad motherfucker—*bad* motherfucker, I'm sayin. I had a stable of fems pullin in ten K a week, no lie, hope to catch the clap if I'm lyin. I was a high roller oncet. They give me comp in Reno, comp in Vegas. 'Here's the man,' they'd say. Oh yeah. They'd say, 'Here comes the Hank! Roll out the red carpet!' You believe me, kiddy?"

"Yessir."

"I still do all right with the fems, though. Charisma, I got charisma.

Look here, I been everywhere, did I tell youz that? Done everythin. Been a longshoreman in New York. Been a trucker in Tennessee. Less than legal age, I sucked my first pussy in a barn in Kansas, a wheat farmer's wife, he never done it for her. She followed me around like a damn puppy after. You find me a man doesn't munch his lady's pussy, I'll show you a woman I can steal. Munchin poon has been a forty-year habit. It's why my voice sounds like a toilet." He probes Jasper's chest with a blackened finger. "Hope to catch the clap if I'm lyin. I been a prize fighter, went the distance with the great Floyd Patterson back in 1960. You think I'm lyin? It's in the record, look it up. It's from Floyd I learned my peekaboo style. And look here, I been a lumberjack, a thief, a lovable scamp, an urban mystery, a hero in the Korean War. I got a chestful of medals. Youz believe me?"

"Sure."

"It's the God's truth. I blew up bridges in the war. I cracked safes after, did two hundred jobs till I got caught. I took an amateur fool with me, that's why. He had bad nerves, blew himself up and blew a wall out of the building we was in and damn near kilt me. See this notched ear here? Yep, never fuck with amateurs, kiddy, they'll kill you. But I still got the touch." He holds out blackened hands again. "Look how steady. Like a brain surgeon."

Henry looks around, makes a smacking sound with his lips. "Sure thirsty," he says. He pulls at the end of his nose, leaving a streak of commando camouflage behind. "Youz twenty-one yit?" he asks.

"Twenty-three," says Jasper.

"Lucky fuck. Twenty-three and free as a falcon's fart. Man, what I wouldn't give to be that. Say, look here, let's go have a beer and talk some. I like youz, c'mon."

Jasper says he has to work, he has to get back inside.

Henry frowns at the diner. "What time is it?"

"Four-thirty."

"Four fuckin thirty. Whoops! There goes nother second into the eternal zero." Henry's hands flick at the air all around as if he's trying

11.

to catch flies. "Nother, nother, nother," he says. "Can't hold em back, can't catch Now for nothin. Look there, kiddy, tick, tick, tick, Now is flyin by. Sure youz don't want to have a beer with the Hank?"

"Can't."

"Tick, tick, tick." The hands fly, the fingers grasp.

Across the street, a woman runs out of Texas Style and toward a parked car. A man in a Stetson follows her. "Hey, baby, hey, baby, just kidding, baby," says the man.

"I'm no cunt!" she yells.

"Hey, baby, you know me, baby, all mouth."

"That's the trouble!" she says. She gets in the car, starts the engine roaring, drives off in a whir of rubber. The man yells after her, "Stankfinger! That's all I said is stankfinger! What the goddamn hell's wrong with that? Who was to know in the goddamn booth back there anyway? All dark and everything, we coulda. Selfish bitch." The man holds his middle finger up, looks at it, sniffs it. He turns around, looks at two derelicts leaning on a rusty Ford. "What the hell's the problem?" he says to them.

"Got any loose change, man?" says one.

"Vietnam vets," says the other.

"Fuck you," says the man in the Stetson. He goes back inside.

Stankfinger! Yeah, stinkfinger. Jasper knows stinkfinger, she was sixteen, seventeen, thigh drooping open, letting his hand rise. Molly, sister of his buddy Art Trout. Sweet and gooey. Eyes like star sapphires. First time. So special, so special.

Henry is cackling. "Wisdom of the street," he tells Jasper. "Keep that in mind when they got youz confused, kiddy."

"I was born confused," says Jasper.

"I bet you're a *ambitious* young man, pride of the future."

"Not at all."

"I bet youz want to be a doctor or a lawyer."

"Can't stand that stuff."

"Me neither."

"I take classes out at State."

"No shit? A college boy, huh?" Henry smacks his lips. "Youz hear that, kiddy?"

"What?"

"Nother second of dust on a dry throat, skittern into the eeeternal zeeero." He clicks his fingers. "Gone, gone, gone. Youz understand my philosophics? I'm tellin youz, it goes fast. Look here, gimme a couple bucks, okay? Be kind to a vet. My ole wound is actin up. Oh me, oh my. Got shot twenty-two times on Pork Chop Hill. Don't be a noodle, son. I'll pay youz back."

Jasper finds a five and a twenty in his pocket. He offers the five to Henry. Henry snatches both bills. "Market and what?" he says.

"Tenth."

"Tenth. The hardware store. Arthur MacArthur's my friend."

Henry Hank heads across the street, dodging cars. He goes past the two beggars holding out their hands. He looks at the two bills, gives them the five, then hurries into Texas Style. Jasper hears the Western whine of a fiddle bleeding outward as the door opens. He watches the men examine the five-dollar bill as if they don't trust it, like it might be counterfeit, *his* five-dollar bill. He looks at his palm smeared with black from when he pulled Henry to his feet. He rubs his palm on his pants but the black won't come off. "Shit," he says. He sniffs the chronic odor of sewer decay that hangs in the air of east San Diego, and he wonders when somebody is going to come fix that smell. Rot every-where and nobody is doing nothing.

From inside the diner, he hears Fat Stanley yelling. "Jasper! Where the hell is that kid? Ho, boy, Jasper, the dishes!"

☉

At nine Helga says good night and heads to her car. Her feet are killing her. Everything is killing her. She gets in the car and sits a minute, thinks about having a cigarette, hears her doctor's voice warning her not to add insult to injury. A hollow place opens in the pit of her stomach. She remembers death. Sometimes she can go four, five, six hours not thinking about death. It's the nights that are bad, the nights and the quiet bring death back. During the day she stays busy, hustles tables, collects her tips, jokes with the customers, talks to Fat Stanley and Jasper and Mary, feels only the dull cramping of her feet, the ache in her back, the sore spot under her arm where they zap her with radiation once every other week at the clinic.

Blessed be the light, the day, the diner, and staying busy.

She runs her hand over her abdomen, traces the lips of the scar. The tumor was big as a golf ball. It's gone now, all gone, eggs—everything. Dried up, calcified, useless, semiwoman now.

She chokes on her own thoughts. She almost cries and it makes her mad. "Yeah, so what?" she says to her scooped womb. Reaching in the glove box, she grabs a pack of Marlboros. She lights one, sits back and lets the smoke work its magic. A minute passes and the nicotine starts stroking her nerves, putting them to bed.

"Gonna die anyway," she says. "So what the fuck? No guarantees. This goddamn chemotherapy shit could kill me tomorrow. People die from it. It kills their cancer and them too. Ah-hah! There's a joke for you, you little microbe cocksuckers, you fuckin cancer, fuck you . . . fuck you!" She shakes her fist at her belly, threatening to pulverize it for betraying her. After a moment, she opens her fist, rubs back and forth across her abdomen, soothing her colon.

So far so good with the chemo, hardly side effect one. A touch of nausea this morning. Some mild diarrhea. She's had worse, hell yes, lots worse. She hardens her PROPERTY OF MIKE bicep, gives it a feel. She starts the car, heads up Adams Avenue, past the bar, past the movie house called Narcissus, where they show artsy-fartsy films; she rolls past the video store, sees a man coming out, decides he's rented sleazy porno and is gonna beat off on his couch, visions of T and A humping through his head. She knows his type. She rolls past the yogurt shop, the dry cleaners, Great Western Bank, Century 21, Hair Today—all these places where people do their thing, all these places full of people waiting their turn to step up and get whacked just like her. A hundred years from now, not one, not one person she sees walking along the

14.

sidewalk will be alive. Dead, cold, and hard, just like Helga Martin—there is satisfaction in that. She cruises past the park with its thin trees and the dew glistening on the lawn, the playground, where shrieking children swing and teeter-totter and dare death on the monkey bars. Quiet now, the contraptions of play look like the unearthed bones of some extinct thing from the lizard-hissing past.

Driving by the French Gourmet Coffeehouse, she notices a lone man sitting at a table outside. He sips from a cup. His hair is thick. Youth is in his jaw. Makes her think of Mike and the motorcycle and being eighteen. Wild and free. Pure man. What fun. Drove to the Grand Canyon that time and saw grandeur in red, and the tiny ribbon of the Colorado far, far below. Slept in one sleeping bag under the stars, coyotes howling so lonely somewhere. And Mike's warm body there touching the length of hers. Oh, Mikey, Mikey. Memories—the last sweetnesses left. She looks up, half expecting to see him there, her Saint Mike, keeping cool watch from heaven.

She caresses her bicep, thumbs his name—MIKE. All that's left to touch is his sacred name. He was an organ donor and they couldn't even use his organs. She pictures the van pulling out, the motorcycle trying to stop, the skid, the crash. Never coming back—never never never never never. Three children gawking at Mommy screaming with the phone in her hand.

"Fuck, fuck, fuck," she mutters. She tells herself to shut up.

She turns the flow of her thoughts toward her kids, tells herself she's lucky to have them at least. But what will their fate be? The thought clings perversely, forcing her to picture it. Orphans. Official "experts" running their lives. Cogs in the bureaucratic wheel. But Nancy could take over, Nancy could be the mommy. Seventeen is old enough if you have to do it. She is a bitchy one, though, won't forgive her mama for all those men, all the booze and all the men after Mike died—men like Godot. That was a bad mistake. Him and that big thing and all the noise and the kids a wall away. How long would it have lasted had he not exposed himself to Nancy that night, him coming out of the john naked and she standing in the hall gawking, and what did he say? He asked her had she ever seen an agent of creation more beautiful? Poor child, she ran screaming.

Nancy is like Helga at the same age. Overwhelmed, but immortal. Wanting it all. Terrified of it all. Selfish. In denial. She wants a life first. She looks at her mother and says, "What if I die and never know what it is to live, Mama? What if? What if?" Now how does a half-dead woman answer a question like that? How does one comfort a daughter full of bitter memories and exploding hormones?

Helga maneuvers to the curb in front of the apartment. She cuts the motor and sits a moment, rubbing the tender spot under her arm, her mind tracing the course of black spots breaking loose from her womb, running riot through her bloodstream, nibbling here, nibbling there. "Fuck, fuck, fuck," she whispers. "Fuck you, you bastards. I'll win in the end. You watch and see! You watch and see, you pricks!"

She thinks about her kids again. She wonders how in the world they will get along without her. Nancy first, then Katherine, then Michael Junior. All of them literal pains in the ass, bone breakers, hemorrhoid makers, and that goddamn doctor saying she was a big baby and she could wait until she was six centimeters before the spinal block. That was when Michael Junior was on the launching pad. In a rush. Always in a hurry, that boy. Came too fast for the spinal block and all the doctor could do was cut, and she foaming at the mouth and cussing him beautifully, cussing him, using the f-word with the creativity of an artist. Ten pounds of kid followed after, ten pounds of kid squinching up his face and bellowing.

She sees him in her mind's eye now, her little Mikey grown up ten years later and playing flag football, throwing for a touchdown. The cheers that day for *her* son. Her *biggest* boy. "What an arm!" she heard some guy say. Pro material someday. There he is, Mike Martin! Yay! Then she remembers she won't be there to see him. Fuck, fuck, fuck! Hot tears spill from her eyes for the millionth time in the past year. There's no one to see, so she lets them go. She beats the steering wheel and sobs real good. From her purse she takes a hanky and blows her nose, wipes her eyes. She sits breathing, willing her composure to come back. Don't let them know, she tells herself. Last thing they need is for Mama to fall apart. Take your lumps and keep it to yourself.

She sighs big, calms down, thinks of pretty Nancy. Nancy is the hope. Grow up, Nancy. If she could meet a nice boy, someone steady and kind. Someone like . . . like Jasper, maybe? He's a nice boy. Such kind eyes. If he would just hurry up and graduate and get a job, they could make a family for Kathy and Mikey. Give them security.

Helga fantasizes a wedding. Jasper and Nancy down the aisle. It wouldn't be so bad to die if she knew her kids were going to be all right, that's the thing.

Jasper and Nancy. Work on it.

She gets out of the car, slams the door hard, walks to the terrace. Her stomach boils and she vomits. In a moment it is over and she has her breath back. "That's all I need," she says. "That and my goddamn hair falling out. Man, that's all I need." She starts a word-run full of fucks, then she stops. She examines the word and finds it doesn't punch the air like it used to. It blows from her mouth and breaks into fragments. "Fuck!" she says once more and watches it lose its potency, watches it fizzle into atoms.

✛

Ten o'clock and Jasper finishes steaming the dishes in the sterilizer. He goes to the big sink and starts scrubbing pans. On the other side of the wall he can hear Fat Stanley pumicing the grill and humming to himself. Mary Quick comes over. "You didn't give the Hank any money, did you, Jasper?" she says.

"No . . . well, yeah, a little."

"Don't give him no more."

"Okay," says Jasper. He runs the wire scrubber over and over a burnt grease stain. "The Hank's a funny guy," he says.

"If you only knew," she tells him.

After a minute she says, "It's hard to see now, but twenty years ago he was a knockout, a killer stud. Women couldn't keep their hands off

17.

him. He had, I don't know . . . magnetism. Is that the word I want? Women went for him like addicts go for heroin."

"Hard to believe," says Jasper. He is thinking of that one tooth sticking up, those red gums, the grooved face, the melting polish running down the Hank's neck.

"He didn't take care of himself," she says. "Let it be a lesson. I'll tell you something, though. Me and him, we were damn near millionaires once. Well, maybe not that rich, but we drove a Cadillac Coupe *Dee* Ville and ate at four-star restaurants. Get this, we had green satin sheets and pillows on our bed." She sighs. "We were something."

"So what happened?" asks Jasper.

"Happened what happens. You get on the wheel of fortune, it goes up, and one day it goes down and you fall off."

"Had some tough luck," says Jasper.

"It's always been ups and downs with us. I mean, we didn't think we'd live to get *this* old and have to worry about *retirement*. What the hell's that? We were supposed to die young. Ain't everybody? Fifty. I never thought I'd see fifty. It's ancient, and I've seen it, plus two. Henry and me were supposed to go out in a blaze of glory somewhere along the line. I think that's what he was thinking too, but who really knows what the Hank thinks? He's a ride on a roller coaster. Finally it was going down, down, down. I don't know. He had some girls working for him, a little stable of good ones, and he sold them to another pimp for a stake in a million-dollar poker game." She raises her hands in a gesture of helplessness. "Lost it in ten hours, the whole thing. Gone. Poof. If it wasn't for my savings, we couldn't have even got out of town. We'd had to rob somebody."

"His luck run out," says Jasper.

"That's the truth," says Mary. "But you know, I'm okay with it. In fact, I'm relieved. My life is much quieter now. I didn't know I was aching for quiet. I'm too old for that high-roller shit. Twenty-two years of it is enough for me."

She keeps staring at Jasper, making him feel peculiar. Her eyes always seem to be searching his face as if he's got answers written there. She has a bottle of beer in her hand and is sipping it through a straw. It occurs to Jasper that when a woman looks that way at a guy all the time, she is hoping he will make a move. But he doesn't know if he wants to. There is a lot of age in Mary's face. But then again, those were a pair of handsome handfuls he saw today. *Whim-whams* the Hank called them.

He puts the last pot on the drainboard. She sets her beer down and grabs a towel. She talks to him in her whiskey voice, a voice that lightly matches Henry's, the kind of voice Jasper has heard from women who smoke and drink too much and go to cowboy bars and laugh too loud and get melancholy at midnight, end up bawling about some rotten man what done her wrong. He checks out the two safety pins holding her blouse together, sees that kissable bubble of blue-veined skin in the shadow of her Celtic cross. She makes some moves with the towel, polishing the pot in her hand, and the bubble jiggles, and he is beginning to take a liberal view of her age. His ears get warm.

Stankfinger.

He assures himself that in dim light Mary will be pretty. He can see she was a fox in her day. A fifteen-, sixteen-year-old yum-yum, like stankfinger Molly Trout was.

He pulls the plug in the sink, watches the gray water whirl away, tells himself that Mary Quick is just another loose-goose, harebrained broad he can bop, but doesn't have to take seriously. Glancing at her again, he sees that question mark in her eyes. He knows she is thinking what he is thinking. She probably wants to do it right there, standing up, against the sink. His ears get warmer. His pants crowd him. He glances toward the back, toward the storeroom, where he could lock the door and it would be nice and quiet. Do it fast. Fat Stanley's in opera-land, his voice coming on louder and louder. He'll be belting one out in a minute, making believe he's on the stage. He would never know what the two of them were doing.

Mary wets her lips. She says, "My heavens, you're so young."

"Young?"

She says, "You remind me of someone I used to know. A boy." She stares toward the humming, rattling freezer. "Young and sweet like a rosebud."

"A boyfriend," says Jasper, keeping it friendly.

"No, someone else. A little boy who died."

"Bummer."

"He would have been tall like you, I think. Don't stoop," she tells him. "You'll get round-shouldered." She moves in real close and stares up at him. He is about to kiss her when she says, "It's your mouth mostly that's like him. That hanging upper lip. It's uncanny. It's just like his. Do you believe souls can migrate to other people?"

"What're we talking about?"

"Does the water ever talk to you?" she says. "Sometimes currents in the water seem to tell me things. It's like a sign. We're talking about J.J., Jimmy Jack Quick. He was ten. My son. He drowned."

Jasper backs away. "Geez," he says. "Ten?"

"Ten."

He wants to get away from her now. He doesn't like being compared to a dead kid.

Turning her back to him, she skirts the wall and hangs the pot on the overhead rack near the stove. Jasper gets the push broom and sweeps up. He thinks of little J.J. and hopes drowning is quick as people say it is. One big gulp and it's over. All those people in the Genesis flood, one big gulp. Bam! Like a sledgehammer in the chest, and a second of knowing you're done for, then you're done for. He has read a statistic about the flood. It said the rain had to fall thirty feet an hour for forty days before it could fill the earth to the tip of Mount Everest. Thirty feet an hour pouring on your head and forcing you under with the fishes, and the fishes see your eyes roll up, they dart in there and nibble you to molecules. Pass you through their guts and sprinkle the ocean floor with strings of human being and the waves wash you to shore, and you get punched into the earth, where a sprig springs up that is eaten by a goat and deposited upstream, from which a tree rises and is cut down and made into a pencil, with which a writer writes a book on prayers and . . . That poor bugger probably never even bopped a girl. Ten years old.

"It's like a spirit is trying to contact me," she says, "the electricity in the water. It almost stops my heart when it happens. Do you believe in life after death?" she says.

"Sure."

"Don't you think it would be terrible of Jesus not to raise a little boy from the dead? I think that would be terrible."

"Yeah, terrible, it would."

"Delicate matters, you know, the workings of the Lord's mind. Mysterious ways his wonders to unfold."

"That's what I've heard," he says.

"It's true, Jasper."

He sweeps fast and watches from the corner of his eye as she rubs absentmindedly at a spot over her heart. Suddenly she unties her apron, throws it in the laundry bin, scoots over and grabs her purse from under the counter.

"See you," she says.

She steps outside and heads across the street, haunch bones rolling, skirt fetching.

Leaning his chin on the broom handle, he takes her in. All woman, that, he tells himself. She is taking her braid loose, letting it fall over her shoulder. But maybe too peculiar? She pats her hair, tucks her blouse in her waistband, pauses to light a cigarette. What was that about talking water? Weird. Weird. When she opens the door of Texas Style, Jasper hears the mandolin whine of bluegrass. "But weird or no I'd give her a go," he croons.

Godot comes in, as usual. "Your Harley's leaking oil," he tells Jasper. He jerks his thumb toward where the bike sits at the curb.

"The rear seal is shot," Jasper tells him.

"Rear seal is shot," says Godot. "Sounds like me."

21.

Fat Stanley comes out with a pitcher of beer. He slides into the booth across from Godot. "So what happened about what's her name?" he says.

Godot frowns. "She's gonna get me fired, Stan. She's the power broker now. She's gonna get me fired."

"That's bad."

"Bad? It's a disaster, Stan. What am I gonna do? Who the bleep is gonna hire an old fart like me? Look at me. Nobody wants you when you're old and gray. Look at my hands." His hands are trembling. "I'm losing weight. I'm . . . I'm . . . I don't know. I've got no answers. There's nothing but this abyss in front of me. You're looking at an untenured professor of religious studies who hasn't got a chance in hell of finding a job. Simple as that. Might as well cut my balls off."

"Maybe it won't be that bad," says Fat Stanley.

Godot combs his fingers through his beard. He has an Old Testament sternness in his eyes. "Women are waiting out there like vampires in the dark, waiting to suck our blood, Stan, waiting to suck us dry, waiting to make us into little dried-up smudges they can step on. Bertha's one of the ringleaders. She gave away her heart when they made her director. It's a common phenomenon. Once they step into our world, they lose that softness we love them for. They lose their sense of justice, I'm saying. They come on all fired up for revenge, getting after us for aeons of fucking them over. This one, let me tell you, this Bertha Tatem, is into the worst sin of all. She writes confessionist poetry about men who have betrayed her. She gets these little breast-beating pieces of verse published in the lit mags. I've read some of it. Precious, limp-wristed, passive-victim stuff in trimeters." Godot rolls his eyes, purses his mouth. His silver beard shivers with disdain. "Confessionists—bah!"

"Confessionists," says Fat Stanley.

"Trimeters, for Christ's sake."

"God save us," says Fat Stanley.

Jasper knows they have pooled their wisdom. There are deep

things you'll know when you're older, he tells himself. "My girl Didi, she's a poet," he says. "She wants to be."

"They all want to now," says Godot. "They can whine to high heaven and call it art."

"God save us," says Fat Stanley.

Godot waves his hand in front of his face as if driving away a fleet of gnats. "I should have tried harder somewhere for a tenure track. All these years on one-year contracts, I was cutting my own throat. How could I believe it would last forever? So stupid." He pauses, sighs, digs at his beard like he's digging for a bug. Then he says, "I am that I am. But not long ago, you know, Stan, women weren't in competition, especially not in religious studies. Now . . . now they're everywhere, into everything. It's a conspiracy."

"What will you do?" says Fat Stanley.

Godot blows smoke into the air. "Who the bleep knows? Cut my throat. Make them happy." He pauses, grimaces, says, "Horseshit, I don't want to make them happy, that mob of shit smears. What I ought to do, you see, is cut *their* throats. Yeah, her and that little tart Mary Mythwish."

He continues to unload his heart. He calls women spiders, demons, fiends, devil turds. He says they have made a holy citadel of themselves, says they are out to store a billion frozen sperm and do away with the current race of men altogether, start over with themselves in charge, build themselves a new world on double-X-chromosome principles. Yes, and the dopes in government and the bigger dopes at the universities are letting them get away with it, throwing away our heritage with both hands as fast as they can. This thing is snowballing, he insists. We are going to get buried beneath an avalanche of feminine whimperers, whiners, and witches. The new gods will be Pulchritude, Coiffure, Mindless Chatter, Buns of Steel, Sculptured Thigh, Militant Mammary, and Multiple Orgasm. The male of the species will have his penis snipped off and put on a pike over the doorway to the humanities building as a warning to all that those dead white European chaps had damn well better stay mum in their graves. Other movements, other voices, are taking over.

He points at Jasper mopping the floor and listening. "Poor boy. Poor, poor boy, he'll never know what it is to be a man in a man's world!" The last words come out as a cry. There are tears in the professor's eyes.

Jasper feels suddenly very sorry for himself. Grim, the situation is grim.

Fat Stanley says, "Well, in matriarchal societies it's worked out okay. Look at Micronesia and Melanesia. I read the other day in *National Geographic*—"

"She called me a craftsman! Can you imagine that? She says I'm a mere craftsman." He lowers his brows at Fat Stanley and clutches his arm. "What about that book I wrote, huh? I'm a creator, Stan, an artist. Am I not?"

"Amen," says Fat Stanley.

"Godot's days are numbered, my boy. Numbered, numbered. Out with him! Throw him on the streets. You see those two bums over there?" He points out the window. "It's gonna be *three* bums when the semester is over. The new Trinity, them and me. That's what they're waiting for over there. Waiting for me."

"They're always over there. I'm sick of them," says Fat Stanley. "They turn away business."

They all look in the direction of the two men leaning on the hunk-of-junk Ford.

"I'm deteriorating just like that," says Godot. "Inside I am pure angst. Angst is eating me up. I feel it in my stomach and my chest."

"You should go to a doctor. You should check it out."

"Maybe I should just die," says Godot. "I'm obsolete now."

"That's no way to talk. Just talking that way is bad for your health. People who talk like that go downhill fast. I know you're a better man than that, Godot."

"Bad, bad, bad," says Godot. "I feel really bad." He stands up, looks across the street. "I'm going to Texas Style," he says. "You coming?"

They leave together. Jasper cleans up the table where they were sitting. As he wipes the table off, he looks out the big bay window, at the false lights, purple and red and blue, lighting up the bar and the marquee of the Narcissus theater, and beyond that the dark night, the smog-encased stars.

♡

In rush-hour traffic the next day, Didi Godunov hunkers on the Harley, her pelvis flush with his behind. The wind blows her dark hair back. She knows she looks good that way. She looks very fatal. She sees herself as if from a parallel plain. She sees a woman passing by in a generic Honda, seeing this cool chick on a motorcycle with her hair streaming in the wind. The Honda woman is jealous of that chick. She wants to be that chick. Didi smiles to herself and feels pity for the poor dear in the Honda. A BMW pulls even with the Harley, an older man driving. He looks longingly at Didi. He wants a wild time with her. He wants to be Jasper in a leather jacket with this cool chick clinging to his back. All the men want her, all the women envy her, Didi can tell. She wants to tell them how great it is to be Didi Godunov. She hopes her face shows it as she glances left and right, tossing her hair, letting it stream like wild grass in water. She is sweet, adorable, athletic, divine, aromatic. She is femme fatale extraordinaire. She writes brilliant poetry. She has a lover who is orally fixated.

There is a mild surge forward and the sound of the pipes backing down. She watches his left hand squeeze the clutch, feels his leg rise slightly, his toe catch the shift bar, the left hand letting go. They are in third gear, slowing. Cars on both sides are slowing too. She strains to see around his shoulder. In front of them is a sea of red lights. What now? she wonders. This place is getting more and more like L.A., she tells herself. He takes the Harley to the far right lane and scoots between cars. He is in second gear now, being careful.

Didi feels privileged. Everyone else is creeping along, but she is gliding by like the wind itself. He drives neatly down the middle of the traffic. It makes her think of Moses parting the Red Sea. "Actually the Sea of Reeds," said Professor Godot. " 'And the Lord drove the sea back by a strong east wind . . . and the waters were divided.' Now there's a God for you!" Didi chuckles into Jasper's back. Godot is a goof. That silver beard, those big, expressive eyes. Everybody says he's trying to be Jehovah. "I am that I am," he's always saying. But not much longer. They are letting the old boy go, discarding him like an old fable. The wise ones wink knowingly, but she feels sorry for him. He may look ancient, he may sound out of date, but he still knows his stuff. He speaks Hebrew and Greek and languages nobody's even heard of. Didi is always impressed by people who speak lots of languages. All she knows is American, and it's hardly enough sometimes to express what she feels. Now and again when she's writing her poetry, the words abandon her and a huge nothing opens up in the center of her brain. It's like those black holes in outer space sucking up all the light.

Red and blue lights flash ahead. A pair of police cars are stopped by the side of the freeway. Officers are outside standing next to a downed motorcycle. A Yamaha, a punk bike. The cops are writing on narrow pads. At the edge of the concrete, not far off in the dirt, is a body covered with a blanket, the booted feet peeking out forming a listless V. Didi thinks she sees blood on the concrete. Oil and gas form a drifting puddle running away from the bike.

Jasper doesn't stop. He inches past, then cracks the throttle. The clutch whirs for a moment, then catches and the Harley leaps forward. Didi feels the heat from the engine between her legs cooling off as the wind rises. She shakes her hair out again, lets it fly. On the opposite side of the freeway, she sees more flashing red lights, sirens wailing. An ambulance races by. She clutches Jasper tighter, leans her face on the warm leather. He's strong, he's good on this thing, he knows what he's doing.

When they reach her apartment in Pacific Beach, Didi still has the vision of the listless feet and the form beneath the blanket. Omens for others. Didi Godunov has destiny on her side and miles to go before she sleeps.

She and Jasper get off the Harley and stand for a while, watching the neighbor's kid playing in the street. Her name is Kelly. She is wearing filthy panties and nothing else as she pedals her tiny bike in circles from the gutter to the edge of the traffic and back again. Cars dodge her. Horns honk. It happens all the time. Didi swears that one of these days she is going to call the Humane Society. She closes her eyes, shakes her head, leads Jasper up the walk. Inside, she drops her pack of books on the sofa and gets the lemonade she promised him.

When she gets back, he is sitting next to her pack, glancing through a *Cosmopolitan*. He puts the magazine on the end table and smiles at her as he takes the glass of lemonade. She loves his smile. She loves especially to see his tongue so pink and glistening. She considers his mouth a marker of good health. With so many diseases out there, it is important to know the signs. She bends down and gives him a peck, tastes the lemony residue on his lips. Cars honk outside. Someone yells, "Kelly, goddamn you!" Didi turns the radio on B-100. Hard rock fills the living room.

Didi lies on the rug in front of him and does her exercises. She was going to be a gymnast when she was younger, but she grew too large. Breasts wouldn't quit. Butt got big. No diet could keep her gymnast slim. It was heartbreaking until she found she was a poet. She has kept the exercises, kept herself limber as a weasel. She is able to contort her body, create impossible pretzel shapes. It wows everybody, especially Jasper. She glances at him as she moves. He has that greedy look. He checks her everything, then pretends nonchalance as he looks around, takes in the print of Matisse's *Blue Nude* on the wall, the easy chair, the case of books, the desk cluttered with poems, lecture notes, and yellowing copies of *American Poetry Review*. She puts her left leg behind her head, her foot draping over her shoulder. His eyes slide back to her, soaking up her intimacies.

She tells him there is a poem in that dead man's feet and those cop-car lights. She makes up two lines on the spot: *What's left of him is canvas covered / lights light up his feet—*

Nudging Jasper with her toe, she adds that he should sell his bike,

27.

get a car. His eyes are glued to where her thighs fork, the mound in the denim there. He has told her she is a bovinity of a girl. He doesn't go for these reeds with boy bottoms and breasts no bigger than lemons. She fills his eyes like a Rubens woman, he has said. Real woman. All woman, he has said. He praises her curvy bigness every time they are in bed, running his hand appreciatively over her hip, like a skier sliding down the slope to her waist, then up her side and to her breasts, one at a time hefting them, thumbing the nipples, murmuring, "Marvelous, marvelous—" He is the first man who has looked with such pure adoration on her lushness. When his face is between her legs, his eyes peeping upward, it reminds her of believers in church praying to the cross.

When they first met, she was sitting on a marble bench outside a classroom, and he was sitting there too, reading a paperback that had a red-and-yellow sunset on the cover and SHELLEY across the top. She lied to him, told him she liked Shelley. He read her "Indian Serenade"—*I arise from dreams of thee / In the first sweet sleep of night*—and bam! she wanted him. That was when it was always best, in the beginning, when the promise was pending. She had let her myopic eyes do the talking. Her eyes, she knew, gave her whole face an innocent, spacey air. She is always practicing this air in the mirror and has brought it to perfection.

She rests a moment, then turns down the music and quotes him a line from one of her latest poems, a free-verse song about a woman trapped in a loveless marriage and longing for the real thing to happen to her before she dies. As she quotes its first sad line to him—*Love could teach my ass to dance*—he listens politely, but then he begins to drift, his eyes become opaque, and she knows, as usual, she's lost him. It is a major source of irritation about him, he doesn't appreciate her poetry the way he should. She doesn't understand how he can love Shelley's verse and not hers. In fact, she thinks most of Shelley's stuff stinks. Keats and Byron, they stink too. Wordsworth? Coleridge? *Puleeze!* The real poets came later. Sylvia Plath. Anne Sexton. She doesn't bother to finish the poem about the lonely woman who wants her ass to dance.

Instead she tells him about this old friend of hers named Wendy Williams, who had pretensions to poetry. Now she is fat and is married to a lawyer. But once upon a time Wendy got involved with a married guy who had four kids. It turned into a mess. What happens is she writes this guy a poem and sends it to his house and the wife opens it and there's this poem to her husband. The wife reads this thing that says, *He drives through every orifice of my trembling, willing body / loving me with the thickest tool I've known.*

Didi bursts into laughter.

Jasper is shaking his head, saying wow, geez.

Didi holds her hand up for silence, then she finishes Wendy's love poem. It goes—*In the mirror I watch myself go down / to make his limp stalk walk / oh, there's nothing quite as thrilling / as Wendy sucking Kendall's cock.*

Collapsing in laughter, legs kicking, Didi shrieks out the fate of the terrible triangle. Wendy caught gonorrhea from some guy, and she gave it to Kendall, who gave it to his wife! Wendy's ovaries burned out. She can never have kids!

Abruptly, Didi quits laughing. Maybe that's not so funny, she tells herself. She decides that Wendy deserved VD for writing such a horrid poem. Jasper has leaned back on the couch. He asks about the wife. Didi doesn't know about the wife. He looks at *Blue Nude* on the wall, his lips puckering with distaste. The look on Jasper's face makes Didi second-guess herself. She wonders if she's made a mistake telling such a pathetic story. She switches the subject to herself, tells him she has thirteen poems circulating because thirteen is her lucky number, it has the sound of destiny. She asks him if he believes in special destinies for special people. He shrugs.

She tells him that all she wants is to be famous. She doesn't need to be rich. Oh, it would be nice to be rich, but she wants fame more, the name Didi Godunov on a book of verse, winner of the Yale Younger Poets Award. Her picture on the back. A blurb from a critic saying the new Plath has arrived, the new Sexton.

She rocks and talks, her legs still crossed behind her neck. To win him back to the right train of thought, she bends her face forward and kisses her own butt. She has done more. She wonders if he would like to see it. Of course he would. Men like to look and look. Glancing at him, she sees to her horror that he is yawning.

Unrolling, stretching out, she spreads her legs and arms. All he needs to do is come shuffle her denims down.

He is checking his watch. He doesn't like to be late for work.

Just a quickie, she thinks. Mental messages flash toward him. If he loves her, he'll know what she needs. She closes her eyes. She waits for him to do it. She wants his weight. She wants his kisses. Another one of her poems comes to mind and she tries to say it in a tone of voice that will make him want to comfort her: *Smoke and fog rolls me over like a log / and the tiresome weep of memory / ruptures my soul incessantly / I coulda been your answer.*

When she opens her eyes he is gone. On the end table is an empty glass. She hears the motorcycle start, the pipes rumbling. She hears the clutch spin. She follows the sound of the engine fading away, and she is pretty sure now that she shouldn't have told the story of Wendy Williams. Horrid Wendy. Burned-out ovaries, ish.

Feeling mildly depressed, Jasper pulls away from the curb and heads toward the freeway. He thinks of Didi's fragment of poem about the dead guy under the blanket. The image dives down thirty feet to the fish bait J.J. Quick. Godot's voice is there. "What is crooked cannot be made straight." Jasper drives carefully. He remembers when he was younger and how he made himself believe that life was his own dream. He would close his eyes and the world would vanish. Open them and the world would reappear. He was a god. From the beams of his eyes worlds coming and going. Worlds died, he didn't. Maybe he never would? Little J.J. Quick, ten years old, sleeps in the deep. He was not immortal, but maybe J.J. Jasper John is.

ANYTHING IS POSSIBLE, says a billboard advertising a cruise. A happy couple, arms around each other, stand at the ship's railing staring at an Alaskan inlet. God's country, thinks Jasper.

30.

He moves onto the freeway in fourth gear. He moves under the speed limit in the slow lane, cars passing him. The sun shines on his head. His head feels like an eggshell drawn to the pavement. The chill in his bowels angers him, makes him want to tempt fate, show them all he is not J.J. Quick, nor the dead cyclist under the blanket either. Throttle down, clutch whirring, the bike barks, dashes forward, speedometer climbing. Jasper John weaves to the fast lane, hangs on, and lets the rpm's rip.

2. SUPERFLUITY OF NAUGHTINESS

He buses those dishes and glasses and cups, washes them, racks them, runs them through the sterilizer, recycles them for the waitresses. Everybody's in tune, working together like a well-oiled machine. Or maybe not so well-oiled. Helga misses a beat now and then. She keeps running to the bathroom. The bathroom is behind the wall where the steel sinks are, and when he stops to scour a pan, he can hear her retching noises. It takes her only a few seconds and then she is out again, wiping her mouth with a hanky, stuffing the hanky in her pocket, shuffling on sore feet into the dining room, murmuring, "Fuck, fuck, fuck," as if it is an incantation. When she enters into the lights, her smile switches on. All business, she takes care of her tables, pours coffee, brings the dessert tray, chats, recommends.

By nine o'clock, traffic thins. Fat Stanley has the remaining customers frozen in awe as he stands in the middle of the floor singing something sad from *Tosca*. His voice fills Jasper with longing for he knows not what. For love, maybe. For a big life, a big, important life? It feels strange to Jasper that a beautiful voice raised in song could fill him with ambition for some unknown *thing*. The purity of the chef's instrument seems to enter Jasper's soul, sends it rising like a balloon, expanding over the earth, arms out in benediction over the entire cosmos. Now he could change water into wine. Now he could feed five thousand with five barley loaves and two fish. Now the blind would see, the lame walk, the dead rise. He listens. He listens for something profound, a voice inside the voice telling him something he cannot name.

When the aria is over and the people are clapping, Jasper goes back to gathering dirty dishes. He hums to himself, reluctant to let the sweetness go.

"Did you see the new ad?" asks Fat Stanley. "Check it out." He points to the corkboard.

Hot, mature, playful SWF, carnal as hell and into kink, dreams of tall, handsome, willow-limbed youth, with honeysuckle hair and burn-me-down eyes. Spread your nectar over wee Lily, petite sweet from Lemon Grove. Write me at Adam and Eve Possibilities, please.

"She'll get lots of letters," says Jasper.

"Letter like that makes me fall in love," says Fat Stanley.

Jasper knows that Lily will get a letter from Fat Stanley. He imagines himself writing her a letter and she contacting him, having him over for drinks, making love to him in front of a fireplace. Sweet petite Lily, yeah wow, wild pussy, stankfinger, take it to the max, go down, Moses. Ummm. He wonders why she has to advertise if she's so sweet petite and into kink. The good ones shouldn't have to advertise. Maybe a face like a camel? Thighs like ricotta cheese? But sometimes you don't care, just so it's feminine and soft and has that smell and can touch you there with those delicate fingers. Sometimes, oh sometimes like right now this minute, you just ache to be touched no matter what. And so grateful when they do.

He feels it now, partially tumescent, aching. He pushes against the counter as he unloads the dishes into the sink. He feels a vague wetness on the inside of his thigh. His hands work automatically at rinsing the dinnerware while the rest of him dreams of Lily on a rug.

"Jasper, make sure you do the mats tonight," says Fat Stanley. "Filthy. Look at em."

Jasper looks down at the rubber mats. He hasn't scrubbed them in a while and they are gathering little cobwebs of dirt between their nipples. What if she's another prostitute? he asks himself. It happens to Fat Stanley all the time. Suddenly Jasper knows Lily *is* a prostitute, but he doesn't care. He's in that mood where anything goes.

The customers are leaving. Fat Stanley is playing with the till. Jasper is ready to jump out of his skin. He wants to hop the Harley and run flat out on the freeway, let the wind blow his fidgety, horny self away. Good Christ, it's terrible! It's a sickness. It's something he cannot help. He's like a bottle of champagne someone has shaken. The pressure is rising, the cap is ready to blow, the contents ready to spray all over the place.

Fat Stanley says good night and leaves by the back door. Mary takes her apron off and throws it in the laundry bin. Helga is in the bathroom. Mary listens at the door, her eyes worried.

"Helga," she calls.

Mary and Jasper can hear her gasp, cough, spit, retch. She coughs again, and again. "Helga?"

"I'm okay," she says, her voice raspy.

"Is there anything we can do?"

A pause. Heartbeats drift by. "Get me Dr. Frankenstein," she says. "Tell him to prepare the body." She laughs sarcastically. The toilet flushes.

Jasper is on the way out the door when Mary catches him by the arm and asks him if he wants to step over to Texas Style for a beer. "Such a hot, sweaty day today," she adds.

"Mary," he says, "do you like motorcycles?" He points to the oil-dripping Harley.

"They scare me to death, I love em," she tells him.

"Want a ride?"

To his surprise she says, "Okay."

She hikes up her skirt, and off they go, rumbling along the street, creating breezes to cool their faces, she clinging to him tight, her breasts against his back feeling like warm bread. He takes her to Balboa Park and cruises the outdoor concert. They stop a while, listening to Fat Stanley-type music, full of violins and cellos. They go downtown, down Broadway, busy with cars and buses, people prowling the sidewalks. Some sailors wave at Mary.

"They probably think I'm some young biker chick," she says, giggling.

He cruises the front of Bee-Jay Plaza, the little one-block park there, picks out the gays waiting, their eyes full of quiet desperation and false promise. Lots of them have mustaches. Lots of them have bee-stung lips. Jasper has noted how hard they work to make that area as voluptuous as a vagina. When he first came to town, he ran out of gas one night and had to hitch a ride. A guy picked him up, a chatty fellow with a furry mustache and pulsing lips. He was young, brown-eyed, with swept-back hair that made a little pig's tail on the back of his neck. He drove to a gas station a mile away and even provided the can from his trunk, waited for Jasper to get a gallon, then drove him back to the bike. A very nice guy. Afterward, the guy, his name was Paul, invited Jasper to stop by his place for a drink. It was on Twelfth, a block away.

Paul brought out marijuana, mixed a quart of margaritas, and the two of them got high. Soft music was on. Paul pulled out a stack of *Penthouse*, and they looked at the naked girls, read the nasty letters aloud to each other, laughed, got horny. Paul was upfront with it. "You jack me off, I'll jack you off," he said. Jasper had passed the point of no return. He sat with Paul in mutual masturbation, staring at a glossy blond looking over her shoulder, showing off her bottom, a finger touching the Spot. When the cum made its loading gesture at the base of his penis, he told Paul to watch out.

"So soon?" said Paul. "Want me to suck it?"

And without waiting for an answer, he bent over, took Jasper in his mouth. Milked him.

Jasper had felt pleasure mixing with guilt and a nip of self-disgust. He realized as he watched Paul's bobbing head that he had expected just this to happen. He was no innocent. He was no fool. When it was over, Paul looked up at him as if expecting him to reciprocate.

Jasper hesitated. Then, not knowing what else to say, he said, "Thank you."

"It's okay," said Paul. He patted Jasper's leg. "Wait here," he said. "I'll be right back.

He went into the bathroom. Jasper heard the water running, heard Paul brushing his teeth. Spitting. Brushing and spitting. Jasper pulled himself together and tiptoed out of the apartment. He never saw Paul again, but it was hard to put the experience in its proper place. He didn't know what to think of himself, didn't know if he should loathe himself and Paul, or just be angry, or not be anything much at all. Just take it as another notch of experience, no harm, no foul.

Down a back street near Market he goes slow and lets Mary get a look at the streetwalkers in their miniskirts, perfumes thickening the air. Some of them are talking to customers pulled over in cars. Some are leaning against storefronts, some are walking, wiggling their asses. He wonders if Mary is offended.

He glances back at her. Her hand is up, she is waving at the sisters. They are waving back, giving off big smiles, like, wow, nothing in the world bothers me. Jasper cuts west on Market Street, then goes north, passing nightclubs, hawkers in shiny jackets, more streetwalkers, movie houses with marquees advertising XXX—*Naked Nanette, Scent of Heather, Slip Up, Wicked, Nightdreams*. There are posters of starlets, thighs inviting, names plastered brightly above: Merry Suckling, Pia Pudding, Constant Honey. On a corner two men kiss.

"Smack me upside the jaw if I ever get fuddy-duddy about all this," Mary says in his ear. Her sweeping hand takes in life.

36.

Up First Avenue they ascend, all the way to Washington and then to Park, and the back way to Fat Stanley's, and Mary is saying, "I've seen lots heavier action than your downtown. New York. Chicago. L.A. is way worse. People . . . will do things, you know?"

Jasper feels her round chin digging into his shoulder, her cheek brushing the back of his neck, her breasts squishing up. She feels sixteen on his back.

Before they reach the diner, they go by Helga's car parked at the curb and see her in it, just sitting behind the wheel, smoking a ciga-rette. Jasper makes a U-turn and pulls in behind her. He and Mary go to the window.

"You okay, honey?" asks Mary.

"Sure, I'm just thinking." Her eyes are compressed, like someone fighting a headache. "I'm just remembering things, that's all. Taking it easy." In the streetlights, the rims around her eyes are purple. Her cheekbones look as if they have been honed with a file.

"Whyn't you come get a beer with us?" says Mary.

"I can't drink no more," says Helga.

"Have a ginger ale or something. Relax. Listen to some music. The band is good, Helga."

"I know," she says. "I've been there."

"C'mon, take your mind off things."

Helga thinks a second, then she gets out and goes with them. They walk on each side of her, close, ready in case she falls.

Texas Style is long and narrow. Long bar, half the length of the build-ing. Stools and a place for barmaids to pick up orders. Behind the bar is Arthur, big and bald and busy. Behind him is a mirror that's as long as the bar. There is a cash register in the middle. There are abundant bottles of brews sitting on glass shelves climbing to the ceiling, any-thing you want, name your poison. There are a few tables and chairs crowd the middle of the floor, and a row of red vinyl booths. In the back is a small dance floor and a stage, and a cowboy band called Reap the Whirlwind is warming up. There is a pretty lady in Western dress, tightening the strings on a fiddle. Behind her is a fellow tapping lightly on a set of drums, while two men tune their guitars.

Jasper finds a booth near the door and orders a pitcher of beer for himself and Mary. Helga asks for Seven-Up. The waitress leaves a bowl of popcorn on the table. At the bar are some men. One of them is waving at Jasper.

"There's Godot," he says.

"Where?" says Helga. "Oh no, anybody but him. He isn't coming over here, is he? Don't encourage him, Jasper."

"What's wrong with Godot?" says Jasper.

"I don't like him," says Helga.

After the second mug of beer Jasper feels real good. This is his kind of place. The boozy smoky smell fills his nostrils and he is back home in Colorado, checking out the bars from Denver to Boulder—Red Earth, Pike's Place, Garden of the Gods, Slim Pickens, all of them big on honky-tonk dances, Coors beer, restless women in painted-on jeans, hot-eyed men with heavy fists and soft beer guts. Texas Style might have come straight from Colorado or anywhere north or south. If an urban cowboy learns to drawl in one of them, he speaks the dialect of all.

Mary crams her mouth with popcorn, says, "It's too salty," but she keeps eating it. Helga tries some, one little puff at a time as if she is weighing them on her tongue. She swallows, has another, then another. Pretty soon she is cramming in handfuls. She eyes the beer greedily.

"This was my life," she says. "Me and Mike. The only time I ever felt immortal was when I was with him in a bar and the music was playing and we were tanking up. Something almost holy about that, you know."

"Makes you feel fixed somehow," says Mary.

"It's a little world separate," says Helga. She wonders aloud if she dares try a beer. She says she's dehydrated from all the upchucking and no doubt needs lots of liquids.

By the second pitcher, she has her own mug. Popcorn and beer.

"Ahh," she says, "this is *it*. I'm relaxing now. If I closed my eyes I bet I'd sleep like a baby."

Jasper feels suddenly like some kind of Good Samaritan for bringing her along, like this is what the doctor ordered for sure. The music is playing, and he can feel life coming on sweet and heavy for all of them, like syrup filling all their nooks and crannies. Helga might look like a tattered dress on a stick, but something ready has entered her eyes.

"Listen to the music," he tells her. "Pretty good stuff, huh?"

Helga listens but her attention is not on the music. She feels suddenly immensely exhausted and she wonders if she's going to melt all over the table right in front of her friends. So tired. Eyes are burning. Light-headed. She rubs a place in her armpit that seems swollen.

Couples are getting up, dancing close. She and Mike once. Where are your revels now? Play the fool, she tells them, it don't last. That sweet young thing in your arms, that broad-shouldered cowpoke, both of you are decaying even this very second. Helga knows she could tell them a thing or two about living, about not being coy with life. Grab it like a tit in your teeth, suck every drop out of it. Anger enters her heart. She looks at buxom Mary and feels an impulse to punch her right in the nose. What right has Mary to be so goddamn healthy? Look at those fat tits, those firm arms. It really makes Helga mad to think that Mary is older than her by twelve years. Helga wants everybody above forty to show some putrefaction that approximates her own; but this Mary Quick, except for the bags under her eyes, looks like she could polka all night and still take the measure of any twenty men in the house.

Raking her with envious eyes, Helga settles on the Celtic cross hanging like some shield between Mary's breasts, and she decides she especially hates *it*. Helga has said prayers. Done no good. There's no God, and if there is one and he allows this evil thing to happen to her, then he is evil himself and not worthy of her respect. Screw him. She looks at Jasper, remembers that Jasper must marry Nancy soon. Time is wasting.

"Jasper, you've met my Nancy, haven't you?"

"Huh?"

"Nancy. My daughter Nancy. Didn't you meet her one time when she came in with my other two?"

Jasper shrugs. "Nancy," he says, screwing up his eyes.

"You should," says Helga. "You two would hit it off."

"Uh-huh."

"So how's the college? You getting the grades, Jasper?"

Jasper makes a face. "I flunked a physics exam the other day. It was all kinds of formulas and stuff about the quantum world. I don't like the teeny-weenies I can't see. I like the big stuff, the macrocosm. Know what I mean?" He stretches his arms out like he's going to enfold the universe.

"I was never no good at that," says Mary. "Math, whew." She shakes her hand like there's something sticky on it.

"That's not what's important," says Helga. "What's important is, are you a good man, Jasper?"

"I don't know."

Helga coughs. "Just treat her right, that's all I'm saying. You don't, I'll come back and haunt your young ass. You savvy me, Jasper John?" She coughs again. She puts her fist in front of her mouth and bathes it with coughs. She grabs napkins, presses them to her lips, hacks into them. Jasper and Mary look at her with alarm. Half standing, Jasper reaches his long arm over the table and pats her on the back. The spasm subsides.

"You okay?" he asks.

"Fuck no," she says, a chain of phlegm rattling in her throat. "What do you think? Pour me a beer, goddammit. Why the hell are you so young? Look at his young face. Don't you hate him, Mary?"

Mary chuckles. She says, "No, I couldn't hate him. Jasper's my sweetie." She gives him a kiss on the cheek, a squeeze on the upper thigh.

Helga coughs again. "It's this smoke," she says, waving her hand.

"This smoke," Mary agrees. "My lungs are shot too. When I get up in the morning, you won't believe how much I cough."

40.

Helga brightens at the news. "Yeah?"

"Oh yeah, I just cough my lungs out. I have this pain comes and goes in my jaw and here in my neck too, on the left side. What do you think it is?"

Helga is feeling better and better. She takes out her own cigarettes, offers one to Mary. They light up. "It sounds serious to me," says Helga. "Pains in the jaw. Coughing. Ever have a pain down your left arm?"

Mary nods. "The other day I did."

"I'll tell you what, Mary. I'm not saying it is for sure, but those are heart symptoms. I know my medicals these days. You get in my position, you know your medicals."

"Heart," says Mary. "You know, I had a notion."

"Let me tell you the symptoms I had when—"

Jasper looks into his beer, studies the bubbles rising like little secrets from the bottom. He wonders what he is doing with these two old broads talking about their health problems. His eyes shift away to the couples on the floor. He watches a cowgirl in tight jeans, bulbous ass, cascading hair. He pines for her.

A fresh pitcher of beer arrives, and the waitress says it is from Godot. Jasper waves him over and is grateful to note how quickly the two women break off their dialogue on ovaries, bowels, lymph nodes, and other bits of anatomy.

"Thanks for the pitcher," he says. "Sit down."

"I've only got a minute," says Godot. He fluffs his beard and takes the seat next to Helga. He looks at her. "So you're still alive," he says.

Her mouth twists.

"She loves me," he says, grinning.

They give each other looks. Helga breaks it off. She reaches in her purse. "Let me show you this," she says. From her wallet she takes a picture and snaps it like a card on the table. "That's me when," she says. They see a young woman with piles of auburn hair drifting to her shoulders. Her smiling eyes are shaped like crescent moons, her nose is

41.

dainty. Her mouth is lush with lipstick. She wears a blue-and-white polka-dot blouse.

"That's you?" says Mary.

"Hubba-hubba," says Jasper.

"That's when I could make a strong man weep," says Helga. "You remember that, don't you, Godot?"

"She was a looker," he admits.

"Well, we all have our day," says Mary. "I was quite a little turn-on once myself."

Jasper takes his cue to tell her she is still a turn-on. She rewards him with another squeeze of his upper thigh.

Godot takes out his wallet, shows them a picture of himself as a young man. His hair is thick, his beard is dark, his eyes are mesmerizing. From his mouth pokes a pipe. "That was for my dust jacket," he says. "For the back of my book."

"You wrote a book?" says Mary.

"Yeah, I wrote a book," says Godot.

Jasper has read Godot's book. He found it poetic and odd. "I've read it," he says. "It's in the school library."

"And what did you think?" asks Godot.

"It was brilliant," Jasper tells him.

Godot nods. "That was the consensus among the critics. Some of them said I was a man to watch." Godot sighs. "But that was years ago. I've been set aside for other literary gods."

Mary gets Godot talking about his book. He tells her the title, *In the Beginning,* and that it was a work of scholarship, but it also had some popular appeal. It was a work which attempted to interweave the history and myths of the Middle East and in so doing show the roots of Western Scripture. Godot used Sumerian and Babylonian myths, added some Zoroastrian duality, mixed it well with archeological evidence on monotheism, Egyptian love poetry, Canaanite proverbs and fables of magic trees, temptation, fast-talking serpents, redemption and resurrection. It was reviewed in major newspapers. It had a cult of followers. Years after its publication, he got a letter from the infamous

Moon Poo Murphy saying that the book had become the sacred text of the Moon Poo Movement. There was talk that Godot was one of the most important religious thinkers in America. He was called as comprehensive as Thomas Aquinas. One critic went so far as to say Godot showed "promise of Augustinian proportions."

But then it all began to fade when Rama Gautama's book, *The New Path to Virtue,* came out, saying that it was no good getting caught in a time warp and thinking of the traditional way to salvation. Rama Gautama called Godot's book a tool of the establishment, a philosophical apology for conservative politics and the agenda of blind obedience. Reviewers everywhere jumped on the bandwagon, calling Rama Gautama's message lyrical and inspirational and exactly what was needed in a world headed for an apocalypse. Godot and his book were eclipsed, forgotten by all but a handful of diehards.

"When did all this happen?" says Mary. "Where was I?"

"Oh, years ago," says Godot. "Actually, I've come to lean somewhat toward Rama Gautama myself. My message *was* conservative. It did subtly advocate blind obedience. The years have changed my understanding of things. I'm not so dogmatic as I was. Which is not the way you're supposed to get as you age. The young me was ancient history before the old me got wise. I'm searching for new ways of defining it now. I wish I could take back my old book, break it down, and remake it again in a more modern image."

"The last thing you look is modern," says Helga.

"You too," he says.

Jasper feels he must say something to defend Godot's book. He tells them about the chapter on magic words, words that *became* themselves. Kinetic words, tactile words, words that expanded the universe, words that moved upon the face of the waters, words that said "Let there be," and there was. "That was a fine chapter," he says. "The power Word that became the thing itself. That was a good one, Professor."

Godot nods gratefully. "So you understood that notion," he says. "Hardly anyone really understood what I was saying there. We've lost that, you know. We've lost the power Words." He combs his fingers through his beard. He looks at the picture of his youth on the table. "You know how things are. I'll tell you how things are. This is it. Listen up, this little idea contains all you need to know about words in our time. Once, long ago, we used to speak in pentameters. Read Shakespeare and company, you'll see what I mean. Then in the nineteenth century we began to speak in tetrameters, four feet to the line. You follow me? From five-foot lines we went to four-foot lines. And now where are we? Trimeters. Trimeters. Somebody shoot me. Mark what I say now."

He pauses mysteriously. He leans forward, his pug nose just inches from Jasper's own. *"Dimeters,"* he says. "Just listen and you'll hear the young people speaking dimeters. Sometimes, I'm not lying now, sometimes I hear monometers. Oh yes, it's gotten that bad. One more generation and you'll hear nothing but grunts and growls and snorts. There will be lots of pointing with fingers, and hand gestures in place of punctuation. I'm telling you, we are witnessing the decline and fall. Our end as an intelligent species is imaged in the Word."

Helga shakes her head. She says, "That's what you think you know." She elbows Godot. Her lips thicken, her eyes mock.

Godot taps his forefinger on the table, scanning the number of feet in Helga's sentence. " 'That's what you think you know.' Trimeters, Helga. You speak trimeters."

"Hmmph," says Helga.

"And monometers," adds Godot.

An awkward silence follows. They listen to the band playing. Godot hangs around till the end of the tune, then rises and says good night. He stops to talk to Arthur for a few seconds. When he goes out the door cold fog swirls round him, tumbling through the opening, breathing a chill on those in the booths.

"I can't stand that man," says Helga.

Round about midnight, Helga is snoozing in the corner of the booth and she hears this voice full of cough balls saying, "Flamin legs, look who's here! Hump me if it ain't handsome Hank. Look here, kiddy, I got somethin for youz."

When she opens her eyes, there's that guy who popped the buttons on Mary's blouse. He's all in black still, and he's handing Jasper some money. He says to Jasper, "Bet youz never thought to see that again."

"No, I never did."

"I added a little somethin extra for the loan."

Jasper counts forty bucks for the original twenty-five. "Hey, thanks," he says.

Henry looks at the ladies. "Hi, Punkin," he says. "Hey, who's the sleepy head there? Do I know youz?"

Helga sits up and tells him who she is. He slides up next to her. "Heard bad news about youz, heard youz got the big C. Look here, sweet stuff, my grampa he had the big C in his pustrate and he lived to be eighty-one. Don't count yourself out."

He chucks her under the chin.

"I'm not counting myself out. That'll be the day." She loves everything about this man, loves his big, pocky cheekbones, his brambly beard, his smell of booze and tobacco. This one's like Mike, this one's all *man.*

"I'll buy us another pitcher," he says, and from his shirt pocket he brings out a wad of bills would choke a hippopotamus. "Had a lil luck," he says. His fist is shaking as if he holds a pair of dice. His smile is broad, all but toothless, wet, gummy, a wee unicorn horn of a tooth rising like a mistake from the corner of his mouth. Wetly he laughs, evilly he laughs. He winks at Helga. She tells herself that this is the face of a rogue for sure, his hair slicked back and shiny as licorice, his big black nostrils sucking up the air like a predator sniffing prey. The surface of his nose is contoured like cottage cheese. He shifts his gaze over to Jasper. He slugs Jasper on the shoulder and the boy rubs the spot, says, "Hey, ooch."

"I never did catch the name, kiddy. What's the name?" Henry cups his ear.

"Jasper John."

"Uh-huh." Henry's mouth works on the name, chewing it. He taps a knuckle on his forehead hard enough to make a hollow sound, and he finishes by telling Jasper that his name is locked away in a mind that is like a steel trap. He turns to Helga and repeats the process with her name. "Steel trap," he tells her, bonking himself on the head. "Locked up tight as a nun's buns."

The waitress brings the fresh pitcher and he hands her a two-dollar tip and tells her to keep the booze coming till he hollers uncle.

"Have I ever let you down, Henry?" she asks him.

"Sweet stuff," he says. He takes a whack at her bottom as she walks away. "She's a good kid," he says. "She knows me. Everybody here knows the Hank now."

Standing up, he shouts, "Who's the Hank?"

The people at the tables and at the bar turn to look at him. The waitress and Arthur MacArthur shout back, "You are, Henry!"

"See what I mean?" he says. He chucks Helga under the chin. "Hey, sweet stuff, what about a dance? Youz look like a ballerina. C'mon, shake that thing."

"Me?"

"Youz."

"Oh no, Henry, I'm all washed up. I ain't got no *thing* to shake no more, honey."

"Yes, you do." He reaches under her and pinches her butt.

Helga loves him like a god. "Legs, don't fail me now!" she says.

Out she slides on his arm. He does a heavy, boot-stomping shuffle all the way to the dance floor. His chrome toes flash like strobe lights. "The Hank is comin," he growls. The other couples give him room. He takes Helga's hand and guides her into a pirouette, then he lets her go, pulls his elbows into his sides, his hands drooping limp at the wrists, and he works his hips and knees and feet into a hoedown rhythm all his own. Helga watches him getting carried away with himself, doing a little twirl, throwing his arms out like helicopter blades. He comes back round facing her, jerks his elbows up and down, sends his belly into spasms over the lip of his belt. She decides he looks like a bull seal galumphing on the shore. People are laughing. Helga is laughing too, harder than she's laughed in years. She's dancing in front of him, trying to keep up, prancing forward, back, and sideways, but she's laughing so much it's making her stumble, making her giddy. And when he changes his stance and starts hopping toward her like a vulture, she can't move anymore. She puts her hands on her knees to keep from falling and she shrieks with laughter.

"You're gonna make me pee my pants!" she cries.

"Go, Hank!" yells someone in the crowd.

"Get it on, Hank!" some are saying.

Henry gives off his one-fang grin. He waves at the people urging him on. Picking Helga up, his arms tucked under her fanny, he whirls her the length of the floor. She looks down into his sweaty face, the lights passing behind him like dubious halos.

When the music ends, he sets her down and walks dizzily backwards into some men at the edge of the floor, who steady him. "Whoa, sweet stuff, babycakes!" he howls. "Youz is some hot number!"

She comes to him. "Hunk of man," she says. She gives him a slurpy kiss. His hand squeezes her emaciated bum, and for a brief, shining moment Helga feels a rush of glory and she believes in miracle cures and that all things are possible.

When they get back to the booth, she asks Mary, "Where the hell you find this wild thang?"

"Where else but in a bar?" says Mary. "What you see is what he is. Twenty-two years and it's always the same Henry Hank." She looks at him affectionately. He wiggles his eyebrows. Mary taps the roll of money he has left on the table and asks him where it came from.

"I got my ways," he tells her.

"Is it legal?"

"Hell yeah, Punkin. You know me."

"Is it legal, Henry?" she says, her voice stern.

"Legal as fishing off the pier in Baja," he says. He looks at Jasper. "Where you think I got this, Jim?"

"Market Street?" says Jasper.

47.

"This boy, this kiddy, is my buddy, my pal. He steered me right. I said I'm a friend of Arthur MacArthur and they let me right in. Everybody down there knows who the Hank is now. I could tell youz some stories about Vegas would make youz drool like Pavel's dog. Am I lyin, Punkin? Hope to catch the clap if I'm lyin."

"Henry knows Vegas," says Mary.

He swallows a mug of beer without pausing, slams it down, burps hard enough to rattle the glasses, then lets them know what a gambler he is and how he's made Vegas, Reno, Tahoe, and all the slot machines in between tremble with fear at the sound of his voice. He's held the world in suspense on a million-dollar roll of the dice, been in poker games with the stress factor so high dentures nearby have melted and B-girls have had strokes. He once took two hundred and ninety thousand dollars off of Ten-Gallon Gary, did it in two hours, all cash, no deductibles, no taxes. Ten-Gallon Gary hasn't been the same since, a broken man, broke his spirit. That's what happens when the wrong man messes with the Hank.

Henry pauses for breath. He pours himself another beer, winks at the waitress, indicates with his twirling finger that they need another round, then picks up where he left off. He's been everywhere, done everything. Born in the Garden State, a wild brat of the streets, gave his mother so much grief she got gray-haired before she was twenty-five. His mama was the one special darling in his life. If she ever got down and depressed and moaning about life, he would tackle her, strip her shoes off, and tickle her feet till she roared like a hyena, oh yeah, *tickle* that woman till she cried like a crocodile. His mama loved him—big-time loved her little man. A man can't be all bad if his mama loves him that way. When she died it sent him into a tailspin. He joined the All-American Eighth Army and parachuted behind the thirty-eighth parallel, played cutthroat commando for six months and won a Silver Star and a mess of other medals. He was at Pork Chop Hill and killed fifty Chinks with a machine gun, took out a tank single-handed, won a cluster for his Silver Star, and was promised the Medal of Honor, but never got it, because the IRS charged him in 1954 with owing back taxes and the Republicans said he was a slacker. But anyway, the army ran him over to T-Bone next to help break the Chinks' hearts. He turned the tide at Heartbreak Ridge and got a second cluster, the only second cluster ever given for a Silver Star. It was at Heartbreak Ridge where he gave General Dwight D. MacArthur himself lessons in hand-to-hand combat and showed him how to outflank the maneuvers of the yellow peril. Wherever the Hank went he turned the tide. The boys would see him coming and give three cheers because they knew they were saved. The Chinks would throw down their weapons and skedaddle.

"Ah, the war . . . nothing like a good war," Henry tells them. "Gets rid of the clutter."

"Did you really do all that?" says Jasper.

Henry leans into Jasper, gets face to face with him. "Jim," he says, "do I look like a man who would lie about his war record?"

"I don't know," says Jasper.

"I hope to catch the clap, AIDS, syphilis, rabies, crabs, herpes, and the creepy crud if I'm lyin."

"That's good enough for me," says Jasper.

"You believe in the Hank?"

"I believe in the Hank."

"Look here, youz probably think Audie Murphy was the most decorated soldier of all time, don't you?"

"Is he? I don't know."

"*Was* he? He's dead now, God love the little southern-fried sonofabitch." Henry pokes himself in the chest. "I'm the second most decorated soldier in history. When the Korean War was over, they decorated me so much I shined like Halley's comet. I damn near toppled over from the weight. Look at the record, Jim. My name is there. Henry Hank, the baddest marine since John Wayne took Iwo Jima single-handed."

"I thought you said army?"

Henry doesn't miss a beat. "Both. I was in both. They couldn't spare me. I was like a prize football player, I went both ways. Did half the war as a marine, half as army."

"Wow," says Jasper.

Henry isn't finished. He rolls out the rest of his life. After the war he came back to the States and went into larceny, then into gambling and prostitution. He met Mary Quick in a bar in Urbana, Illinois, took her to Chicago, and gave her a Cadillac.

"Didn I, Punking?"

"You did, Henry."

He says somebody ought to write a book of his life, he's so damn interesting, doesn't know anybody more interesting than the Hank. He finishes with a flourish, telling them he is *muy* ugly, *muy* macho, *muy* lovable, *muy* mysterious, and the last of a dying breed that tamed the old West. "Those are my references," he says, "what's yours?" He drills a finger into Jasper's ribs.

"I thought you spent the war blowing bridges," says Jasper.

"Who tole youz that?"

"Youz. You did."

"Me?"

"That day I lent you the money, that's what you said."

"Well then, it's true. Look here, I blew up the bridge-too-far. Ever heard of that one? Yours truly give it the coupe de coupe. A jack-of-all-trades. President Truman thanked me personally and said I was a credit to the American dream."

The band comes back from its break. They play a cowboy waltz. Mary and Henry get up and dance. The dancers move the same way this time, couples shuffle along stiffly, hands on each other's shoulders, looking like a series of boxcars. Jasper watches them. He has lost count of the beers, but he knows he is good and drunk. He doesn't give a flying Philadelphia about nothing. His sights are set on doing Mary. Mary looks good in the low lights, looks scrumptious. She felt warm and ready clinging to his back on the Harley, she's like something hot from Sweden, with big hips that will keep a fellow from slipping over the side. He watches her hips swaying to the music. Her skirt swishes enticingly. He knows she is doing it just for him. Squeezed his thigh twice, didn't she? Can't keep her eyes off him.

But then Jasper spies a fault. Its name is Henry Hank. The Hank is throwing a wrench in the works. Only thing to do with a guy like that is drink him under the table. Rising from the booth, Jasper travels to the latrine to prepare himself for some serious competition. He stands over the urinal letting go. His pee looks like liquid crystal. Pee gets pure with beer, he tells himself, chuckling. It's why the sea is salty. Oceans of it running through the sewers to the salty sea, out to sea far, rising with the sun, forming clouds, coming over land and raining, raining pee on people's heads. No wonder the air stinks! Sewers everywhere are farting pee! *Lava las manos!*

When Jasper gets back to the booth, Henry is at it again, booming forth his philosophics, saying how men were men in Korea. His beard pocks out bulldog fashion, his one tooth is fanging his upper lip, belligerence is in his eyes. He talks about being the only real man left in the world. Everywhere he looks are punks with fucking earrings in their fucking ears and fucking ponytails and fucking baggy clothes like three-year-olds wear. "No wonder we lost the Vietnam War! No wonder they chased our sorry asses out of Lebanon. No wonder all that's left for us is to pick on little hunta countries like Panama and Grenada."

"You'd show em, Henry," says Mary. She is leaning on her elbows, cheek to fist. Her eyes droop Irish setter sad.

"Damn right I would, don't youz forget it."

"Operation Killer. Ain't he bad?"

"I make the world safe for women and children." Henry leans back, stiff-arming the table, his gaze haughty.

"Fawk you," says Mary. "You big blowhard bastud."

Henry points an accusing finger at her. "Punkin's dwunk!" he says.

"Fawk you," she repeats. Her head sways. "Crummy world," she says. "Crummy fawking world, too good for this crummy fawking world, good die young, get to be with jolly baby Jesus. Tell em about it, Henry. Ain't that where all the veal goes?"

"Naw, let's not talk about *that*," says Henry.

"Talk about J.J.," she orders.

"Naw, c'mon, we're havin a good time here, Punkin."

She pokes Jasper's arm and she says she wants to know why he lets this guy Satan go to and fro over the earth—"and *you* don't do nothing about it. Why the hell you say to him, 'Sic em, big boy'? Why you say that, huh? Then he come and get my J.J., you rotten shitsner."

"Don't bawl," says Henry.

"Bawl? Who? Since when you goddamn whozit, since when?"

"She'll cry, just watch her," says Henry.

As if on cue, Mary cries buckets of goo into her hanky. The three of them sit watching her. Jasper takes a look at Henry and sees Henry is crying too. "Aw, man," he says.

Getting up, he drags Mary from the booth and makes her walk with him to the dance floor. He makes her dance.

"Tears ain't a sexy thing," he tells her.

Wiping her eyes on his shoulder, she says, "Who's cryin, you fawk!"

Round and round they go with the others. Henry and Helga join them. They come together, all four of them joining in a ring. They sing along with the band, and by the time the song ends, they are laughing in each other's faces. Mary tells them she is having the time of her life. Helga says she feels immortal. Henry gooses Helga and she howls. He gooses Mary and she howls. Helga and Mary goose Henry and he howls. Jasper is trying to get in the goosing but his brain won't send the signals in time.

Jasper decides to take command of the situation. He slides up next to Mary and starts kissing her neck. Helga screams with laughter and points at him. "Look at this upstart prick! Look at this horny sonofabitch! Son, she's old enough to be your mama!"

Mary pushes him away. She says, "Boy, I'm beat. My heart's pounding like a piston. Don't crowd me, honey. Give a girl air."

"You better not try that shit on my Nancy," says Helga. "I'll punch your lights out." Helga takes a swing at Jasper, cuffs the top of his head.

"Hey!"

"You listening to me, Jasper John?"

"What?"

"You respect my Nancy, or I'll have your hide."

"All right, all right," says Jasper.

Glumly Jasper drinks another beer. He turns away, watches the dancers. He makes a plan. He is going to act like he is too drunk to drive home. Mary is going to insist he stay with her. He will follow her home docile and such, and when they get inside her house, he'll pretend he doesn't know what he's doing and just go for those titties, down they'll go in a heap on the floor, him and her ripping clothes off, all hot as jalapeños, and he'll give her such a balling she'll want to be his sex slave ever after, yeah.

Images of conquest work through his brain. He gazes toward the tables, and he sees a pretty girl with flowing hair, fine forehead polished bright above a pair of dreamy eyes. Hey, who's that? He thinks a moment, then he remembers her on the dance floor, remembers her chewable bulbous ass. He stares at her. She stares at him. Love! Oh love!

But beside her is the boyfriend. The boyfriend notices where she is looking. He stares too, eyes hard. Jasper rises and goes forth in quest. He stands over her. "Excuse me," he says.

"Fuck off," says the boyfriend.

"Didn't we meet in another life?" Jasper smiles at his own glibness. He feels smooth, original, irresistible, charismatic. "Does the name Lancelot ring a bell, princess?"

"No," she says. She is nervous now. Her smile flickers. She knows she started something.

"She walks in beauty like the night," he quotes.

The boyfriend stands up. "Back off," says the boyfriend.

Jasper measures him coolly. They are of a size, but the boyfriend is heavier, has a wishy-washy belly, soft. Hit him there and it's over. Jasper's own belly is flat and hard. It can take a punch. "If I had her and you had a feather up your ass, we'd both be tickled," he says.

Her lips part. Jasper can tell she wants to laugh. He winks at her. The boyfriend kicks his chair back and cocks his fist. She puts her hand on his arm. She says, "Eugene, come on, he's drunk."

"I'm tellin you to fuck off!" says Eugene, his breath blowing in Jasper's face.

Jasper stares at him bemused. "If I whip your ass, I get her," he says. His fingers caress her hair.

Next thing he knows he is on the floor and there is this vacuum in his head, there is infinite empty space. Did Eugene hit him? He doesn't know for sure, but he thinks so. A pair of hands pull him up by the armpits. People make way for him. The door opens. Cool air bathes his face. The air is nasty. It smells of sewer. The lights above have halos.

"Kicked your scrawny ass," says Helga, guffawing hard, her hands on her knees. "You shoulda seen yourself go down! Haw-haw!"

Henry is chuckling.

Mary is looking trembly, like she's ready to cry some more.

"Didna feel nothin," says Jasper. "Think I slipped settin up, that's what. He never touched me."

"Haw-haw!"

"Settin up to go down," says Henry. "You're all right, Jim. That's some stupid thing I woulda done at your age."

Jasper is leaning on Henry. Henry has an arm around Jasper's waist. "Wasna she booful?" he asks Henry. "See her shmile? Know what? Know what? She wants me put hickey on her ass."

Helga jumps in close, her face an inch away. "I won't have no son-in-law talking that shit in her presence," she says. "My Nancy's a good girl, she is. Am I making myself clear? You come to my house, you be a gennleman."

Jasper's mind feels like mud. He nods. He smiles. He wants to cooperate. He wants everybody to be friends. There is this throbbing in his jaw now, and yes, his left ear is ringing.

"I don feel good," he says. "I wan go home."

☺

Next morning Jasper eases up, sits, holds his head steady. He looks around at unfamiliar walls. He is on a strange couch. Old couch, worn armrests, once rose-colored, now faded pinkish blah. Dusty beige curtains hang on a window that lets in filtered sun. He sees itty-bitty dust worlds drifting in a shaft of light. He focuses in front of him, on a gray cat lying atop a coffee table among scattered magazines. Another gray cat curls in an overstuffed chair opposite the couch. A third gray cat sits preening itself on a recliner. There is a wall unit, holding a television, a stereo, and a pair of speakers. The front door is close by, a candlestick lamp sits on an end table. The table is ringed with cup stains.

Jasper feels as though his brain is as hard as a peach pit. His jaw has stiffened. Tenderly he runs his fingers over the surface of his jaw. There is some swelling. His back teeth ache. He remembers the girl with cascading hair. He remembers being thrown out of Texas Style, and Helga yelling, and Mary and Henry holding him up. They walked him through the fog to this house. Mary put him on the couch, gave him a pillow and a blanket.

He stumbles out of the living room into a dining room, finds there a table and chairs, a braided oval rug, a print of something Cubist on the wall that looks vaguely like a fragmented woman. There is a fan over the table. A hutch is practically empty except for a few cups and some chipped plates. It is a spacious room ending in a passageway to the kitchen. To his right is a wall and three doors. The middle door is green. The walls are white. The other two doors are walnut color.

"Head," he says.

Opening the first door, he sees Mary Quick sprawled across a bed, Henry next to her, covers piled like drifts of snow, clothes on the floor, pale blue panties lounging on the headboard. Mary's panties. She lies openmouthed, snoring lightly. Her hair drifts wildly over the pillow. Her breasts lean outward along her biceps, wide yolks of her nipples floating asymmetrically. She has a leaner waist than he would have figured. There are stretch marks running silver-sided into her pubic hairs. The hairs themselves are so thinned out he can see skin shining through. He looks closely and sees that some of the hairs are gray. Gray pubic hairs. It is something he has never considered, that people get gray hairs there the same as they do on their heads. She is old. She has a bloated varicose vein working down her calf and onto her foot. She has thick toenails, painted orange. A scab on her knee is cracking. She has nothing of Didi's fresh limbs or tight skin. But still, there is something sexy about her, something receptive and warm in the way her leg is cocked, the way the lips of her vagina lie open. He can tell she is one of those women a fellow wouldn't have to work over for hours to get her bell to ring. She would know how to get in touch with her feelings.

He looks at it. The treasure. Says it in his mind. *Pussy.* Hmmm, *pussy.* What a word. *Pussy.* Fits the thing exactly. The little lips form one. The lips curl up like so and make a pussy mouth. *Poos,* the lips say, *pooseey.* Can't wear it out. Snaps right back time after time. Gets a grip.

Stankfinger. Do *that,* but nothing more, she said. What was her name? The girl from Littleton, what was her name? Mushy mouth, no fun to kiss, all warm spit, slimy and no suction so that it was like wiping his lips over tepid grease. Do that okay, but don't intercourse me, she said. Got her rocks off on his finger sitting in a stolen Camaro, two gears gone, nice leathery seats, radio on. Battery wore down that night and the fucker wouldn't start. Cold night in Colorado. Had to hitch it home. Ellen! Ellen Gardner, that's who. Where is she now? Never nothing but stankfinger from her. Funny how they come and go.

He is warm of loin now, thinks about slipping on top of Mary for a quick one. Get real, he tells himself.

Henry Hank lies partly on his side like a walrus, one heavy fin over the edge of the bed, the other drifting at his side. He has a mass of gray hair covering his chest and belly. Swoops of hair cover his shoulders, his arms, the half-moon of his butt that Jasper can see. Hair is practically matted on his legs and feet. He is hammertoed. He has a faded tattoo on his chest that says MOTHER. Down his left arm are tattoos of a panther, a naked woman, and a pair of dice showing seven with the words BORN TO WIN beneath them. The blue edge of another tattoo is peeking around the curve of Henry's right arm pressed against the sheet, but Jasper can only make out the letters FI. The tail of a scar pokes out from a crease of skin that runs from Henry's shoulder to the FI letters. His belly shows scars that look like nicks in a volleyball.

Jasper leaves the bedroom. He goes to the next door, the green one, and tries to open it. It is locked. He checks the next door and finds a spare bedroom. The spare is empty, save for some cardboard boxes and a rolled rug lying in a pool of sun. A short hallway leads him finally to the bathroom.

He does his business, washes up, splashes cold water over his head, slicks his hair back, brushes his teeth with his index finger. Looking in the mirror at his stubble, he decides to grow a beard. He tells himself a beard will make him look like Jesus, or better yet, like Robin Hood, a short one on the chin, a little mustache.

He goes to the kitchen, opens the refrigerator, and finds a jug of orange juice. He drinks it half gone. The cats curl round his feet, he gives them a bowl of milk. He goes outside. In the backyard is a flower garden, daisies, dahlias coming up. There is grass at the borders. An apple tree shades the garden. A pair of old, withered apples still hang on the tree, looking like gnarly faces. Jasper thinks an apple tree in San Diego is a dumb idea. Too warm year-round for apple trees, but people will keep dreaming.

The house itself is faded beige stucco with white trim. There is a narrow garage at the end of the driveway. Jasper looks it over. In the back he finds a rusty shovel, a mattock, and a dirt fork. Inside the garage he finds an unfinished room, with a small stove and pieces of furniture. Wallboard is nailed up. A little work and the place could be cozy. There are piles of empty boxes, some tools, a pair of threadbare tires, discarded clothes, a bed with a rolled mattress. In the driveway is an aged Chevrolet fastback, '66 or '67.

He lights a cigarette, goes around front, sits on the steps in the sun, absorbing warmth and rubbing his sore jaw. Coming toward him down the street, he sees a bearded man with a guitar and next to him a smallish woman in a helmet haircut. She is wearing a white shirt and faded denims with the knees out and butterfly badges stitched to the pockets. The woman is a mystery, but the man with the guitar is Pirate. There will be music in the park today.

3. GRAY HAIRS WITH SORROW

Pirate makes the rounds and every few days he plays guitar and sings golden oldies from the Beatles and Elvis and the Everly Brothers at the park in east San Diego. He has experimented and found out that tunes from the fifties and sixties bring in more money than any other eras. It is the comfortable sentimental sanity of the older songs, he theorizes. The people who frequent the park can process "Cathy's Clown," or "I Want to Hold Your Hand," the simple emotions of their youth, whereas the music rapping the airwaves with percussive instruments and in-your-face lyrics only agitates them, sets their teeth on edge, makes them kick the dog, snarl at each other, and holler at their kids. The park is kept clean for families, especially women with children. There are shade trees, lots of grass and benches, a sandy playground filled with swings and seesaws and slides. Pirate will find a spot on the lawn and take out his guitar, leave the case open for dollar bills and loose change. He will play and sing. Jasper John will come by and prime the pump. People will see him putting money in the case and feel that they should put something in too. Pirate always gives Jasper his money back, and a little something extra for the trouble.

As Jasper suns himself on the porch, Pirate stops to talk. He sits on the step next to Jasper, takes out a packet of Zig-Zags, a pinch of marijuana from a Bull Durham sack, and rolls a joint, twisting it at the ends.

"Who punched you?" he says, pointing to Jasper's jaw.

"Can you tell?"

"It's blue."

Jasper fingers the spot lightly, feels a tender lump below his ear. "Jealous husband, I think. Over at Texas Style last night. It's all a blur."

"Hope she was worth it."

"Naw," says Jasper. "I can't hardly remember even what she looked like."

The woman in the helmet hair hangs back near the terrace, nesting under an olive tree, her back against the trunk. She is eating M&M's, popping them into her mouth one by one and chewing carefully, while she stares across the street toward the park. Streaky blond hair, a man's white shirt knotted at the waist, baggy blue pants and butterfly patches is what Jasper sees. She is thin, tiny, undernourished. Pirate indicates her when he says quietly, "She don't look like much, but she's okay."

"Where'd you find her?" Jasper asks.

Pirate has a way with women. He has a method, a formula. They come home with him and he plays old Beatle tunes for them. They think it is romantic. They drink wine, eat cheese and apple slices, smoke marijuana. Pirate claims he has never had a failure. He has lost count, but he thinks he has bedded at least five hundred women with what he calls the Beatle Method. The song that puts them into the sheets is the one called "Eleanor Rigby," about all the lonely people. Pirate thinks women fear loneliness more than they fear death or AIDS or anything.

He says that this latest thin one came home with him one night after a gig at Balboa Park. She stopped and sang a duet and the people applauded, so they sang a few more. "She's a natural," Pirate says. "Got an emerald voice." Pirate points a callused, guitar-picking finger at her and says, "She's gonna stick around and sing with me some more till she finds a steady job. She's lookin for some waitressing. I thought maybe Fat Stanley could help out." He raises his voice to the woman. "You got experience, right, Ruby?"

She nods.

Pirate winks at Jasper. "Ain't I lucky?" he says, his voice low as if he and Jasper are two conspirators. "They fall in my lap all the time. Just come outta nowhere. I never lack for something slick to dip my wick into. I'm tellin you, Jas baby, you needs to get a guitar."

"I know," says Jasper. He is jealous. He has long observed Pirate and wondered why women go for him. As far as Jasper can see, Pirate is too hairy and his nose is too big. He wears a stupid patch over an eye that isn't even blind. He has a low forehead and a beard so thick he looks like a man peering through a bush. His hair falls in back to his elbows, it enfolds his shoulders and meets up with his beard. The effect is that of a monk's cowl. What can it be that the women go for? Is it just the music, the romance of the Beatles, as Pirate says?

"Wee bit of a thing, ain't she?" he says. "It's like ballin a ten-year-old."

"Petite," says Jasper.

"Sweet," says Pirate. "Look at her left cheek," he says.

Jasper sees a dent there. Pirate says it came from a husband who beat Ruby one day with a pipe, fractured her skull too, kicked her in the belly and caused an abortion. "It ain't too bright. I mean, if some sonofabitch did that to you, would you stay with him? Neither would I. But ole Ruby did. Stayed on, in fact, till he brought home another woman and did her in Ruby's bed. Caught him at it, didn't you, Ruby?"

Ruby nods. She keeps eating her M&M's.

"I can't phantom that, can you, Jasper? I mean, he beats her half dead, but she stays. Then he brings home another woman and she goes, 'I'm not puttin up with that shit. You can beat me, but don't you ball no other broads.' How come women are so stupid?"

"It's a mystery," says Jasper.

61.

"The two halves of her brain are like a pair of Twinkies."

Pirate grins wickedly at Jasper. Jasper is slow to catch the wit about Twinkies, but he acts like he understands.

"Watch now," says Pirate. "Ruby!" he says.

"What?" she says.

"Ruby honey, alphabetize those M&M's, will you?"

She looks inside the bag. "Okay," she says. Then she goes on nibbling them.

"Ain't Ruby funny?" says Pirate.

Pirate lights the joint and the sweet smell of cannabis fills the air. He passes it to Jasper, who takes a hit, holds the smoke in his lungs for a few seconds, then releases it.

"Ruby Rush," says Pirate. "Ruby Rush. I love her name, don't you? It fills the mouth like the word 'flesh' or the word 'lust.' I'll make you a preposition, Ruby. You tell me how to make a woman commit suicide in a bathtub, and I'll buy you a double bacon cheeseburger at Fat Stanley's."

Ruby doesn't stir.

"Put a mirror at the bottom of the tub, that's how." Pirate winks at Jasper. "Doesn't get it," he says. "Hey, did I tell you I changed my name? My name is now Pirate Pomegranate. What do you think of that?"

"Catchy," says Jasper.

"Has a certain ring, don't you think? Look here, man, if you don't want them radicating you from memory, get a name that sticks. Pirate Pomegranate sticks. One day you'll see it on a record label." His thumb and forefinger create a label in the air. "Pirate Pomegranate Sings the Classics."

Again he passes the joint. Jasper takes another hit and a calm wisdom enters his soul.

"So who lives here?" says Pirate. "Pretty lady?"

Jasper tells him about Mary and about how drunk he was last night when she took him home.

"You devil," says Pirate.

"I didn't get any," says Jasper. "I fuckin passed out, man."

"You nimrod," says Pirate.

Across the street, a man comes out of his house, disappears for a moment in the garage, comes back trailing a lawn mower. He adjusts a lever on the push bar, then pulls a self-winding rope. The motor coughs. Three pulls later it starts. He lets the motor warm. Next door, an old lady who looks like a walking sack of potatoes comes out and waves at the man. She goes down the walk and adjusts a homemade sign on her lawn. It says ESTATE SALE—BARGAINS.

Pirate says, "A woman is like a lawn mower." He raises a cryptic eyebrow and looks at Jasper as if they shared the secret of how a woman is like a lawn mower. Jasper calmly, sagely nods. Pirate takes another deep hit, holds the smoke, and says, "Women are like caterpillars, they metastasize." Again the cryptic eyebrow wiggles, and again Jasper in his infinite peace nods. The toke goes back and forth until there is nothing left but ashes.

"Ruby," says Pirate. She turns around. Her face makes Jasper think of orphans. Sad mouth, defeated eyes, clingy bangs, dented cheek. She needs a makeover. "Shut up," says Pirate. She shrugs, turns her attention to the man and his mower making rectangles on the lawn.

Jasper stares at the exclamations of grass spraying from the mower. He wonders if he could learn to play the guitar and make women turn to putty the way Pirate does. Jasper knows he is not getting his share. Guys like Pirate get it all, greedy guys with guitars that leave nothing for the Jasper Johns of this world.

When Pirate heads on to the park, Ruby in tow, Jasper goes back inside the house. He smells bacon and eggs and coffee. Mary is in the kitchen. She gestures for him to sit at the table. She serves him breakfast, and while he is eating, Henry Hank comes out of the bedroom. He is wearing a silky maroon robe with the letters H/H over the breast pocket, a sign of better days. Lowering himself heavily into a chair at the table, he yawns, he scratches his beard, he looks at Jasper as if he can't quite place him. There are nests of gray in Henry's beard, especially over his chin, where it is almost white. Across his forehead are fissures that curl downward and become cobwebs circling his eyes. He looks pale as death and every minute of his fifty-eight years.

"Youz eatin all the bacon," he growls.

"Quit that," says Mary. She whacks him on top of the head with her spatula.

He rubs the spot, grimaces at Mary, says, "Ouch, what you do that for, goddammit?"

"Cuz you make me feel so ornery," she tells him.

"Youz give me a headache."

"Good."

He looks at Jasper. "She's not a mornin person."

Mary says, "Drink your coffee. How many eggs you want?"

"Lots."

She serves him six and the rest of the bacon and a pile of toast. He has four cups of coffee laced with sugar and cream. As he eats and drinks, his face takes on life, plumps up, gets pinkish. His wrinkles fade into finer lines.

"Youz look familiar now," he says to Jasper. "Youz was outta focus there." He points his fork. "Jack or some suckin fool J of a name it was." He raps his head, shouts, "Jim!"

"Jasper," says Jasper.

Henry squints like he doesn't believe the name. "Who would name a kid *Jasper?* What the whozit kind of name is Jasper? Rhymes with Casper. Jasper Casper. I bet youz hate it, huh, Jim? Kids make fun of you?"

"I never thought about it," says Jasper.

"Casper Jasper. Now a name like Henry Hank, that's a real name, that's a *man's* name." He reaches over, slugs Jasper on the arm. He looks at Jasper's bruised jaw. "Hey, what about laster night? That son-ofabitch. I thought youz was gonna kick his ass, haw, haw, haw! Knocked you over like a pin in a bowling alley. It was fun to watch."

"I'm glad I could entertain you," says Jasper.

Henry shakes Jasper's arm and laughs and tells him he's okay. Mary comes into the room and starts cleaning off the table. Henry lowers his voice. "Youz okay now, Punking? How's them pains?"

"I'm fine," she says.

"Can youz breathe better?"

She takes a drag on her cigarette and blows a stream of smoke at him.

"Guess she can breathe. Laster night she is outta puff and I'm thinkin artificial restoration." His chest swells. "Too much man for her, ain't it so, Punkin?"

"Must be," says Mary.

Henry asks Jasper if he's going to finish the toast on his plate. Jasper gives it to him. Henry swirls the toast in leftover yolk, crams it in his mouth. There is a moment of silence after he swallows, as if he's listening for something. Then he rises and heads toward the bathroom. "Coffee is just like a enema on me," he says. "Cleans me out like clockwork every mornin. That's why I'll never have cancer of the bowels!"

✛

After Jasper leaves for work, and while Henry takes one of his long showers, Mary cleans the house. She makes the bed, she dusts, she runs the vacuum. Mary has till five o'clock, a whole day to herself. She goes out on the porch and feels the sun on her face. For a moment she is happy to be alive. Such moments are very rare for Mary. They remind her of those sudden surges of joy she had in childhood when she was at the lake and the doves were gathered round her, taking bits of bread from her hand. The warm wind, the smell of still waters, gnats rising and falling on the soft wind over the muddy shore, the evergreens nearby and the sound of the doves. All of it once had the power to make her believe in life, and that beauty existed and it was good. The nibble of dove bill on her palm, the warmth of the sun on her face, these were the little mercies that made it all worthwhile.

She looks down the street and sees the sign advertising the estate

65.

sale, and she decides to go see if there really are any bargains as the sign promises. Maybe she will buy some little thing. She passes by the new-mown grass and its smell reminds her of the golf course near the little house by the lake. She remembers the man riding the mower over the greens, blades whirring. She sees the early-morning risers waiting to tee off. She sees white balls arcing above, climbing into the sun and out of sight. Her mama is watching. She and her mama shade their eyes and watch the white balls rise into the blue sky. She feels her mama's hand, long, thin, bony. She misses her mama. She is fifty-two, but she still misses her mama.

She pauses to look over the little house where the people are selling their "estate." It is a tired house, its trimming is chipped, it is grayish. There are rose bushes tangling the porch posts. The steps show the effects of wear, of many years of weathering and countless feet dimpling the wood. The screens are rusty and full of holes. Mary opens the door and steps into the living room and is relieved to find it homey, filled with a comfy sofa, two stuffed chairs, a coffee table, a rug on the floor, curtains with sheers on the windows. Along the walls are rows of bookshelves crammed with books. There is a lived-in aroma in the air, the smells of pipe smoke clinging to the carpet, and coffee wafting from the kitchen. Behind the dining-room table is an elderly lady with a tuft of white hair, glasses, a soft, imploding face. She has a shoebox in front of her, out of which she is making change for a customer who is going off with an armful of clothes.

The lady raises questioning eyes toward Mary. Mary smiles. "Just thought I'd have a look," she says.

"Everything marked must go," says the lady. Her voice is thin, all throat and taut nerves. "Clothes, furniture, chinaware, books, everything with a price tag, you'll see." She nods several times for emphasis.

Mary returns the nods. "Everything," she says. "Moving out of town?"

"Oh no, just a ways over to La Mesa. The home."

"Ah, yes," says Mary. The *home.* She turns away from the lady and walks down a row of books, but they don't interest her. How can anybody read so many? Why would they want to? Too many writers writing. There is a bust of Shakespeare on an end table and a pipe rack full of pipes. She grabs the bust, turns it upside down and sees a price sticker. She gives the lady fifteen dollars for the bust.

"It's for a friend," says Mary. "A nice young man, he's in college."

"Willie the Shake," says the lady.

"Pardon?"

"My man always calls him Willie the Shake. We got this thirty years ago in an antique shop in Tucson, Arizona. My man will be glad to know a nice Shakespeare lover got him."

"Thirty years," says Mary.

The lady snaps her fingers. "Thirty years." She smiles wistfully.

"I'm sure my friend will take good care of it," Mary tells her.

"Are you close by?" says the lady.

"Four houses down, across from the park."

"The beige place?"

"Yes."

"That was Irene and Freddie. They had the nicest garden out back. You keep the garden?"

"Oh yes. Full of flowers. You should come see." Mary is pleased to report her industry.

"Watch out for gophers. Freddie was always gassing gophers. It's a graveyard for gophers, that yard."

"I'll keep an eye out."

"There's plenty more." The lady gestures outward, her hand indicating the potpourri of a lifetime.

Mary wanders about and buys a few more things. She picks a portrait of the Madonna framed in old brass carved with vines and leaves. Holy Mother Mary wears a blue robe. She has her hands folded across her chest. From an angle she seems to be crying oily tears. From straight on, she looks peaceful. Her eyes say, "Fear nothing, I love you."

67.

"What a strange picture," says Mary. She moves to the side and the Madonna cries. She stands in front and the Madonna's benevolence shines upon her.

"*That* has been here for forty-two years," says the lady. "It was here when we moved in. It was in a closet stuck away. We're not Catholics, but we thought it was so beautiful, we hung it on the wall. My man says it reminds him of Rembrandt's work, the somber colors."

"Yes," says Mary. "Hmmm." She examines the work with respect.

"So glad an art lover got her," says the lady.

Mary also buys dinnerware, a complete set, including saucers and cups. The lady claims it is fine china, very expensive in its day. She puts Mary's purchases in cardboard boxes. She leans the picture of the Madonna against the wall.

"Anything more?" she asks.

"I'll just look around."

She goes down the hall and turns into a bedroom, looks on a bed piled with clothes, each article marked with a price tag. She sees his and hers matching nightstands and lamps. Spread over the vanity are a clock radio, costume jewelry, antique bottles in purple, amber and green, a gold-framed portrait of a man and woman. They are young, smiling, in love. He has thick hair grazing his forehead, his eyes are mischievous. She is shy, her face says he's my man, I'm his gal. Their clothes are forties war era.

Mary walks into the hall and looks left. There is another door. It has a sign on it that says PRIVATE. She eases toward the door, turns the knob. She means no harm, all she wants is just a little peek. As she looks in she is caught by an explosion of light. She squints. She shades her eyes. Stepping into the room, Mary looks around. All over the room are burning candles. Candles burn on top of a chest of drawers. Candles burn at a desk. Candles burn on a long, foldout table. Candles burn in a ring around a bed in the middle of the room. Melting wax drips off everything, piles up in cloudy nodules. It has hardened on the furniture and at the base of the candles on the floor. There is a hum in the room of an exhaust fan whirling above her head, sucking the smoke, but barely able to keep up.

She sees a human form lying in the bed. All around her are ivory walls. There is track lighting in the ceiling, every bulb blazing. There is a sliding glass door hung with gauzy curtains through which the sun pours.

"What the . . . ?" she says.

But then she thinks she understands. The candles, the lit lamps, the sunlight, and a white bed are keeping the darkness away from a very old man at the center. He is as hairless as a skull. He lies amid a cloud of white, one blue eye resembling a fixed star. The other eye drifts. Mary feels her heart slamming inside her chest. She is panting. Her stomach flutters with fear.

"He looks like Death," she murmurs to herself. "He looks like Death."

Death's mouth is twisted. Death is grinning hideously on one side, the side with the intense blue eye. Death has a wide reflective forehead, covered with a cold sheen of sweat. Death's neck looks like melting putty; his body is so thin it barely makes a ripple in the sheet.

Mary feels a pain, as if a little rock has gotten stuck deep in her chest. She puts her hand over the pain and presses. She closes her eyes a moment and takes deep breaths. "He's a man," she tells herself. "Just a poor, sick man."

The warmth and the waxy smell of the burning candles rising around her make her feel faint. She knows she'd better go. She opens her eyes and looks at the man again, and she says, "You poor dear, you poor, poor dear." With so much light falling on his face, he looks like a suspect being questioned about his crimes. His eye is fierce, it is nonrepentant.

She inches closer to him, until she is at the edge of the candles and can feel their fire. She sees the glistening pores in his nose, the broken veins, the black dots in his shaven chin. She smells him, the mildew of him rising. He does not move. He doesn't even blink. Only the shallow rise and fall of his chest and the glittering eye say he is alive. She knows this is the man in the picture in the other bedroom, the one with the mischievous look, the one who smokes all those pipes and who calls Shakespeare Willie the Shake, the one who has read all those books on the shelves in the living room. He is no doubt a very smart man. She puts out her hand, touches his chest timidly. She wants to make him feel better. "You are glowing," she tells him. "All this light."

There is no response. The eye is on her. Perhaps the eye is talking, but she cannot hear it. She starts for the door, pauses, turns to take in the scene once more, hears the old man cough, stares at him, watches his eye grow dimmer and dimmer as if some internal plug has opened beneath the iris and the colors are draining away. She hears a short, fluttering sigh.

"Oh my God," she says. "I think he just died! I think he just died right in front of me like that. Don't you dare do that to me. I won't have it."

Returning to the bed, she kicks over a few candles, sends them sputtering over the floor. She puts her head to the man's chest, waits, waits, waits.

"Oh no," she says. "Oh Jesus," she says. Her own heart is pounding so hard now she can see the folds of her blouse trembling. A pain runs down her left arm.

In a panic she heads for the sliding door. She wants to get outside before someone comes in and finds her with the dead man, connects him with her. "I'm such bad luck," she says. "I walk in a room and he dies! Jesus Christ, just like that. I'm such bad luck!" The door will not open. Looking down, she sees it has a bar lock that runs the length of the runners and is clamped at both ends. Her throat and jaw hurt terribly. Her arm feels as if it is being crushed. She wants to cry out. Her mouth is open, but no sounds are coming out. She stumbles toward the bed and notices her left leg is dragging.

I'm dying, she tells herself. It's a trap. It's a—

Mary feels her heart detonate. She feels herself falling, feels herself

70.

hitting the floor. There is a sensation of something floating pillowy beneath her. Visions of the lake confront her. Her son flailing in the water. The upturned boat. A stake through her heart. Her jaw explodes, her bladder lets go, there are sensations of flame and falling, the smell of hot wax. And then from nowhere comes a sweet, sweet peace. Everything is lovely. She knows she is smiling. They will find her that way.

♡

Henry stops by the restaurant. He has this brass horn in his hand, this *trumpet.* He nails Jasper by the sinks and asks him can he sing? Does he know "Saint Louie Woman"? Does he know "When It's Sleepy Time Down South" or "Sittin in the Sun"?

"Huh?" says Jasper.

"Check it out, Jim," says Henry. "There's this guy over the park with this gittar and he and his little toot-toot are makin a fortune, a fuckin fortune, Jim. I ain't lyin, hope to catch the clap if I'm lyin. Piles of greenback'a dollar in his gittar case. Hey, I can make sweeter music than that cat. Let me put it to youz this way: If that cat tried to play that pissin half-rock, half-folk horseshit in New York, well, Lucifer have another soul cuz the Yorkers would eat him alive! They'd stomp that tone-deaf cretin to pieces, they'd reach down his throat, pull out his lungs and use em for basketballs, they'd—"

"I get the picture," says Jasper.

"He's a cat-tastrophe!"

"He's Pirate," says Jasper.

"Friend of yours, Jim?" Henry raises a suspicious eyebrow at Jasper.

"You could say that, sort of."

Henry runs his tongue round his one fang. He takes a slow look at the kitchen, the grill, the counters, the packed shelves, the meat locker, the sinks, and the steamer. "Yeah," he says, "youz know what, Jim.

Check it out, there's better ways of makin a livin than this." He waves away the kitchen. "I'll tell youz what, youz come with the Hank and together we'll make some competition for that noodle. I'll teach youz 'Saint Louie Woman' and I'll ply my horn while youz sing big-hearted for the peoples."

"That'll be the day."

"Free fuckin money, honey!"

"I gotta job."

"Aw Jesus, lissen to the man." Henry snorts in derision. "What the hell am I gonna do with youz?"

"Just let me get back to work, will youz? Will *you?* Damn, man, you're addictive."

"Haw, haw! Youz don't know the half of it, precious. Crack cocaine ain't got nuthin on me! Youz might as well give in to my charm, son, let it happen. No sir, no use fightin the call of the wild, not when its name is Henry Hank."

Jasper sighs. He turns his back on Henry and starts scrubbing pots. He feels gluttonous eyes scanning him, but he doesn't turn around. Finally Henry leaves out the back, the screen door slamming behind him.

"Wacky sonofabitch," says Jasper. He turns to the bulletin board.

Serious relationship to be had with SWM, Sweet William from Wales. My locks are gray but my heart is young. I have my own teeth and can still do handstands and balance a eel on the end of my nose. These practices have given me an uncommon wit and a precocious body. If you are between 25–50, with firm skin beneath your chin, teeth that don't go in a glass at night, no mustache, no dowager's hump, like hiking, biking, aerobics, candlelit dinners by the sea, you're for me! Contact Sweet Will, Adam and Eve Possibilities.

"Is that better than mine?" says Fat Stanley. He stands next to Jasper, his whiskers trembling with indignation.

"It's good," says Jasper.

"Wish I could write like that. That kind of stuff gets their attention, 'balance a eel on the end of my nose.' Why can't I think of stuff like that?"

Fat Stanley waddles to the counter and digs his hands into a pot of chopped raw cabbage with shredded carrots. He adds pineapple and mayonnaise and stirs, digging deep, bringing the bottom pieces to the top over and over. He grumbles while he works, tells Jasper about his date the night before, how she had a bald spot at the crown of her head. You could see in the light how she had tried to hide it with strings of her hair. She had cheeks like a cadaver. He wants to know what is happening to women, why are they all looking like refugees? He is discouraged, very. It's as if the American woman has turned into a different species. "If they're not ripping me off, they're bald and built like hunger artists. And they've all got attitudes. Man, do they got attitudes."

"A disappointment, huh?" says Jasper, not knowing what else to say. Fat Stanley looks beat, looks like a man who has had too many doors slammed in his face.

Fat Stanley adds that he might give it up. Looking for love is too depressing. He's getting nowhere fast. He comes home each night to the same empty house and the same empty bed. He's too old now to find love. All the ones in his generation are jaded, they've seen too much. He should have gotten one when he was young, gotten someone innocent, someone uncorrupted.

"Are there any of them left? Have you found any lately?" he asks Jasper. "The sweet ones who still believe?"

"I'm still looking too," says Jasper.

Fat Stanley's hands whirl the coleslaw. Some of it is flying out of the pot and over him and the floor. "Twenty years from now, you'll be just like me!" he says. "Life is cycles. You'll be the one with the ads in the paper, you'll be the one going to bed cold and empty!"

"Baby back rib special!" shouts Helga. She places the order on the carousel and twirls it toward Fat Stanley. He pauses to look at it. Taking his hands from the cole slaw, he washes them at the sink, dries them on his apron.

"Medium salad," he says to Jasper. "Heat up some breadsticks."

They have a good lunch crowd, which includes Pirate and Ruby in a booth. They order double bacon cheeseburgers, french fries, beer. When Jasper passes by with a tray of dirty dishes, Pirate reminds him to come prime the pump on his break.

"Business is okay today," he adds. "They like Ruby. Ruby's got the voice. Mellow emeralds."

Jasper looks at her. She looks at him. He thinks her face is like a little moon, the dent in her cheek like a tiny moon crater.

"Two o'clock, the poker game at Texas Style," says Pirate. "You coming, Jasper? My good-luck piece here is coming." He pats her head, gives her a scratch behind the ear. "You my little good-luck piece, Ruby?"

"If you want," she says.

Jasper says, "No cards for me. Me and Helga are going to the movie." Jasper points out the bay window, toward the Narcissus marquee, where it says WINTER LIGHT.

From the kitchen, they can hear Fat Stanley warming up his voice. Customers are smiling, ears are perking. His song flows from the kitchen, through the slot where the carousel drips with tickets, and into the dining room.

"Ahh," says Ruby, perking up. "Opera."

"You like that stuff?" says Pirate.

"I used to go. My dad, he took me when I was a kid."

Her eyes have widened and Jasper sees an unexpected clarity there. She no longer looks detached and half awake. Jasper thinks he sees some depth, like there is more inside Ruby than Ruby lets on. As the notes fill the air, the wings of her nose quiver, her features grow more open, more receptive, more innocent, almost childish. She smiles and her teeth look too large for her mouth.

"Oh, beautiful, beautiful," she says.

Fat Stanley's song climbs an octave higher. He holds the note over them like a benediction.

"Oh, wonderful, wonderful," sighs Ruby. She is clutching her neck in one hand, her other hand reaches upward, her face is tilted toward the ceiling, her eyes are closed. She listens with a completeness that

Jasper has never seen before. Abruptly, he changes his mind about her, thinks she might be worth getting to know better.

When the song ends she says, "What's his name?"

Jasper hurries to answer. "Stanley Lipton," he tells her.

"*Fat* Stanley," says Pirate. "Fat as a tuba."

"He's a chef," says Jasper. "He used to sing in the chorus at opera houses all over the country. He's a great guy." Jasper wants to play Cupid, wants to sell Fat Stanley to her. "He always wanted to go solo, but he never got his shot."

"It's a shame," she says. "It really is. He gave me goose bumps." She points to her forearms.

"You want to meet him?" Jasper says. It crosses his mind how tickled Fat Stanley would be to meet a woman who wasn't out of the want ads. "I'd be glad to introduce you, Ruby. You guys could talk opera. Does he know his stuff!"

From afar, they hear a sound that resembles an air-raid siren. It is climbing. It is weird. It is out of place. "What the hell is that?" some customer says. People are craning their necks to see out the bay window. The noise is coming from the park. It falls off, takes up a lower note, and within seconds they recognize the brassy rhythm of a trumpet.

"Henry," says Jasper.

Helga is leaning out the door, staring toward the park. "It's him," she says.

"That's my goddamn spot," says Pirate. He throws his napkin down and hurries outside. Ruby, Helga, and Jasper follow.

When they arrive at Henry's spot, he lowers the horn and sings to them in his phlegmy voice, "Saint Louie woman, with youz di'mun wing, youz pull that man a-wound by his apwun stwing—"

In front of him is a small box with a dollar in it. People picnicking on the grass are gawking, looking at him and at each other with raised brows and frozen smiles. Children are pointing. Henry sings off-key with all his heart, belts out his song, lathering it with his pebbly throat, quacking it into the air like a lonely duck.

"Oh, Saint Louie woman—"

Pirate listens a while, hands on hips, shaggy mane quivering with indignation. He raises the patch on his eye and tries to stare Henry down. Henry is unperturbed. "You saw me here," says Pirate. "Hey, I'm talking to you! You saw me here! This is my spot here. You saw me here." He points to his guitar case. A small boy is sitting on the grass next to it, guarding it for Pirate.

Henry looks around, checks behind him and to the sides, says, "Don't see youz name, noodle."

"Everybody knows this is Pirate's spot," says Pirate. He waves his hand. "Everybody knows, just ask them."

Henry scratches under his beard. A trickle of shoe polish runs over his Adam's apple. "Public property," he says. "Free country."

"My spot," says Pirate, pouting.

Helga slides over by Henry, gives him a pat on the behind. He shows his tooth. He says, "How's it going, sweet stuff?"

"If it don't go, I push it," she tells him.

"My spot," says Pirate.

"Shut your face," says Henry. "I don't see your name nowhere."

Pirate snorts. He rolls his shoulders. "One of them troublemakers," he says. "That's what this is."

"I said, *shut your face,*" says Henry.

"I'll shut *your* face," says Pirate.

Again Henry surveys the grass around him. "Nope, I don't see your name, I surely do not see your name."

"You'll see this," says Pirate, holding up his fist.

Henry grins. He shifts his weight from one foot to the other. He flips his horn on end, holding it like a club. "Half a bust some chops, I see," he says. "Put one right between those blueberry pies, I see. Best youz know I was once in the ring with the great Floyd Patterson, best you know I can tickle your catastrophics, noodle. Youz heard of Floyd, boy?"

"I don't give a fuck who you fought," says Pirate. He reaches inside his guitar case and brings out a billy club about a foot long, smooth and black.

Henry's eyes get big. "Whoa, this is a serus man," he says. He moves his trumpet back and forth like a sword. He warns Pirate not to take him on, not a man that went ten rounds with Floyd Patterson.

Arms out, weapons raised, they circle each other and now and then take a swipe at each other. Within a few seconds of swinging, both men are already panting. Pirate takes a dive at Henry, catches him waist high, drives at him like a football player until Henry loses his footing and goes down. The trumpet flies from his hand. He catches Pirate by the collar and rolls him over, takes hold of his wrist and bites it. Pirate howls. He drops the billy club and tries to scoot away from Henry. Henry grabs Pirate's leg and climbs up it to his chest, gives him a punch on the jaw. Pirate calls him a sonofabitch and grabs his beard. He grabs Pirate's beard. They start yanking each other around by the beards and squealing and swearing.

"You fuck!"

"You fuck!"

"Goddamn sonofabitch!"

"You cunt-licking cocksucker!"

"You—"

"Yoouuu—"

They roll over and over each other, try to knee one another, try to bite the hands that hold the beards, try to punch, do punch, try to gouge, do gouge, and finally end up off the grass on the sidewalk, panting and puffing and flopping around like a pair of beached whales.

At last, Henry rolls off Pirate and lies next to him, arms stretched, his hand still holding the beard. Pirate keeps his grip on Henry's beard too. They look at one another.

"You let go, I'll let go," says Pirate.

"Youz fust," says Henry, gasping.

"Don't you fuck me," says Pirate.

"I'm a man of my word," says Henry.

77.

Pirate eases his fingers open, slides his hand away. Henry hesitates. He smiles. He gives Pirate's beard another yank, then lets it go. Before Pirate can react, Henry moves away. He sits up, laughing wetly, and he says, "Youz one tough dude, Deadeye."

"You too," says Pirate. He runs his hand over his face, smooths out his beard with the palms of his hand. "I'm tuckered out," he says.

"That's it?" says Helga, leaning over the two men, her hands on her hips. "That's it?"

They look at her. Pirate says, "What the Christ's sake you want, woman? Blood and guts?"

"At least a bloody nose! C'mon! Jesus, I don't know what the hell's the matter with men these days? Look at you, you pair of punks. If you'da fucked with Mike like that, you'd be wearing your nuts for a necklace. Nobody's got moxy no more. Look at me, I'm down to ninety pounds, got one lung left, missing half my colon, one tit, and all my reproductive organs, but I could give a better account than you two."

"Aw, go on," says Pirate.

"If I'da had a steak for lunch, he'd be dead now," says Henry. "Lack of lunch what made me run outta gas."

He holds his hand out for Jasper, and Jasper helps him up, then goes around him brushing off the grass and dirt.

"Get my horn, will youz, Jim? Get my box too. Let's go see if the boss has got a filet mignon for the Hank."

They move down the street, Henry limping, Jasper following with the trumpet, Helga bringing up the rear grumbling. Behind them, they can hear Pirate tuning his guitar.

Around two o'clock Henry rises from a row of beer cans and a licked plate, and he goes over to Texas Style for the poker game. Pirate packs up and heads there too, Ruby-good-luck-piece in tow. A bit later, Godot shows up at the restaurant. Fat Stanley closes down for the afternoon. He and Godot go to Texas Style. Helga and Jasper go to the Narcissus for *Winter Light*.

———

Afterward, they sit in the seats a while and talk about the movie. Jasper tells her it was one of Bergman's deepest, but Helga is not impressed. She doesn't get the point of the pastor saying God is a spider.

Jasper feels important. He is a college man. He knows more than Helga and he thinks he can explain how God is a spider. "Like a spider, God spins a web and when you get caught in it, he comes along and anesthetizes you and wraps you up in his web and sucks you dry. Your husk he throws away. Then your essence becomes a part of God. See what I mean?" Jasper is proud of his critical abilities.

Helga looks him over. "Is that what school is teaching you?" she says.

He nods.

Helga says, "So Bergman thinks God sucks you dry, huh?" She bites her lip. She squints at the white screen. "Like a parasite," she says. "God the parasite. And when the pastor says he is free at last, he means he's free of the spider, he's ripped himself off the web."

"Free at last when you have no beliefs," says Jasper.

"And the other way you're just a insect stuck on his web. What an image, all wrapped up in God's silk. Bergman's going to hell for that. God the spider. Wait'll he gets up there and has to explain that one." She touches his arm, clears her throat, and she says, "Half the time I don't believe in anything. And half the time I'm like some born-again fanatic. I go round and round. I say to myself, Why would a good God let such evil things happen to me? What's he trying to prove? Then I think of all I've done, and I know I deserve it. Then I change my mind and I think, Hell, I haven't been so bad, I haven't killed nobody, I haven't robbed nobody, all I've done is live a little. I've prayed a lot these past months, but I've yet to hear a whisper from Mr. All-Good."

"Heaven is always silent," says Jasper. "It's what we all bitch about."

There doesn't seem to be anything more to add. They stare at the blank screen a while, then get up and leave.

Fat Stanley is at the diner when they get back. He tells them Pirate is cleaning everybody out, has taken a bundle from Henry and Godot.

"Pirate knows his poker," says Fat Stanley. "He and Henry might kill each other before the night is over, that's my guess. Henry's looking furious."

"I wouldn't worry too much about it," says Helga. "I seen those two in action. One don't want to fight and the other's damn glad of it." She walks to the back, gets her apron, starts after the salt shakers. They get to work. They start preparing for the evening customers.

At five Mary Quick hasn't showed up. At five-thirty Jasper offers to run to the house and see what's keeping her, but people are coming in and Fat Stanley says it's time to get busy. He says he had his doubts about Mary all along, her face is the face of a lush, those bags under her eyes give her away. He says she probably spent the day wrapped around a bottle.

The evening goes by. Helga has to hustle all the tables, while Jasper tries to handle the counter. Both of them are dizzy with exhaustion by nine o'clock. It is then that Godot comes in and takes a booth. He is drunk. He scours them with bloodshot eyes and orders Helga to get him a steak and a pitcher of beer. He says that Pirate Pomegranate is a crook, but Henry Hank is a bigger crook. The two of them cleaned him out, then they got in a fight over who was cheating and Henry hit Pirate with a chair, grabbed the money on the table, and ran off. Pirate has gone home to get his gun.

Godot holds up a twenty-dollar bill. "All I got left, them sonsabitches."

Jasper and Helga stare at one another. "I'd have paid to see that," says Helga. She laughs.

"Gone to get his gun," says Jasper. "Oh boy, what now?"

"He says he's going to blow his fucking brains out," says Godot. "But I got a feeling Henry can take care of himself. That old boy has been around. Pirate better watch it."

While Godot is waiting for his order, he takes out a pen, grabs some napkins, and starts writing on them. "I'm inspired tonight," he says. "Crazy stuff like those two inspires me!" He writes and writes, covers the napkins with blue scrawls, until his food comes out. He bolts his steak down and goes back to writing. "Look out, I'm hot," he says.

"What the hell's he doing?" says Helga.

Jasper shrugs.

"You writing me a love letter, Godot?" she says.

"I'm writing a movie," he says. "I'm embarking on a new career, haven't you heard? I'm a screenwriter now."

"No shit?"

"Going to give a whole new meaning to the words 'porno movie.' "

"Oh yeah?"

"Going to create it new, the whole sucking thing. Just you watch what happens now, Helga. Just you watch."

Helga rolls her eyes at Jasper. Godot catches her look. His voice takes on a new pitch, a kind of desperate whine, "Don't you know what's happened to your poor Godot? They've given me notice, Helga. They've *rejected* me!" His face twists toward the light. Shadows play among the furrows in his brow. He looks scorched. "I am the sacrifice. I am the one forced to pay for the sins of the fathers who have oppressed the mothers since Adam slipped his IQ up Eve. So be it." He waves his hand like he doesn't care. But the look on his face says he's devastated.

Fat Stanley comes out of the kitchen wiping his hands on his apron. "You got fired?" he says.

"Not renewing my contract next semester," says Godot.

"Who did this to you? Is it Bertha Tatem?"

Godot nods. "She and her sidekick, Mary Mythwish. Pair of warthogs," he mutters. "Mary Mythwish hit me with a broadside in her Christian newsletter, that *Daily Savior* thing she hands out. She calls me 'a pernicious proselytizer for an allegorical Bible.' Her words, 'pernicious proselytizer.' " He laughs without mirth. "Where did that little nemesis come from?" he says. "I mean, from the beginning of time I have said Yahweh was an allegorist. And now it's like it's brand-new to her. Has she been living in a cave in Burma? Who ever knew in their wildest dreams there would be Mythwishers who would take Scripture as concrete fact in the late twentieth century? She says my interpretations turn Scripture into gibberish. Hah! Only for a gibberish mind." Godot snorts in disgust. "The little ditz wants us to accept every syllable as literal truth, can you believe it?"

"Tell her to grow up," says Fat Stanley. "Tell her this is 1990."

"In other words, a serpent seduced Eve, and don't call the damn brute a phallic symbol. No sir, he smooth-talked her into eating forbidden fruit and the forbidden fruit opened her eyes to nakedness and shame. Correct me if I'm wrong, but are these not symbols of self-consciousness coming awake? That's all I said in class. Just trying to get the kids to think a little bit, you know. I'm saying we were like all the other animals, and then the fruit of the tree made us see. It commemorates that point where the light flicks on and you say, 'Holy shit, that's me in the mirror.' That's all I said. It wasn't E equals MC squared. Nothing complicated. And I wasn't attacking her personally. Did I attack her personally, Jasper? You were there."

"Nope."

"Well, Mary Mythwish don't see it," says Godot. "The whole Garden story is literal fact and a lesson to us to be obedient to authority. She says the Exodus actually happened, the Red Sea, the manna, the tablets with the commandments, the forty years' wandering. She even believes Moses wrote the Pentateuch, for Christ's sake! What am I supposed to do with that? I said to her, I said show me the data."

"None of that's true?" says Fat Stanley. "Moses didn't write Exodus?"

"Oh, come on! Not you too!"

Fat Stanley's shoulders slump in shame. "Sorry," he says, "I read a lot, but I don't know history like you do."

"There's the problem in a nutshell. Nobody knows history. Nobody bothers to find out the truth. Everybody wants to go with the same old flow—and it ain't working! Somebody needs to write a new set of revelations for the times." Godot raises his forefinger and sights along it toward the overhead light. "We need the New Word made flesh, something that moves upon the face of the waters with all the formulas in its hand."

"A new god?" says Helga. "Make him a butterfly. The old one is a spider, right, Jasper?" She is teasing. She thinks Godot is funny.

Godot frowns, nods his head several times, bites his lips. "A new *Word,*" he says. "The Word made flesh for our time. Laugh if you want to, but I know what I'm saying."

He muses for a moment, twirling the tip of his beard between thumb and finger. "They used to take me at face value," he says. "I had them in the palm of my hand. Now every dimwit out there has to argue." He points to Jasper. "Bring on the hard data, boy!"

"Me?"

"All you need is to find the power Word, the kinetic Word, the Word that *is* the thing you utter. Sit, chosen one. Sit down and let me straighten you out."

"Bullshit, I'm no savior," says Jasper.

Godot blesses Jasper. *"In nomine Patris et Filii et Spiritus Sancti."*

"You're drunk," says Helga. "Look at your eyes. They're swimming."

"I see more clearly when I drink. I see *you* more clearly, Helga. 'Come into my parlor,' said the spider to the fly." Godot grins like a ghoul. He says to Helga, "Helga, you want to see something?" He looks down at his lap. "You want to see the monolith? Helga knows the monolith, don't you, Helga? Helga's prayed to the monolith many a blessed night."

Godot unzips his fly. Helga's lips press into a challenging smile. "Go ahead, I dare you," she says.

Fat Stanley shakes his finger at Godot. "That's enough of that," he tells him. "You pull that thing out in my restaurant, friend or no friend, I'll throw your ass out the door."

"Fucking guy's no fun, is he?" says Godot. "Gimme nuther pitcher of beer."

"No."

"Well, fuck me, everybody hates Godot. Did I tell you what she said, Stan? Did you hear the bitch speak? She says to me, 'When the semester's over, you're out of here, Godot.' She says to me, 'Things have changed, Godot. We're in charge now and you and your brothers are going to pay for the sins of your fathers.' If I'm misquoting one syllable, you can cut my balls off. 'You and your brothers are going to pay for the sins of your fathers.'" He leans forward, elbows on table, head in hands. "Oh boy, oh boy, are we in trouble now, fellas. Oh, uh-huh, and you know what else she says? She says, 'If you had any decency, you would be ashamed of being a man of the twentieth century!' Verbatim, verbatim. I shit you not."

Fat Stanley thinks it over, then he says, "Well, you know, you may not want to hear this, but in some ways Bertha's got a point. I mean, women might not be any great shakes, but truth is, sometimes I look around and I am ashamed of being a man of this century."

Godot explodes. "What point! What point, you fat twat! What point! Can't you see what's happening? It's a conspiracy." His fist beats the air. Words spew from his mouth like dragon's fire. "There will be licking of lye. Women are gearing up for maximum ovary production. Artificial insemination is the wave of the future. Why is that? Why are they doing it? I'll tell you why, to get rid of this!" He cups his crotch. "Babies are going to come pouring out to be whips for women, to menace society and inflict maximum damage on the ecosystem. Men, real men, are already becoming an endangered species. It's as clear as the nose on your fat face, Fat Stanley."

"Now watch what you're saying," says Fat Stanley.

Godot glares at him. "I have enemies," he says.

"Not me, Godot."

Godot points his finger. "You, yep, you. Always been something strange about you. You've been passing information to the gestapo bitches, haven't you, fat man?"

"Oh, c'mon!"

"Jasper too, I bet." He rakes Jasper with his eyes. "And Helga, of course."

84.

She gives him a two-fingered Irish salute.

Godot grins horribly. "Did you guys know that Stanley Lipton is a closet queer? Did you know that? I swear on a stack of Bibles. Did you ever notice how he lisps when there's a fairy around?"

"I don't lisp!" says Fat Stanley.

"We've all heard you," says Godot. "And Jasper there, Jasper's got that look too. Funny lips."

"I do?" says Jasper.

"Leviticus says you should be put to death."

"You liar," says Helga.

"Look it up," says Godot. "Look at Stan's mouth. Look at it, a bearded pussy."

"You sot!" yells Fat Stanley. He hauls the professor out of the booth and throws him to the floor. Godot lies there cackling and making faces. Fat Stanley sits on him, tells him to apologize, but Godot just keeps making goofy faces, twisting his lips, pretending to suck on something.

"Kill him," says Helga.

Fat Stanley catches Godot's beard and makes him be still. "Instead of disintegrating like they want you to," he says, "you should vindicate yourself. You should write another profound book. You stupid, self-pitying sot. It would shut them up. Look at how you're acting. You make me sick. You make me want to weep."

Fat Stanley rises. Godot jumps up after him and pulls a razor from his pocket. Everyone gives him room. He flips the razor open and makes teasing motions with it in the air. He says he will be revenged. "Vengeance is mine," he says. "You'll see, you'll see."

"Sit down and put that away," orders Fat Stanley. "You're drunk. You're going to hurt someone."

"Well, that's the idea, fat man. You know, you know."

He backs toward the door. He opens it and goes into the night. The gleam of the razor in his hand catches the cold moon on its blade. The blade looks for an instant like a firefly or the figure of an idea flitting above his head. He looks left and right, his head jerking, his face the face of a man looking for trouble. He spots the derelicts across the street and shouts at them, "Run, you motherfuckers!"

The men jump. They back off. They watch him as he slashes the air with the razor. They watch him turn round and round, then go west. He runs.

"Maybe we better call the cops," says Helga.

Nobody calls the cops. Fat Stanley tells them to get back to work. He mutters as he stares across the street at the two men warily inching again toward their derelict car. He says he's going to sell the diner and move back to England where he belongs. America is just too much for a civilized man to bear.

"It stinks out here," he says. "When are they going to fix those sewers? Look at those bums. Those bums are ruining us. Go away!" he shouts to the men.

The men look at him over the roof of the car. "Free country," says one.

"Vietnam vets," says the other.

Fat Stanley slams the door. He turns and bustles toward the kitchen.

"That Godot," says Helga. She has her hand over her abdomen. "He gives me the shits," she says. She heads toward the bathroom and Jasper is alone.

He starts cleaning up where Godot was sitting, gathering the napkins scattered over the table. He unfolds one and reads:

TITLE: GOLDEN SHOWER

He knew a woman had no beard
But what he kissed was mighty weird
"Foo, what's this?" quote he. "Alas!"
"Tee-hee," said she, "you've kissed my ass."
She filled her bladder with Earl Grey tea,
And on his bald head took a pee.

On another napkin is written the line: *O Romeo, O Romeo, why don't you reem my hole, O Romeo?*

"Crazy shit," says Jasper, chuckling. "Goes to show you, Ph.D. or no Ph.D." On the next napkin he finds:

Multimillion-dollar moneymaker comes to Hollywood: make way for *ReemHerHole and JuleeTit,* screenplay by Willsuck Snakeshit. Story of passion and young lust! The feud. The cunt that can't say no. The Cock a doodled who! The mad bard strikes again. Yahweh dies of apoplexy. World flies into sun. Sun ejaculates in Venus' face. Ultimate climax, spewing volcanic and Roman candle fountain gushing visuals of semen. The only Shakescene rolls once, twice, thrice, in his grave. "Cursed be he who moves my bones." If you write for fools, you're sure to have a vast audience, Professor Godot. Yuzza, yuzza, hubba, hubba.

The whole thing just tickles Jasper to no end. His chuckles won't stop. He reads and chuckles, rereads and chuckles more, breaks into wild laughter, sinks into the booth, lies on his back, kicking his legs, laughing so hard it nearly kills him.

"Jesus, Jasper," says Fat Stanley, leaning through the order slot. "You sound goofy as Godot. Must be something in this cuckoo-land driving people nuts."

The expression "cuckoo-land" sets Jasper howling. "Now you quit that," Fat Stanley orders. "I mean it, I'm serious. Dammit, boy, dammit now!"

Jasper shrieks, he kicks his legs, he waves Godot's napkins.

Fat Stanley threatens him. "I say stop! By God, you better stop that before I come out there! Jasper! Come on, won't you stop, Jasper? Won't you, for the love of God, son? Won't you? Won't you— Helga! Something's wrong with Jasper!"

"I got my own troubles," yells Helga from the toilet.

"Listen to this," says Jasper, gasping, holding Godot's poetry up, shaking it like contaminated Kleenex between his thumb and forefinger. "Oh, boss, you gotta hear this! You gotta hear these professorial pronouncements. Eeee-weee! Whew! The philosopher speaks! Listen to what he says! Listen to what he says now—"

4. FALLING LITTLE BY LITTLE

@ ⊕ ♡

After Jasper finishes reading "Golden Shower" and the movie proposal to Fat Stanley, he hears no laughter. He hears snorts of derision and then: "You want something that matches Godot's vile mind, read this." Fat Stanley knocks a knuckle against the Dial-A-Date ad. "I'm outta here," he says. He throws his apron in the laundry bin and goes out the back way. The screen door slams. Jasper can hear him spitting in the alley, hawking up something heavy, spitting it out like a wad of gum.

Helga follows soon after, her face pale as concrete. "Jesus, I'm in trouble, I'm passing blood," she says. "What the fuck," she says.

"That's bad," says Jasper. He wants to ask her more about it, but she keeps going.

"I'm fucked, fucked, fucked," she says.

After Helga is gone, Jasper reads the ad, tells himself that Dial-A-Date may be a good thing. Where else can the maimed get laid? Who wants to touch them after all? Darwin's fitness theory. Be gone, gimp. Die, dork.

He looks at all the dishes left to clean, imagines running them out to the trash. The hell with everything. He stands over the sinks. He broods about the injustices of life. He would, if he could, wave his hand and destroy the earth.

Henry Hank finds him that way, staring into greasy water, melancholy as an angel inspecting sin. "Well," says Henry. "Youz heard about Pun*king*, I can tell."

Jasper blinks his eyes, looks up, sees Henry all in black except for his bright chrome toes. "Pirate's got a gun. He's gonna shoot you," Jasper tells him.

"Naw," says Henry. He reaches into his back pocket, pulls out a pistol just barely as big as the palm of his hand. "We made a deal. We cut the cards. He won his winnings, I won this little chickadee. Ole Deadeye is okay. Me and him and the little fem are gonna put together a trio—trumpet, guitar, and warbler. Do youz play an instrument, Jim?"

"Fat Stanley plays piano," says Jasper. "Me, I don't play nothing. I can't even dance good."

"The boss plays piano?"

"Real good."

"This could be the start of somethin big." Henry taps his temple like he's got it all figured. "But lookee here," he says. "I got to take youz to see Punkin in the hospital. She asked special for her sweetie. Youz're like her boy now, her sweetie, she says."

"What happened to her?" asks Jasper.

Henry shakes his head gravely. "Bad, bad, bad. Ole Punkin had a heart attack, a major heart attack."

"A *heart* attack!"

"A *major* heart attack. Never know, do youz? I mean, who'da thought? Women, ain't they supposed to be immune to such circumstantials?"

What more can happen this awful day? Jasper feels like just giving up, just falling down dead. Mary Quick is suddenly very dear to him. She seems now to be his only true friend in the world. Just this morning she fed him bacon and eggs. He pictures her with the spatula in her hand, her eyes showing lavender saddlebags underneath. *Signs.* There had been a bluish rim around her mouth. Sure signs if only he weren't so stupid. He thinks of how he almost climbed on top of her when she was lying open on the bed, and the memory fills him with shame. She is dying of a cracked heart. Godot is losing his job, writing pornographic poems, planning porno-movie revenge. Fat Stanley wants to sell out, wants to go in quest of something better than hopeless America. Helga is passing blood. What a world, what a world. "I need to get drunk," he says.

"Later, I promise," says Henry. "First let's go see her. She wants youz, Jim. Maybe it's her dyin request." Henry puts his hand over his heart and makes a boo-boo face.

Jasper doesn't have to think it over. He closes his eyes to the mess around him, unties his apron, casts it aside like a false personality. He throws the switches, locks the door. Suddenly there is a sense of purpose inside him. He feels like a hero rushing to the rescue. He wants to get there and lay on the hands, let Mary know she can count on him, her sweetie.

They cruise down El Cajon Boulevard in Agnes, Henry's Chevrolet. The front end is bouncing like the prow of a boat over choppy water. Jasper asks Henry has he ever heard of shock absorbers, and Henry says, "Are youz a mechanic, Jim? Look here, put some shocks on old Agnes and youz can borrow her anytime. Look at that back seat. That back seat accommodations two."

"I got my Harley," says Jasper.

"Flamin legs! Them things'll kill a man. I rode one seven years and that's why this shoulder is higher than this shoulder." He points to his right shoulder. "Went down finally and broke my wrist, my elbow, and this shoulder. Youz know what they say about bikers, Jim? There is them who's gone down, and them who's goin down. Sell that iron coffin before youz die."

"No way," says Jasper.

Henry shrugs. "Nobody could tell me nothin neither. We all find out the hard way. Life is piss youz off lessons, and when youz finally wise up, it's too late to give a flyin fuck."

He is silent for a few blocks, then in a soft, almost timid voice, he says, "I hopes my Punking don't die. I'd hate that worse than fuckin a heifer. Truth is, though, she's had a weepin-weak heart since that little dipshit drowned. She went all to pieces over that. Cared nothin about nothin." Henry scrunches up his face and shakes his head from side to side. "Aw, fuck that," he says. "Look at me now, sad as cooked cabbage. Let's talk about somethin happy, Jim."

Henry doesn't hesitate to start a new subject. He talks about being a safecracker. He was an expert. His fingers were as finely tuned as a surgeon's. But since that punk amateur blew half the building down with nitro, he's lost his taste for safes. He's more creative now. He falls down in stores and collects insurance not to sue. He gambles in dens of iniquity and mostly he wins. He says Deadeye is the biggest cheater he ever seen. He spent the game rubbing Ruby's ass for luck and hiding aces in his beard, until Henry got wise and wreaked revenge. "Never trust a prick with a beard long enough to cover the bib on his bib overalls," Henry concludes. "Mine's just right." He fluffs his Lincoln with the back of his hand.

"I've done time," says Jasper. "Judge kept me in jail once for stealing cars." He knows he's bragging, but there's this feeling in him that he has to keep up with Henry.

"Youz?"

"Meez."

"Well, I'll be goddamn." Henry grins at him. "I'll be goddamn and go to hell. You know what? I knew you'd be interestin. Look here, Jim, there's this dry cleaner place, Calvin Cleans. It would be easy money. Now, let me tell youz—"

"No, don't tell me," says Jasper. "I don't want to know. I don't steal no more. I promised the judge I would knock it off if he didn't put me in reform school, and I haven't stolen so much as a Tootsie Roll since."

"How much time you done?"

"Forty days."

Henry blows it off. "Do forty days standin on my head, fartin 'Hello, Dolly!' Try five years, noodle. They'da give me more, cept I'm so sweet." He opens his mouth and laughs hard in Jasper's face. Jasper sees wet gums and big, hard-looking molars in the back of Henry's mouth. "Look here, Jim. Youz have charmed the Hank. I see a real man here, a man's man. We be buddies to the end, Jim." He pauses as if waiting to hear Jasper confirm their undying friendship.

"Yeah," says Jasper.

"A car thief," says Henry. "I tell youz, I got radar for ex-cons. My own kind just gravitates to me like God's little angels."

They park on Florida Street, near the hospital. Henry takes Jasper the back way, through the hospital library and up some stairs. They cross a hallway and enter the first room on the right. Mary is there bathed in fluorescent light. She lies under a sheet, her arm at her side taped to a board, an IV dripping something into her vein. Her hair, lying lifeless as straw, is spread across the pillow. Her face is waxy smooth. She looks like a corpse for a moment, until Henry shakes her shoulder and whispers in his phlegmy voice, "Hey, Punkin, is youz dead!"

Her body jerks as though he has zapped her with a cow prod. "Damnation, Henry," she moans. "You trying to give me a heart attack?"

Gleefully, he points to Jasper. "Look what I brung," he says.

"Jasper," she whispers. "My sweetie."

"I'm here, Mary. I'm here for you," he tells her. He takes her hand, pats it, finds it bony and cold. "Boy, who would've thought?" he says. "How'd it happen, Mary?"

She clears her throat several times, then she says, "I felt it coming a long time now. Weeks. Months. Between my shoulder blades this feeling. I felt it in my throat and down my arm too. I knew what was happening. I seen Death, Jasper. I was in a room of candles. The light trying to keep away the dark. This old man died while I was standing there. All that light didn't work."

93.

"Who died?" says Jasper.

"This old man, *her* man."

"Who's her?"

"The lady who sold me Shakespeare and the Madonna."

Jasper looks at Henry. "That house down the block having the garage sale," says Henry.

"Estate sale," corrects Mary.

Jasper remembers the sign. BARGAINS it said. "Somebody died while you were there?"

"*Her* man. In this bed all shriveled up. She had put candles all over, but it did not a bit of good. I heard his last breath, Jasper. I heard his death rattle."

"Whoa, jaggers. No wonder you had a heart attack."

"Yeah." She coughs wetly. She makes a face at the taste in her mouth. She swallows. She clears her throat.

"Youz sound pitiful," says Henry.

"I left some boxes of things at that house. I bought a bust of Shakespeare for you, Jasper. You guys get my boxes. Will you do that?"

"It's good as done," says Jasper. He thinks about owning a bust of the great bard. He doesn't know if he really likes him all that much. Difficult reading. Reading Shakespeare usually makes Jasper feel stupid.

Her eyes close for a moment. The lids look russet and rough, like the skin of baby birds. She smells a bit like a gamey pork chop. Jasper no longer feels heroic. He knows there is nothing he can do for her. Slowly, he eases his hand out of hers.

Henry starts chattering. He gives her a rundown of the poker game and how Pirate cheated, how he rubbed Ruby's ass for luck but kept aces hidden in his beard. He says how he socked Pirate and took the money, and Pirate came after him with a gun, but they sat for a shot of Incorrigible Ike instead. Pirate was supposed to shoot him after one farewell drink, but it led to another and another, and then Henry talked him into cutting cards for the gun and for the poker winnings.

94.

"And I got the gun," he says, tapping himself on the chest.

"Are we broke?" she says.

He says, "That's okay, I got remedies cookin."

Mary looks at Jasper. "Watch out for this guy," she says. "Don't let him get you in trouble."

Henry gets defensive. He says the world is full of rascals. Bad company has been the ruin of Henry Hank. He claims he was a man of Puritan potential once, but it meant giving up his soul, it meant giving up his freedom, it meant bowing down to pricks and potentates, and paying taxes, it meant selling out and going commercial. "Better to rule in hell than serve the system," he says.

"Yeah, yeah," says Mary. "Did you ask Jasper about watching the cats?"

"I forgot."

Mary sighs. "This one isn't dependable, or I'd get him to do it. His brain is four-fifths pickled pig's feet and the rest is Incorrigible Ike."

"She understands my philosophics," says Henry.

Jasper is thankful to offer something. "I'll watch the cats," he says.

"Fresh water every day," Mary tells him. "There's a bag of Princess underneath the sink and cans of cat food in the cupboard. They like a little of both. Feed them once a day. And if you would, keep an eye out for Lummox. He's my tom, an orange tabby. He's got one eye. He looks meaner than hell, but he's really very sweet."

"Not to the Hank, he ain't," says Henry.

"That's true, he hates Henry. Henry put his eye out when we were doing the garden."

"On accident," says Henry. "Nicked him with the sod fork. I never meant to, but he don't listen."

"He was just being a cat. He was just curious about what you were doing."

"Well, he found out."

"Oh, you're so mean."

Henry grins. "He don't like me and I don't like him."

Jasper can't recall an orange cat. The three grays were draped over the furniture like tired children, he remembers. And they came into the kitchen when he opened the refrigerator. "I haven't seen that one," he says. "Lummox, I haven't seen him."

"He's off in the canyons. He'll come back," says Mary.

Then there is this other favor she asks him for. The doctor has said she'll need someone to help out when she gets back home, someone to keep an eye out. Will Jasper be that someone? She knows it's a lot to ask, but will he move into the spare room for a few weeks till she's on her feet?

Henry jumps in. He says, "Free room and board, Jim, and I'll give youz somethin under the table now and then, if my luck is holdin. What youz say?"

"I guess I can do it," Jasper tells them.

Mary's smile is grateful. "You don't know what a relief it is," she says.

Henry says it would have been catastrophic for him to play nursemaid. He pulls the sheet back from the bottom and starts tickling Mary's toes. "Let's see if we can get a giggle outta her," he says. "Laughin is the best medicine, they say."

"Not tonight," she says.

"Flamin legs, I bet youz don't wanna dance neither. Look here, don't be mopin, woman. Youz depressin me, youz bringin me down. I want youz better now, or I'll have to commit suicide." He pretends to stab himself in the throat. He gurgles and gasps and falls over the foot of the bed.

"Yeah, right," says Mary. She coughs again, phlegm rattling in her throat and chest.

"Whoa, listen to that. It's ugly. We gotta go. We got things to do. Youz keep calm as mutton, Punking. Don't worry about nuthin. Me and Jim's got it under control." Henry reaches up and squeezes her cheeks between his thumb and fingers, making her lips pucker like a pleated flower. He sings, "Punkin's sweet, she's my meat, when she's well I'll lick her feet."

After the two men leave, Mary lies listening to her heart. It thumps slowly, keeping time with the drug dripping into her arm, giving off a lazy ta-dum, ta-dum. Her lungs feel like sponges. Her hands and feet are cold. It keeps hitting her every few minutes that she is mortal, Mary is mortal—is going to die. She remembers the first time death seemed real, when the telegram came saying her father was killed in action. The year was 1944. She was six years old. She remembers her mother fainting, the telegram twirling like a feather before it settled on the floor.

Outside in the hall she hears a cart going by. She hears the tinkle of glass. Somebody is talking. She has to keep telling herself that she is in a hospital, lying in bed with a serious heart condition. She is fifty-two and in a hospital. Little Mary Quick, the lake girl, has had a heart attack and is in a hospital. It does not compute.

"How did it happen?" she says. The way to the heart attack is lost somewhere in the tapestry of her life.

She was Mary Strand. She lived with her mother in a cottage by Long Lake in Illinois, a green lake that lapped her feet and brought wild doves in season to take her bread. The doves would come right up and pick the bread out of her hand. They would coo. They would even sleep beside her as she lay in the sun listening to the swish of water, the tish of trees. Her mother said she was special because the doves trusted her, the doves recognized a good soul.

She tries to picture her mother's face, but it is difficult. Vague impressions rise, a long face, soft lips, big eyes. She was a tall, gaunt, blond woman. Mary wonders how it is that some women can't get over the loss of one man. Mary has had *so many* men she can't even begin to count them. They come by in a blur, hundreds easily, probably thousands. Tom Quick was first at fourteen, a horny kid four years older than she. He had busy hands. Ever since they were little, nine, ten years old, he had his hands on her, brushing on her somehow, making out like it was casual, an accident. Tom Quick. He came into her room one night and she was ready, but his sex convulsed all over her legs before he could get it inside, gushing from him while he moaned, there in the guest room with his parents sleeping on the other side of the wall. She married him when she was eighteen. His parents were ecstatic. She was the daughter they always wanted. And then she disappointed them. A silly thing, she thinks, looking back on it. All because she was after something, God knows what. Tom never improved much in bed, and so she took a lover, and after that she took another, and a third one too. A psychiatrist once told her it wasn't better sex she needed, she was searching for her father. Mary had her doubts about that theory, but she didn't know anything for sure. Henry Hank became her fourth lover. And that's when she left Tom, and that's when J.J. died soon after in the lake, and that's when she became a prostitute, and Henry was her pimp. In the end, after twenty-two years, all they had was each other. Money gone, good times gone, drugs gone, health gone, endless rows of men wanting her, their hundred-dollar bills out, all that, all of them nothing but coagulated memory. Gone, gone, gone.

She sums it up and knows why she is in the hospital, why she's such a rickety old broad. Everything makes perfect sense. They went fast, those years, and soon enough now *she* would be a blip in the cycle of life, lost among a yillion million other blips. She wonders if in the other world where J.J. is and Jesus Christ, in that world of pure love, if she will be able to find her mother. Suicides don't go to heaven, she has heard. People who fill their pockets with rocks and jump off the ends of docks don't see the face of God. Jumped in, made a little splash, rings on the aquaface vanishing, blub, blub. Mary had been staying in town with the Quicks and no one knew for a week that her mother had jumped in the lake. When they found her shoes on the end of the dock, they dragged the lake and came up with a body unrecognizable, its head filled with baby freshwater eels.

Mary lived on with the Quicks and married their son and took lovers. She had a child but didn't know who the father was. Ten years later her child drowned in the same lake that took her mother. The horror of it made her run, run, run. But she could not run away from her son. Her son she carries with her everywhere. She knows his soul is in heaven, but the rest of him is with *her*. She thinks the arrival of Jasper might be a sign of absolution. For several days she has felt some sort of message trying to get through to her every time she takes a bath or does the dishes and feels electricity surging in the water. She has this conviction that her son has forgiven her for what she did to him. He has sent her his image.

She folds her hands and prays, "My son who art in heaven—"

That same night, driving east on El Cajon Boulevard, Henry slows down, pulls over to the curb, and points to a dry cleaners. CALVIN CLEANS says the sign. There is a bay window and they can see night lights inside casting reflections over a counter and strings of clothes on racks. Henry says the owner leaves out the back door every Friday afternoon at four forty-five, and he goes along the alley and comes out by the bank a block away, and he goes inside with his packet of receipts. It would be like stealing candy from a baby. He gestures with his hand toward the cleaners and tells Jasper to say the word and the Hank will lay the world at his feet.

"Don't even try tempting me," Jasper answers. "Not a chance."

"Gone soft," says Henry.

"I don't care," says Jasper.

Henry takes hold of Jasper's chin and stares him eye to eye. "Which world youz livin in, car thief? Youz want to lay down for the cocksuckers can stick it up your ass? Youz want to be a good boy? Youz want to pay taxes and let em say on your tombstone what a fine citizen he was? That robber baron there, that Calvin Cleans, nickel-and-dimes us all to death. All of em do, Jim. And we take it. They eat us like foxes do the hens. But lemme tell youz what, noodle, when they come to my coop, they meet the big bad wolf. I eat *them*, Jim. And that's the only question for a man in this godforsaken hellhole of a country—is youz the eat*en* or the eat*er*? Youz got to make up your mind, Jim. Do youz understand my philosophics?"

"I've read Darwin."

"Fuck that dope. I'm talkin real world now, rob or be robbed, I'm talkin here."

"Yeah, I know."

"Youz think it over."

Henry drives on. They go to the drive-through at Jack in the Box, order burgers and Cokes. While the two of them are sitting in the parking lot, eating, they watch a gang of teenagers goofing around with each other, talking, laughing. There are twelve of them, seven boys and five girls. One of the girls is leaning against a car while her boyfriend presses against her. They kiss.

"Sweet young pussy," says Henry. He sighs like he is remembering old times. "That kid don't know how lucky he is. When I was his age I was dumb as a rock. I think about some of the sweet buds I coulda picked back then, and I could kick my ass, you know. What a dope. It takes practice to learn the signals, don't it, Jim?"

Jasper nods.

Henry's eyes narrow as a woman in a loose dress walks by carrying a bag with the restaurant's logo on it. She gets in a car and sits there with a man sharing french fries and drinks.

"What youz spose her looks like under all that shimmy-shake, Jim? Anythin new?"

"Be new to me," says Jasper.

"These fems lettin it all hang out don't know nothin about a man's mind. They don't leave nothin for meditation! Damn stupid, weepin shame, Jim. Youz would think the fems would have better instinctuals, they're spose to be so goddamn mother-earthy. All that poetical poop-cock they want us to believe about em, what a load of rot, hey? Men are the ones close to nature." Henry makes a fist and shakes it at the cosmos. "Men just won't get tamed, know what I mean? Mud and blood and thunder. Bones thick as drive shafts. Fems don't get it. All fems know is hairdos and manicures, Jim. Hey, yum-yum, gimme a nibble, look at that little broad with her shorts up the crack of her ass. Cute little previews, huh?"

100.

Jasper is looking.

"Youz want her?" says Henry. "Youz want her, I'll make it so."

"Go on."

"I ain't lyin. Hope to catch the clap if I'm lyin. Say the word and she's yours. Hot pussy tonight, Jim. Hot, young pussy. Umm, tastes like tapioca."

"Don't tempt me, Henry."

"Is *that* Jim's weak spot? Is pussy his weak spot? I'll have her over here in two minutes." Henry opens the door and starts to get out. Jasper panics.

"Hell no, man, hell no!" He grabs Henry's arm and pulls him back. "You don't proposition someone like her. That's jail bait. I bet she ain't sixteen even. Come on, let's just go before you get me in trouble."

Henry shakes his head with disappointment. "Youz don't know how to live, son. That's what *real trouble* is, not knowin how to live. Youz can have no fun in life if youz don't take chances. Who cares if she's sixteen or six or sixty? What I'm saying is, don't pass nuthin up. What youz saving for? When the juices dry up, Jim, they're gone extinct. Spring turns to winter, youz get me? Real life is at the edges, see? Make somethin happen, Jim. Look here, I'll show youz what I mean."

Again Henry starts to get out, and again Jasper grabs him. "I mean it," he says. "I don't want her. That's not my style."

"I'm not doing that," says Henry. He jerks his arm away. "As the peter said to the pickle, 'Watch and learn.' "

Henry walks down to the sidewalk and stops at a mail drop. He opens the slot. He looks in, then he looks around to see if anybody is watching. The kids in the parking lot are preoccupied with each other. No one is noticing Henry.

Opening the slot again, he shouts, "Come outta there, youz whozit! Oh, lissen to him bawl, now it's too late. Papa was right, wasn't he, whozit? But no, we don't lissen to Papa!"

A bald man passes by with a Chihuahua on a leash. He stops a few feet from Henry and watches him. The dog makes vicious, squeaky noises. Henry indicates the mail drop.

"Sniffs him in there," he says. "Sniffs my baby boy."

"What's that you say?"

"Set him on top." Henry pats the mail drop. "And I turn my back for two seconds to see if the bus is comin, and down he goes. Kids are like weasels, they're like snakes, wiggle their way into anythin. This one's done it before. He thinks he's funny. Don't you think you're funny, little Henry!"

"You better tell somebody," says the man. He looks around as if there's a hero standing by, ready to come to the rescue.

While the bald man has his back turned, Henry grabs the pop-eyed Chihuahua, unhooks his leash, and drops him into the mailbox. He yells down the slot, "Pet the doggy, little Henry! Pet the doggy now."

The man gawks at Henry. "What have you done?" he says. "My God, what have you done?" He touches the mailbox, blinks at it, and looks around as if he's not sure of what is going on here, like maybe it's *Candid Camera*, or maybe Henry is one of those sidewalk magicians and it's all an illusion, the dog is up his sleeve or something.

"Everythin is fine," Henry tells him. "Be cool."

The man's mouth gapes wide as a fist. His eyes are saying, wait a minute, this can't happen to a man just out walking his dog, what's the trick here? He opens the mail slot and calls softly, "Filbert? Filbert?" Filbert squeaks a few times, then comes unglued, barks like he is going insane, goes "yi-yi-yi!" "What have you done?" says the man to Henry.

"A boy and his dog," says Henry. "A boy and his dog."

"Good God, this is terrible!" says the man.

The teenagers have stopped molesting each other. They are catching on to something happening. They move closer to listen. The dog's bark has turned into a faint squeal, a wee howl, ghostly and mournful, like the soul of a puppy passing by: *oowoowoowoo*.

Henry drapes his arm over the mail drop and runs a hand up and down its side. "It'll be fine as fish on a line," he says. "We'll gets youz outta there. Don't cry, little one." His eyes roll upward. He says, "I tole him to behave, didn't I, Lord? Oh, the damn dwarf, don't make him suffer, Lord! He don't mean harm."

"Dwarf?" says one of the boys, cocking his head curiously.

"What's going on?" says one of the girls.

"Someone chucked a baby in the box," says the boy next to her.

"A baby! Oh my God!" says the girl.

"Filbert," wails the bald man.

"Filbert," she repeats.

Voices whirl in the air. The word goes around. "Baby in the box. Baby Filbert."

Eager-eyed boys and girls descend on the mail drop. Henry has the slot open. "Say what? Say what?" he says. "He's cryin. I can hear the little wee-ness cryin."

The thin, ghostly squeal of the dog bleeds upward: *wooo, owwooo.*

"Ohhh," the girls whine.

"Better do something," says another boy, his voice all business.

"Baby's dying?" says someone else. "Is that what I hear?"

Filbert's owner takes over the slot, crams his head halfway down it, and croons, "Daddy's here, precious, Daddy's here."

"Oh, won't somebody help the pitiful thing?" says Henry. He takes out a hanky and blows his nose, wipes his eyes. He pulls his beard. He beats on the mail drop with his fist, and the bald man jumps back.

"You trying to break my ears?" he says. His eyes say he's had it with Henry.

"My heart can't take it no more," says Henry. "I'm crackin up. It's the stress. My wife left me for a piano player. Dumped the kid and run off. I'm crackin up! Can't stands no more!"

"What's he say?"

The word goes around as a larger and larger crowd gathers. "Dumped it!" "Brand-new infant!" "Crack baby!" "The mother run off!" "Umbilical cord wrapped around its neck!"

Henry beats more against the steel sides of the drop. "Why me? Why me?" he cries.

"Careful," says one of the girls. "Don't scare him."

"You're right," says Henry. "We gotta stay calm."

"Daddy's here, Filbert. Daddy's here," sings the man.

It goes on for some minutes, everybody trying to decide what to do. Some boys want to tear the drop off its foundation and turn it over. Others say it's too dangerous, they might kill the baby. More and more people come by, asking what's going on. Cars slow down, stop; there is a traffic jam. The crowd grows and grows. Jasper hears one man in the back tell the person next to him that there is a chopped-up infant in the mailbox and the killer is its mother. She jumped on the bus and got away.

"You know, the thing of it is," says the other man, "I'm not shocked. Nothing surprises me anymore, that's the thing."

"I hear you," says the first man.

The manager of the Jack in the Box comes out. He hears that the teenagers stuffed a dwarf down the mail drop. He runs back inside and phones the police. In the midst of it all, Henry slips away. He and Jasper watch the people gather deeper and deeper. The bald man is still talking down the slot. A girl is yelling for everyone to shut up, she is trying to hear the baby. The manager comes out and all his employees follow him. They're all talking at once. They're mad as hell. They want to kick the shit out of those teenagers. The teenagers don't know what's going on. Everybody is shouting at them. They shout back, they make rude gestures. Threats are made. Fists fly. Bloody noses sprout like red carnations. Cries and shrieks, bellowing and cussing corkscrew through the air. In the distance, the sounds of sirens can be heard.

Climbing back into Agnes, Henry starts her up, and Jasper gets in. They drive onto El Cajon Boulevard. They drive east. The sirens get closer, and soon a fire truck goes by blasting on its horn, red lights flashing. An ambulance screams by, followed by a black-and-white swooshing. It's a sight. Everywhere are wailing, clanging, glistening, glittering, scintillatingly shimmering bubbles of effervescent lights fizzing against the backdrop spectacle of sleepless San Diego hell-bent to rescue the little whozit nooked in a mailbox.

"These is good people," says Henry. "Fine Americans."

———

104.

They stop by Jasper's room to move his things to the house, his books and bookshelves, his portable TV, his clothes, toiletries, and bed. They tie the mattresses to the top of the car and let the rails hang out the window.

After they unload and set up the bed in the spare room, Jasper takes care of the cats, while Henry brings out his trumpet and warms up in the dining room. He plays scales, then breaks into something bluesy, something southern and sad. When he finishes he says, "Satchmo taught me that. There was the finest horn-blowin ebony nigger ever lived. Man, could he blow the horn! Youz too young to know who Satchmo is, Jim? Do you know Pops? He was a god, black and beautiful."

"I heard of him," says Jasper.

"Don't youz never say nothin bad about Pops," says Henry, his eyebrows lowering, his voice threatening.

Jasper says, "What did I say? I didn't say nothin. You the one called him nigger, Henry."

"From me, nigger is okay. Nigger is a love word in the mouth of the Hank. Pops used it all the time. He called me nigger every time I ad-libbed a riff on my horn that he couldn't match. We was in a Creole jazz band, you know. You ask him, he'd tell you I was better than Dizzy Gillespie. Pops would say to me all the time, he'd say, 'Nigger, youz is better than the Diz.' Let me tell youz somethin—one time him and me sang 'Blueberry Hill,' a duet, and Fats Domino was in the audience, this was in New Orleans, and ole Fats said it was so inspirin he went home and turned it into R and B and made a million dollars, just findin his thrill on blueberry hill. What do youz think of that? Me, I shoulda got some percentage for inspirin that boy. But once he got them gold rings on his fingers he wouldn't even give me no credit. Said it was all Pops what inspired him. There's gratitude for youz." Henry pouts. He squints hard at Jasper, like he is trying to read Jasper's brain waves. "Youz believe me?" he says.

"Is that all true?" says Jasper. "Did you really do all that?"

"True as a turkey drownin in a downpour, Jim. Youz think I'm a liar?"

"I don't know. You've sure done a lot for one lifetime."

"Better believe it, Jim. Look here, the Hank won't never lie to you unless you turn Republican. Tell me somethin—youz ever heard of Illinois Jacquet or Cannonball Adderley? How about the Duke?" Henry taps an index finger on his chest proudly. "Personal fuckin friends of the Hank. How about Oscar Peterson or Thelonious Monk? ' 'Round Midnight,' youz heard of that, Jim? Bet youz don't know John Coltrane neither nor Chick Corea none. Never even heard of Bird? What kind of education is that? Cryin shame. I say it's a cryin shame! Youz don't know nothin, man. Me, I've sniffed so much cool-jazz nigger sweat I'm half black blood by now. Look here, don't I sound like Satchmo? Tell me the truth. Don't I sound like Pops?"

"Kinda do," says Jasper.

"Damn straight." Henry lowers an eyelid, still sizing up Jasper. "Can youz sing at all, Jim?" he says.

"Sing? Me?"

"Howz about 'Birf of the Blues'?"

Jasper declines. He declines on "Hello, Dolly!" and "Saint Louie Woman" too, but Henry keeps coaxing, keeps pushing, keeps telling Jasper not to be shy, tells him he's got the kind of voice made for singing the blues. Jasper keeps shaking his head, but finally Henry has had enough nonsense and pounds the table. "Sing!" he orders. The trumpet goes to his lips, he blows, noise comes out, and Jasper makes an attempt to accommodate.

"Saint Louie woman with your diamond ring—"

"Oh yeah! Oh yeah!" shouts Henry. "Smooth as the silk of a debutante's ass. I knew youz had a voice! Let's go, let's get it on, cool-breeze."

Jasper waits for his cue, then joins in again, but this time with more confidence—"Saint Louie wo-man! with your dia-mond ring, oh, you pull that man around—by your apron strings—" He gets into it, lets it fill his veins with liquid ebony, lets it load his soul with empathic black rhythms. Henry's sweet horn sounds weave in and out of Jasper's voice. They blend like whiskey and soda and a dash of bitters, they roll the notes together, make them into one caduceus kissing and tie them in a bow. When it is over, tears are running down Henry's cheeks, and Jasper feels that with one more whining note on the horn he'll be weeping too.

"Booful, booful," says Henry, sniffing, wiping his nose on his sleeve. "Just pure blue cool youz. I ought to take us to New Orleans. We'd have em howlin, Jim."

"Yeah, it was good," says Jasper. "A little practice and we'd be real severe."

Henry lifts the trumpet and blows a heart-wailing B flat, drops down an octave, then spirals upward. Jasper listens, while outside, not far away, a dog howls. As the last trumpeted note fades away, a man outside can be heard yelling. "Have mercy, for Christ's sake, over there!"

"Aw, fuck that noodle," says Henry. "Nobody understands us arteesimo-delicate types." He sets the horn on its mouth, reaches over to the hutch drawer, and takes out a pack of cards. "Hey, youz wanna play some blackjack?"

They play blackjack and drink beer and smoke a joint. Henry cleans Jasper out. Jasper borrows twenty, and Henry takes that too. They play for Jasper's motorcycle jacket, which Henry also wins. Jasper cusses and throws the cards across the room. "I never win," he says. He can feel his lower lip pouting a foot long.

Henry tries to soothe him, tells him to keep the jacket, it won't fit no way anyhow. Jasper mellows. He puts his jacket back on and feels much better. Henry gets the Incorrigible Ike from the cupboard, pours each of them a shot, lifts his glass, and insists they drink to their deathless friendship.

Bravely Jasper takes a swallow. He coughs.

"Equal parts Drāno and antifreeze," says Henry, laughing. "Guaranteed apoplexied liver! Tickle your catastrophics."

"Gawd," moans Jasper.

"Gonna be sick?"

"Gawd." Jasper coughs so hard he feels his ears flapping. His tummy boils. He stands up to go to the bathroom and walks sideways into the green door.

"Young men are too dainty these days," says Henry.

"Poisoned," gasps Jasper.

"Don't be a pussy."

Jasper gives the knob on the door a twist, but it won't open, then he realizes it isn't the bathroom. "What is this?" he says.

"None of your bisness," says Henry.

"How come it's green?"

Henry shrugs and says it just came that way.

Jasper rattles the knob again. "I wanna see," he says.

"Off-limits till the end of time," says Henry.

"Sez who?"

"Sez Mary. It's her bisness, noodle."

"What business? What's she got so valuable in there?"

"Her conscience," says Henry.

Jasper says he doesn't get it; Henry tells him to never mind, there are more important things to think about, like where's he going to get some smokes? He crushes an empty pack of Camels. "All done," he says. He holds up the bottle of whiskey. "Incorrigible Ike getting low. Condition critical. All systems red alert."

They go out on the porch and stare across the park. They stare above the trees at the moon, so lopsided and orange it looks like some god punched it in the face, made it bleed. "Youz know what I'm thinkin? I'm thinkin this is a night for vampires and motorcycles. Let's take a ride," says Henry.

"But you hate motorcycles," says Jasper.

"I love em like I love my own cock," says Henry. "C'mon."

They go to the diner and get Jasper's Harley. Jasper is just sober enough to feel sly. He wants to scare the hell out of Henry. He straps on his goggles, kicks the engine over, tells Henry to hang on, pops the clutch. The clutch whirs, then catches, the engine chokes, coughs, catches up with the gas, and finds its roar. They are off. Jasper bends into the wind and pulls a fast, heel-eating turn down the cloverleaf to the freeway. Once in the open, he winds the Harley out. In his ear he hears Henry making weird noises that might be eeps of terror or of ecstasy, hard to tell. As always when the night blows in his face and the orange blossoms and jasmine smells of Mission Valley whiff up his nose, and his bike is full of pep, begging for endless gears forward, Jasper understands the iron horse syndrome.

Let em fly! Waaa!

Change gears—zing! whoosh!

The throaty sound of two serious cylinders growl beneath him, leaving a trail of bass macho rumbling far behind in the night. The warmth of the engine eases into Jasper's calves, the vibration rising through the saddle, tickling his rosebud, sending radiations of immortality up his spine, straight to the buzz point at the base of his neck, stroking the basic brain, making it quick as a lizard's tongue.

Down 8 they glide, dipping left and right as they rocket by cars that seem to stand still and deliberately stagger themselves across the lanes, providing a slalom round which the Harley weaves toward a distant, invisible finish line. Jasper is sure all those drivers are cussing him, saying in their hearts how he is crazy as Caligula and wishing he would crash and burn and get what is coming to him for tempting fate. But to those fearing his fearlessness, he flashes a mental finger and tells them to go home, go veg, go couch-potato it, go protect every precious day like it's made of brittle glass; but don't wish that tippytoe horseshit life on Jasper John living like he has a Roman candle up his ass. He wants to taste the purity of unsucked air, melt the wafer moon on his tongue, fill his eyes with bright white conflagrations of stars.

"We is dang-er-wusss!" screams Henry in the teeth of the wind.

White moths and other bugs tick off their heads, go wobbling like ashes left and right. "We're meteorites!" shouts Jasper. "On fire! Flaming ozone! Yeah!"

He doesn't let up until they reach the town of El Cajon ten miles away. They back off, heading down Main. They stop at a red light, then turn left on Mollison, heading back toward the freeway. Henry points to a liquor store and tells Jasper to stop. Jasper pulls into the lot, does a U-turn, and positions the bike toward the street again. Henry runs inside, while Jasper sits warming his hands on the valve covers.

A minute later Henry is back. He hops on the bike and shouts, "Go-go-go! Get us the fuck outta here!"

Jasper's reflexes engage. He revs the engine and pops the clutch. Again, there is hesitation before the Harley can get moving.

"Crappy clutch!" yells Jasper.

"Go-go!" says Henry.

When Jasper shifts to second gear, he hears an unfamiliar popping noise behind. Little cracks seem to open in the air around his head. The sounds of teasing smiles sizzle by. Jasper looks back and sees flashes of light playing around a figure standing at the entrance to the liquor store.

"I think he's shooting at us!" says Jasper.

"He *is,* noodle! Crack it! Crack it!"

The Harley leaps like a scared bunny. They race past cars and through lights and turn west at the freeway, fly up the ramp and into traffic. Jasper revs up, then flows among the vehicles, slipping along, using them to hide beside as he plays peekaboo from lane to lane. Henry pats him on the back, calls him a crafty devil, says he would marry him if he only wore a D cup.

At College Avenue, they turn off and cruise the back way to the house. When they get there, Jasper pulls far up the driveway into the shadows of the garage. He cuts the engine. He and Henry listen for sirens, but all they hear is the ticking of the motor beneath them expelling heat.

Finally Henry says, "Youz done good, son."

"Goddamn you," says Jasper.

"Hey now, don't get bent, Jim. That old fart couldn't hit the broad side of a buffalo at two paces. We was never in real trouble, not from no antique noodle like that."

"It really pisses me off, Henry."

"Don't fuss, son. Hell, we made his day. He got to shoot his gun. They'll put him on the news, make him a hero. He'll tell his grandkids what a bad ass he is. Look here, he feels alive right now like he never felt before. I bet he's thankful to us. Bang! Boom! Did youz see him? Bet he thought he was Wyatt Earp."

"Youz big stupid," says Jasper.

Henry ignores him. He gets off the bike and shows Jasper Pirate's gun, says how he slipped it neat out of his pocket and shoved it against the man's nose and told him not to have a stroke, just empty the cash register quick. The old guy slammed the money in Henry's hand and called him a dirty rotten sonofabitch. Henry cackles at the memory, but his eyes are cruel, his mouth bitter. His forefinger traces the outline of the gun in his hand.

"Don't this make your heart beat fast?" he says. "What if I point it at your head, Jim?" The hand moves and Jasper feels the nose of the gun against his temple. "Scares you, don't it? One little wiggle of my finger and youz is history."

Jasper tries to swallow but can't. "Fuck you," he croaks.

Henry lowers the gun. "Man, I love this boy!" he shouts. "Love him, *love* him! Youz fearless fuckin, wild flamin eagle! Youz run go-to-hell-copper down the fuckin freeway, fearless as Sa-*tan* his own damn self. And I'm sayin to the Hank, I'm sayin, 'This fire-breathin boy is youz back when.' Sweet balls, honey, I been just like youz my whole all-out life. Livin on the peaks, out to eat up the world like a sugar lump. I know youz! Don't tell me no different. Look here, tell me the truth, didn't youz get a stiff dick when them bullets was whippin by?"

"Scared me witless," says Jasper.

"But fuck yeah, and youz never felt better in your life!"

"That's damn sure debatable."

Henry says, "My bangin-whangin, bad-ass motherfuckin blood brother boy unto the *death* do us part, that's youz, that's meez! Come here, lover!" He pulls Jasper in and gives him a crushing hug, kisses him wetly on the cheek, calls him "my boy, my *alder*-ego."

They go into the house. Henry won't come down off his high. He

111.

talks and talks until the words mean nothing to Jasper, just so much bullshit, so much noise, noise, noise. He pretends to listen. He nods and smiles. He watches Henry toss the stolen money in the air and swat it with lefts and rights, hooks and jabs. After a while, Jasper even joins Henry in another round of "Saint Louie Woman" and then they do "Mack the Knife."

But all the time he is thinking his own philosophics on the subject of Henry Hank with his narwhal tooth, his Kiwi natural wax, water-resistant, rebuffable hair, his pit viper eyes, his jug ears with the dynamited notch in one, his pocked nose, his Harlem basement voice. He is Pandora's box, the Book of Damnation, the prophecies of Nostradamus, the apocalypse, a Rorschach symbol of the concept Catastrophic. He is a walking advertisement for birth control. A six-foot, paunchy package of unstable nitroglycerin best avoided by anyone, any twenty-three-year-old Jasper John especially, hoping to get threescore and ten and die in his bed.

5. OUTER DARKNESS

Henry shows up every night and helps him tidy up the diner, then they go get drunk again. They spend most of their time at Texas Style paying beer rent on a booth and flirting with the waitresses. It is one of those drifting-through-the-fog, smirking-like-a-politician times. Jasper finds he hardly understands himself. He goes along with whatever Henry wants. Henry is like a magnet and Jasper is a hodgepodge of metal filings.

In the midst of a fifth of Incorrigible Ike and beer chasers one night the notion hits him that he cannot live another minute without Didi Godunov. This he confesses to Henry, who says he must seize the feeling along with the girl, go to her, open his heart, sue for her pity—do it all in a suffering tone of voice and groveling posture, and if the Hank knows fems like he thinks he knows fems, Didi will open up her whim-whams and her sniffable snatch. Henry gives him a stiff-armed hail-Caesar salute and says, "Cross the Rubee-can!"

With a sense of heroic mission urging him forward, Jasper cruises to Pacific Beach, finds Didi's apartment building, parks the Harley on her sidewalk, lurches to her door, and bangs it with his fist. When she doesn't come, he shouts, "Didi! Didi! Didi!" and hammers the door some more, and at last he hears the lock turning. The door opens a crack and he can see a pair of sleepy-eyed angry eyes peeking out.

"What the fuck do you want?" she says.

"Didi!"

"What?"

"Let me in, I have to tell you something!"

"Oh, *God,* now what?" she says. She hesitates. He sees her rubbing her forehead with her fingertips like there is cramp in her brain. Finally, she steps back and beckons him inside. "Make it quick," she says. "I was sleeping."

As soon as he's in the living room, Jasper falls on his knees and confesses his love. Reaching out, he grabs her nightgown, then her knees, leans his face against her knees, kisses them, kisses up her legs, sniffs her, whispers in strangled accents that remind him uncannily of Henry's Satchmo voice, "Didi, I need *youz!*"

He can hear her snickering. She puts the heel of her hand on his head and pushes him away. "You guys and your ideas," she says.

"Didi, Didi," he says. He crawls after her, tugging at her nightie, exposing one whim-wham with a tattoo of a pansy round its nipple. "Let me sniff your flower, please!" he begs. Begging is good, Henry has told him. But dominatrix Didi eyes him coolly and tells him how pathetic he looks on his knees, like Quasimodo on the whipping wheel, she says. And she adds that drunks are disgusting, and she would never sleep with one unless she was drunk too.

In desperation, Jasper rolls onto his back near her feet, tugs at the border of her gown, and implores her to sit on his face. She looks away from him. She tells him she doesn't sit on faces unless she's in the mood. Certainly she is not in the mood to sit on the face of a thug who bursts into her apartment stinking like a brewery and wearing a prickly ugly beard that would chafe her tender peach.

114.

"Where the hell have you been for the last three days?" she wants to know. "Missing all your classes. Not even a phone call. This is love, Jasper? You don't know the meaning of the word. You're just like all the other stinking men I've known. You've probably been to a topless bar and gotten yourself all horny, and so you come here thinking I should do something about it. Men! You're all a bunch of jerks!"

Jasper John looks upward, along the plushy undulations of pinkwear, toward those eggplant-contoured breasts and that disdainful Slavic face—love, oh love! She is a walking wet dream. He closes his eyes and imagines the two of them like boa constrictors wrapping around each other, every little muscle undulating.

". . . come in here thinking just because—"

Incorrigible Ike and beer chasers and Henry's philosophics soak up her words like sponges, dulling their effect, putting him into a semiconscious snooze. He turns on his side, folds his arms, assumes the fetal position . . . drifts. He does not know how long she lectures or he sleeps. A second? A minute? An hour? It is Didi's toe digging into his ribs that wakes him.

"What?" he says.

"You fell asleep, you dirty pig. You were snoring, you horse's ass! How dare you?" She moves away. She sits on the couch, crosses her legs, kicks her foot nervously and glares at him.

"Where am I?" he says.

Her tone is that of the insulted and injured. "You tell me to sit on your face, then you fall asleep. I don't call that a compliment, Jasper John."

Jasper remembers his mission. "I'm a damn fool," he says. "There's a whirlpool in my brain," he says. He squints to keep his eyes from wobbling. He tries to concentrate on poetry that might soothe Didi. He clears his throat, prepares to speak.

"Bird thou never wert," he says with feeling.

"What did you call me?" says she.

"Unclench your floodgates."

"You're gross!"

"A shape with lion body and the head of a man is moving its slow thighs toward Bethlehem."

She leans over her knee and peers at him. "Are you quoting something?"

"I think so," he answers.

There is a moment of silence. Didi takes a deep breath. She says, "I don't do drunken orgies no more. I made a vow, never again, no more drunken, druggy sex. Wyatt Puck and his band were the last, and that's it, I mean it. Just like you, Jasper John, they were all drunk and nasty just like you. You could at least brought some grass, or come early and gotten me chilled out on wine. How would you like it if I did this to you, huh? Showed up drunk and horny and trying to bite your crotch. What would you think of that?"

Jasper considers it for a moment. He thinks he would like it fine if Didi would show up drunk and horny and biting his crotch. But he cops a plea, says he hasn't been himself lately. His friend Mary Quick had a heart attack and is dying, and he and this cool cat named Henry Hank are keeping drinking for three days to drive away the blues.

After he finishes narrating his woes, Jasper thinks his story sounds pretty sad. He wonders if he should cry to show how hurt he is, but then the bobbins of his brain spin and he remembers something she just said about some orgy with a band.

"Punk," he says. "Who's this Punk band?"

"Wyatt *Puck*," she answers. "Heavy metal, it was shit."

"And did you say him and his band was your last drunken orgy? Did I hear that right?"

She bites her lips and looks away. "None of your beeswax," she says.

"I'm not judging you," he says.

"Oh sure."

"I love you, Didi, Scout's honor."

"Oh sure, uh-huh. Men can have orgies and that's okay, but women are sluts if they do."

Jasper rises on all fours and crawls to her, eases his head onto her lap. He waits, hoping she will pet him. "All my good intentions is undone," he says, whining. "All my good intentions and look at what I've become. I was gonna show em all I had *ambition,* but now I'm gonna flunk college and Mama will know she's raised a fool. I was gonna show her I'm better than she thinks, but she's right, I got no ambition, I'm a *loser."* An unforced tear squeezes from his eye and runs onto his nostril. "Loser, loser," he echoes. "Oh, I'm so tired of myself, Didi, so tired of being no good. You're right not to fall in love with me. I'm gonna end up like Henry Hank, an old lush just hanging out."

He waits for her to say something soothing, but she is silent. He can hear her breathing. He can smell her flavor rising through her clenched legs. His cheek against her nightie feels on fire. "Boy, does my face feel hot," he says.

Pulling his head up by the hair, she tells him that his face is red as ketchup and he should get his blood pressure checked before he drops dead of a stroke. "And who is Henry Hank?" she adds.

Jasper blinks in confusion. "Don't know," he says. "Can't tell," he says. "A safecwacker from God knows where. He packs a pistol, a little twenty-five semiautomatic, he's a gambler, he's a war hero, he's a big bastard with a tooth like a unicorn's horn, he's a devil, his beard soaked in shoe polish. When he sweats, black rivers run down his throat. He painted my goatee too, see?" Jasper shoves his chin at her.

She tells him she hates it. "You look vicious in that thing," she says.

"Henry's fault. He told me to. Bad influence, Didi. Why am I hanging out with him? He stinks. He smells like . . . I don't know, like something from Borneo mixed with sweet marijuana and cheap booze. He robbed this store and I was there on my bike waiting for him. I was the getaway guy. The owner shot at us. I coulda got killed, Didi!"

"What?" she says. "You robbed a store, Jasper John?"

"Yezza."

"No shit? Really?"

"Yezza-yezza."

117.

"How much did you get?"

Jasper can't remember. "Couple hundred bucks maybe? I don't know. Enough to keep us going these past three days."

"You robbed a store," she says, and there is a note of awe in her voice.

Jasper picks up the note and runs with it, "Oh yeah, hell, near got my head blowed off, but I went like Evel *Knee*val, zigzagging all over the place, you know, and I could hear those bullets whizzing by my ears. It was close, baby."

"I didn't know you could be so wild as that," she says.

Jasper raises a cocky eyebrow. "That's the real me, baby. I'm an outlaw." He is feeling more optimistic now. It seems to him her knees have parted a hair's width against his chest. On impulse he leans in and kisses her decorated nipple. Immediately she shoves him away.

"You should smell your hair," she says. "Pee-you. I can't stand to make love to a man who smells. You could at least have taken a shower before you come over here."

Jasper is embarrassed about stinking. "Gawd, he's rubbed his smell off on me," he says. His lust unwinds like a dying cobra. No longer in the mood, he pushes himself up and stands swaying before her. There is a ring on his finger, a ring he bought from an Indian at a roadside stand in Arizona. It is silver with an etched roadrunner on its surface. He bought it because it symbolized his new freedom, he and his motorcycle going west, going to golden California. Jasper John the roadrunner. Dramatically, he pulls the ring from his finger and hands it to Didi, telling her it is a symbol of yours truly. With head high he spins toward the door, bangs against it, fumbles for the knob, opens the door, turns back, and points at her with a commanding finger.

"Didi!" he says. "Remember me whenever you see that roadrunner!"

Stiff-legged, he walks to his bike, climbs on, and turns the key in the ignition. Behind him Didi leans out the door and shouts, "Jasper, don't dye your beard! It makes you look like *Satan!*" The door slams. He starts the engine and sits for a moment thinking of his beard. He touches it. Portions are prickly. Other portions are beginning to soften with length.

"You gotta give it time," he says. "It ain't bloomed yet. Things like beards take time and nurture." He bends a bit and checks his face in the rearview mirror. The moonwash gives his skin a bluish tinge. He thinks he is handsome in a spacey sort of way. "Look like Satan, my ass. Satan wishes he could grow some noble quills like these. Makes me look cool. Jazzland Jasper." Lovingly he strokes his beard and says to her whom he no longer loves, "Prettier than your bearded cunt, Miss Didi-orgy-with-a-rock-band-Godunov."

As he drives away, he thinks of her lying naked beneath a heavy metal bunch of freaks, their faces grotesquely painted black and white. All of them with blood-red lips and spiked hair. He sees her lusciousness lying open and invaded at every orifice. His true love with long-haired druggies, all fingers and pricks and devouring mouths, bopping her, leaving their icky-sticky fluids in her. The sight makes his heart mourn, and he almost crashes into the back of a VW van that has a sticker on it that says BE A DEADHEAD. Swerving just in time, he scrapes the side of the van with his handlebar.

"You dumb shit!" the driver yells.

Jasper doesn't care about him. Fuck him. Another greasy-haired druggie in a greasy old VW piece of shit from the dishonored past. His middle finger salutes the guy. The guy honks his horn. Jasper cranks hard on the throttle and is flung into the night.

Didi goes back to bed. Too keyed up to sleep, she thrashes about for a while, then finally goes to the kitchen and pours herself a glass of wine, drinks it quickly, waits for the warmth to set in. She pours another, takes it to the couch, sits staring out the window at the filmy lights, the little mauve flames going by on Balboa Avenue. All those cars, those people, where are they going? she wonders.

The silly gawky boy, so stupid, she tells herself. What was he thinking? God, that awful chin beard. Can't he see in the mirror what it looks like? Oh, if only the Lord would give us the gift to see ourselves as others see us. "Bobby Burns," she whispers. "Oh, to have that much power, that eye for detail, and to be read two hundred years after you're dead." That's all she wants, that's all she's asking.

She thinks of the shoe polish on Jasper's beard and laughs. He is a *goof*, there's no doubt about it; but cute as the dickens. Lovely mouth. His tongue so pink, so slick and pink. He wanted her to sit on his face. He likes that stuff. She thinks now she should have done it. A little now and then is relaxing, and she wouldn't be up sipping wine if she had let him have his way, maybe. She squirms a bit, thinks of her vibrator, crosses her legs, squeezes. "See what you done?" she says. She knows he will never amount to anything. No ambition, no drive. Goes where the wind blows. Types like him always end up hand-to-mouth drunks. Fun when they're young, but they never grow up. They just get old and ugh. Drink and fuck, that's all they know, that's all life is. Wyatt Puck was that way. She was eighteen, a stupid groupie who thought rock and roll was a religion. Music can make you do anything. Music and marijuana and Southern Comfort.

She goes back to the kitchen, rinses the glass, sets it on the drainboard, goes to the bathroom, pees easily, long and heavy, with a slight afterburn. She goes back to bed, turns the light off, and lies there listening to her blood surging, hearing its power and impatience.

Faintly at first, then with growing intensity through the walls comes a muffled pounding—music, the bass cranked up. She knows she'll never be able to sleep now. Little Kelly's mother has come home with her boyfriend. Every goddamn night lately. Party, party, party. She was once a party girl herself, crazy Didi, drugs, booze, rock and roll, Wyatt and those two guys, Dick and— She cannot think of the other boy's name. God, you're really something, she tells herself. Wyatt, Dick and . . . it will not come to her. She sees him making his moves, but no name is written on his face. Running her tongue round her lips as if trying to pick up old flavors, she remembers all of them taking turns kissing her. One with his tongue in her mouth, one on her breast sucking so sweetly, making her belly button crinkle, and one below taking little nibbles. Just let yourself go.

120.

She did.

Women in the Middle Ages were prized for high foreheads and tiny mouths. Now it is big soft lips, *bee-stung* lips. *She* has a high forehead *and* big soft lips, but the rest of her is big too. Few men appreciate her size the way Jasper does. When they make love, he acts like he wants to eat her all up. Reaching down, she traces the outline of her pubic hair. She likes Jasper's mouth a lot, his twisting, prehensile lip. She wishes she had sat on it.

Ummm, yes, on her tongue was a slightly fruity, mildly sweet taste. Wyatt was watching one of them do *that* to her. That's when she knew he didn't love her. No man can love a woman and want to watch her suck another man's cock. He was a voyeur in the chair chewing her panties, his *thing* in his hand, while the others did the work at both ends. And he said, "You're so hot, you're so hot—"

A writer needs to play at the edges, she tells herself, needs to gather those rosebuds while she may. Experience life so she can tell about it. "I absolve thee," she whispers.

Bum-bum-bum goes the wall behind her. Bum-bum-bum.

"Inconsiderate assholes!" she yells. The music plays on.

She recalls her thirteen poems circulating out there in literary-land. Over and over they come in, they go out. Thank you for sending us your work. It does not fit our needs at the present time. Stupid magazines. Stupid editors. One of these days they'll all be sorry. She knows how times have changed, how transparent and thin and commercial everything must be these days. No hard read. Make it minimal. Make it slide down like an oyster shooter. Make it resemble a soap opera, a sitcom, a cop show. Those women she's competing with, they never had to battle vapidity. Stupid Plath. Stupid Sexton. What did they know about rejection? She decides she hates their work. Both women were phonies. Then it occurs to her that Plath and Sexton committed the

121.

ultimate rejection and she likes them again. Rejected the world. Suicide. The great ones are like that, they say, Fuck you, world.

Cool.

She is going to kill herself someday, when she is on top. Make it
spectacular. No head-in-the-oven stuff, no pills, something unique.
Self-incineration maybe. *She flamed out!*

*English 2000: Plath, Sexton, Godunov, the Poetic Trinity: a
graduate course (see professor for prerequisites).*

"That's all I'm asking here," she says. "Not a bunch of years to rot
away molecule by molecule. Brief let me be, but let the name of Godunov live on." She selects a modestly prim smile for the photographer.
She sees her face on the dust jacket, the italicized critical blurb: *An
immortal work!* Hard-core feminists wander the world wearing under-
shirts bought from Barnes & Noble printed with her poetic face.

Flipping from one side to the other, she remains restless and uncomfortable. Music in the walls is like an itch she can't scratch. Party
people, no artistic sensitivity, no dedication to the call. No respect for
others. Party, party, for tomorrow we die. A mean woman, that one.
She always shouts mean things to her kids. Kelly, goddamn you! she
always says. And she uses the same tone of voice in the bedroom when
she's having sex, yells at him, tells him what to do. That's what they're
doing, Didi decides. A wall away, they are fucking in time to the music.
Didi can hear the woman going, "Uh, uh, uh . . ."

"I'm going to kill myself soon as I've lived," she says. "I'll know
when to do it. At the top of my game, go off like a flare, poof! *Godunov
was a comet in the sky.*"

Turning onto her back, she kicks the covers off, stares at the ceiling. Bum-bum-bum goes the wall, spongy, maddening, stupid. They're
fucking. "You bastard, Jasper John, look what you've done," she tells
him. She would still be asleep now but for him. She decides to write a
poem about him called "Sit on My Face." She sits up. She reaches over

to the nightstand, takes out the smooth-tube, battery-operated spot massager, lies back, and lets it work while she dreams up a phantom lover, dark and handsome, sucking her toes, making them burn, making the top of her head tingle, the warm liqueur runs through her veins, honey hot like Fra Angelico. Oh, she thinks, oh, oh, I ought to spank your bottom.

"Ride me, Daddy!" shouts the wall. The woman's voice joins Didi's erotic mirage, and with it the profundo bass bum-bum-bum provides the rhythm of her lover. Didi listens and gets more and more excited. She hears him giving it to her. She is getting it too, deep inside. The cicada hum of her vibrator increases as she finds the exact *spot*. With her free hand she thumbs her breasts, first one, then the other. She wants Kelly's mother to say something more, and she does, she shouts as if she knows Didi needs to hear it. She says, "Ride me, Daddy! Oh yeah, Daddy! Ride me like we're going somewhere!"

By the time Jasper enters Texas Style, Arthur is announcing last call. Jasper shoulders his way between two men on stools at the bar and he tells Arthur to give him a pitcher.

"Not you," says Arthur. "You've had enough."

Jasper has had enough all right. Recklessly he says, "A pitcher! Now!"

"Get lost," says Arthur.

Turning around, he yells at Henry in the booth, "Henry! Ardur won't suv me, Henry! Sic em! Sic the sumbitch, Henry!"

Henry's head jerks back, his eyes roll, he advances from the booth puffing like a locomotive. A few feet from the bar, he stops beside a table, picks up a chair, and throws it to the floor. The chair bounces. It comes to rest with its legs in the air, surrendering.

"Refuss the Hank and youss die!" says Henry.

Backing up, he pushes tables and chairs aside, making a clearing in which he begins to dance and shadowbox, throwing fists at opponents attacking him all around.

"God elp the man whoos say the Hank can't ta hole ess licker! The Hank has bwokes the backs of bears and crockeedials. The Hank has gone the distance with Floyd Patterson and Minos the Mangler. He et the ahm of Fred Grendal and pulled the balls off Billy Wolf. He has drunk the blood of his enemies! So don't fuck wiss me if youss wanna see youss chilren tonight. Gimme boose, Aht, else I'll huff and puff and blow this joint down!"

"Lissen to that bird warble," says a man at the bar.

Arthur tells Henry to shut up, go home.

"By gawd!" Henry backs up to make room for a charge, but he bumps into a table and falls over, legs and arms flailing in the air. The men on the stools laugh, slap their knees and point. Arthur comes after Henry, his bald head leading the way like a battering ram. Jasper thinks Arthur is going to stomp Henry. He throws himself in the way and gets socked in the eye. Henry, on all fours, wobbling about and groaning, is raised by the collar and held face to face with pissed-off Arthur.

"Go easy on an old man with pockets full of woe," Henry tells him.

Roughly, he is taken through the door and deposited on the sidewalk. Jasper follows behind, his hand over his eye. He and Henry put their arms round each other and stare at the retreating back of Arthur. Henry shakes his fist.

"Youss lucky I'm in a gud mood, youss low-liv'n flybar," he says. "Fliver flitters, gibber twitters, giblets in gravy, snivelin snucker, shifty shitter, toad tit, brain-dead barnacle, youss queen of Bee Jay Plaza youss!"

"Look at me eye," wails Jasper.

Henry squints at him. "Where hoom? Take me hoom."

While Henry holds on to Jasper's shoulder, they walk home in silence. Jasper's stomach is churning. He hangs behind at the door and tries to calm himself by taking deep breaths.

Henry sneers at him. "Don't make mens like they use ta. In my day—" He puts his foot on the step, pauses, whirls around, and pukes on the lawn. The sight and the smell is a catalyst to Jasper. He joins Henry.

124.

"Fock!" says Henry, retching.

"Fock!" says Jasper, retching.

It takes a while to get it all out, but at last Henry is in control of himself. He goes into the house. Jasper hangs back, uncertain if he is through, then he too starts up the steps. Halfway up, something gives way beneath his foot. There is a sensation of softness. Looking down, he sees a dead rat at least six inches long. The rat has no head. Jasper jumps away. "What the—" he says. He looks behind him. He looks all around. He looks at the rat again. Its tail is like a pixie's whip.

Is it a warning? he wonders. Is someone out to get me? Headless rat—the symbol of . . . Jasper John? The Deadhead in the VW comes to mind. Didi and the Cossacks? What has he done to create enemies who would put dead rats on the steps? The last three days are unclear to him. He is sure he has acted awful, made a fool of himself many times over, left in his path a dozen or more who want revenge.

"Where be these enemies?" he whispers, paranoia bound.

A movement catches his eye. He looks into the dark at the edge of the porch. Something is out there.

"Henry!" he calls in a hoarse voice. "Henry—"

"Megyow!" A cat comes over and looks up at him as if about to ask a question. The cat is orangish, with a pair of proud jowls and one unwinking eye.

"Lummox?"

"Megyow!"

"Well, you sumbitch, where you been?"

Lummox takes a sniff of Jasper's offered hand, then allows himself to be petted. He likes Jasper. He winds around his legs in a figure eight, arches his back, and lets Jasper scratch him. He goes to the vomit, sniffs it, shakes his ears, turns to the steps, sniffs the rat, and looks at Jasper with expectation.

"Yum, yum," says Jasper. He takes the rat by the tail and pretends to drop it in his mouth. Lummox goes gooey with ecstasy, swarming Jasper's legs and trilling forth a series of musical cat notes.

They go into the house and Jasper opens a can of tuna for Lummox. While the cat is eating, Jasper goes outside and buries the rat behind the garage.

Afterward, in bed, he lies there watching the room spin. His eye is pulsing, his heart is racing. He feels like a broken-down old bum, like he has moved forward in time and is experiencing his future. Whoom, whoom whirls the bed. The mathematical laws of the cosmos have no pity on him. He thinks of what he did to Didi, thinks of her disappointed eyes and the face she made when she said he smelled.

"Stinker," he tells himself. "I'm just a stinker."

The cat appears at Jasper's side and rubs against him, finds a niche inside the armpit, and snuggles down. Suddenly Jasper doesn't feel so lost. Reaching out, he pets the cat, is comforted by soft purring vibrations. "Tomorrow," he tells himself, "yep, tomorrow things are gonna change around here." He yawns. *A new leaf.* Yawns again. *New life.* Yawns once more, smacks his lips, pets Lummox, hears the sounds of sirens far, far away. *New ssneww . . . who—*

☺

It is late morning, the air already hot. He stumbles to the shower and stays under water twenty minutes thinking about how he is destroying himself, how he must stop drinking with that old goat, how brain cells by the millions are dying every night, drowning in alcohol. He will never become a scholar cum laude at this rate. How many classes has he missed? Too, too many. He is a slow student. He needs all the lectures, all the notes, all the studying and memorizing possible just to pass his courses with a simple C. He swears to himself he has reached a turning point. He is going to knuckle down, get serious, take care of business.

Turning the water off, he grabs a towel, rubs himself viciously, until he glows pink as boiled shrimp. Checking himself in the mirror, he sees what looks like a leech under his left eye. It is not as bad as he thought it would be, more discolored than swollen. He brushes his teeth, combs his hair back, trims his beard, cutting free the connection between the mustache and the triangle on his chin. He likes what he sees, thinks he looks like Robin Hood. Going back to his room, he dresses in fresh clothes, blue jeans, undershirt, soft white socks. He takes a can of antifungal foot powder from his kit bag and sprinkles it inside his tennis shoes.

In the kitchen he fries baloney and eggs, makes toast. Lummox enters, swishes his tail hello, and sits waiting for breakfast. Near the doorway, the three grays gather to watch. Their faces are sulky. When Jasper sits down to eat, Lummox mounts a chair and stands, paws on table, waiting for tidbits. Jasper feeds him some baloney and crusts of toast dipped in egg.

"We're pals," Jasper tells him. "You and me."

Lummox winks in agreement. While he is occupied, the three grays enter the room and sniff at their empty dishes. Lummox hisses at them. They hiss back. Then they run to the living room, pause beneath the coffee table, heads together, talking it over.

Later, as Jasper sits on the sofa reading the text for Godot's class, Henry walks in and says, "Guess who's here, Jim! Bet youz can't guess!"

Hearing Henry's voice, Lummox wakes up mad as a killer bee. He flies at Henry feet-first, claws extended, fangs bared. Jasper can't believe what he is seeing, a cat taking on a man, and all business about it too, coming at him sideways, all four feet hopping boing-boing-boing, like a kangaroo, and the man giving ground, going backwards fast, and out the door, slamming the screen in the cat's face.

Henry stands there holding the door closed. "When did that whozit show up?" he says. "Grab him, will youz, Jim?"

Jasper is chuckling. He catches the cat and tucks him under one arm. "Shouldn't have poked his eye out, Henry," he says.

"Was a accident," says Henry. "What about the thirteen years me and him got along? Don't that count for nothin? If I poke your eye out, Jim, would youz forget I hauled youz over this godforsaken planet, and it was me what fed your ugly face for thirteen years? There's gratitude for youz."

Slowly up the steps comes Mary Quick. She motions to Henry to open the screen. He steps back and lets her in. "Hello, Jasper," she says.

"I didn't know you were coming home," he says.

"I couldn't stand it anymore," she tells him. She takes the cat from his arms and starts cooing, calling Lummox her poor kitty, her poor baby. "The bad man, the bad Henry," she says. She tells Jasper that cats never forgive anything.

"Juss a accident," mumbles Henry.

Lummox shows his fangs at the sound of Henry's voice. Henry slides by and goes to the kitchen. "Make me one too," Mary tells him. "How've you been, J.J.?"

Jasper says he's been tip-top. He looks her over. She is wearing a loose-fitting dress, pale green, with a tan jacket. The jacket has deep pockets that hang open and he can see rumpled tissues inside. She looks thinner. A wattle of skin trembles beneath her chin. Her nostrils are red, tender-looking. He can tell she has been blowing her nose a lot. She has been crying, and she looks infinitely tired. Her skin is grayish. There is a medicinal smell eddying from her, which reminds him of Helga.

"I feel like I look," she says, reading his mind. "What did you do to your eye?" she says.

"I fell," he says.

"On a fist?"

He thinks maybe he will tell her about his small act of heroism in trying to stop Arthur from getting to Henry, but it suddenly doesn't seem so heroic or like something he should bring up at the moment. "Zigged when I should have zagged," he tells her.

Mary sits down. She places Lummox on her lap and strokes him as she talks. "They sent me home to die. You going to be able to take care of this old gasbag till then, J.J.? Can you stand to have me on your hands. I'm an invalid now."

"Are you?"

"I'm done for," she says. Her lips twist like lemon peels and he wonders if she is going to start weeping. "It's what the doctors said. They told me, 'Baby, you got parchment paper for a heart. It could blow any second.' Hearts are supposed to go lub-a-dub. Mine goes shoosh-shoosh. Make your will, Mary Quick, get right with the Lord."

"That's what they said?"

"In so many words, yeah." From her pocket she takes a wad of tissues and coughs into it. Phlegm rattles in her chest and throat. She clears her throat and spits into the tissue, puts it back in her pocket. Jasper grimaces. He wonders himself if he can stand being around her, watching her spit, watching her move toward death like an inchworm.

She bends toward Lummox, kisses him on his blind eyelid. The cat's mouth curves in a contented smile. He looks at Jasper and his face seems to be saying, "Things don't get any better than this, pal."

Henry returns with her drink, a vodka-rocks. "They give her nitro," he says, sounding like he's talking through a throatful of dust. "They wanna do a triple bypass. Fix her up. She won't do it. What youz think of that, Jim?"

"I don't know," says Jasper. "I'd hate to have em do it to me. They saw your chest open. They open you like cracked crab."

"You hear that, Henry?" says Mary. "What did I tell you? They stop your heart and put you on a machine."

"Youz just being dramatic," says Henry.

"If I'm gonna die, I'm not doing it on no operating table hooked up to a machine. Screw that. I'm dying on my terms. I'm dying upright with a drink in my hand."

Henry looks at Jasper, gives him a wink. "Just being dramatic," he repeats.

She takes the vodka in one defiant gulp. "Did you guys get my things I bought?" she asks. "Did you get my china and my Madonna?"

Yes, they got everything.

"Come here," says Henry. "I'll show youz somethin."

Mary follows him into the bedroom. He has hung the Madonna on the wall opposite the foot of the bed. Mary smiles, she says, "Her face is so peaceful. Thank you, Henry."

"I figure when youz wake up in the morning, youz can first thing say hello."

She nods. She sits on the bed and takes her shoes off. She looks down at her calves, her feet. "I used to want to be a ballerina," she tells them. "God have mercy, with these feet."

"Youz a good dancer," says Henry. "She's the best," he tells Jasper.

Suddenly Mary is crying. She is looking at her feet and crying. Big tears are streaming down her cheeks, running into the channels at the edge of her lips and chin, falling, spattering her jacket, her wrists, her skirt.

Jasper squirms.

"Aw, Punkin, don't," says Henry.

"I don't want to die," she says.

"Aw, youz ain't gonna die, Punkin."

"I don't want to, I don't want to. I'm gonna die a big nothing. I never done nothing with my life, Henry. Nothing." She weeps into another wad of tissues.

"She's juss depressed," whispers Henry.

"We'll take care of you," says Jasper. "Don't worry about nothing, Mary. You just concentrate on getting well."

"My little boy's dead cuz of me," she says. Big sobs, big shoulder-heaving sobs break from her. "My little boy, my little boy—because of me, because I'm a coward. I'm a whore, Henry!"

"Aw, don't, Punkin."

". . . because I didn't have the guts to—"

"That's nuff now. Now, youz juss stop doing that to yourself, Punkin. I'm not gonna let youz do that no more. Quit beatin yourself up over that. It's twenty-two fuckin years, Punkin. Let it go!"

"I can't, I can't."

Awkwardly, Henry and Jasper stand beside her and pat her on the head and back, trying to soothe her.

"What the hell is life all about?" she says. "What the hell we go through all this for?" she says. "Papa gets his head blowed off, Mama drowns herself, I drown J.J., you make me a whore for twenty-two

130.

years. Would somebody please tell me the point? I hope I do die. I hope my heart blows up!"

Henry leaves her side. He goes to the window and stands looking out. He says, "I never said youz had to do it, Punkin. Youz was game."

She nods in agreement. "I was game," she says. "I'm not blaming you, Henry."

They make her lie down. They put a blanket over her and tiptoe out of the room. She hears them mumbling behind the door. They mumble, they mumble. She hears the men leave the house. She hears the men running away.

For several hours she sleeps. When she wakes it is dusk outside and a pale light is coming through the window. She looks at the Madonna and says a little prayer. She says, "Help me, Mother Mary." She remembers her mother's room and sleeping in her mother's bed and waking up in the night to hear the breath of her mother. It seems as though the past is all she can think about lately. She keeps going over it, sorting out the details, trying to remember the color of the water and how the trees shivered and how the doves ate from her hand, the feel of their tiny beaks on her palm. Comfort, comfort. Her mother's long body standing on the dock. The sad eyes searching for him who would never return.

It has slowly dawned on Mary what is wrong with her picture of the past, what is really wrong at the core. It is something she has always known, but never consciously considered until her heart attack. The cottage by the lake, the mother taking her to bed out of loneliness, the mother looking to her to fill the huge hole made by *his* death—"Dance, Mary, dance, little girl"—the mother standing like a woman in a gothic novel staring out to sea, the mother who did not love her enough to stay, who said, in effect, she wasn't enough to live for, left her to fend for herself—that mother chose death instead of her daughter. And she, the daughter, chose life instead of her son.

"We are both rotten in our own rotten way," she whispers.

The tears flow again. She just can't stop crying these days. She has no control. Emotions, nerves, everything is shot. She folds her hands and asks the Madonna to forgive her. She asks the Madonna for a sign. "Tell me what to do," she prays. "A sign. A sign," she prays. "Holy Mary, Mother of God—"

The image of a man wearing black stockings enters the room. He is naked except for the stockings. He comes toward Mary gripping an erection. His pale body floats easily over the bed. He sits on her chest. He squats with his buttocks over her breasts and places the tip of his penis over her lips. She looks into his face and recognizes him. He is the first one, the one in Chicago, the man who took off his suit and hung it on hangers and put it in the closet, the one who took off his underwear, folded it neatly on the chair, who put his shoes under the chair and put his watch on the stand beside the bed. He is the one who would not touch her with his hands, who made her do it all with her mouth, while he watched his watch. She remembers him, his soft, pale body, his hard, pale cock, his smell, his breath, his gasps when he finally came. She remembers her own sense of triumph after, mixed with disgust and sadness. He was the first of many. More than she can count. His face is the face of all. His body stands in for all their bodies. She touches him. She touches his skin. She caresses his sex, the new-ness of it, a man whose name she doesn't know, a man who moans and watches his watch. He stays on her chest. He rams her mouth. He pushes so far in, she can feel his penis nubbing the back of her throat, closing off the passage. This is what she is for, this is what he is paying her for. She doesn't want to complain, but he is hurting her. He is making tears start in her eyes. He is making her gag. Come! she wants to tell him. Please, for God's sake, mister. Come! Come!

Mary sits up. The pain runs through her chest and into her back. Her left arm is tingling. I'm dying, she tells herself. "Let it come," she says aloud. "Come on, come on then." As she urges death on, she also searches nervously through the tissue in her pockets for the pills. She finds the bottle, opens it with spastic hands, slips a pill beneath her tongue. Seconds tick away, then she feels a wee burning sensation in her anus, followed by the pain easing off. In a minute she is breathing easier. She lies back, turns on her side, wonders why the vision of her first trick should follow a chaste prayer. Close by, hovering, she can feel the Madonna's eyes.

✛

"I want to settle it up now, see if we can come to some conclusions about the human condition, see if we can't figure out what this course has taught us about the human condition, you see."

Godot closes his notes. He sits on the table and crosses his ankles. For several heavy seconds he just stares at them, his students. His eyes shift to Jasper, then to Mary Mythwish. He picks at his beard as if picking ideas from it.

"Where have we been? Where are we going?" he says. "We have been to the Greeks, to Socrates, Plato, Aristotle, and we have compared their views with the ancient mythos of the Bible, and we have seen these two great conditions, or rather traditions, collide. We have seen Christ getting absorbed by Neoplatonism. We have seen the pagan gods turned into Christian saints. We have seen the Word nearly die in the Dark Ages. We have seen the Church prevail but also lose touch with its own soul and eventually produce the likes of Martin Luther and John Calvin, and over four hundred denominations of Protestantism, all of them with truth in their hip pockets. I saw a bumper sticker that sums up what they want us to believe: 'God said it. I believe it. That settles it.' Well . . . maybe not. I mean, God said *what*? It's not entirely clear."

Godot pauses. He looks directly into Mary Mythwish's clear blue eyes. "It's the *what* that no one can tell you."

Mythwish lowers her head. She writes something on a notepad. Godot hesitates. His cheek twitches. The twitching gives him an unraveling look. He waves his arms like a man leading an orchestra. His voice rises. "It got lost somewhere," he tells them. "Once the Word was real. It had power. It created things." He looks down, his eyes searching the floor. "Once," he says. "Once . . . but now, like Pascal, the eternal silence of infinite space terrifies us, and so we turn to Jesus or Buddha or Mohammed or— 'Make it not so,' we say. 'Save us,' we say. 'Take us back to the glory days when there was no such thing as reason and science, and all men believed.' What have we got here? What have we learned as we've approached our own age? We've learned that Christ serves Mammon, that it's" (Godot makes quote marks in the air) ". . . the *American way*. We've learned that we've all got price tags on us. We've learned that this country has about as much spirituality as napalm. We've learned that God is as dead as moon dust. We've learned . . . we have learned . . . what? That the Moral Majority is really the *Moron* Majority? Oh dear, have I said something?"

Mythwish is glaring at Godot. He chuckles nervously.

"I look around me and I say, 'Why are you people here? What are you people after?' I mean, look here, people, I've taught you something this semester that can save your soul. Why don't you get the bleep out of here and find something legitimate to do? Why do you go on participating in this . . . in this system? So you can bow down and serve that *merde* money? Why don't you rebel? Why don't you tear down this institution that's making you into robots? Why don't you demand something better from it, demand that it give you something meaningful? Why does this generation never make demands? Are you broken? I don't know. You don't know. No one knows. Are you all zeros, are you all ciphers?" Godot's eyes are as round as targets. His head is tilted to one side. He is looking at them as if they are enigmas wrapped in riddles.

"Oh, shut up!" says Mary Mythwish. "Just shut up!"

"Except her, she knows," says Godot. "She knows *everything*."

"It's people like you," says Mary.

"Yes, you're right," he says. "I better shut up. I'm not popular around here, I know." He looks away from her. His beard shivers.

"It's your own fault," she says. "Listen to you, listen to what you've been saying all semester. You hate God's country, you hate its religion, and you're trying to make us hate it too. We're not going to let you. God bless America. Jesus bless us." She looks around at a number of students who are nodding in agreement. "What's he got to offer?" she says. "Somebody tell me what he's got to offer."

Shoulders bow submissively. Chins lower. Eyes look away. The entire class shrinks before Mary's challenge.

Godot's head is nodding as if he has suddenly developed a palsy. He launches into a long, rambling statement that Jasper, for one, finds difficult to follow: "Not a very good deal, is it? Old man Godot offers you nothing but your selves. You'd have to be crazy to listen to him. Follow old man Godot and you'll suffer for it. Mythwish gives you spiritual candy canes to suck on. Follow her and there will be bliss, there will be no more of that annoying suffering. Godot says it's going to hurt. But he also tells you, you can take it, and when it's finished burning off the coats of many colors you wear, and there is nothing but the core of your true self left, you will be ready for bigger and better things. You will have evolved spiritually. You will be worthy. None of you is worthy now. There is not one formula of the universe I would give to anyone in here. You're all a bunch of yams. I've shown you the equations of religious history and you still can't do the math. I give you truth and you make a taffy pull out of it. I am that I am, and you are not worthy to kiss my feet!" He leans forward, he grips his beard, he grinds his teeth at them, he continues: "And yet, still, I do what I can to unearth the gospel buried beneath a chorus of infinite opinions held by the Mythwishes of this imploding world. But you know, you little *shits*, you've worn me out." Godot's voice cracks. He has to take a few seconds to regain control. He finishes by saying he can think of nothing more that might magically enlighten them. He says that what they are seeing is a beaten prophet with a mouthful of Jeremiah and a few symbolic gestures left in his duffel bag. He touches his forehead with shaky fingers. He glances toward the door. He sighs. He says, "Let me give you a preview of coming attractions." From the pocket of his jacket he takes a safety pin, unclasps it, holds it with the point touching his palm. His face is ashen, his eyes pulse like embers in an angry wind.

Jasper feels anxious. His skin feels prickly. He has a sense of anticipation, as if Godot is about to reveal some tremendous secret that will make everything clear. The class waits. Then they watch as Godot pushes the point of the safety pin into his palm. There is a quick, very slight quiver in his thumb, but otherwise nothing betrays if Godot feels pain or not.

The students gawk at him. Some look puzzled as if they've witnessed some tremendous thing but can't say what it is. Mythwish looks like she is about to blow a vein. The pin in Godot's hand catches light from the window. It glimmers like the ghost of a tiny, triangular wing, and Jasper is reminded of the razor in the moonlight gleaming above Godot's head as he ran down Adams Avenue.

"You've just driven the last nail in your own coffin," says Mythwish. She taps her notes.

"A small exhibition of my infinite possibilities," he says. He winks at her. Then, abruptly, he stands up and leaves the room.

When the door closes, the students look at each other and someone says, "What was that all about? Wow!"

"That man's crazy," is one answer.

Jasper feels disappointed, not in Godot, but in himself. He feels like a big fake. He is young, in college, and docile. He is in lockstep with all the other students, but he feels bad about it, feels uncomfortable, feels like there should be more of the rebel in him, the iconoclast, the questioner of authority. Like the rest of them, he is chasing paper. Behaving himself, going through the motions, so he can reach the promised land. He is afraid to express himself. He is afraid to say out loud that Godot is right, that they are all wearing coats of many colors. *The layered look. Hip-hop. Slop-slop.* He listens to his classmates, their voices buzzing as they talk things over. *All fakers,* he tells himself, *would-be and wanna-be, dressed for the parts they play.* There is no anarchy in their hearts, no furious hunger to smash walls or rules or laws. There is only a mind-numbing conformity, a longing to finish their four years unchanged, intact, and with an embossed diploma in their hands, so they can take their place in the American dream. He hates them all. He wishes there were some way to remove their masks and to wipe their faces clean, start all over again.

And offer them what? Godot? Himself?

A slower speed, he thinks. A set of different formulas. A list of different words. A different definition of success. All the details can be worked out later. For now it is enough to know that this thing, this system they believe in so much, is the apocalypse unfolding.

"Godot is right!" he tells them. "We should rebel, we should break down the walls, we should . . . we should, ahhmm—"

"Shut up, Jasper," says Mythwish. "You don't know what you're talking about. Until you know, just shut up! That's Godot's whole problem, and you're just like him. A pair of cons, you two."

"What did the pin mean, Mary?" asks the girl next to her.

"Nothing! Can't you guys see what he's trying to do?"

Jasper stands up. "It means Godot's going to do something *tremendous*," he tells them.

He hurries away so he doesn't have to hear Mary's reply; but he hears her anyway, hears her shouting, "Oh sure!" and he hears her laughter.

As Jasper is leaving campus, Godot hails him from behind. The professor still has the pin in his hand. The area around the pin is dark blue, but there is no blood.

"Did you like my swan song?" he says.

"It was . . . it was wow, man," says Jasper.

"It was an act of atonement," says Godot. "And my last-ditch chance to penetrate their thick skulls. Do you think anybody got it?"

Jasper feels like lying to Godot, but he can't. "I don't think so, sir. I think Mythwish has them where she wants them."

Godot pulls the pin from his palm, looks at it, folds it together, and throws it away. A drop of blood forms over the tiny hole and sits there quavering. He and Jasper look at it together. He says, "You know, guys like us, we have to stick together. They're out to make us irrelevant. They're going to populate the earth with automatons. It'll be like Iran and Iraq."

He turns to go, then spins back and catches Jasper by the arm.

"Listen, you're my last hope. You write them a letter. You tell them what a good teacher I am. You tell them to keep me."

"A letter?"

"Counter the acid of Mythwish."

"Oh. Okay."

Godot looks left and right as if searching for spies. "I'm going to show them," he says. "I'm going to make them wish they had never messed with me. I'm going to bring such notoriety to this campus, the walls will come tumbling down. I'm going to do something no one will ever forget. Why did they reject me, Jasper?"

"I don't know, sir."

"Thunderbolts, plagues, firstborn sons."

"I'll write a letter. I'll tell them," Jasper tells him.

"I'm lost. I'm done for. I don't get what happened here. How did I get so old so fast? How did I get so out of date? When did they stop believing in me? When was I turned into garbage? Don't get old, Jasper. It's the worst thing. Not only are you invisible to youth, but nobody thinks you've got anything to say anymore. They turn away when you talk. They kill you one mini-bite at a time."

Jasper nods. He thinks of Mary Quick and Helga Martin, and he trembles to think one day he will be that old and the young will avert their eyes. Godot's eyes are moist. He is feeling pity for Godot. Poor old man. Poor unwanted old fart. A wave of sorrow runs through Jasper. He decides to write that letter for Godot, though he also knows it won't do any good. Everybody knows what is happening. Godot has fallen into outer darkness, the slough of despond, the abyss of no return. The wheels of progress have gone too far to turn back now. The old man is done for, and Jasper is sure Godot knows it too, that all these frantic movements are just the flailing of wings that will never take flight again.

6. CRYING IN THE WILDERNESS

☺ ✚ ♡

Helga goes down on her knees and clutches his pants. Startled, he pulls back, slapping her hands away, sending her spiraling to the floor. She vomits. Fat Stanley cusses into his beard, "Now what the goddamn hell?" Jasper comes from the back and stares at the commotion. Fat Stanley yells at Jasper to call 911. He tells the customers that Helga is sick, she has cancer, it's just a normal cancer collapse. She hears him mutter, "Oh, please no, not another one." She hears him whisper, "What is happening, what's going on? Why me? Why is everything happening to me lately? What have I done? Is there a curse on this place? Was this a burial ground for ancient peoples? Don't you dare die, Helga. Heaven and hell, not another dead waitress in prime time. I'll be *ruined.*"

Helga is embarrassed for herself and for him and because she cannot get up. She feels clearheaded, but detached from her body. Her body seems to belong to a raggedy doll. It flops about, it vomits, it sweats, it freezes. Up above are curious gods leaning over, looking down at her, interested in her condition. They want to suck her fluids. They want to leave her a dry husk that can be blown away. She can hear the door opening, the bell. The gods scurry to an epicenter, abandoning her for a moment to the web of life. Beside her is the kid, the one for Nancy, whose name slips her mind. He is holding her hand, telling her that everything will be all right. He is not afraid of her like the others. He pats her shoulder. Fat Stanley leans down and offers her water slopping over the rim of a glass.

She wakes in the ambulance. She hears something hissing and sees that it is a transparent snake burrowing into her arm. She reaches for its head and tears it away. Someone shouts at her. Someone slugs her in the arm. Someone puts a gag over her mouth. Someone ties her hands down.

Help, she says, but no one hears her.

A radio crackles. Commands fill the metallic spaces around her. She can hear tires sizzling on the pavement beneath her head. The ambulance goes over dips in the road and there is a pulsing sensation, like floating on a water bed.

The ambulance stops and the doors fly open. She is rushed through double doors and down a hall. She is put into a room filled with wheezing instruments and lights. She is transferred to a bed. Hands work on her. Faces come and go. Am I dying? she asks. The words get stuck in the tube in her throat.

The motorcycle vibrates beneath her, its immense power filling her with intimations of mortality. She clings to Mike, his hair whipping at her face. They soar. Then the hair is no longer hair. Her face is full of feathers. These are Harley-Davidson wings. She drives the motorcycle alone, stretches out on it, lying back, her head resting against the sissy bar, her feet forward on the yoke. She is letting it take her where it wills. In the tattoo shop the man runs something shaped like the stem of a water pipe over her arm and in fresh blue-black letters appears PROPERTY OF MIKE. He shows her the one over his heart: PROPERTY OF

HELGA. In the coffin, no longer the devil in his eye, he looks clean-cut, angelic, saintly. He smiles and says there is nothing to it, this dying thing. Don't be afraid, Helga.

Open your eyes, he says.

"Helga Martin, open your eyes!"

She opens her eyes and sees the oncologist standing over her in a white coat, a blue shirt, a blue tie. "You're dehydrated, Helga," he says. "We're going to stop the chemo for now, get your electrolytes back on track. Your blood chemistry is way off. Nod if you understand me."

She nods.

He pats her arm. "I'll be back later," he says. She hears words coming from far away. "Dangerous hemorrhage." She hears the air leaking around her.

Above her, in the high corner of the room, hovering there and smiling benevolently, is Mike. He crooks his finger at her. It's nothing, he says, it's nothing.

"What's she doing?" says a voice she recognizes.

"Pointing at something," says another voice she recognizes.

"I don't see nothing up there," says a third voice she recognizes.

Her bony arm and bony hand are raised at an angle. She sees her bony finger pointing. He is telling her to hurry up. Yes, why waste time? Good idea.

"Mom . . . Mom," says Nancy. "We're here."

"Hi, Mom," says Kathy.

"Hiya, Mom," says Mikey.

They wait for her to speak, but she is too attached to the image of Mike. He looks wonderful. I've missed you, Mike.

Me too, baby, I've missed you.

I never married again.

I know, baby.

"Is she gonna die now?" says Mikey.

Someone is crying, grabbing her hand and pleading with her not to go. She feels tears on her hand. She feels a smooth palm stroking her forehead. "Fight it, Mom," says Nancy. "We need you. We don't want you to die."

Well, you see how it is with these kids. What am I supposed to do?

He nods. He says there isn't much time left. She tells him she'll hurry.

His image vanishes. She murmurs comfort to her children. She whispers to Nancy that she has seen Daddy and that everything is okay. Nancy looks impressed. "It's just a little relapse. A couple of days and you'll be home again, Mom."

"We love you," says Kathy. "Does she hear me?"

I hear you, says Helga.

"You're scaring us," says Nancy.

She is alone and she doesn't know if it is morning or night. A long row of beds stretch out as far as she can see. The beds are full of people. All of them are so still they might be dead. She wonders if she is in a morgue. Beside her, pinned to the blanket, is a form letter. In gold letters it says: CURE FOR CANCER. What follows are row upon row of letters so small and crowded she can't read them. She tries with all her might but the words are gobbledegook. Then further down the letters get big again. They tell her what she doesn't want to know: TERMINAL EPISODE—INVOLUNTARY CONVERSION OF A HOMOSAPIEN BEING—NEGATIVE PATIENT OUTCOME—NOT THE MEDICAL ESTABLISHMENT'S FAULT—I, THE UNDERSIGNED, RELIEVE THE HOSPITAL AND ALL MEDICAL PERSONNEL OF RESPONSIBILITY FOR MY DEATH. Everything else is too, too fine to read. She thinks it may be written in Latin or Greek. Under the line marked for her signature is another bold statement that says she promises to pay a yillion dollars if she is kept alive through the miracle of modern medical science. Your life is worth a yillion dollars, isn't it? says the addendum to the form.

To who? she asks.

And as if divining her reaction, the addendum says, TO YOU, WHAT PRICE LIFE? To others, a few bucks. Maybe they would donate a dollar. Some would donate nothing. Some would as soon kill you as look at you. Your own children have been eating you for eighteen years. Flies and beetles have made homes in your feces. Microorganisms are even now breaking down your cell structure and sinews and preparing you for implosion. Your bones are as tasty as pig bones—wild dogs are waiting to scatter them over the world. We, the forms of your form, watch you walk to the edge and leap. In our thousands we watch others fall with you, and we move forward step by step, knowing it is happening to us too. We wait our turn. Those behind us wait their turn. Such is the program.

Hours later, after type O has been dripped into her vein, she sits up and drinks water through a straw and asks for a mirror. The mirror shows her a balding old woman with red hair, sharp cheekbones, sharp nose, and haunted eyes. She tells the nurse that Helga Martin used to be beautiful. The nurse says she is still beautiful. The nurse smiles at her as if she is smiling at a needy child.

Once upon a time she wasn't such a ravaged piece. Boys fell over themselves to dance with her at the sock hops. They all wanted to get in her pants. She lost her cherry when she was fifteen. She often thinks of the image of herself raising her skirt, letting him have his way. She bled and cried and he went outside the car and smoked and paced. His eyes were wild. He rushed her home and drove away like a madman. Then a week later he was back and they did it in her basement, in her father's darkroom, with the infrared light on. After that, he brought other boys over, and she didn't know how to say no. Once, her father came home unexpectedly and caught her doing it with a boy she loved named Jerry. Jerry fled out the back door, pulling up his pants as he ran. Her father made her bathe, then he sat her down with a book full of colored pictures and he showed her all the diseases boys could give you. For four years she didn't let another boy touch her. And then came Mike. And he blew her away. He came on his motorcycle, bringing his wild ways, his sexy ways, his commanding ways, and her father could no longer hold her back. The bar scenes followed, the drinking, the dope, the parties full of desperately happy people and deafening music, Bob Dylan's stuff, the Rolling Stones, the Beatles, Jimi Hendrix, Janis Joplin. Always in her heart, throughout her twenties when the kids were born, and her thirties as she tried to keep a grip on the wild spirits tempting her, she would play the music and play her life over again, and it seemed that nothing, not the kids, not the cars, not the clothes, not the furniture or the movies or the country bars, the country sounds, nothing could fill in the gap of those free-spirited years with rock and roll and Mike and the motorcycle, going wherever, doing whatever, lost in a fog of self-indulgence, all of it somehow merging with the erotic. She did *love* to make love to him. Oh yes! Never anyone else, never any of the two or three dozen after his death, made her feel the way he made her feel, not even Godot with his monstrous monolith. She and Mike went to a palm reader and the palm reader told them they were eternal lovers, that they had had other lives and had met and loved in those other lives and would always meet and love again ever after.

Helga has no more fear of going *there*. She has seen him, talked with him. He is waiting. She is anxious to get on with it, but she must hold back a bit, until she is sure Fat Stanley will take care of her kids.

♡

Fat Stanley says, "It's pret-ty bad. Pret-ty bad. They don't think she's gonna make it. The kids, I'll tell you, they're devastated, they're scared. I do my best to comfort them. I've got them at the house, staying with me. Least I could do. Poor brats got no one but her. If she goes I don't know what."

Pirate strums his guitar. Ruby sits in the shadow of a tree. Henry exercises the keys of his horn. He complains about his lip being worn out. They have spent the afternoon in the park entertaining the people. Henry's got them leaning toward jazz. He keeps pushing improvisation on a theme, a little spontaneity please. If he could dig up a drummer and get Fat Stanley to play piano, he could get them a gig, he swears. If they would just listen to him, they could go places as artists. Fat Stanley won't listen. Fat Stanley says no way. Henry says there are too many musicians with no *vision* and that's a damn shame.

It is past eight o'clock now, a warm spring night, a Sunday and they have earned sixty-seven bucks and change. The streetlights are winking. There is not enough darkness in the sky to make the lights stay on, but it won't be long now.

"She's tough," says Jasper. "If anyone can pull through, Helga can. She's tough."

Fat Stanley agrees. "But the big C's into her bones, into her brain," he says. "Gets in the bones and they start breaking. I knew a guy who broke his ribs just rolling over in bed. He had to have sponge rubber taped to him. It's a hard death."

Pirate picks at the guitar, filling the air with restful chords. Down the block the door to Texas Style opens and they hear laughter. Henry yawns. He asks for the time.

"Twenty after eight," says Fat Stanley.

Pirate asks why Henry gives a damn about the time. Henry says he doesn't give a damn about the time. Ruby Rush stands up, says she's going home. She looks at Pirate to see if he's coming. He waves at her. As she walks away, Henry remarks that her voice doesn't fit her pitiful figure, that she looks like some starving waif, but she has a big girl's voice.

"She does have a voice," says Fat Stanley. "If I could teach her *O mio bambino caro,* she would tear our hearts out. Maybe I'll do that, have her sing it for the customers some night. She's a good waitress. She stepped right in when Helga went down."

He calls after her, he says, "See you Tuesday, Ruby."

She waves.

Leaning back, his arms behind his head, he looks into the darkening sky, and he says that pretty soon he'll have more than Sundays and Mondays off. He's put the diner up for sale. There's a couple buyers already interested. He's talked about this before. Everybody knows he's going back to England to what he calls the last bastion of civilization. Henry says it's a joke. Henry says there is no bastion of civilization nowhere.

"Let's go play some poker," says Pirate.

"Not with no cheater," says Henry.

"Tub-o'-guts, you're the cheater," says Pirate.

"Flamin cheater," says Henry.

They argue over who cheats, who hides aces in his beard. Henry denies cheating at anything in his life. A natural-born winner like the Hank doesn't need to cheat nobody nohow.

"Ha!" laughs Pirate.

Godot drives by. He goes into the Union 76 and gets some gas, then he drives across the street and parks at the curb down the hill.

"What's he want?" says Pirate. "That cat gives me the creeps."

Henry says, "Can't stand them Ph.D. punks."

Godot gets out of the car and climbs to where they sit. He stands in front of them, staring at them like someone looking for a fight. He is a mess. His coat is torn, the sleeves are split across both shoulders, the front pocket is hanging by a thread, his pants are ripped at the knees. There is a rim of dried blood on his lower lip. Crusts of blood ring his nostrils. Tracers of blood have dried over portions of his white beard. He clenches and unclenches his fists. His eyes are fiercely aggressive.

"What happened to you?" says Fat Stanley. He reaches in the case and hands Godot a beer.

Godot takes the beer, twists the top off, drinks. He flops down and removes his shoes and socks, wiggles his toes in the grass. "Told me not to even come back and finish the last two weeks," he tells them. "They got a restraining order."

"Who? Tatem?" asks Fat Stanley.

"The department, the whole university," says Godot. He laughs. "They're scared to death of me," he says.

"What'd you do?"

"Tore the place up. Got drunk and tore it up good. Tequila makes you crazy, did you know that?"

146.

"Tequila," says Fat Stanley.

Godot looks at Jasper. "Did you write that letter?" he says. Then he says, "Never mind, I don't care. I don't give a flying fuck about anything anymore."

Jasper has forgotten to write the letter. He feels vaguely guilty, but what the hell, it wouldn't have done any good anyway.

Godot takes off his suit jacket, rolls it up, uses it for a pillow. He sniffs the air. "When are they going to fix the sewers?" he says. "The air is so damn heavy in this town, a man can hardly breathe." Taking out a bloodstained hanky he picks at crusts of blood on his nostrils. "I tried being nice, you know. I tried reasoning with them. They wouldn't listen, so I sent a trash can through the front window at the admin building. The campus cops beat me, they had me arrested by the SDPD."

"Jesus, Godot," says Fat Stanley.

"Good for youz," says Henry.

He shows Henry a nasty cut on his lip, says he gave tit for tat. "I had to post bail. They think I'll pay for those windows, but I'll rot in hell first. When I think of all the wasted years I gave them, ungrateful bleepin cocksuckers—"

"Jesus, Godot, you're an educated man. What the hell you doing drinking tequila and throwing trash cans through windows?" says Fat Stanley, and he says, "Jesus, Godot, snap out of it." Fat Stanley is shaking his head with disappointment. "You're getting crazier and crazier, man."

"What's being educated got to do with it?" says Godot. He shows off his knuckles, all skinned and swollen. "I didn't go down without a fight," he says. "When I was in the navy I was division middleweight champ. Had lightning in one hand, thunder in the other. They called me SOS Godot. I used to have a picture of me with my guard up, ready to punch your lights out. Wish I could show you that one. You'd see a different Godot."

Henry is impressed. "No shit? Youz? A fuckin fighter?"

"I was young then, a little thunder god. It was aeons ago."

147.

Pirate wants to know how Godot became a professor and he tells them it was the GI Bill. After the war, he went to college and just kept on going until he got his doctorate. It wasn't good for anything but teaching, so he taught. "But I'm no teacher anymore," he adds. He clears his throat, spits. "I got bigger, better plans now. Don't ever count Godot out."

Jasper thinks he'll take Godot's mind off his troubles by telling him about Helga, about the cancer going wild, so he runs it through, what happened to her.

"Well, that's a blow," says Godot. "Helga's had a tough life, and now she's dying. I'll miss her, I really will. She's real people. Not like the ones who did me in; they're not real people. Backstabbers. Sneaks. Jealous of me, that's what, ever since I won that Outstanding Professor Award. Wish I'd never won it. Assholes have been scheming against me ever since, I swear. Been chipping away at my foundations, the little bleepin bugs." He smashes his fist into the grass. He tells them, "There are no real people in academia. They think what they're doing is important. It's not. None of it's important anymore. It's not like it was when I was in school, a degree meant something then, meant you were educated, meant you were deep. Now it's all just abstract antiseptics. What's really important now is making money. Lots and lots of money. You don't need an education for that. All you need is cunning and moxie. You want to know how to make money?" he says. He winks at Henry.

Henry bites. "What makes money?" he says.

"You want to know?"

"Hell yeah."

Godot looks at the sky as if reading the answer there. "Sex and violence make money," he says.

"Well, yeah, everybody knows that."

Godot bends closer to Henry. "Movies," he says. He winks again, gives Henry the thumbs-up and the A-OK.

"Movies," repeats Henry. "Yeah? Yeah? Youz got somethin up your sleeve, I can tell."

"I do. I really do. I've written a screenplay. I've written a knockout sex and violence screenplay, a sexy, brilliant screenplay." A nearly hysterical laugh bursts from him. He points at them and giggles like a girl. "You should see your faces!" he says.

They look at each other. They are puzzled, but intrigued. Their focus centers on Godot again. He says, yes, he has written a screenplay and he is going to make a movie and become a millionaire. He has taken *Romeo and Juliet,* rewritten it in free-floating blank verse with a twist. He has married Will Shakespeare to pornography down and dirty. ". . . Juliet as nymphomaniac. Romeo as well-hung stud. The two of them as light through yonder window breaks caught doing it sixty-nine, imagine that, and imagine an overvoice talking dirty in your ear—half of sex is talking dirty, you know. My actors will speak verse—iambic pentameter, blank verse—and end up screwing themselves to death on a tombstone. Obsessional sex and death, a violent combination. Perfect formula for making money. It's what the world wants. It's in, baby."

"Porno's hot!" says Henry.

"Damn sure is!" agrees Pirate.

Godot explains. He gives them the philosophy behind his inspiration. He is going to write a series of plays adapting Shakespeare to pornography. He will write bottom-of-the-barrel bawdy art for America's infamous look-down-their-noses society. He will create dirty movies that come across as brain food. XXX-rated Shakespeare, huzza, huzza, something you can take the wife to, something the intellectuals can slip into their VCR and whack off to without feeling guilty, something at the cutting edge of the New Culture.

"Hot damn!" says Henry. "I like to hear this cat talk!"

"This has got teeth in it!" says Pirate. "It's got mileage!"

Godot raises his forefinger and says, "It is our striving that redeems us, boys. It is our striving that vindicates us. If you succeed, all sins are forgiven."

"That's a fact," says Henry. "Flamin legs, Professor, youz is spittin on a tidal wave. A movie like that, it could be big, very, very big. Look here, what happened back in the early days when those noodles made *Deep Throat?* Fuckin flocks of people went. Fems was opening up their mouths from coast to coast. Cocksucking went serus with that flick. It was in, it was a gazillion-dollar flick, man. This is what I'm sayin, Professor, youz come up with a *potent-motion* idea—Shakespeare's down-home fuckin? It's got legs, it's got flamin legs, man!"

"Naked Nanette," says Jasper. "I hear they made that for peanuts and its brought in twenty million dollars so far this year. I read that somewhere. Imagine it, people paying twenty million dollars just to watch."

"I can't believe what I'm hearing," says Fat Stanley. "I mean, come on, Godot, *come on.*"

Godot chuckles wickedly. He gives Fat Stanley's shoulder a playful shove. "Wake up, innocent one," he says. "Wake up and smell the porn. Porn is *now,* porn is the future, porn is forever. The people are used to it, they just want it more sophisticated. I'm saying, let's face it, you can't go out and free-fuck anymore. It's not the seventies or the early eighties. Sex with strangers isn't safe. Sex kills. But are we any less horny? Hell no. We want it more than ever. So what are we supposed to do?" Godot ticks the choices off on his fingers. "These are the seven ages of man now: One, we masturbate; two, we pile on the condoms; three, we get blood tests before we go to bed with whoever she is—"

"Fuck that," says Pirate. "I take my chances."

"Four, we take our chances." Godot nods toward Pirate. "Five, we get married and stay faithful; six, when she turns into Pork Chop Patty, we rent movies and fantasize; seven, we forget the whole thing and turn celibate. Now, there's no market for celibacy; but for the right kind of movies, the sky's the limit, boys."

"No end to it," says Henry. He spreads his palms expansively toward the cosmos above them.

"It's a fuckin fact," says Pirate.

"My movie is timely," says Godot. "Perfect timing for once in my life. My movie will fill a niche. Listen to me, there are no worthwhile pursuits left. Everybody knows there is nothing worthwhile anymore.

150.

We've gone as far as we're going intellectually, morally, ethically, and what have we found? No absolutes. Not a goddamn thing, boys. Zero, *nada*. We've left old Godots behind, we've gotten rid of old laws, old traditions, and fallen into a bottomless hole where we're all squirming in confusion. We've outsmarted ourselves. Nothing left to do but go with the flow, get in on it, make some coin, kick back on the balcony of our mansions, sip Moët, and watch the whole thing come tumbling down."

"It's wrong, you're wrong," says Fat Stanley.

Godot points at him. "The pot calling the kettle black. He runs an ad in the papers and gets himself laid twice a month by a prostitute posing as a lovesick bitch. Now, what the hell are you looking for out there, Stanley? You looking for love, honey?"

Fat Stanley's tone turns belligerent. "Yes . . . yes, I'm looking for love."

"But in the meantime you take what comes along. What is love?" Godot takes a handful of groin and gives it a shake. "It's a bone for some hot young thing. I can prove it. Look here, once you get much older do you think you'll still be advertising? Hell no. If AIDS doesn't get you first, you won't care. Why won't you care? Because *love* is hormones, honey."

"It's more than that, Godot. But there's no use arguing with a cynic. I'm not gonna argue with you. I got kids at home. I've got responsibilities," he says, standing up to leave.

"Let him go," says Henry, waving goodbye. "We got to have juss true believers in on this thing."

"You want in?" says Godot.

Henry's face is full of admiration for the professor. "I wisht I had thought of it, it's a gem," he says. "Hell yeah, I want in."

Pirate wants in too. They make a deal. Godot tells them he needs a thousand bucks apiece to get started on production preliminaries.

"Done!" says Henry.

"Done!" says Pirate.

There are details to be discussed. Godot runs to his car in his bare

151.

feet and returns with a quart of Incorrigible Ike and a manuscript, which he throws into Henry's lap. He does a little dance for them, a kind of jig, while he sings:

> *Oh, I'm losing my mind and I don't give a damn*
> *I've got a fine notion to make me a man*
> *And from his fifth rib I'll bring forth a pig*
> *I'll make it walk upright and wear a big wig*
> *Hi-ho, here I go, playing with creation*
> *Fiddlededee, it's only* me! *full of inspiration!*

Godot grabs his shoes and flings them into the air, one after the other high over the grass and onto the sandlot. "Let's get serious, boys."

They go to Henry's house. When they get inside, Godot washes up in the bathroom and comes back with Band-Aids on his forehead and across his nose. His lower lip looks raw. His knuckles are swollen.

"Youz look like a prizefighter," says Henry. "I can see it in youz now. Shave off that beard and I bet youz got a fighter's chin."

"I can take a punch," says Godot.

They sit around the table and talk about how this thing should be done. They talk about locations and cameras and angles. They talk about getting the right actors. The actors have got to be turn-ons for the audience, young and juicy.

"That's gospel," says Henry.

"I second the notion," says Pirate.

Somehow everybody gets to looking at Jasper in a critical way. "What you lookin at me for?" he says.

"Young enough," says Godot.

"Got that look," says Henry. "Tall, rangy, got long hair like the fems want."

"Ruby says he looks sexy in his jeans," adds Pirate.

"She said that about *me?*" says Jasper. "Sexy in my jeans? Really?"

"Swear to God," says Pirate. "Women think long legs mean long cock."

Godot puts an arm around Jasper and tells him quietly that with a little work and proper direction, he could be a knockout Romeo.

Henry agrees. "Youz'll have them chicks creamin their pants."

"How big is it?" says Godot.

"Got to have six inches at least, that's what I've heard," says Pirate. "You don't have six inches, they won't hire you."

"Camera angles can make it look bigger," Godot assures them.

Jasper's face feels hot. "I never measured," he says. "But I've never had any complaints."

He laughs. There is an increasing giddiness racing through him and he wonders if he can keep from falling on the floor and roaring with laughter. These guys are perfectly serious. They mean to make him Romeo. He keeps smiling, keeps chuckling at how solemn their faces are. It's as if they are planning to storm the walls of Jericho. They bring up the girl to play opposite Jasper, and Pirate offers Ruby. Ruby is juicy. Ruby will do anything Pirate says.

"I'm not doing it with Ruby," says Jasper. "No way."

They look at him as if they can't believe their ears.

"What?"

"Huh?"

"Don't be a noodle, Jim."

They lean over him, put their hands on him. Pirate says dirty things about Ruby, her ass, her breasts, her pussy all hot. "She'll suck you off," he says.

"You won't have to buy a share," says Godot. "You'll be the star and reap the profits with us, right, boys?"

"There youz go, what more youz want, Jim?"

Godot turns Jasper and gets him nose to nose. "You could end up the most famous man on the planet," he says. "*Romeo and Juliet* is just a start."

"The tip of the tit," says Henry.

"I've got plans for *The Taming of the Shrew, Measure for Measure,*

153.

A *Midsummer Night's Dream.* There are thirty-seven plays to choose from, all of them crying for revision. Listen to me, I've got X-ray eyes into the human heart, and I'm telling you Porno Willie is as surefire a hit as PCs, software, and MTV. Don't you want to be famous, son? Don't you want to be admired all over the world? Don't you want to be known as one of the avant-garde in the new, sophisticated culture of fuck flicks?"

"I don't know," says Jasper.

Henry refills Jasper's glass, coaxes him to drink. They all coax him.

"I'm of two minds," he tells them. "Two voices are talking in my head."

"Two voices?" says Pirate. "Is he dangerous? Are you dangerous, Jasper?" Even Jasper laughs at the idea of him being dangerous.

"I'm dangerous," says Godot.

"Me too," says Henry.

The two men look at each other. Henry says that a middleweight isn't as dangerous as a heavyweight. Godot replies that he could have kicked Henry's ass back in his boxing days. Henry says it would have been the day hell freezes over and the heavens fall.

While they go beard to beard, Jasper slides out and walks into the kitchen, runs his head under the water. The Incorrigible Ike has created a vacuum in his head. He can't think straight. His lips and tongue feel numb.

"Jas baby, can we count on you?" Pirate calls out.

"Our pal."

"Our boy."

He comes to the doorway and leans with his arms out, his hands clutching the jambs. "I'm . . . I'm—"

"He says 'yes'!"

". . . sick," says Jasper.

The three men go back to talking among themselves, saying that they've got some real planning to do, some pooling of resources, some strategies to work out.

"I'm not the one," says Jasper. "No, I mean it. Everybody from here to who-knows-where seeing my pecker and all. I mean no, thank you, fellas, that's not my style."

"What do you know of style?" says Pirate. Pirate pulls Jasper into the room. The others tug at him too. He slaps their hands.

"Leave me alone, you fucks," he tells them. But they won't leave him alone. They keep coming after him. Godot has the manuscript and is holding it out, shoving it in his face, pounding on it with his finger.

"The words," he says. "The words. You're not allowed to say no till you read the words," he says. "C'mon, read it. It's a work of art. You don't bleeping say no to a bleeping work of art! Who do you bleeping think you are, sonny?"

"Work of art," echoes Henry.

"Bleeping work of art," echoes Pirate.

Fat Stanley walks up Kensington Avenue. When he gets to his house, he stands a moment and takes in the porch with its swing and the hanging pots dripping with plants. He notices mostly the lights on in the house. He's not used to lights being on when he comes home. He's not sure if he likes it. It's awfully different. He hears the faint voice of the television and it's like it isn't his home anymore, not *all* his, not the place where he comes into the quiet and the dark and gives it life in his own good time. For the first time since he was a boy in New York there is someone waiting for him to come home. The children are waiting. They are expecting him. They are already calling him Uncle Stan and looking to him for security.

Breathing deeply, he closes his eyes, then looks again at the scene, the house, the lights, and he wonders why it depresses him. He had suspected he would feel good about having the kids there, bringing *their* life into his home. But he doesn't feel good. He feels nervous and dispirited. He resents being forced to cope with them right now. He misses his quiet nights with his wine and his piano. That television, it's always on. That kid Mikey is always lounging in front of it with his baseball cap on backwards and his doo-wop clothes hanging on him like a bunch of sacks. He's got a dirty mouth too. Ten years old and he already sounds R-rated.

"I'm not so lonely as I thought I was," he says, pondering this new revelation. Of course, part of his lack of patience with them is the circumstances, that these are the children of Helga, and that she may very well die and leave them on his hands. Then what would he do? Such a thought fills him with an almost overwhelming anxiety.

Looking left and right, he takes in all the houses in their parallel rows. Most of them have lights in the windows. Porch lights are on here and there. Cars shine with dew in the driveways and on the street. Palm trees line the terraces, like sentries watching. It's a good neighborhood. The déclassé elements have been kept out, but they are pressing at the borders. Nowhere to run anymore, nowhere to hide, unless you can afford a house in La Jolla with stone walls, iron gates, and security patrols. But so far things are okay this far east. So far it is still a place for families. He had chosen the house long ago, the three bedrooms, bath and a half, with family in mind. That was 1976. He had not dreamed back then that fourteen years later he would still not be married, that he would still be searching, that he would, in fact, be so desperate for *someone* he would keep a running advertisement in the *Union*. But there it is. Life never goes the way you think it should.

Inside his home, Helga's kids sit on the couch, watching a rerun of *Mary Tyler Moore*. She's gonna make it after all. Those were better days, everybody says. To hear people talk, those were golden years of togetherness and commitment. People had something worthwhile to do. Stop the war. Peace, brothers and sisters. Love ye one another, mellow yellow, be cool, love animals, don't eat them. The long hair and love beads, love flowers, the hippy look, the music with a be-political message—it was a minor revolution, an interesting time filled with sentimental possibilities. Nothing like *now*. Now is . . . Fat Stanley can't explain now, all he knows is that now is like nothing he's ever heard of. Now is a colorless inequality, a bloody bloodlessness, a dry isolation. No one seems to believe in a future, no one wants to grow up. Look at that Jasper John—there's a boy just going through the motions, and he can't even tell you why he's doing it, or where he's going, or what he wants out of life. It's the culture of confusion, the culture of the dazed and bewildered. The Jasper Johns don't have any ambitions except to get laid or get numb. What the hell happened?

Don't think about it—that way lies madness, Fat Stanley tells himself. He blinks his thoughts away. "What's up?" he says to the kids as he enters the living room. "Did you eat?" he says.

They ate.

Fat Stanley can smell the lingering odor of tortillas and refried beans. He sits in the easy chair, stretches his legs on the ottoman, and watches television. Before the show is over, he is catnapping. He hears them turn the station. They argue over what to watch, then settle on flipping back and forth between a number of talk shows. Each time a commercial comes on, the kids change the channel. Some happy guy is sleeping with two sisters, they like sharing him, but the mother of the sisters doesn't approve; someone is a woman in a man's body, she/he is going to have an operation to fix nature's faux pas; another is a crackhead and wants understanding for bringing a crack baby into the world, the drugs made her do it; a dying wife has caught AIDS from her husband but she forgives him, he is already dead. Fat Stanley keeps his eyes closed, but as he listens to the parade of woes going by, he wonders if people really need to know all this stuff.

At ten-thirty he gets up and tells the kids it's time for bed.

"I'm not tired," says Mikey. "Ma let's us stay up long as we want."

"I'm not Ma," says Fat Stanley.

"No shit, dude."

"I've told you about that kind of talk, Mikey."

Mikey sneers with contempt. Fat Stanley wants to slap the little bastard.

"C'mon," says Nancy. She turns off the TV. "Get up, Mikey. Go get your pajamas on." Her voice is stern. Her face says *no nonsense.*

"Aw, shit," says Mikey. But he rises. As he passes by, Fat Stanley smells stale cigarette smoke. Mikey slouches, his shoulders are rounded like a little bear cub. He drags his feet on the oak-wood floor.

"Pick up your feet," orders Fat Stanley.

"Yeah, yeah." Now he exaggerates his walk, like he is stepping through tires.

Kathy is right behind him. She is carrying a stuffed Orphan Annie doll. She pauses to give Fat Stanley a hug. "Good night, Uncle Stan," she says.

"Good night, sweetheart," he says. He wants to take the doll from her. She is much too old to be hauling it around. It reminds him of the little boy who comes to the diner with his mother every Friday night. The boy is five and always has a pacifier in his mouth, and Fat Stanley has to fight an impulse to snatch the pacifier away every time he sees the boy sucking it.

When the children are out of the room, Nancy asks Fat Stanley about Helga. She wants to know what the doctors are saying now. Do they give her any chance at all? Nancy is a tall, pretty girl, with a saddle of freckles across her nose, nice legs, graceful lines, but too thin in the shoulders. Her collarbones are prominent. She is mildly flat-chested, with just the hint of breasts pressing against her tank top. She has a vulnerable neck, a slim face, large lips, and interesting eyes, overly large and liquid, like a Pekinese. Her hair is short and parted on one side boy style. It hangs just to the middle of her ears. She wears big round purple earrings. At work, Helga often complained about Nancy's attitude, her sassy mouth, her laziness, her contempt for all things adult; but Fat Stanley has seen no evidence of these characteristics. On the contrary, she has been quite the little lady and the only bright spot in all that's happened lately. She has taken charge of her brother and sister. She has kept the house clean and made the meals. She has shown Fat Stanley affection and respect. He likes her very much.

"They still think your mother can go on a while. Dr. Rutledge says he's seen worse than her go on for two, three months. I saw her today. She was real calm. No pain. They've got her on something."

"Did she say anything?"

"Asked about you and the kids. Made me promise to feed you and get you off to school. She'd be lucid a while, then she'd drift off."

"We should've gone with you," says Nancy.

He tells her the doctor would rather wait another day or two, till she's stable. "She got awful agitated when you guys came that day. It scares her, I think, that she can't get up and take care of her own children, knowing how you need her and all."

Nancy looks away, toward the wall, then the floor. Her arms are crossed in front of her. Her eyes are wet. When she speaks her voice is so soft Fat Stanley can barely hear her. "It took cancer to make her a real mother."

"Did it?" he says.

"It's almost too late," she says.

"For what?"

Nancy shrugs. "I don't know." She looks at him. "Good night, Uncle Stan."

"Yes, good night, dear. Oh, Nancy, I asked your mother if you had other relatives and she said there was no one left. I thought maybe, you know, in her state of mind, she might not remember things too clear. Don't you have grandparents or uncles or aunts? I've never heard her mention any, but I thought—"

"No," says Nancy. "None. Ma always said she burned her bridges. If there are relatives, I wouldn't have the faintest idea who they might be or where they are. It was just us all these years. She said these are the things you will do for a man, if he's the right man. Ma is stubborn, you know. She said if they didn't want him, they didn't want her. 'I told them all to go to hell,' she said. Even after Daddy died, she wouldn't ask for help. She said she didn't need them, her mom and dad. She would get drunk and trash them all the time. Maybe they weren't such good parents, I don't know."

"She's always been a tough cookie, your ma," he says.

"Tough on all of us," Nancy tells him.

He watches her until she disappears into her room, then he sits down and broods on his predicament. He tries to remember if Helga ever talked of her parents or her husband's parents and can't recall anything but what Nancy said, the thing about cutting loose from everything, of going off with Mike and burning her bridges.

Getting up, he goes into the kitchen and opens the refrigerator, takes out a bottle of zinfandel, pulls the cork, and pours a glass. He gets some water crackers and some cheese and goes back to the living room. Sipping the wine, he lets his mind drift. He remembers when his mother took him to the ship. She took him aboard and pinned his name and his uncle's address to his coat. She told him when the war was over, he could come home. It was early 1944. He was only four years old then. But he remembers it. He remembers the bombs. He remembers the ones that buzzed, then went quiet, and you knew there would be a hit somewhere soon. He remembers the shelters, the fires, the constant moving from place to place. He remembers dead people. When his mother left him on the ship and blended into the crowd below, he didn't know it would be the last time he would see her. A burning wall fell on her. His father died in North Africa.

He lived with his uncle, the two of them in an apartment in New York. His uncle was a bachelor, a gourmet cook, a cultured man. He took Stanley to museums, plays, concerts, operas. He sent the boy to private schools. When Stanley grew out of a brief flirtation with rock music and acquired a passion for opera, his uncle paid for voice lessons and eventually got him into the chorus at several concert halls. He thought he was on his way. It was a hectic, exhausting life, but there was always this hope, this expectation that his big break would come any day, any minute. But it never did. As the years went by, he began to realize he wasn't quite good enough, he didn't have that extra something to be a real standout, a tenor extraordinaire. He would always be in the chorus. He would always be chasing from opera house to opera house, never belonging anywhere, never admired and catered to, never one who would bring the house down. He was good, but not good enough. It was like a curse God had given him. He had just enough talent to succeed at the middle rungs of his profession, but not enough to triumph, not enough to experience the ultimate fulfillment he was seeking. Finally he decided if he couldn't excel, he didn't want to participate. When his uncle died and left him some money, Stanley moved West, bought the restaurant, and became Fat Stanley. He cooked, he sang for his customers, he looked for love, he grew older and older. He was now fifty. He was terrified of being *old* in America.

Standing up, he goes to the window and looks at the night. There is mist around the streetlight. A skunk is on the lawn. It is sniffing something in the grass. It digs a little hole, shoves its snout in, pulls back, its teeth snapping, chewing on whatever thought it was safe beneath the grass. After a moment the skunk ambles away. Fat Stanley thinks of the prostitute who answered his last ad. She took him to a hotel and charged him a hundred and fifty dollars. Her perfume was overpowering, stuck in his mouth and nose like chokecherries. He almost couldn't respond because of her smell. One hundred fifty dollars. Twenty minutes of touchy-feely and then the act itself. Unutterable shame afterwards. And yet he does it over and over. He can't help himself. No woman has made love to him from a free and giving heart in his life. But he still wants them badly. It's as if they have the key to unlock the meaning, the purpose, the secret of existence, to open the door and show him why he is alive. Magical creatures, when they aren't whores, when they are like . . . like Nancy, for instance, so fresh so sweet.

Turning from the window, he paces the floor, he thinks of the children again. "What do I do?" he asks himself. "These aren't *my* kids. Why should I be saddled with them?"

No sir, he is going back to England and that's that, no ifs, ands, or buts. The real estate agent says it looks good, looks like a sure thing, an offer will be coming in a few days. Capon Enterprises, they're *very* interested. Fat Stanley will take it and *sayonara,* sweetheart. He will end his days in a decent country. It would be unfair of Helga to stick him with three kids at this stage of the game. He won't do it. Sometimes you've got to be tough, you've got to think of yourself.

Stopping by the portrait of the white cliffs of Dover on the wall, he reads the inscription below:

Glimmering and vast, out in the tranquil bay.

He remembers the last stanza and quotes it softly to an imagined love:

> *. . . let us be true*
> *To one another! for the world, which seems*
> *To lie before us like a land of dreams,*
> *So various, so beautiful, so new,*
> *Hath really neither joy, nor love, nor light,*
> *Nor certitude, nor peace, nor help for pain;*
> *And we are here as on a darkling plain*
> *Swept with confused alarms of struggle and flight,*
> *Where ignorant armies clash by night.*

As he turns from the picture, he sees Nancy standing near the piano, watching him. She is in a white nightgown. It floats about her body like a diaphanous cloud. Her lips are pressed together in a smile.

"I thought I heard you calling me," she says. She leans against the piano, places one bare foot on top of the other. She holds herself by the elbows, hugging herself as if she feels a chill.

"I was just seeing if I could still remember a poem. 'Dover Beach.' I used it at my uncle's eulogy."

"It's beautiful," she says. " 'We are here as on a darkling plain.' That's beautiful. I wish I knew poetry by heart like that. I have such a bad memory." She looks down as if considering something. She bites her lower lip.

He says, "What is it, dear?"

Her eyelids rise. She looks at him, into him. The two of them, the man and the girl, stare at one another for what seems to Fat Stanley a heart-racing, intimate moment. Love, oh love. When she speaks, her voice is subdued, tremulous. "What's going to happen to us, Uncle Stan? What will they do to us when Ma dies?"

162.

✚

Each time he wakes up he feels like his head is made of cast iron and won't come off the pillow. His stomach is queasy. His throat hurts. Sleep keeps coming in sonic waves. He feels like one drifting in and out of a coma. Once, around noon, he forces himself to rise and go to the toilet. He has diarrhea. The bathroom fills with the oily-ammonia smell of Incorrigible Ike. For a long time he sits with his elbows on his knees, his head in his hands, straining to get the poisons out of him. He thinks of the night before and of Godot showing him the script, of Godot reading it aloud, taking all the parts. He had Jasper and the others half sick with laughter. Mary Quick had come out of the bedroom and she had laughed too.

He wonders about it. Maybe making a porno movie wouldn't be so bad, not if it was a kind of comedy-tragedy as Godot explained it. Jasper had left them with the impression that he would be Reem-HerHole and it was okay for Ruby to be JuleeTit. It had made him feel good to give in to their pleas. But now, in the midst of his own stink, he isn't sure about being ReemHerHole. He really doubts he can get an erection in front of a camera, not with those three happy warriors looking on. He's just not sure of himself. He's never seen himself as a stud. His technique includes lots and lots of foreplay, but he's no good at holding back once Mr. Cyclops is inside. Five, six minutes and it's over. Those guys in those movies, they go on forever, they go on so long sometimes it gets boring. Drugs help. He's done better that way. They'll have to get him high on grass. Grass works good.

But the last thing he wants at the moment is to be high on anything or in bed with anyone, not even Didi Godunov. Finishing his business, he stumbles back to bed and falls instantly asleep. He sleeps the rest of the day.

It is nearly seven before Henry Hank comes in and makes him get up. Henry pulls him out of bed and shoves him into the shower, says they have things to do, places to go, people to see. Investment money to make movies doesn't grow on trees. They're going to have to earn it.

"I'm sick," Jasper tells him.

"Kids these days, soft," says Henry. He turns the water on cold and has Jasper doing a little dance.

After the shower, Jasper dresses in fresh clothes and goes into the kitchen, where he makes himself a bowl of Cream of Wheat. He puts a scoop of butter on it and lots of sugar. He eats it slowly, savoring its warmth in his mouth. After he finishes eating, he gets a glass of orange juice and takes three aspirins. He goes to the living room, flops out on the recliner.

"My head," he says to Mary.

She is stretched out on the sofa, the floor lamp bathing her in a ring of light. There is a vodka-rocks on the coffee table. The gray cats are draped over the back of the sofa. Lummox is on her lap. She is reading the Bible. She turns the pages quickly and reads something, then turns the pages and reads something else. This turning of the pages goes on and on, until Jasper thinks it will drive him crazy.

"What are you looking for?" he asks her.

"I don't know," she says.

She stops. "Listen to this," she says. " 'Raging waves of the sea, foaming out their own shame; wandering stars, to whom is reserved the blackness of darkness forever.' What do you think?" She looks over the rim of the book at him. "Is that us, do you suppose?"

"What?"

"Raging waves, wandering stars."

"I got a headache, Mary. What're you reading that stuff for?"

"I *need* to. I want a sign. People say all the answers are right here in this book, all you need is faith."

"Uh-huh."

"Did you know that David had Bathsheba's husband killed so he could marry her? See, I didn't know that. I'm so ignorant. I know a prayer or two, but what's that? That's nothing. I've heard the names, David, Bathsheba, but I never knew the details."

"It was a long time ago, Mary."

"So what's changed?"

Jasper thinks about it. "Nothing," he says.

She is quiet for a moment. Jasper hears the cats purring. Then Mary says, "He saw her naked and lusted after her and she got pregnant and her husband wouldn't have sex with her because he had taken a vow to be pure for battle."

"The purification ritual," says Jasper. "Ask Godot about it. They refused to cut their hair or sleep with a woman or get drunk. Godot says that's where the idea comes from that the body is a temple for worshipping God."

"I like that," she says. "*Is* the body a temple?" she says.

"I don't know," he tells her. "You're asking the wrong guy."

"Samson cut his hair for Delilah and that was the end of him," says Mary. "There is so much *sex* in this book, it's really something. They had a thing about the power of sex. Always it's like they're saying, 'Watch out!' "

She turns the pages, stops, reads for a moment. "Listen, this is what I mean. I'm just skimming along and what's it say? 'Abstain from fleshly lusts, which war against the soul.' See what I mean?"

Jasper says, "Hmmm." And he says, "Samson gets his muscles back and kills the Philistines. He pulls the pillars down, that's the best part."

"That's redemption," says Mary. "You always get a second chance from God." She taps the Bible. "That's what's all through here too . . . redemption."

"Hmmm." Jasper wonders if Mary is going to become a born-again freak-zoid. "So you're really getting into it, huh?"

The book lies on her chest, open like a pair of wings. She is fingering the Celtic cross at her throat, tracing round and round its hub. "I've been praying for a sign," she says.

"Like a voice?" says Jasper.

"Anything. A voice, a vision. They say, knock and the door will open."

Henry is heard coming in the back door. His big feet pound on the

165.

floor as he crosses the kitchen. The floor trembles, windows rattle. He enters the dining room. "Guess who's sleeping in the garage?" He doesn't wait for an answer. "Godot. He's unrolled the mattress. He acts like he lives there."

"I know," says Mary. "I gave him breakfast this morning. He was sleeping on the couch when I got up. I fed him."

"Is he gonna live there permanent?" says Henry. "Did youz say he could have the garage?"

"I said I didn't care."

Henry looks as if he is calculating some law of physics in his head. "Did he ask about that screenplay?"

"No."

"Didn't ask where it was?"

"No."

He looks at Jasper. "Get up, youz lazy whozit," he says. "I can't do everythin by myself."

"Do what?"

"C'mon."

"I'm sick, Henry."

Henry doesn't care. He grabs Jasper by the arm and pulls him out of the chair. They go out the front, where Agnes is parked.

Henry drives them downtown. He parks in front of the Imperial Room, where the well-to-do go for dinner. He tells Jasper what the plan is. Henry is going to be hit by a Cadillac, a Lexus, a Mercedes, or maybe a BMW, one of those big, expensive kind. Jasper is there to be the witness passing by.

"We be lookin for some old fart with a young quim," says Henry. "It'll take a finessin eye to spot the right one. Youz leave it to me. He's got to have a guilty face. I got extrasensories for pickles like that."

They sit in the car, watching the couples arriving along the curb at the Imperial Room. Men in black suits. Women in furs. Blond women with paunchy, tired-looking men.

It's a slow night. They have watched for an hour and only about a dozen couples have arrived. Henry asks if Jasper is making mental notes of the choices.

"My stomach feels like shit, Henry."

"Flamin legs." Henry shakes his head in disgust. "No aptitude. When I was your age, Jim, I could put away a fifth of crude down-home and still pass a drunk test. Hope to catch the clap if I'm lyin. I did it oncet. I walked a straight line and stood on one foot wavin my hands in the air, and the cops had to let me go. Those were the days before these chickenshit breath tests. Man ain't got a chance with those sonsabitches. Technology is takin all the fun out of life. Technology is killin off urban mysteries like me, makin us extinct species like the dodo bird. Youz know why so many noodles is out there shootin each other? Cuz technology's got em by the balls. It won't let em blow off steam like they use to do. Youz can't go get drunk and get in a fight and blow off steam, it's nothin like before technology. Have one drink and youz got to worry about some whozit pullin youz over and shovin technology in your face and takin youz off to jail. I'll tell youz somethin, Jim. I know plenty of cats, myself included, who can drink all night and still drive a car better than some of these Mothers Against Drunk Drivers. Yours truly has never been out of control or hung over a blessed day in his blessed life."

"Have you ever been sober a day in your life?" says Jasper.

"Funny man. But look here, if we was in a snowstorm and it's a hundred below, I'd last hours longer than youz before my blood freezes. Why? Booze, Jim, booze. It pays to keep the blood thinned with booze, ask any doctor." Henry stops talking. He is alert, staring out Jasper's window. "There he is, Jim. That one there. Him and her."

Jasper sees a long Cadillac, and next to it a balding man, short and stout. He is handing his keys to the valet. On the other side of the car is a tall blond cliché wearing a white dress with a mink wrap. As the valet drives the car away, the man and woman walk beneath the awning toward the double doors. The man's hand is possessively placed on the woman's waist.

"Young enough to be his granddaughter," says Henry. "He's the one. We wait and watch till they come out. Then we strike."

The time passes, while Henry talks about the porno flick and his earthquake destiny, how he will hobnob with the rich and famous in Hollywood, how he will throw big production parties and lavish pool parties at his estate in Beverly Hills and get laid by starlets who want to be in his movies. Women will be coming out of the woodwork. They're always ready to drop their drawers for a man that's got money and power and movies to offer. There will be limos and yachts. There will be expensive wines from all over the world. There will be a private gourmet chef.

". . . and youz can be my executive right-hand man. I'll make youz famous, Jim, so stick with me, don't get lost. Did youz ever measure to see if youz got six inches? We can't be overlookin the details."

"Oh, shut up, Henry," says Jasper.

"Art is in the details," says Henry. "Let me tell youz somethin—"

Two and a half hours later it is time to pluck the pigeon. Henry sends Jasper up the street to hide in the shadow of a house. Henry passes by Jasper and takes up a position behind a palm tree that is next to a mail drop and a stop sign. A minute later, the long Cadillac pulls out of the Imperial Room driveway. It accelerates, then slows down and comes to a stop at the crosswalk. As the car starts forward again, a large shadow falls across its windshield. This is followed by a body. There is a thud of the body against the fender and hood of the car. A cry of pain rips the air. The body rolls over the hood, looking oddly like a wailing blot of ink. The Cadillac has stopped. For a moment the body on its hood is still and there is the sound of the engine humming. From behind, exhaust vapor can be seen rising over the bumper and trunk. Seconds tick by. Henry lets out a moan.

"Paralyzed," he says. "Oh, what happened, what happened?"

Brusquely, the Cadillac leaps forward and turns left, its tires sizzling as it throws Henry into the street. Henry flies like a discus for a moment, whirling round once before he hits the pavement and rolls toward the gutter.

"Jiminy fuck!" he yells.

Jasper breaks from the side of the house and runs to him. "Are you hurt?" he says, bending to see. "Are you hurt, Henry? What happened?"

"What the fuck youz think, noodle? Goddamn! Get my flamin lawyer, sonsabitches! Get my flamin lawyer! I'm gonna sue that rollin catastrophic! Hit and run. Hit and run." He stands, shaking his fist at the vanished Cadillac. He tests his legs, walks in a circle, and complains about his knees being on fire. His pants are bloody and torn at the knees. His palms, his elbows, are bloody.

"Lucky I'm all muscle," he says. "I'd be dead now. Flamin legs, Jim, everywhere I go things are upside down. People don't give a shit, know what I'm sayin? For all that prick knows or cares, I'm in the gutter bleedin to death right now. It's makin me lose my faith, know what I mean? Know what I mean, Jim?"

"I thought he killed you, man. You should have seen yourself fly off there." Jasper giggles.

Henry raises an eyebrow. He grins. "Take a damn sight more than that old cheatin heart in his goddamn Cadillac to kill the Hank," he says. He puts his arm over Jasper's shoulder and they start walking back to Agnes. "Ow, fuck! My hip too, my ribs, my shoulder. That lead-footed whozit. Did youz get his number, Jim?"

"It was too dark."

"I'll find him if it's the last thing I do. I'll find him and dice him with a hatchet. Dirty dishonest fuckin whozit noodle. Call himself a man? I'll have his balls for my pool table, Jim." Henry hobbles along, cussing and making threats. When they get to the car, he eases himself into the passenger side and lays his head back on the seat, closes his eyes. "I feel like that fuckin old geezer Methuselah," he says. "If I didn't know better, Jim, I'd say I was gettin old."

"Naw, Henry. No way, not youz," says Jasper.

169.

7. SEEKING AFTER A SIGN

⟲ ✚ ♡

Tourmaline-minded man wanted. I know where vast deposits of tourma-
line lie. If you are the spelunker type, looking for a lover with potent night
vision and a fearless commitment to the underworld, then come explore
my cave. You will meet someone 33, with black hair, black eyes, and a
body hardened by years of handling picks. I want a bare-forked animal
loaded with assets and no moral liabilities. Write P. Pit, c/o Adam and
Eve Possibilities.

"They are nothing like their advertisements," says Fat Stanley. With a
pair of tongs he turns the steaks. Each steak sends micro balls of grease
to dance in the air, like champagne fizzing above a glass. Smoke rises
too, and the savory aroma of burning flesh. "She was a compulsive
talker," he says. "One of those high-strung types, full of herself, yak,
yak, yak."

"Uh-huh. Did you get any?" says Jasper. He is in charge of french
fries tonight. He takes one basket out of the bubbling grease, shakes it,
bangs it on the sides of the stainless-steel deep fryer, hooks the basket
on the edge, and lets the fries drain. He checks to see if they are deep
golden brown. Fat Stanley said they should look caramel-colored to be
just right. There are some thin ones on top, with blackened edges.
Jasper picks them out, blows on them, and eats them, crunching them
between his teeth and enjoying the burnt flavor.

"She was hot," Fat Stanley tells him. "She had that 'when you
gonna make your move?' look all night long. Right off the bat she tells

me about her ex, how he started running around on her because she got a fat ass. You ask me, she went overboard the other way. Parts of her, her extremities, were all bone. I think she had those plastic inserts in her cheeks. Everything was askew . . . right eye higher than the left, mouth puffed up like a blowfish with about seven layers of lipstick on, and that tiny chin and neck, and bony wrists, bony knuckles, and, well—" Fat Stanley makes keep-away gestures with his hands. Then he tilts his head to the side and says, "But she was also very curvaceous between here and here, and then nothing but pipe stems hanging out. It was bizarre. I don't know, maybe she appeals to some men, but she didn't appeal to me. She drank too much. She was patting my belly, asking me was I pregnant? She thought she was funny. She laughed like a goddamn horse. She goes haaw, haaw, those big teeth sticking out. Ugh. I didn't like her, Jasper. She's the first one I've had in ages who was legitimate, but I didn't like her one bit."

"Man, boss, you've got the worst luck with women," Jasper tells him.

"Tell me about it," says Fat Stanley. "What I'd like to know, though, what I wish somebody would tell me is, you know, where have the *real* women gone? I look at Helga's girls, at Nancy and Kathy, and I see how unspoiled they are now, and I say, why can't they stay that way? What happens to them when they get out here with the rest of us? I mean, they're so sweet and then something happens and they're like beasts of prey. They start whining about being a woman in a man's world. They start stereotyping us, saying our brains are in our pants, things like that. They start experimenting with sex and get fanatical about orgasms. And of course it's our fault, you know. It's in *all* the magazines. I saw Nancy reading one of those articles. 'The Oral Way to Orgasm.' I wanted to tell her to burn it. I wanted to tell her to slow down, read *Little House on the Prairie,* or something. Time enough when you get older for stuffing your head with garbage. I hate to think of it, of the young ones and what this world will make of them. There's no more innocence, Jasper."

Jasper feels bad for Fat Stanley. Such a man so unlucky in love he

171.

has to advertise for it. Aging and going bitter. Jasper has wondered several times how he might lean Fat Stanley toward some weight control and exercise. What woman wants to deal with five foot nine, two hundred fifty pounds of muscle and lard? It's not enough that Fat Stanley has a handsome face and a heart as big as a cow, everything else has to be handsome too these days. It's the total package people buy, not just the good parts. But every time Jasper thinks to say something to his boss, he can't bring himself to do it. It would hurt Fat Stanley's feelings too much.

Fat Stanley removes the steaks from the grill and puts them on plates. Jasper adds the french fries, sets the plates on the counter, and dings the bell. Ruby Rush takes the plates to a booth on the far side of the diner, next to the window. She looks at the steaks, crosses her right hand over to the customer on the left, and slides the plate in front of him, then gives the man on the right the plate in her left hand. She does it smoothly. She picks up their salad bowls and puts them in the bus tray.

"She's good," says Fat Stanley, standing next to Jasper, watching.

"She's good," says Jasper. "You like her?" he says. "I mean, do you think she's pretty? I think she's kind of pretty, don't you?"

"She's pretty," says Fat Stanley.

Ruby returns with a ticket, puts it on the carousel, and turns it around. Fat Stanley grabs the ticket, places it on the narrow bar next to the grill, reads it, and goes to the meat locker. Ruby grabs both coffeepots from behind the counter and makes the rounds. She looks fetching in her full skirt and puffy blouse. The skirt swishes against her legs as she walks. Her hair is different tonight, pulled straight back off her forehead and sides, her ears showing, dripping with rings of gold.

Fat Stanley returns with a pair of sirloins. "She's a quiet one," he says to Jasper. "Still waters run deep."

He forks the steaks onto the grill. He drapes half his bottom over the stool and hums a little, then breaks into an aria from *Romeo et Juliette*. He sings praises to Juliette's beauty. He compares her to the rising sun. Her radiance makes the evening stars grow pale. Love, oh love.

The patrons stop eating. Their jaws stop grinding. They turn their heads, ears cocked. Fat Stanley's disembodied bell tones glide through the aperture and over the room as if they are spiritual chords trying to make contact. Jasper leans his elbows on the counter and watches the effect. He sees Ruby sit on a padded stool and turn toward the kitchen. She closes her eyes. She raises her face toward the ceiling like a sunbather worshipping the sun. Jasper gets a sense of the notes washing over her, bringing a tiny smile to her lips, a flush to her cheeks, a radiance to her brow. There is a sepia glow throughout the room. It is like an old photograph, the stillness, the time freeze. Jasper knows how they are feeling, how their hearts are beating faster, how something immortal in them is longing for a grand, passionate love à la *Romeo et Juliette*. He feels it too, and the accompanying melancholy, the sense of loss, the emptiness of the real world that comes rushing in as soon as the aria is over.

The patrons clap for Fat Stanley. They go back to their dinners. He goes back to the steaks, pressing them with his thumb to see how done they are. Jasper gets busy, he buses the dishes, spreads them in the racks, raises the door of the sterilizer and shoves them in, closes the door, presses the red button near his hip. The washer comes to life, hissing, gushing, pumping, spraying, scalding those germs. As it runs the cycle, he hurries to the carousel and reads the new ticket. Baked potatoes. He brushes up two potatoes, stabs them with a fork, puts them in the microwave, times it for ten minutes. He moves back to the sterilizer and pulls the rack out. Ruby comes through the double doors. She grabs a fresh towel from the cupboard. For a moment, she stops, her eyes fixed on Fat Stanley on his stool, one hand bunching his beard, his other hand playing with tongs, making them snap like lobster claws. He looks sideways at Ruby.

Ruby says, "I wanted to tell you how much I love your voice. It's just so . . . so moving, Fat Stanley. I just wanted to tell you that."

"Thanks," he says.

"It's really beautiful. It's . . . *really beautiful.*"

They stare at each other. Jasper remembers a line from some play where it said, *They have changed eyes,* and he wonders if Ruby might be the one for Fat Stanley at last. For everyone there is someone, he has heard. He wants to believe it. He wants it to be true for Fat Stanley, but mostly he wants it to be true for himself. After she leaves the kitchen, Jasper goes over to Fat Stanley and says, "She likes you, boss."

"She likes me?"

"She does."

"You think?"

"I'd put money on it."

"*She* likes *me?*" Fat Stanley's eyes are quizzical, like he is trying to figure out if Jasper is fooling him or not. He looks away, his gaze following her as she does her job. "Me?" he says. "Her?" he says.

"I'm telling you, boss."

Ruby enters again. She has a folded piece of paper in her hand. She hands it to Jasper. "I forgot, someone dropped this off for you," she says.

"What?"

She hands him the note.

"When?"

"It was this afternoon. I put it in my purse, and then we got busy and I forgot. Sorry."

He unfolds the note and reads:

Jasper John,
Come to me tomorrow morning, ten o'clock. I have to tell you
something important.
Your Didi

His heart quickens at the *Your* Didi. What could it be? *Come to me
. . . have to tell you something important.* She is seeking him out.

174.

What for? He remembers how disgusted she was with him that night he showed up drunk. He hasn't seen her since, and now she comes all the way from Pacific Beach to deliver a note. It must be very important. Must be— His mind spins like a slot machine. And then he thinks he knows what it is, and he wonders if he should get on his horse right now this minute and head for Colorado or anywhere but here, before it's too late.

Mary closes the Bible, puts it on the coffee table. She sips her vodka and takes a long pull on a cigarette. It is, she decides, a very confusing book. She has just stopped at a place in James that says, *Faith without works is dead.* Earlier she had read in Paul, *The just shall live by faith.* Well now, which is it? She has read until her eyeballs feel like they are falling out of her head, and she is no closer to the answer to things than before she started. Especially, she is confused about the nature of God. Is he the Old Testament tyrant or the New Testament disciplinarian with the schizophrenic voice? She's definitely made up her mind that the Old Testament one isn't for her. He comes across as a pissed-off old fart, a spoiled brat, a monster. She's got no use for that guy. I AM THAT I AM. And at his command Joshua utterly destroys everything in his path, men, women, children, even the oxen, the sheep, and the poor innocent asses.

But then Jesus speaks out of both sides of his mouth. He comes in peace but with a sword. Love ye one another, do unto others as you would have them do unto you. I'm here to cast fire on the earth; son against father, daughter against mother; the world is ending very, very soon, the apocalypse is just around the corner, and the Lord Jesus is coming to judge the quick and the dead, so everybody better get squared away. But then the world didn't end soon. It's still here as nasty as ever, and no Jesus. Slower than the Second Coming of Jesus Christ, she really understands that now. What is the message we're supposed to get? It's a crazy book, a book that needed better editors. Is God all-powerful *and* all-good? she wonders. Then how can evil things happen? If evil things happen, God is either not all-good or not all-

175.

powerful. If he is all-good, he must be sharing power with something wicked. Nothing else makes sense. She read the Book of Job and it gave her an answer. It told her flatly to shut up, she was too stupid to figure it out, so cool it, you worm! Leave it in God's hands, you insect. Actually, there is some small comfort in that—in her insignificance and his greatness. Her sins seem trivial when she thinks what a speck she is. *He* laid the foundations of the earth.

"What have I done?" she says.

And she answers herself. She says, "Hmm, what haven't I done?"

Leaning over, she opens the cover of the Bible to the first page and the dedication written there to that unknown suicide:

To our beloved daughter Sister Augustine, who took her vows of chastity, poverty, obedience at Our Lady of Peace, Tulsa, Oklahoma, 3 June 1965. From her proud parents, Martha and Ray Little.

Mary watches Sister Augustine for the ten thousandth time as she leaps into the abyss. What was her story? Mary has no idea.

Rising from the couch, she goes into the dining room and stops before the green door. She takes out her keys, finds the right one and inserts it, then changes her mind. It hasn't done her much good lately. That old sense of comfort, of still having *him* with her, just isn't there anymore. She removes the key, puts it back in her pocket. She goes to the kitchen and freshens her drink. Standing at the sink, staring out the window, she can see the garden bathed in the porch light. The flowers are drooping. They are panting for water. A pair of shriveled apples from last year still hang on the tree. There are some apple blossoms, but they don't look healthy. Mary lights another cigarette, inhales, blows the smoke over the windowpanes. She thinks about going out and watering the flowers, but she doesn't go. She wonders how she will get through the night without screaming. She needs to be busy, but there is nothing she really wants to do.

Back in the dining room, she goes to the hutch, opens the bottom drawer, and takes out the Scrabble game. She sits at the table and places words on the board. She does this for a while before she notices the letters are telling her something. Among other words, she has vertically spelled out the word BOOM. Then she notices she has three E's and I-V-L. With trembling hands she places them horizontally after the B in BOOM and the word BELIEVE appears. A hot flash runs through her veins. Warmth pours into her chest. BELIEVE. She touches the letters, adds up the score—33. Her heart hammers harder at the number 33. Christ died when he was 33.

"Is it a sign?" she whispers. She has been praying for a sign, but she doesn't want to be a fool, she doesn't want to look like an idiot ready to leech off of anything that comes along. Still, it seems pretty significant, this BELIEVE adding up to 33.

The back door opens and she hears Jasper's tennis-shoe tread. He enters the dining room. "What's up?" he says. "Playing Scrabble?"

"Look," she tells him, pointing at the letters.

Jasper stands behind her and reads, "Believe, boom, man, nope, pot, tail. You're doing pretty good."

"This one says *believe*. It adds up to thirty-three," she says. "See, a bonus on V."

"Lucky you, Mary."

"I think it's significant."

"Yeah?" Jasper goes into the kitchen, grabs himself a Coke. "You want a Coke?" he says.

"I want to tell you something," she says. "I *have* to tell you something."

"Oh, oh, that don't sound good. *Have* to? Your heart messing with you again?" He sits at the table, takes one of her cigarettes. She sees his mild eyes focused on her. His hair falls over his ears. It brushes his shoulders. The overhead light glistens in his hair and beard, and it strikes Mary that he is just the person to hear what she has to say. She can trust him.

"Screw this old heart," she says.

Rising from the table, she goes to the couch, retrieves the Bible, and brings it to him. She shows him the dedication.

"Who is Sister Augustine?" he says. "Friend of yours?"

"I swiped this Bible from a woman who killed herself," she tells him.

"Oh?"

"It's a story how I got this thing. I'm not a good person."

"I've done worse, I'll bet, lots worse," he says.

He doesn't know what real sin is, she says. She tells him about her youth, about her mother dying, about living with the Quicks, about her husband, about her affairs and the birth of Jimmy Jack and how ten years later he drowned. "But you know about my son," she says. "What you don't know is that my husband forgave me for the affairs and for not knowing J.J.'s real father. It was his forgiveness that drove me crazy. There is nothing worse than a goddamn forgiving, loving man to make you feel how icky and awful you really are. I hated his goodness. I had nothing but contempt for it. I wish he had beaten me. I wish he had come down to my level."

She takes a moment to let her message sink in. Then she tells him how, after abstaining for ten years, she took a new lover, and this new lover was a heroin addict doctor, who carried a .357 magnum in a shoulder harness because he was afraid he was going to be assassinated by hippie freaks who wanted his drugs. He had a cabin in the woods, where they would get high and make love. One night in the cabin, he overdosed. There was no phone. They were next to the same lake that had drowned her mother and would also drown her son. It was two miles to the highway, three miles to town. First she tried to get her lover in the car, so she could drive him to the hospital. But he was too heavy for her. She put her head on his chest and didn't hear a heartbeat. She panicked. She took the .357, went outside, and fired distress signals into the air. Three shots, then a pause, then three more shots. She kept reloading the gun and repeating the same pattern until the police came. They called an ambulance. By the time the ambulance arrived the lover was dead. She was arrested for possession of narcotics. She spent three days in jail. Her story was printed in the paper. Her son, her mother-in-law, everybody read her story. Her husband stood by her, but he now slept in the basement and ate his meals at his mother's house. His face was the face of a martyr.

"There is nothing worse than the face of a martyr," she says. "It was while I was waiting for the trial that I met Henry Hank, and was I ever glad. He was so . . . *earthy*. Nothing sanctimonious about that son of a bitch. I left my husband and son and moved in with him. I couldn't live up to them, they were too much for me. I couldn't be what they wanted. But then the worst thing happened one day when I picked up my son and took him out on the lake. I should have known better, all the bad things connected with that water, I should have known better. It was that day he drowned. The boat was going too fast and the sail caught the wind too hard. I don't know. How the whole thing happened exactly, I can't say. But we went over and he drowned, and when I got home I took a bottle of sleeping pills but threw them up. So I took some rope and tried to hang myself, but Henry came home and found me hanging from the door and took me down. Henry brought me back to life, I don't know what for."

For a while she sits with her hands covering her face. An entire minute ticks by. Finally, she lowers her hands. She lifts her glass, drains its contents. She tilts her head and stares at Jasper, trying to read his thoughts. She reads repulsion in his face. "You think I'm a bitch," she says.

"I don't think anything. I'm making no judgments on you, Mary. The longer I live, the more I see how there's no black and white, and how everybody is floundering, how everybody is trying real hard, but fucking up right and left. Me too. Me as much as anybody." These words sound fine to her, but his face still has that judgmental look. He wants to be cool about it, wants to be sophisticated about sin, but his eyes give him away. There is no forgiveness in his eyes.

"I never really meant to kill myself," she confesses. "I hung myself on the door, but I never really put my weight down. The thing I have to

179.

live with, J.J., is what a coward I am. I am terrified of death. There, I admit it. So there."

Jasper says he doesn't want to die either, not ever.

"Is there an afterlife?" she asks.

"Maybe, maybe there is."

"I think so. I think my boy is there, his soul is there. He's doing important things."

"I bet he is," says Jasper.

"I left town after that. I didn't wait for the trial or nothing. Maybe I'm still wanted in Illinois, I don't know, twenty-two years, do they keep after you that long? I just left. Me and Henry together. I ran like a rabbit, ran away from my troubles fast as I could. We went to Chicago first and lost ourselves in the crowd, and that's where I had my first trick, actually my first dozen, then we took off to New York. It was in New York I got this Bible. I followed this woman into the subway. She was carrying this Bible and a purse, and I wanted to steal the purse. She went through the turnstile, and she puts the Bible on a bench, puts her purse next to it, and she goes to the edge of the platform. When the subway comes along, she jumps in front of it. It was incredible. She just jumped in front of the train"—Mary snaps her fingers—"just like that. Everybody ran over there to see. I didn't go. I grabbed the Bible and the purse and got the hell out of there. You get hard. Life happens to you and you get hard. I took her money and the Bible and I stuffed the purse in a mailbox. Now what do you think?"

Jasper shrugs. "Like you said, 'life happens and you get hard.' What do you want me to say?"

"I don't know. I've got no excuses. When you're a whore, you're putrid. Everything is putrid. You smell putrid. When you go to the toilet, you think, Everybody is like this, everybody is putrid, they're all full of shit, they all deserve to die. You see the worst, you expect the worst. Is Sister Augustine in hell, do you think?"

"What for?"

"Suicides go to hell, they say."

Jasper considers the matter. Then he says if God is really love, there is no hell. It would be a contradiction and God cannot contradict himself.

As Mary listens, she plays with the letters in front of her. She picks up y-h-w, and another h. yhwh. She tries to find a place for them on the board, but they don't fit. "God cannot contradict himself," she repeats. "My trouble is, I worry about everything, that's my problem. A regular worrywart."

Jasper smiles. "Me, I don't worry about much of nothing," he tells her. "What happens, happens. It isn't like worry is some kind of payment to get off the hook. Maybe I'm like my mother. She's a free spirit. Maybe that's me." He gives Mary the thumbs-up sign.

"I've never been a free spirit," she says. "People think I am, but I'm not. I carry too much luggage to fly." She hesitates. She fiddles with the letters. She says, "Terrified as I am, I still want to get it over with. Get rid of the burden. I bet you I die soon, Jasper. I bet my world comes to an end pretty damn quick now."

"No, you'll live a long time," he says.

"What makes you think so?"

He shrugs. "You still got wishes in your eyes, Mary. Your eyes say they haven't seen it all yet."

She takes heart. "You really think so?" she says. She feels a little tremor of hope that he can see so much in her eyes still.

He nods. He slides off the chair and stands up.

"Where're you going?" she says.

"To bed," he says. "I'm beat." He stretches. He drains the last of his Coke, crushes the can.

"Good night, Jasper."

"Good night, Mary."

"Thank you for listening to my bullshit, Jasper."

He leaves her alone. She plays with the letters. She smokes another cigarette. She wonders what Jasper really thinks of her now. People say what they think you want to hear. He probably hates her. Fuck what he thinks, she doesn't care, what does it matter?

She goes into her bedroom, and as she enters, she sees another *sign.* One hand flies to her mouth in astonishment, the other reaches out. There across the bed, on *her side,* is an elongated cross. Her chest pains start, and she digs in her pocket for the bottle of nitro. First the Scrabble spells BELIEVE and the score adds up to Christ's age when he died, and now she walks into her room and there is a cross on the bed. If these are not signs, what are they?

Glancing at the window, she notes that it is flushed with moonlight now, and that the light coming in is throwing off shadows of more crosses, picking them off the window moldings and planting them on the floor. Another cross climbs the wall. Things like this don't just happen. These cannot be coincidences. At the edge of the bed, she sits in the wash of crosses and looks at the portrait of the Madonna. It is crying. It seems to be saying, "What more do you want, daughter?"

♡

Sometime after Jasper falls asleep with Lummox curled under his arm, a noise wakes him. Jasper looks into the darkness and sees the outline of two heads across the room. His scalp prickles.

"Who is it?" he asks.

"Me," says Mary Quick.

When she comes closer, he sees that the second head was Shakespeare's on the block-and-pine bookshelf. Mary is in a nightgown. Her arms hang like sunless roots at her side. Her hair is down, curving round her neck and partially over her breasts.

"What's up?" he says.

"I can't sleep. I'm cold," she tells him. Her voice is whispery, like the hum of a freezer. He offers her one of his blankets, but she wants to sleep with him. "Can I?" she asks meekly.

Sliding over, he holds the covers back and she gets in. She turns her back to him, drawing up her knees, her body shivering. Turning on his side, he holds her cold body against him. Her spine feels like the knuckles of a fist digging into his chest. He curls his legs against the backs of her legs, his arm goes over her ribs, and he cups one breast.

He holds it docilely, while his warmth moves to her and she stops trembling. He can feel her body relax. Her breathing softens. Her breath saws rhythmically in and out.

Jasper wonders what to do with her. He doesn't know if he should just hold her like this, or is she expecting him to make love to her? He is tumescent. His penis went hard as soon as she pushed her bottom against him. Her breast in his hand feels wonderful, so heavy, so mature and experienced. He runs his thumb over the nipple, but the nipple doesn't perk up. It would be an easy matter to slide her nightgown up and slip inside her. He leans his erection against her to see what she will do, but she neither pushes back nor pulls away. He tells himself that the only reason she would get in bed with him is because she needs some loving. She probably needs it real bad, and she's probably wondering if he is a man or not. Women don't forgive guys that let them down when they offer themselves. She'll think you're queer, he tells himself. A real man is always ready to go for it.

He reaches down to adjust her nightgown and is about to raise it, when he hears her snore. Soft nasal snores fill the air like a flirting housefly. He winds his fist in her gown, then lets it go. He doesn't know if he is angry, or hurt, or just confused. Finally, he decides he doesn't know a thing about women and he probably never will.

Rolling onto his back, he makes room between himself and Mary for Lummox to lie, as if in a little nest, and feel toasty warm. Jasper stares at the ceiling and thinks of Didi and the last time with her when they made love, when she sat on him and wiggled, and he felt the tip of his penis rubbing against some organ way up there. He masturbates in honor of the memory, hurrying himself to completion. Afterwards, he is thankful he didn't push it with Mary. Now that his orgasm is out of the way, he can think more clearly. He knows now he was being sensitive. He knows now she just needed someone to hold her, and he was there for her. He reaches across and pats her hip. "Mmmm," she murmurs, as if she understands.

When he wakes in the morning, he smells coffee, cigarettes, and pancakes. She is in the kitchen making noises. The radio is on, the announcer is saying more hot weather is on the way. Jasper gets out of bed, goes to the bathroom.

When he enters the dining room, Henry Hank is there at the table with a pile of pancakes in front of him running with butter and syrup. Henry nods to Jasper and keeps eating. Mary tells Jasper to sit and she'll get him breakfast. He pours a cup of coffee and sits across from Henry. He feels groggy this morning, like his head is full of warm pudding. In the hutch glass he watches the profile of Henry eating, watches him take gargantuan bites, watches his jaws work, his beard shudder. Henry's image is partially transparent, ghostly in the glass as it weaves among the cups and saucers. Soon the whole stack of cakes is gone. Henry leans back and burps; he leans forward and burps again: he raises his leg and farts and says what he says every morning after breakfast, "Ahh, just like clockwork, that's me. It's why I'll never have cancer of the bowels." He gets up and goes into the bathroom, closes the door.

Mary brings a plate of pancakes for Jasper. He butters them from the bottom up, lifting each one and shoving the butter under, until he comes to the top, where he smears butter to the edges, then repeats the same process from bottom to top with the syrup. When he has everything drenched he begins taking big bites, washing them down with coffee. With each swallow, he feels better and better. By the time he is finished he is ready for the day, ready for Didi, whatever her *have to tell you something important* might mean.

As Jasper is running his finger over his plate, gathering up the last of the syrup and licking it off, Henry returns to the table. He lights a cigarette, blows a slim stream of smoke into the air. "Youz shoulda been with us yesterday," he tells Jasper. He says that he and Sam-bam Godot started out on a major hunt for investment money, and it ended up ". . . wild as wolves, man, wild as wolves!"

He says they took two pints of Incorrigible Ike and drank them on the way, and got all the details worked out about their movie. Henry figures he knows everything there is to know about homemade movies. After a while, Godot went off on his enemies and talked about how he

184.

was going to ruin the motherfuckers when he got rich and powerful. Godot drank nonstop, talked nonstop, all the way to Riverside, where they started looking for likely places to contribute to their cause. At that point Godot's head was wobbling and all he could say was "Kill them. Kill them all."

Henry stopped off and bought a case of beer, and they drank from the case while they checked a number of places to rob. They picked seven convenience stores. Henry timed how long it would take to get from one to the other and back to the freeway. He estimated the time would be an hour and ten minutes if things went right.

At each stop, Godot kept getting out of the car and pissing, standing behind the open door, directing his spray and saying, "Piss on you, piss on you." Henry says he never saw anybody piss so much as Godot. After every beer he pissed. Then he would get back in the car and mumble about killing this enemy and that enemy. His head would roll, his mouth would wrap around another beer. It was Henry who had to do all the work. Henry says he wishes Jim had been there. Jim, he knows, would have held up his own end.

Jasper feels proud that Henry thinks so much of him. This is what people think now, that Jasper John is dependable. Jasper John has never been dependable, but now he is. It's what moving to another state can do, it can give you a fresh personality.

With Godot about as helpful as a potted plant, Henry took over and worked his way down the line, methodically knocking over the stores. He got to the freeway inside an hour, but he only hit four of the seven stores he had staked out, the other three being too crowded for safety's sake. So he had some cash and he was pretty satisfied, but things didn't work out too well once they got to San Diego and Henry took Godot to pick up his car at the college—

". . . where he sees these two fems and he says they're his enemies and he's gonna kill them. They're in this car in a parkin lot and Sam-bam gets out and he fuckin jumps on the hood. And he's callin them pigs and bitches and filthy whores, and they're lockin their doors and huggin each other like Hansel and Gretel, and Sam-bam's the witch what's gonna eat them." Henry guffaws loudly over the memory. "They won't come out for nothin! He's dancin on the hood, throwin punches at them, tellin em to come get their medicine, he'll take em both at the same time, with one arm tied behind his back. Weee! what a sight! And he tells them, he says, if he and his brothers have to pay for the sins of their fathers, then they and their sisters have to pay for the sins of their mothers. He says that fifty hundred times. Just screamin it at em and kickin the fuck outta that car. Man, you know them foreign cars can't take it. Thin as paper, them things. Buy American! Youz shoulda seen how scared them two was, Jim. Flamin legs, I bet both of em crapped their panties. I know they did. They was sure their time had come. Must have been like a drum inside that car." Henry bangs the table to emphasize how hard Godot was beating on the car.

He laughs about it, puts his head back and bellows, "Oh, Sam-bam, Sam-bam, what a man! That sonofabitch, what he done next is, he pulls out his crank and he pisses on the windshield! Can youz see it? Look here, Jim, Sam-bam has a crank like nothin I ever seen. It hangs to his knees, Jim! It fills up both his hands and got this much hangin over." Henry measures off another four inches or so on the table. "I ain't lyin, hope to catch the clap if I'm lyin—to his knees, Jim. It's like he can piss on the windshield, then use his crank as a wiper after. It's *that* long! A major piece of work. Awesome! Awesome! If it's that big when he's takin a leak, imagine that baby on-screen when it's up and angry! Whoa, Jim, ever see the crank on a jackass when he lets it hang? This is what I'm sayin!"

Jasper tries to picture Godot with a giant cock, but he can't. Such a skinny old man and so nervous and fragile-looking, it's impossible to imagine him with the kind of equipment a Jasper John or any other guy might actually envy.

"The cops got him," says Henry. "Someone called the cops and they come and arrest the noodle. Those two *quackin* aspens are demandin they lock Sam-bam up forever, sayin he's crazy and a menace to society, and the cops are sayin they got him this time, got him for indecent exposure this time, like it was some major big deal, Jim, murder or arson or somethin. Let me tell youz the naked truth—that world-class crank of his ain't no indecent exposition. People will pay good money to see that thing or I'm a plate of spaghetti."

"So they took him to jail?" says Jasper.

"That's all right," says Henry. "I got him out. I took my day's work and bailed him out. Dumb sonofabitch, because of him, I'm broke again. He's in the garage, in the bed out here sleepin it off, the goose. And here I am, still haven't got the money to make my movie. After all that too!"

The back door slams and they can hear stumbling footsteps, and then Godot comes into the room. He is holding his head between his hands, his face is as pale as his beard. He looks an age beyond calculation. "Ahggg," he says. "Jesus, my bleeping head. Water, where's the water?" Turning around, he stumbles back into the kitchen and puts his head under the tap. They can hear him drinking water, choking it down, coughing and spitting and swallowing. Finally, he turns the tap off and eases his way back to the dining room. He spots the coffeepot on the table.

"Coffee," he says. He sits, while Mary pours him coffee. His hands are shaking as he raises the cup and sips. He looks at Jasper, then at Henry. "What happened?" he says.

"Youz pissed on em," says Henry.

Godot nods. "I pissed on em."

"Then the cops arrested youz and I bailed youz out."

"The dirty cunts," says Godot. "Excuse me, Mary."

He sips again. His hands are shaking so badly he spills coffee on his beard. He brushes at the stains with his hand, then takes the corner of his shirt and wipes up and down. He lowers the cup and stares across the table with leaky, reddish, infinitely old eyes. "Where's my screenplay?" he asks.

"I got it safe," says Henry. "Don't youz worry."

"Get it," orders Godot. "I'm ripping it up. I've got better ideas. *Whores of Babylon,* that's what I'm gonna do. Get my screenplay, Henry."

Henry shakes his head. "No way, pal. No way I'm lettin youz tear up the masterpiece of the century. Knock that idea outta your noodle right now. Youz can write the *Whores of Babylon,* and that's fine, but *ReemHerHole and JuleeTit* is sacred property."

"I've made up my mind," says Godot. "And when I've made up my mind, that's it!" He tries to stand up, but can't. The chair kicks out from under him, and the professor goes down, disappears over the rim of the table and hits the floor with a sound like scattering Tinkertoys.

"Wounded," he murmurs from below, "in the housh of friends I am wounded. Can't you see I can't do it, Henry? Can't blashpheme my main man. Won't do it. This is Shake-*speare* we're talking about here, Henry. Gimme manuscript. Burn it, Henry. I don't wanna the goddamn thing as my legacy!"

"Not burnin nothin," says Henry. "That screenplay is the Hope Diamond to me. Look here, when we're sittin in Beverly Hills with starlets on our laps and gold Cadillacs in the driveway, youz'll thank me, Sam-bam."

"Oh, gawd." Godot's head bumps the floor. He closes his eyes. "I think I'm dying," he whispers. "And you're fucking me, Henry. I'm dying. Give a man his dying wish."

"Youz'll thank me," says Henry. "Just wait and see."

In less than a minute, the old man is sleeping. Henry and Jasper take him by the arms and legs and haul him back to the garage. They fling him onto the bed. He lies with arms crucified. His white hair spread upon the pillow. His white beard spread over his chest, his body and his clothes reeking to high heaven. His mouth is open, emitting thunderous snores.

"Some partner this guy's gonna be," says Henry.

Jasper looks at the garage. At one time, someone obviously had plans for making it into a real home. There is a shabby blue rug on the floor. Beneath the window, there is a gas stove. A porcelain sink streaked with rust is next to the stove, followed by long counters and drawers and a set of unfinished cupboards above. Near the bed is a bureau and a table with three folding chairs. The unfinished wallboards are ornamented with water stains, their amoeba patterns reminding Jasper of modern paintings, the babble of artists. Cobwebs drape every corner. Old clothes powdered with dust hang from a wire, which itself hangs from an open joist. The air is heavy. There is an odor of decomposition, of wood rot and mildewing cardboard and unwashed flesh. Along the west edge of the floor, a slash of light reveals the crumbling foundation of the entire structure.

8. TAKE THIS CUP AWAY

↺ ✚ ♡

He parks the Harley at the curb. In front of him is the long walkway, then the apartments. On both sides of the walkway, weed-infested grass is dying. Jasper watches as Kelly rides her tiny bicycle over the grass, kicking dandelion seeds into the air. She brushes past him and into the street. She pedals along the gutter, looking over her shoulder at him, her eyes daring him to chase her.

An older boy comes out on the porch of the apartment next to Didi's. "I'm telling Mom," he says. His voice is listless, bored.

Jasper wonders if he should interfere this time. Cars go by. Drivers stare at Kelly as if they expect her to dash in front of them. She rides in circles, ignoring the cars.

"Is this your favorite game?" says Jasper.

The little girl doesn't answer. She rides close to him, turns, makes circles, glances at him. Her eyes flirt with him.

"I mean it," says the boy on the porch.

Drivers tap their horns. Some of them stare at Jasper as if it is his fault. "Oh hell," he says.

He chases her. She likes it. Her little legs pump like mad as she tries to get away. She heads toward an oncoming car. The driver slams on his brakes and starts to skid sideways into her. All around, Jasper can hear the squeal of brakes. He lunges for Kelly, catches her. The back end of the car slides by so close it brushes Jasper's leg. He picks her up, bicycle and all, carries her to the grass. A man gets out of the car and looks across the hood at them.

"Is she all right?" he says.

"Yeah, she's fine." Jasper feels his heart racing. He is panting. *It was close. Another foot and—*

"God, that was close," says the man. He shakes his head. He gets in his car, straightens it out, and drives off.

When Jasper puts her down, she looks up at him and says, "Who're you?"

"I'm my sister's keeper," he says. He musses her hair.

"Hey, what's your name?"

"J.J.," he says.

She thinks it over. "That's not a name. I broke my wrist," she says. "When I was little, I fell off my bike and broke my wrist, see?" She holds the wrist out. It looks fine to Jasper. "I have headaches," she continues. "I throw up in day and walk in my sleep in night. I'm deaf in this ear." She points to her left ear. "Mama doesn't know what to make of me! I'm a little bitch!"

The boy on the porch sits down and ties his shoe. "She's crazy," he tells Jasper.

"I'm going to die of kidneys," she says proudly.

"She's gonna get run over. Are you supposed to be watching her?" says Jasper.

The boy gets a sullen face. He doesn't answer. He comes over and yanks Kelly off her bike and hauls her toward the house. "Let me go, you bastard!" she shouts at him.

"We're not supposed to talk to strangers!" says the boy. He pulls her by the arm, she tripping on her toes behind him. When they get on the porch, he throws her into the house. The door slams. Jasper stands hands on hips, breathing heavily, his heart still beating hard. He wants to knock hell out of that boy.

"I know what you're thinking," says Didi. She is outside, shading her eyes, watching him. "Couldn't you just *kill* that mother? Some people—there ought to be a law against them having kids. She's a trashy bitch. You should hear what I hear some nights."

"She almost got killed."

"I saw."

"The kid's a hypochondriac already."

"I know."

"How old is she?"

"Six . . . maybe seven." Didi beckons to him. "C'mon, you've done your good deed for the day. There's nothing more you can do."

Jasper knows it's true. He looks at Kelly's apartment. He thinks about what she'll be like in a few years, out there with the rest of them, taking her chances.

"C'mon, forget it," says Didi.

Following her into the apartment, he goes first to the kitchen, gets a drink of water, then leans against the counter looking at Didi. "So what's up?" he says. He looks at her stomach to see if there are any signs. She is wearing shorts and a halter. Her feet are bare, the toenails glossy red. Her thighs look tanned. The shinbones shine.

"Look at you looking at me," she says. "What's that look for?" Her head is cocked to the side, she is smiling. Opening the refrigerator, she takes out a bottle of wine, hands it to him. "Pull the cork," she says. "I want to get drunk."

"Oh, oh."

"Oh, go on, there's a corkscrew in that drawer." She points.

He finds the corkscrew. As he drills it into the cork, he looks around the living room to see if he can find any clues. On the end table, below the lamp, is a small bouquet of flowers in a vase. There is an ashtray full of butts on the coffee table and a half-empty pack of Virginia Slims. There is also a stack of *American Poetry Review,* and a pamphlet with the title *Living with AIDS.* His stomach gets queasy. He feels his penis shrivel. He notes the couch and the rumpled pillows where she has been sitting, waiting for him to come, waiting to nail him with something. He puts the wine bottle between his legs, squeezes it, and pulls the cork. She has a long-stemmed glass in each hand. When he fills them with wine, she hands him one, then raises her own. Her smile is perplexing. He wishes she would just say what the problem is and get it over with.

"Fuck the world!" she says.

They click glasses, they drink.

"Why are we fucking the world?" he says.

"You should see your face. Don't you know what's happened to me, Jasper? No, of course you don't."

He glances at the AIDS pamphlet. "Why're you reading that?" he says.

"What? Oh, God help me, it's not that! Jesus Christ!" She laughs at him.

"All right then, what is it? You're pregnant, aren't you?"

"Jasper! God forbid. That's how much you notice things, isn't it? You thought I was *pregnant?* Jesus, nothing but negativity. How come you always think the worst?"

"I don't. Yeah, maybe. I mean, we haven't been very careful, Didi."

"Man," she says. "Man, Jasper, you just don't know what's going on, do you? You, like, walk around in a fog, don't you? I'm not dumb, Jasper. Any girl gets pregnant these days is dumber than dirt. I'm on the pill, I'm not pregnant. We're here to celebrate my first publication, you silly boy!" She goes to the desk, picks up a letter. "I'm for real now, baby," she says. "This is a letter of acceptance." She shakes the letter at him. "There was a check inside for thirty dollars! I'm bona fide published, Jasper, that's what I'm talking about here. That's why I had you come over. What, you thought I was *pregnant* or that I had *AIDS?* Oh, Jasper!" Peals of laughter break from her. She points at him.

Joy enters his heart, it comes quick as lightning. "Wahoo!" he yells.

"Way to go, Didi Godunov! I'll be a suffering bastard, you got published!"

She hands him the letter. It is from *The Polestar Poetry Review*. It says they are pleased to notify her of the acceptance of her poem "Deliquescent Love," which will appear in the December issue. They want a short biography from her, and they hope she will keep them in mind for any future work.

"A real live poet," says Jasper.

"Ain't it wonderful?" she says.

They clink glasses again and drink. Jasper keeps repeating himself, saying, "Great news, great news—"

"You thought I either had AIDS or was pregnant," she says again. "Ohhh, Jasper."

"Let it go," he says. "The pamphlet threw me off."

"You dope."

"I'm a dope," he says. She can call him anything, he doesn't care. They have another glass of wine and he tells her that it's just a matter of time before she's famous, he can see her name on the magazine covers, he can see her name on a book of collected poems, and he'll be able to say he knew her when.

"Will you still remember me when you're famous?" he says.

She assures him that she will always be the same old Didi. Money and fame will never spoil her. Whirling round with the glass in her hand, she dances about the room, dances up to him, kisses him, dances away. She tells him that one poem is only a beginning, but she feels it in her soul that from now on things will be different. Poetry prizes will follow. An agent will want her. There will be a book contract. All the work and dedication to her craft will pay off now. Didi Godunov is about to become the newest star in the poetic heavens.

Putting her glass on the table, she takes him in her arms, kisses him deeply, tells him that at last, at the ripe age of twenty-one, her real life begins, and she knows no one she would rather share the news with than Mr. Jasper John.

"This is too much," he says. "This is so great." Warmth floods his veins. He takes her in both hands, squeezes her, murmurs against her mouth, "I love you, Didi."

Mouths meet. The kissing starts for real. His hands get busy. He tastes wine on her tongue. He runs his finger under the leg rim of her shorts and feels moisture. Her mouth breaks away and she sings in a whispery voice, "Des-tin-y and me—"

They make love on the couch, only it is hard for Jasper to concentrate because Didi talks the whole time. He works hard to please her, playing on her like a pianist, and she opens to him, allows him all liberties, but she talks and talks, and he finds it very distracting. She says she's had a sense of destiny ever since she was a little girl. She had this secret understanding deep inside herself, the door would open one day and destiny would stand before her with open arms like a mighty god. She says the future is a line of magic words stretching from here to eternity. He inserts two fingers. Hammers them in and out, notes the clarity of her juices, the aroma of her sex. Her eyes are shimmering like drops of water. Her mouth glistens. He kisses her mouth. He kisses her ear, her neck. He smells suntan lotion. Love, oh love.

Busying his hands in gooey places, he keeps the kisses coming, slipping his lips over her breasts, first one, then the other, then running his tongue downward, to her belly button, to her vagina. She cocks one leg over the back of the couch. She plays with his hair. She talks. She says she has a feeling about the poem she sent to *Sewanee Review,* that they're going to take it, and lately she's been getting vibes about the one that went to *The New Yorker*— ". . . and I'll get my verse together in the fall and submit it to the Yale Younger Poets thing. God, when I win that, look out! It will be the making of me. I'll be a hot property . . . a hot property."

The fingers in his hair tighten. She pulls his head up, her blistering eyes looking at him. "Doesn't somebody want to fuck me?" she says.

He's all right now. He just hopes she won't keep talking, the talking makes him feel separated, makes him feel there are two unrelated things going on here. Sliding his jeans down, he gets on top of her, plunges in.

"Oooo," she says.

"Oooo," he says.

Words start pouring from her again, something about prizes, Pulitzer Prize, National Book Award. He stops her mouth with kisses. He runs his tongue along the inside of her lips, the back of her teeth. Their tongues foil. She pulls her mouth away, turns her head to the side, breathes.

"It could happen," she says, her voice raspy. "It's all I've ever asked of life. It's all I want. After that, I don't care if I die! Uhhh! Don't stop!"

He tries to hold back, tries to wait for her, but it doesn't work. The process has started and there is nothing he can do.

Didi tells herself she's out of sync with him, he's not the one. He gets her right to that penultimate point and then he can't last. He will rest for a moment, then he will try some more before his penis deflates, but for her it is over. She is already beginning to feel like a sopping, unfillable wound. She lets her mind roam while he goes at her down there, his hips desperate. The area is so wet now she can't feel anything, can only hear the slap of their bellies meeting. An idea has been in her head since the letter of acceptance came and she wants to think about herself and how she can make her idea into something real. She knows now for sure that she is more than just an average person. She has accomplished something only a tiny minority of the population ever accomplish. She can call herself an *author*. When people ask her what she does, she can say she's a *writer*, a published *author*, a *poet*. She thinks there must be about her certain subtle marks of distinction. Probably she has a poet's face. Certainly she has a poet's eyes. She feels colossal inside her head, full of potential. And so this idea has come to her that a writer must not let anything stand in the way of success. She has read from Faulkner that "Ode on a Grecian Urn" is worth any number of old ladies, and she agrees. She would add old men as well, and young men too. She would add men of any age and be done with it.

She tells herself that what Faulkner meant is that she must be ruthless, she must sacrifice anything and anyone, exploit whoever will help accomplish her art. And that is where Jasper John fits in. He thinks this is about love, and maybe it is, but mostly it is about exploitation in the name of Didi Godunov's destiny. It is about words, it is about imagination, it is about intellectual superiority having precedence over all other claims. It is about making time to create something of value. It is about *art*. She needs somebody to help. She needs somebody who will support her in her quest. It is decided she needs Jasper.

Watching him pull up his pants, hitching them over his narrow hips as he stands over her, looking at her with that defeated expression, she wonders if he will feel at all manipulated by what she is about to do. His sadness now is reassuring. It has been the rare man in her life who has cared so much. The light hitting him through the curtains is amber. It bathes his beard in a richness that reminds her of golden fields in Nebraska and playing hide-and-seek with her friends, and letting Bobby Richmond find her in the field, letting him paw her, while the other kids searched the wheat. Her virginity went into the earth that day and afterwards she said, "So that's all it is." And he, the skunk, wrote on the sidewalk at school in blue chalk: DIDI DUZ IT.

There came a time years later when she met Wyatt Puck. They all got high on pot the night he gave her as a present to his drummer and his bass guitar player, and between the two of them working her at both ends, the big O happened for the first time. In fact, she had multiple O's that night. She also lost Wyatt. He was gone by morning. When she went to see him later, he couldn't look at her. That was around the time that Wendy caught gonorrhea and gave it to Kendall and Kendall's wife. It was the lowest point in Didi's life, in her self-image and her special sense of destiny. She saw herself and Wendy as nothing more than a pair of sluts. She confused herself even more when she bought a vibrator and started using it and getting satisfaction by fantasizing Wyatt and the boys. She did this over and over. She couldn't stop. She would be sitting in front of the TV, or eating lunch, or doing her hair, or reading a magazine, or doing nothing, and the image of herself under them would hit her, and she would have to get her vibrator and do it. Sometimes she would do it three, four times in a day. It was crazy. It worried her. She even considered going to a psychiatrist. Finally, though, after months of self-indulgence, she had come to terms with her feelings. After all, she told herself, it was her business, and she wasn't hurting anyone, so what was the big deal?

She watches as Jasper leaves the room. She hears him pad down the hall and into the bathroom. He closes the door with a gentle click. Why not him? she asks herself. She really doesn't understand it. He's big enough, he's cute enough, he's willing enough. He has the pinkest, sweetest tool! Why not him? Didi sits up, reaches over the side of the couch, grabs her underpants, wads them up and stuffs them between her legs to catch the drippings. She takes the Virginia Slims from the coffee table, shakes one out, puts it between her lips and lights it. She waits for him to be through, to come back contrite and sit next to her like a lost boy.

She practices her approach. "I'll say I miss him so much all the time. No, I'll say I'm really starting to have deep feelings about him and us. No, I'll ask him how much he loves me. He says he loves me." She pauses to ponder his love. If he loves her so much, then why doesn't he know what she needs and suggest it himself?

"I need someone to take care of me now, someone who will take over the routine stuff and let me write. Maybe I should marry him," she says. "We could get married in Yuma and then he would be legally bound to me."

She feels ruthless. She feels like a real artist, a self-centered bitch. She thinks Faulkner would be proud of her. *I'll live with him. He'll take care of me. I'll wallow in writing. Ergo, I'll be great.* Yes, if he loves her really, he will want to take care of her and let her realize her destiny. She will immortalize him in verse. In the old days, Shakespeare, Petrarch, men like them, they used to immortalize women all the time; now women will do it for men. It is a resolution which brings her some peace of mind. She has visions of herself in total absorption in her work, while Jasper stands worshipfully by, shushing anyone who wants to interview her or take her picture. She sees herself throwing artistic tantrums and Jasper taking her abuse, his eyes adoring her. She is his little genius, his darling, his grand passionate love.

Through the window comes faintly the voice of the brother next door calling, "Kelly! Kelly! Where you going? Get back here, you little shit! I'm telling Mom, Kelly!"

Where are you going, Kelly? Didi thinks Kelly will end up a real femme fatale someday if she survives. Kelly is a miniature version of herself, she thinks, someone willing to go for it, willing to try anything, willing to live on the edge, flirt with danger. Kelly is a kindred spirit. No one understands her but Didi. It is the curse of the artist not to be understood. No one understood Didi. Why is that? she wonders. The answer comes to her from her heart. No one feels as she feels. No one feels as deeply, as many fathoms deeply, as she feels. The Seven Seas cannot contain the potential of Didi's soul. Her creativity comes from those depths. It is a mixed blessing, a lonely life, the life of the artist.

Didi feels sorrow for herself and for Kelly. She thinks maybe she will steal Kelly, take her to the mountains and teach her to be a poet. The idea tickles her, Kelly as her protégée.

Lifting up on her elbow, pushing the curtain back, she peeks out the window, she watches the little girl zooming round and round on her pint-sized bicycle, going nowhere, going everywhere. She is naked. The brother stands with his thumb hooked in the pocket of his jeans. He is smoking a cigarette. He is watching her ride.

Didi remembers herself that small, and the feeling of being closed in, of being suffocated, of wanting to be like Kelly is, naked outside in the big bright world, zooming round and round. She sees her father's used-goods store, the display tables loaded with discards, old pants, old sweaters, old shirts, old blouses, old coats, scarfs, hats, shoes, boots, slippers, bathrobes, pajamas, all of it smelling of vacated body. Smelling of stale skin. She sees herself among all this, wandering in and out of the tables. Sometimes she would take a sweater or coat, use it for a pillow, and doze beneath a table, while customers would come and go, skirts and fat ankles appearing and disappearing. She would dream of a vast life opening up for her. Looking at old magazines, she would have visions of being a model or a movie star, of being Mod, being Cool, of looking like Twiggy, of speaking Cockney and wearing a red miniskirt and having a pouty lip and big eyes. She remembers how little the little Nebraska town looked to her after her parents took her on a visit to Saint Louis. It was the remembered vastness surrounding her town's smallness which haunted her ever after, and forced her to run away several times, until she finally got out for good when she was eighteen. Until then, she was another Kelly going in circles.

Jasper comes back. He flops onto the couch and says, "Is she out there again? I heard her brother."

Didi turns from the window. "Come see Baby Godiva," she says.

Jasper gets up. He looks. "Look at him watch her," he says. "I don't trust that guy." He sits down. "I'll have to go pretty soon," he says.

"I want to talk to you first," she says.

Holding the wad of panties to her, she leaves the room. She goes into the bathroom, sits on the toilet, pees, then wipes herself with a tissue. She checks her panties and the tissue for blood. She flushes the toilet, washes her hands, sniffs beneath her arms, and adds a spray of deodorant. She brushes her hair. She puts on her shorts and halter and goes back to the living room.

It is all different now. She feels subdued. She feels how strange it is that they were naked and making love just moments ago, and he had his face down there, his tongue in there, and he sits almost pouting now and probably feeling slightly awkward like she does. Probably he wishes he could just go. Part of her wants him to, but that would defeat her whole purpose in having him over.

Sitting next to him, she takes his hand, their fingers entwining. She talks about how no one has ever believed in her the way he does. She says they have something special between them. Kissing his shoulder, she snuggles with him. She puts his hand on her thigh and puts her hand on his stomach.

"Don't you think things are starting to fall into place?" she says.

"Seems like it," he says.

"From now on I'll, like, totally dedicate myself body and soul to my art. 'Deliquescent Love' is just the beginning. I'm going to go all out now. I'm going to work so hard. Write and write. Do you think I can do it, Jasper? Do you think I can make it all the way?"

"Sure," he says.

"I only need time," she says. "It's tough to find the time. All the things you have to do, you know what I mean?"

He knows what she means.

"I know this will sound like I'm getting a big head, Jasper, but I feel like I might be a genius, you know, and, honest, I feel the call of my genius telling me to strike while the iron is hot, while my name is out there. By December when my poem comes out, I want to have the entire book done and ready to go. When the calls come in, I want to have the goods. How am I going to do that and have to work and go to school and all the thousand things you have to do just to keep on keeping on? Oh, it's so frustrating, Jasper."

"Hmm, I bet," he says.

Now she is getting upset with him. Why doesn't he see what she's getting at? He is not paying attention. He is not focused on what she is saying. *I need,* she wants to tell him. *Don't you understand how much I need?* She strokes his belly, runs her hand down, feels the lump between his legs, gives it a little press. She keeps her hand there to see if anything happens.

"I don't know, I've just been thinking we should see more of each other. My feelings for you are growing, you know. I mean, I've even thought about what it would be like to be married to you. You know, waking up every morning and having you in bed next to me. We could make love anytime we wanted to. We could read the same books and talk about them. I could read you my poetry. You could be my best critic. You're smart. I need someone like you. I've been thinking about such things. Have you ever thought about us that way, honey?" She gives him another little squeeze. There is some swelling there now. She feels heat on her palm.

"I've thought about it, sure," he says. "I didn't think you ever thought about it, though. But I've thought about it."

He clears his throat. He stretches his legs out, puts his feet on the coffee table. She slips her head onto his chest. Her fingers knead his penis. "Maybe we should try living together," she says. "I don't know, it's just a thought."

"I think we should," he says.

"We could see if we're compatible," she says.

She unbuttons his jeans, reaches inside. He is tumescent now. She sees the head above the rim of his pants. Again he clears his throat. He stretches out farther. She runs her hand back and forth lightly.

"You know, you could move in with us," he says. "With me and Mary and Henry. Into my room. She would be glad to have you there. She's all scared of having another heart attack and having no one there to save her. You wouldn't have to pay rent. I'd buy our food and stuff, and you could be free to write."

"It's an idea," she says. Her head has sunk down to his stomach. She is looking closely at his penis. It seems to be expecting something more from her. If she stuck her tongue out, she could touch the tip of its little mouth. She can smell herself.

"I think you should let me fix it," he says. "There's plenty of room. I'd stay out of your way when you're writing. Artists have to have their space. I'm sensitive to that. You won't even know I'm around. We can put your desk in my bedroom, it'd be *our* bedroom. The rest of your furniture, we could put in the garage."

She says, "Hmm, maybe I should. Maybe it's fate." She squeezes him, listens to him moan. "Maybe it's fate," she repeats.

"It's up to you," he says. He takes a deep breath. "But I don't think you'll find a better deal, Didi. We'll try it out. Things go good, we'll get married whenever you want. I'll take care of you. You'll write your poems and get famous, and I'll take care of you. Oh, God that feels good, Didi."

Love, oh love.

"Talk to me," she says. "Tell me things, honey." A tiny drop of fluid appears on the mouth of his penis.

"It'll be great, it'll be us, it'll be . . . you'll write poetry, you'll win the Pulitzer Prize . . . and this book of yours, collection, this . . . maybe for sure, famous . . . your destiny, your, you know, your destiny— Oh, Didi, baby . . . God."

She gives him a lick. "I'll come," she says.

۵

Modern, mature woman, very political, concentrated, would like to meet mature man, 40–45, for quiet nights of companionship and profound discussions concerning Marx, Gandhi, Boris Pasternak, and the films of David Lean. Can poetry, literature, and humanism survive in a christotechno world? Can trees, butterflies, songbirds, and frogs live beside the chemical industrial complex? Will natural and cerebral beauty be a mythos to our grandchildren? Let's talk of final things, of intellectual loneliness, of cabbages and kings. Write Alice, Adam and Eve Possibilities.

Jasper tells himself that "Alice" sounds like a philosopher, and she would probably drive a man crazy with babble the way Didi Godunov does.

It's been a week since Didi moved in. There are times he wants to throttle her, make her shut up. How can someone talk so damn much? She reads her poems to him in bed at night, and he is supposed to say something about each one, but he's not expected to really criticize. He tried that once and for two days she froze him out. There is this certain look and tone of voice he has learned to be wary of, a furrowing of the brows, the eyes that look away, the voice going flat, words kept to one or two icy syllables. He calls it her snit. When she's in a snit, he does his best to stay away. At the moment, he is glad to be at work because he heard a snit coming on. He had told her that he didn't like Plath and Sexton because their poetry was too confessional.

"Oh, really?" she had said, her voice icy.

He had tried to backpedal a bit, telling her that their poetry lacked the universality of *her* poetry, that was the big difference; but he knew she could tell he was lying. Truth is, he doesn't like her poetry either. He doesn't like her confessions. He doesn't think her life is that interesting. He wishes she would be less dedicated to her *art,* and more considerate of him at two o'clock in the morning when she wants to type and he wants to sleep. If he does sleep, she will often wake him up and read him some lines she has just written. Her words wad up inside his head and he is reduced to handing her clichés—*smooth, clean, terrific, inspired, interesting* . . . What he really wants to say is *too familiar, thin, bloodless, imitative, boring, stupid, trite, what a bunch of shit* . . .

He ties on his apron. He looks into the dining room and sees Ruby filling sugar jars. The new one, the one called Beehive, is making coffee. She is as tall as Jasper. She is slim, with a long waist and a swanlike neck. Her hair is something out of the sixties. It is piled on her head like a Buddhist temple. She wears cat glasses. She is fortyish, a gum chewer, a smoker of cigarillos, a skilled waitress. She and Ruby make a good team.

In back of him the phone rings. He can hear Fat Stanley on the line saying, "Yes . . . My number? . . . He did? . . . No, that's okay. Yes, we're good friends . . . Oh my, oh dear, oh no . . . oh no." There is silence, then he says, "Thank you." He hangs up. He turns around and says, "That was Bertha Tatem. Godot has cut his wrists."

"Omigod, that's awful," says Jasper. "When? Just now?"

"I don't know. Sometime today. He's alive. He's okay. He's in the hospital, same one as Helga."

Jasper remembers Godot when he and Henry put him in the garage, and how Godot looked crucified on the bed, snoring away, with visions of Babylonian whores dancing in his head.

Fat Stanley explains that Godot cut his wrists in front of Mary Mythwish at school, then walked down the hall bleeding, got as far as Bertha Tatem's office doorway, and collapsed.

"Woo, wild," says Jasper.

"I'm going to see him after work," says Fat Stanley. "I said I would.

God, when it rains it pours, doesn't it? Helga and Mary, and now Godot. Makes you wonder who's next."

"Bad luck comes in threes," says Jasper.

Fat Stanley sits on his stool. He reaches over to the porcelain handles on the grill, adjusts the flame. "If he hadn't lost his job," he says.

"It's so stupid," says Jasper, airing his thoughts. "Why don't he just get another job? I'd tell them to go fuck themselves, that's what I'd do. He's making it look like they were right to fire him. Probably they saw something a long time ago. I mean, if he was all there, wouldn't they have given him tenure?"

Fat Stanley says, "Would they? I don't know. A high-strung man like him, it wouldn't take much to make him fall apart. One day he's normal as you and me, then he finds out he's losing his job, finds out he's no longer wanted, no longer appreciated or useful, and he goes to pieces. At his age, I can understand it. Doesn't take much to put you over the edge at his age."

Fat Stanley's eyes are sad. He rests his elbow on his knee. His thumb and forefinger tug at the tuft of hair just beneath his lower lip. He speaks as if from far away. He says, "He would have been fine if they had stuck with him. You know, that school, it was his whole life, and then it tosses him out and goes for the hot young teacher—replaces him with a hot young *female* scholar. That's a double kick up the ass to a guy like Godot. Remember what he said in here that night, he was paying for the sins of his father? Think of being told a stupid thing like that. It would eat you alive."

"Yeah, I guess," says Jasper. "But me, I'd go find new worlds to conquer, that's what I'd do." He squares his shoulders. In his young strength and immortality, he feels contempt for lesser beings.

"That's because you're young," says Fat Stanley. "When you're older, you'll change your tune."

Jasper doesn't believe it. He is disgusted with Godot. He doesn't see age as an excuse for surrender. He decides suddenly that he has a harsh opinion of people who collapse in adversity, who collapse and do savage things to themselves, like that Sister Augustine who killed herself right in front of Mary Quick. And Mary's own mother. Jesus. People like that are repulsive. He liked much better the Godot who showed up the other night with a battered face, bruised knuckles, and a porno movie script in his hand. A Godot ready to spit in Shakespeare's eye, ready to desecrate the very words the academics worship. That Godot he admired, the blasphemous one.

"You want to go with me?" says Fat Stanley. "You want to see him?"

"Not me," says Jasper. "To hell with that."

Fat Stanley makes a face at Jasper. "Jasper," he says, "don't be hard on Godot."

Jasper thinks it over. He sucks his lower lip and wonders if he has changed recently, or was he always so uncompromising? He knows something shifted in him the second he heard what Godot had done, something came up that was all black, that was all wrong. When he was with Mary the other night and being philosophical and cool, he had told her there were no blacks and whites and no judgments in him. Was that a lie? Partly, just partly. Jasper hadn't liked her story—hadn't liked it and was wishing ever since she had kept it to herself. There are things about the rotten end of people that we just shouldn't know. Still, though, she was his friend. She was this fallible, weak-willed, broken old lady—and she was his friend. Godot too. But something about this suicide thing had made him shift off dead center. He knows it really isn't right to condemn Godot so harshly. Godot is in trouble, he is hurting. Mary is hurting. Everybody is hurting. He grimaces. He wishes he were outside so he could spit.

"It just makes me mad at him," he says. "I don't know why, what it is, but it makes me—" He shrugs his shoulders, sucks his lip, searches for the right word.

"Nervous?" says Fat Stanley. "Scared?"

Jasper hesitates. "Is that it?" he says.

Fat Stanley tugs at his ear. His head bobs up and down. "Yeah, yeah," he says, "it scares me too. Ho boy, I admit it. This thing that you can be so broken, so sad, you'll annihilate yourself. Any one of us might do it, given the right push. It's awfully scary to think you can hurt so bad that you'll die from it. Freud said we all have a death wish, you know, just waiting to take us over."

"Not me, not yours truly. Suicide is gutless, man," says Jasper. "The Godot who cuts his wrists is not the Godot I want to know, man. I want people to be what they seem. He seemed hard as wood knots once upon a time. A wood knot is dependable. Then he changed, gone soft."

"Uh-huh. You want actors," says Fat Stanley. "You want . . . illusions."

✛

After work he and Henry go to a nightclub called Bottoms. They are just going for a couple of beers and to relax. They enter beneath blue lights that give the bar a mysterious, alternate-world look as it swims in a sea of wavering smoke. Waitresses float between round tables where customers sit drinking and watching dancers above them on a runway stage. Jasper smells orange blossoms nearby. A girl in a bikini walks past him. She tugs at Henry's elbow.

"Lemon Drop!" he says, turning to her.

They hug. "Over here," she says. She guides them through the tables to a padded bar that surrounds the stage. Henry whispers to her. She smiles. She gives him a kiss on the lips. He hands her a dollar bill and she leaves. A few minutes later she returns with a pitcher of beer and two mugs. Henry tells her to run a tab. He pats her fanny, gives it a little squeeze. She takes another dollar bill from him.

"Youz want some of that?" he says to Jasper. "Let me know. I'll fix it."

"Didi's about all I can handle right now," says Jasper.

Henry gives him a look. "Youz're some bullshitter," he tells Jasper. "Never bullshit a bullshitter."

Henry is right. Jasper knows he would like to give Lemon Drop a go. He looks around the club at the other girls prancing in bikinis and

207.

he knows any one of them could crook her finger and he would follow like a puppy.

"See that," says Henry. He points to a huge chrome hook fixed to the ceiling over center stage. "Wait'll youz see what they do with that," he says.

Jasper stares at the hook, then he looks around some more. He sees a row of booths in the back. The booths are filled with men and women, but only men sit on the stools at the stage. He sees a bouncer in a black suit standing by the door. He tries to make out facial features on the women sitting at the round tables, but they all look smudgy in the blue lights.

Music plays and a woman dances onto the stage. She wears spiked heels, net stockings, a G-string. She has looping earrings that hit her shoulders. In her nose is another ring, tiny, golden. Two more rings glitter on her nipples. When she sticks her tongue out at the men, they can see what looks like a tie tack driven through her tongue.

"Think what she can do with that," says Henry.

"Don't it hurt?" says Jasper.

Henry doesn't answer. He is watching the girl. His tongue massages his unicorn tooth. When she finishes her dance, she walks along the edge of the bar and gathers her tips. Some of the men compliment her dancing. She says, "Thank you." She lets some of them hold her hand a moment, or touch her leg, or her foot. She clenches the money in her fist. When she gets to where Jasper is sitting, he holds out a dollar and asks her if the thing in her tongue hurts.

She kneels in front of him, shows him her drilled tongue. "When I got it pierced, I cried," she says. "But it's okay now. I have to wash it with peroxide or it will get infected, food gets in there and stuff, you know. I know a guy that does it if you want one."

"I was just wondering is all," says Jasper. She takes his money and moves on.

"Youz want some of that?" says Henry. "Think what that fem can do for youz, Jim."

"I wouldn't kick her out of bed," says Jasper. "But she can lose the hardware. I'd be afraid of getting my teeth knocked out."

"Flamin legs, Jim, don't youz know what they do now? Listen to the Hank. She runs that up and down your peter. You ain't been done till you feel that thing pressing on the center vein. It makes youz spout like a whale, Jim."

"I guess you know, huh?"

Henry grins. "Look here, Jim. Youz can sit round waitin for life to come knockin, or youz can go grab it and pull it through the door. Now what youz think is my philosophics? Let me put it this way. The Hank has lived by one rule: If it feels good, it is good, and fuck any mother-fucker who says pain is gain and your reward comes after youz die. Whoever says that is a lyin sack of shit, Jim. Look here, when it's time to go, the last thing I want is to be thinkin I ain't lived. I don't want to have to say, 'Whoa, motherfucker, I ain't lived yet, gimme one more chance, motherfucker.' I don't want to have to say that, Jim. Flamin legs, that would be too damn sad."

Another dancer comes out. The music gets her going. She moves about the stage like a miniature night sky. There are silver stars pasted all over her. She wears silver star glasses and a crown of silver stars, and silver stars over her nipples. Silver stars make a Y-shaped pattern down her stomach. Silver stars disappear between her legs and come up the crack of her ass. Her ass is smooth and white and full of potential. Hundreds of silver stars run down her legs and over her back. The effect is oddly like staring into the Milky Way with two moons blocking out the middle.

"I'm in heaven," says the man to Jasper's right.

Henry whispers, "Fucks like heaven too, Jim. Youz want her? I can fix it. Fifty bucks she'll let youz do it up her anal asshole." Henry's eyes are full of cunning. "Look at her. Just look at her."

Jasper watches her roll and vibrate to the music. The silver stars wink at him. She bends over, spreads her cheeks, and looks at him upside down between her legs. Her ass rotates enticingly.

"Go with the flow, Jim," whispers Henry.

"Not my type," says Jasper. But he watches her a long while and he wonders if she is.

When the music is over, she picks up her tips and leaves the stage. There is a break. Henry orders another pitcher.

"Did you know Godot is in the hospital? Slashed his wrists," says Jasper. Drawing a line on his wrist, he illustrates what Godot did.

"Yeah, I heard," says Henry. "Dumb bastard. But look here, Jim, don't youz worry about it, I still got the screenplay. We're still gonna make our movie, and you're still gonna be our ReemHerHole. Don't be sweatin none of that. We don't need him no way." Henry taps his head, indicating it's all there, the movie.

Jasper sees past his shoulder to a couple in one of the booths. They are making out. Their hands are lost in the dark beneath the table. Lemon Drop waltzes by. Henry grabs her.

"Give my man a kiss," he tells her. "My man needs a kiss." He puts a dollar on her tray.

"You want?" she says to Jasper.

Henry doesn't let him answer. Henry tells Lemon Drop to just do it. She does. Jasper feels soft lips opening on his lips. He smells orange blossoms. There is a gluey moment as their mouths seal, then she breaks away. She looks at him. Her pupils are dilated. She looks excessively mellow. Jasper wouldn't mind some of what she's on.

"Thanks, that felt nice," he says.

"My pleasure," she says.

When she walks away, Henry gets after him, telling him that Lemon Drop likes him, wants him, must have him. Henry's going to fix it up. Jasper smells blossoms on his mustache. He is tempted. Turning on the stool, he watches her weave among the tables. He sees how the men stare at her. They look ready to tear her to pieces. We're all so hungry, he tells himself. They show us some tit, some thigh, some ass, and a raging madman takes control. It doesn't make sense, but there it is.

As if reading his thoughts, Henry reaches over, runs his hand along Jasper's leg. Jasper jerks away.

210.

"Just checkin," says Henry. He wheezes laughter. "Needed to know if youz having a good time, Jim. Look here, what about youz and Didi? That is some serus fem. When youz brung her in the Hank was impressed, his estimations went up ten notches. Any young rooster like youz what has access to that is a man to be reckoned with. Bet she turns youz every way but loose, huh? I can hear youz in there at night. Does she talk the whole time?"

"She talks," answers Jasper.

"Some of em do. I had one oncet, she would say dirty words the whole time—fuck, cunt, piss, shit—the whole way. Women, youz know, they're the same, but then again, they're different."

"Her infinite variety," says Jasper.

"That's right," says Henry. "Variety is the spice of life, definitely." The back of Henry's fingers brush Jasper's beard. It is a caressing stroke. "What's the farm girls say about a man's beard, Jim?"

Jasper doesn't know.

"They say youz can tell by the hay if the pitchfork's good."

"Is that what they say?"

"The pitchfork." Henry runs his hand up Jasper's leg again.

"I love women. Only women, Henry."

"Course youz do, but any port in a storm, Jim." His fingers linger a moment. Then he pats Jasper and straightens up. "Where's the fems?" he says.

A new girl comes on. She prances to the music. She has the bright red mane of a chow chow, it bristles in all directions, forming a frame for her head. She has red wings painted over her eyes and cheekbones. She is bare-breasted. Her breasts are large. They slope gently toward upturned tips and seem to vibrate rather than bounce as she walks.

"Name's Susie Q," says Henry.

She high-steps to the front of the stage. She is wearing flesh-colored panties, so thin Jasper can see the dark, triangular bush right through them. She grinds to the music and pooches her groin in some man's face. He slips money inside her leg band, and she moves on to the next man, grinds for him. Her whole act consists of wiggling her

211.

hips to the beat and pooching her groin at each man. By the time she gets to Jasper, she has several bills rolled up and sticking out. She puts her bush so close to him, he can smell it. He slips a dollar bill next to the others. Henry gets his turn next. Instead of pushing his money toward her, he holds it back, makes her come down farther, makes her come and get it. When the rolled bill touches her, Henry bends forward and buries his mouth in her crotch. People in back and along the bar shout and whistle. Some are clapping their hands. She lets him have two seconds, then she pulls away, moves to the next guy and the next. None of them do what Henry did. By the time the music ends, Susie Q has a skirt of dollar bills protruding from her leg bands. She goes offstage, stumbling a bit, awkwardly plucking her tips.

Henry puts his arm around Jasper and pulls him close. "Smell my beard," he says.

"Powdered pussy," says Jasper, sniffing.

"From her beard to my beard, fair exchange," says Henry.

As the night wears on almost all the girls seem to give Henry special treatment. They call him by name, they smile for him, they dip their fannies in his face, they get their dollar bill. Henry keeps insisting that this one or that one loves him. Lemon Drop keeps coming by with pitchers of beer and kisses. Lemon Drop loves him, Henry says. Henry says he has magnetism, charisma. He can't keep the women off. He's their urban mystery, and women love a mystery. He hypnotizes them like a snake does a mouse. He offers Jasper any woman in the place, he offers to make Jasper a multibillionaire, he offers to give Jasper the world on a platter. All Jasper has to do is be his pal, be loyal to the Hank.

He tells Jasper it's all going to work out according to the plan. The Hank has a cosmic plan, everything calculated to the last detail, and Jasper is a part of that plan. Together they will move mountains, men, women, and real estate. Together they will own the souls of every red-blooded type of the species called North American. It will bow at their feet. Senators, presidents, corporate boards, every piece of the pie and layer of the cake will come under their control. It's all as easy as writing a check. Making the movie is just the first step. From there, they will branch out, they will diversify. They will incorporate. They will gobble up the weak. They will sell off the sick. They will create pandemonium in the stock market and build an empire with ill-gotten gains in the land of the free and the home of the brave. Does Jasper understand Henry's philosophics?

Yes, he guesses he does.

"Wisdom of age," says Henry. "It's the only good thing about gettin old. I'm a wise old fucker. I know life like the head of my peter. I know what makes *everybody* tick. Money, honey, is number one . . . and youz know the other. I got a book for youz, *Debbie Anal and the Pumphouse Gang.* Read it to Didi and see if she don't go crazy. Have money, talk dirty."

"The Muff-Divers of Bemidji," says Jasper, remembering an Evergreen book he once read.

Henry laughs. He punches Jasper's arm. "Youz okay," he says. "Listen here. Talkin about money, when we gonna clean Calvin Cleans clock, Jim? When we gonna? Man, I'm tellin youz, it'll be takin candy from a baby."

"I don't know," says Jasper.

"Got to know soon. Got to get financed. Can't make our movie if we don't get financed."

"Let me think it over."

"Let the Hank know."

"I will."

"My buddy, my baby, my boy."

"Let me think it over, Henry."

"Youz'll do the right thing, I know. The Hank knows your true-blue heart."

Blue lights come on and noise fills the stage. The noise is ear-piercing. It is like a child's scream. Jasper puts his hands over his ears, but he can hear it anyway. In the center of the stage is an enigmatic figure. She wears a black cape, which covers her all the way to her toes.

Her hair is black, it shines like enamel paint. Her face is dusted with ivory powder. Thick black lashes and thick black lips glow amid the corpse white of her skin. She waits until the scream dies away, then she starts doing a slow side-to-side shuffle. While she is shuffling, Lemon Drop comes onstage with a sign on an easel. She props the sign to one side. It says KAREN THE KONTORTIONIST.

"Here she is, guys," says Lemon Drop. She claps her hands. A spattering of applause joins in.

Accompanying Karen is the worst music Jasper has ever heard. It is an unmelodic-unmusic clashing of guitars, drums, dissonant piano, bells, horns, cymbals, and someone shrieking in the background. Karen moves forward, her figure jerking beneath her black cape as if fragments of the music are pelting her. Pausing beneath the hook, she opens the cape. Lemon Drop and the girl with the chow chow hair move to assist her. They take away the cape, leaving Karen alone and naked on the stage, her hands bound in front of her with glistening yellow rope. Karen raises her hands. The hook comes down, and she catches hold of it. Immediately it raises her to the ceiling. For a moment she hangs there, then the hook begins to rotate and she goes round and round, circling above them like a painted bird. Strobe lights hit her and bits of painted flesh appear, bits of Karen the Kontortionist flash in the air. She has tattoos of phosphorescent snakes wrapped around both thighs. She has scallops of leaves and butterflies and flowers and vines in phosphorescent golds, greens, purples, and pinks covering her breasts and belly. Her back resembles the fanned tail of a peacock, a dozen eyes staring from the tips of quaking feathers. A pair of succulent apples are tattooed to the cheeks of her ass.

Near Jasper an awed voice says, "My God, look at that."

"Have a nibble, Leonard," says someone else.

"She's like a storybook," says another.

Henry leans toward Jasper and says, "They ain't seen nothin yet. This is the one I want, Jim. I've had my eye on her."

They watch Karen circling. Jasper focuses on the phosphorescent parts of her. She's a garden of earthly fears and delights. He thinks of

214.

how vulnerable she is, how on a hook like that, a man could do any-thing to her. She is exposed, helpless. Just as we want them, he tells himself. Images enter his head. He runs his fingers over her tattoos. She is young. She is willing. Her skin is a fable. Between the spreading of her ribs and the slow-motion movement of her knees, he sees the luminous point of contact that men have died for, killed their brothers for, given away kingdoms to possess. Mary Quick hangs there. Helga and Didi hang there, Ruby Rush, Beehive, Bertha Tatem, and Mary Mythwish hang there. Delicious . . . delicious. He feels like a flesh-eater, a cannibal. He looks around and sees her hemmed in by his brothers, teeth showing, jaws ready, mouths moist—all of them loving "long pig."

Turning as if a wind is moving her, she does a partial pull-up, her legs go up, her feet slide by her cheeks. The guitars say *ga-whoosh!* A horn bleeds, a bird whistles, a drum makes sounds like boulders collid-ing, the shrieker shrieks. Her feet go higher, her feet slip by her head and go behind her neck, her legs pour over her, her ass follows, she flows over her face and is suddenly upside down, her arms twisting in their sockets, looking as if they are dislocated.

The men applaud.

Ohmmm! Woom! Woooo! says the music.

And the hook spins.

"She must be made of taffy," says Henry.

"Fuckin weird," says a man.

"I feel like I'm on the other side of the looking glass," says another.

"She's wonderland. You're wonderland, baby!"

Karen's head dips down, her spine slithers upward, pouring herself back through her arms again. When she is right side up, she leaves her ankles locked behind her neck. From below, beams of white light, narrow as laser beams, wink on simultaneously as she circles. The lights center on her vagina. Each man at the bar gets an intimate look. They see the wiry beard, the purple lips, the smooth pink flesh protruding, the glistening ingress squinting like a socket for an eye. A smell of earth, of damp soil, hovers like a mist over the bar. Karen's tongue

215.

comes out. She touches her nose with her tongue. She touches her chin with her tongue.

Beside Jasper, Henry is leaning far forward and grinning. "Gonna get you, baby," he says to Karen as she circles by.

Jasper doesn't share his enthusiasm. He doesn't know why, but he feels sick. He is nauseous. His head is light, it is spinning. He wants to stand up, but he's afraid he'll fall.

"I feel dizzy," he says.

"Hush," says Henry. "Don't break a man's concentration."

Jasper looks at Karen revolving on the hook, her apple-tattooed ass sliding by. He sees the men leaning forward in the shadows, their eyes hot and greedy, their eyes searching Karen's body as if it is the living language, the holy book, its symbols saying: *Take, eat.*

"I'm leaving," says Jasper. He waits for a response, but there is none. "I'm going," he says.

Henry suddenly glares at him. "Jim, there are times when youz shouldn't talk!"

"Fuck it, I'm going."

Jasper eases off the stool. He wants nothing more than fresh air now. Carefully he walks the course through the tables. He reaches the door. The bouncer opens it and he spills into the night. A cool mist bathes his face. He sucks the cool into his lungs. He exhales from his diaphragm, purging his lungs. He can still hear the music inside Bottoms. It is coming through the walls. It means something, but he doesn't know what exactly. It is like music from the beginning of time, like before the world was filled with man-made noises. It is instinct music, he thinks, no rhyme, no reason, music made by the wind chafing through trees; music made of lightning, of thunder, of fear; music made by falling rocks and the wind whistling through hollows, the wind rushing through reeds and over the lap of water. It was a long time ago, but Jasper feels like he was there to hear it. He knows it didn't jar him then as it does now. He puts his hands over his ears, but he still hears it.

A bus goes by, slows down. There is the squeal of brakes before it stops. The smell of diesel clears his mind. He trots to the bus, then waits impatiently for an old woman to get off. Her descent is maddeningly slow, one foot at a time, both hands clinging to the rail. Jasper wants to make her hurry. He feels an impulse to shove her out of the way. The music throbs against the walls of Bottoms. He sees Karen the Kontortionist turning as he watches the old woman turn to lower herself from the bottom step to the curb. A sudden impulse makes him reach out and take her elbow. "I've got you," he says. The old woman makes puffy grunty noises. She reaches the sidewalk, glances at him, smiles, then shuffles by. He smells dampness and old roots. Finally he gets on the bus, gives a rolled dollar to the driver, and sits down. In a moment he is moving, going east to home, to Didi waiting.

Helga wakes in near-darkness in a new room. She is alone in here, this room where they send people to die. There is a faint flow from a fluorescent bulb recessed in the ceiling. It sends a soft diffusion of ghostly light into the room. Raising her head from the pillow, she sees over the edge of the mattress, gleaming in the light, the white, sterile floor, the white, sterile walls. Instruments cling to the walls like insects: a long tube on the wall for taking blood pressure, a white lamp with a familiar praying mantis arm, a stainless-steel plate with hose connections in the middle. Under the plate is a sign that says OXYGEN. There are more connections and instruments in the wall and on the floor, but she isn't sure how they do what they do. She smells them in the air, the smell of disinfected metal. She believes they are machines to keep her alive.

Beside her, close enough to touch, is a small table with fake wood grain over its surface. On the table is a phone. There are get-well cards on the table: "We Love You Mom, Please GET WELL!" "I am praying for you every day. Trust in Jesus. Your Friend Mary Quick." "Helga, get the hell out of there, it's no place for a fox like you. Love Pirate Pomegranate." And so on. Her friends haven't forgotten her.

There is a plastic pot full of flowers on the table. Around the pot is a red ribbon. She lies back and runs her mind over her body, checking for pain, and for signs of strength. There is an uncomfortable pressure in her abdomen. She bears down, farts, but the pressure in her intestine won't go away. It is poised at the center of her being, the center of her cancer. Gingerly she touches it. It tells her not to probe, but she probes anyway and is punished with a slick pain that runs from her belly to a point under her right armpit. She cries out and the sound of her voice echoes in the room. A sense of the great hollowness out there fills her heart. She cusses it, she cusses the hollowness. Cussing gives her courage.

Closing her eyes against the ghostly light, she reminds herself that she is dying, and it is not mere histrionics, it is not a melodrama, it is not a depression-inspired death wish, or an outburst of pique. She is really going to what someone called the Great Perhaps. What pleases her at the moment is that she can say it to herself, say death, say my death, my death soon, today, tonight, tomorrow, soon, no more Thanksgiving Day, no more Christmas, no more birthdays, no more children—she can say all this and not feel her insides turn to water. She has cried all she can cry, raved all she can rave, prayed all she can pray. Maybe it is the drugs they are giving her; but whatever it is, she is proud of her control, her calmness, her *clarity* in the face of the absolutely irrevocable promise of leaving this dimension. I'm a brave girl, she tells herself.

She spends most of her waking hours going backward in time. At the moment she sees a child in fourth or fifth grade. The long ago is easy to remember. It is more clear to her than two or three hours ago when Fat Stanley was beside her bed, bending over her, telling her how well she looked. He's an old, fat fool, but she loves him. She wishes now she had married him after Mike died. She wishes now she hadn't been so hung up on trying to find a wild-man substitute for Mike. Fat Stanley would have made a good father and a loyal husband. She could just kick herself for not going after him, but it is too late now.

She brushes those regrets aside and centers herself on the little girl she was. She remembers the kids calling her Birdlegs, and her mother making her wear dresses to school every day, not listening to her pleas for pants. She was Birdlegs through grammar school and most of high school. She didn't get nice legs until she was eighteen, when they and the rest of her filled out. Her legs were her best feature then, for years and years, until the cancer came, until the cancer brought her back in a circle to the scrawny legs of youth. She reminds herself that she would not relive her childhood for anything, not for a million billion dollars. She would live only the years with Mike, the early years, before kids, before guilt, before the rut of three squalling brats and a house smelling of peepee diapers. Before all the whimpering, whining, gimme, gimme, gimme, and drowning under the weight of children. Little parasites. Little leeches. And that goddamn Mike staying at the bars having his fun. Coming home fucked up, and she smelling of baby shit and barf, with her ratted matted hair, burned-out eyes, and hateful heart. She would shriek at him, make him despise her for the bitch she was. After he died, she sugarcoated those early years, made them cozy for herself and the kids. But now she is beyond tricks. She sees what it was like, what some vicious bug in her soul remembers. No, she would not go back to that either. Where would she go? When was her life a worthwhile thing? Does it all boil down to booze and bars and wasted years? Her mother told her she would pay for her sins, she would pay for breaking their hearts, she would pay for going off with that hoodlum Mike, that smart-mouth, drunken motorcycle rider from hell.

Mothers know these things.

Helga is glad the selfish, dirty-minded, vindictive little witch cannot see her now, cannot see that the predictions came true, that life has been a little bit, or larger than a little bit, of hell.

She feels herself frowning. She wonders where such evil thoughts come from, is it a side effect of the drugs they give her? Is it some cancer atom in her brain? She listens to herself breathing, notes the shallow rise and fall of her chest. She checks to see if the pain is still there and is satisfied that it hasn't moved. She tries to pass wind again, but can't. She decides it is cancer madness that has made her think bad things about her beloved Mike. She remembers that he came to her a few nights ago, hovering in the corner of the ceiling, beckoning. Her

Mikey. Her one and only love. Love, oh love. No one ever measured up to my Mikey, she tells herself. He was a real man. Just had too much energy for his own good, too much of the life force. Can't be holding men like that back, it breaks their spirit. Got to let them go, let them run like wild horses. Then when they get older, they settle down and make good husbands. They stick with you because you didn't try to break them.

The pain is waking up again, stretching, yawning, testing. Soon it will start raking her with its nails. It hates her. It wants to hear her cry. But she has news for it. Fuck you! she says. You think you're so high and mighty, you think you rule, you think I'll just let you grow and grow, but you don't know me. I've got a plan now, you stupid bastard. I've decided to die and take you with me. I always said I'd fix you, you cretin. Put your ass in the grave and bury you forever.

As if listening to what she is saying, the pain slashes out. Helga grits her teeth. She pulls a bit of blanket into her mouth and bites it. Her face is fragmenting. Her belly hurts . . . it hurts real bad. She goes with it, lets it show off, lets it squeeze a few tears from her, before it subsides. When it finally eases off, she whispers defiantly, "Hah!"

Leaning over, she picks up the phone, dials 9 and Fat Stanley's number. The phone rings half a dozen times before he answers.

"Hello," he says, his voice sleepy.

"It's me," she says.

He coughs. He clears his throat. "Hello. Who?"

"It's me, it's Helga. Did I wake you up?"

"What's the matter? Are you okay?" he says.

"Stanley, you've got to make a decision. You got to tell me, Stanley. What's going to happen to my kids? My kids, Stanley. My kids!"

He says, "Calm down, don't get yourself all upset now. What time is it? Jesus Christ, it's one o'clock."

"Is it one o'clock?"

"Yes."

"I'm running out of time, Stan."

"No, no you're not, Helga. Helga, listen to me. You're not going to die. Listen, they're going to use this miracle drug on you. It's saving lives right and left. It's practically a sure thing, Helga. I talked to the doctor when I was there tonight, and he's going to use this miracle drug and you'll see in a couple days, you'll be up and snorting like a steam engine."

"You think so, Stan?"

"I know so. You'll live to be a hundred, the doctor said."

"A hundred? I would like that, Stan. Stan, I want to live to be a hundred."

"You will."

"But what if I don't? Just say it don't work on me, then what? I don't feel so good, Stan. I feel rotten. I can feel it eating me. You don't know the pain I'm in, it's like a tiger trying to lay me open. Fuck me, Stan, why couldn't I have got something like Mary's got? She'll go fast when it's ready to take her. Me, it's picking me apart in itty-bitty pieces. It's like how people staked to an anthill die. That's what it feels like. When it comes, I grit my teeth so hard, I almost break my jaw."

"Haven't they given you your shot? You were supposed to have a shot at twelve-thirty. Those fuckers. Hang up, I'm going to call them and tell them to give you your shot."

"Wait, Stan, listen. Tell me something, please. Tell me what's gonna happen if the miracle drug doesn't work on me. I want to know what's gonna happen."

"I don't know," he says. "What can I say?"

"Say you'll take care of my kids. Say you'll take them in and raise them as your own, you'll educate them, get them a decent start in life. Will you do that for me, Stanley? I would do it for you. Listen to me, Stan. Stan, are you listening?"

"I'm listening."

"If I know they're all right, I can die in peace. Give a mother her dying wish, Stanley Lipton. Will you promise me? Promise me."

There is a long pause. She hears him breathing. She feels his anguish, but she doesn't care. She will sacrifice him, she will sacrifice anyone, to her children.

At last he says, "Helga, I'm probably the worst candidate you could find. I'm fifty years old, Helga. I don't know a thing about kids, not a thing. I don't know if I'm up to the job, you see? I might ruin them. It scares me to death. I want to help, but what if I fuck them up? I'd never forgive myself if I fucked up your kids. Kids today, you know, they need somebody who knows what he's doing. Kids today, they're all fucked up because nobody knows what he's doing. Helga, isn't there somebody you trust? Your mother, your father, a sister, or something?"

"I trust only you," she tells him. "You've known my kids for years. You know what they need. I trust only you, Stanley. Will you promise me—no foster homes, no orphanages, no *authorities* or *experts?* Just you. What more do you want from life, old friend? Ever since I've known you, you've wanted a family. Well, here it is, ready-made. All you need do is love them."

"I wish I was married," he says. "I wish I had a woman to look after them. I'd do it then, if I had a wife who was willing."

Helga hesitates. There is a deadness in the line, and she wonders if she's lost him. "Are you there?" she says.

He sighs. He says, "Let me think it over some more. Let me see what I can do."

"You're Uncle Stan to them," she says desperately.

"I know."

"They wouldn't understand if you turned your back."

"I won't turn my back."

"Are you going to let me die in peace, Stan?"

"Jesus, Helga, Jesus."

"Don't give me Jesus. Give me you."

He sighs. He puffs into the phone. "Look, I gotta tell you the truth, honey. No bullshit, I'm moving to England. I sold the restaurant just yesterday. I signed the papers. It's in escrow. Two months and I'm gone. I tell you, I'm not in a position to take on three kids. I won't have a job. I don't know where I'm going to live. All this couldn't have come at a worse time for me. It's awful. It's just awful."

"You will take my kids," she commands him. "You'll get your priorities straight and you'll do it. I know you, Stanley Lipton. I know you don't really give two cents for England. You see right through that merry old England horseshit. What the hell's in England? You and I both know it's nothing but pansies and punk rockers and that stupid parasitic royal family. It's no place for a real man. This is the place for a real man. It's what this country needs. This country needs you, Stanley. Are you listening to me?"

There is a lot of fussing and sighing at the end of the line, but she thinks she's hooked him. She knows him well, she knows his heart. He has a heart big enough to absorb her children.

"Tell me if it's okay to die yet, Stan."

"No," he says. "Now, you just wait," he tells her. "Give me a chance to think." He clears his throat. She can hear him sniffing. She can hear him scratching his beard. "The miracle drug," he says. "You'll be up and around."

"Miracle drug, my ass. There's no miracles for me. Give me a straight answer."

She stops to listen to something. She concentrates. Something is coming. She feels something ominous stirring around her. "Oh-oh, oh-oh," she says. "Wait a minute, wait a minute."

It has started again, the clawing. She is sucking air between her teeth and suddenly she can't talk. The pressure in her jaw intensifies. Her teeth threaten to snap. She closes her eyes, she hears the pain roar. It comes like a vulture from the sky. It comes like a tidal wave. It comes like a flash of fire. It is like gas fumes exploding. There is a fierce, unforgiving anguish inside her belly. "Oh God!" she cries. "Oh Ga-God!"

"Helga! What is it! What is it!"

She opens her eyes. At the foot of her bed a giant spider rises on its back legs, its other legs wiggling, it fangs nipping. She screams. The receiver falls from her hand. It hits the floor with a crack and pulls the rest of the phone off the table. Bells ring. Get-well cards skitter. Faintly, far away, his voice is calling her. "Helga!" he is saying. "Hel-gaaaa . . ."

223.

9.   FROM THE WHIRLWIND

⊚ ✚ ♡

Didi Godunov sits at her desk in the bedroom, pecking away at her typewriter, writing immortal poetry. Discarded wads of poems are scattered about the desk and floor. Lummox sprawls over the desk, his back against the warm motor of the typewriter. Letters pile up on white paper. Word follows word, building toward the heart of the matter.

> *She wears a turquoise Celtic cross the color of the veins*
> *which map the nipples of her breasts. She smells of*
> *burnt rubber; she smells of cheap eau d'Espagne*
> *lathered on to hide the stink of her decay,*
> *the decay of age and heart attacks.*
> *Her toenails thick and orange are filled with fungus.*
> *She is rotting from the bottom up.*
> *Old lady sick.*
> *Her name is Mary Quick.*

When she finishes reading the poem, Didi rips it from the roller, squishes it, flips it in the growing pile of rejects, and inserts a clean sheet of paper in the typewriter. Taking up the poem she has been working on for days, the one that will make her reputation, the one called "Schizophrenic Love," she rereads the last lines, then sits brooding, a frown on her face, trying to think of something more to say. This life she's living does not inspire her. This place, this house and the woman in it, stifles her creativity.

As she sits staring at the wall in front of her, she thinks of Jasper John and how he finagled her into living with him, then dumped his responsibilities right in her lap. Typical man. He goes out having a good time, while she sits babysitting a crackpot. The woman has gone bonkers over Jesus and all that crud. Didi made up her mind long ago when she read Carlos Castaneda that God was far more complicated and unknowable than anything Mary Quick could imagine. Old-time religion might have found him long, long ago, when the sons of God made whoopee with the daughters of men, but having found him, it soon lost him, that's what Didi Godunov knows.

She hadn't realized what the situation was when she agreed to move in with Jasper and his "family." Jasper hadn't mentioned what a state of morbid superstition Mary Quick was in. Didi had expected a sick old lady, weak and docile. Instead she has one who reads the Bible endlessly, and aggressively says, "Listen to this one, listen to this," and quotes some junk written by some dead dork long ago gone to dust. How can people believe such stuff? It's totally barbaric.

But what is far creepier even is when Mary goes in that closet and locks herself in there and mumbles. Didi can hear her through the door, but there is little of what she says that Didi understands except an occasional "forgive" or "sin" or "blessed be." Didi figures the woman is probably praying to her money, counting all the whore money she has saved over the years, piling up a stack of filthy lucre, like Ebenezer Scrooge. Or maybe, like him, she's talking to the ghosts of Christmas, and they are telling her how bad she's fucked up? What a *life* that woman has lived! Didi has heard plenty of dirt on Mary Quick, enough to make a book of poems all by itself.

At the corner outside, she hears the brakes of a bus squealing, coming to a stop. There is a pause, and then she hears the engine roaring, making a sound like a giant whirring fan. "That better be him," she says to Lummox, who raises his head and winks at her.

She visualizes the green door again. Didi is dying to find out what is behind it. She thinks if it isn't whore money, it is something religious, a huge statue of the virgin, or maybe a giant statue of Lord Jesus, something made of plaster, with a robe painted on, blood on the palms and feet. These simpleminded futs will canonize anything! Didi figures Mary Quick is one of those Catholics, one of those cannibals who kneel at the mass to eat their god, drink his blood. This is my body, eat me; this is my blood, drink me. Didi knows the primitive. It is the primitive that makes her feel the world is consistent and recognizable. Ancient warriors used to eat the hearts and brains of their enemies, believing that the enemy's virtues would become the conqueror's virtues. They ate courage and wisdom, just as men nowadays eat powdered prostates and bull testicles, believing they will get a stiff cock from it, and women stuff themselves with vitamins, drink aloe vera juice mixed with bee pollen and royal jelly believing they've found the fountain of youth. Who is it that said the 100 percent American is 99 percent idiot? Didi dribbles laughter into her hand. Whoever said it is a guru after her own heart.

She leans back, lights a cigarette, watches the smoke rise. Though she is living for free in Quick's house, she is full of doubts about whether hers was the better part of the deal. How can one create art in a house where a nut goes around quoting this and that shmuck all day, and asking impossible questions and saying she has seen signs from God?

"Just amuse her," Jasper had said.

And that's what Didi did, that's how she has earned her keep this past week, by *amusing* Mary Quick, by agreeing with her notions.

226.

That's all they really want you to do—say, "Praise Jesus, amen, amen" —go robotic, that's all. Didi sees Mary Quick as an older version of that other Mary at school, the one named Mary Mythwish who keeps the Lord Jesus in her purse. Was it something about the name "Mary"?

Where is that Jasper? Where is that sonofabitch? She knows he's with Henry Hank. If that man isn't the devil, then Didi Godunov has the brain of an oyster. There's a beastie who would make a poem only Tolkien could write. Satyr face. Wicked phallic tooth! Animal cunning in those eyes. An evil troll, that's what he is. She likes him. Shoe polish in his beard and all, he's more interesting than anyone she knows, far more interesting than Jasper, that's for sure. Henry is an outlaw and outlaws fascinate her.

The back door opens and closes. Jasper is home. The long, lanky drink of water is here. "It's about time," she mutters. She hurries her fingers over the typewriter, so he can see how busy she is.

"What's up?" he says, entering the bedroom. He kisses the top of her head. She smells beer. " 'Schizophrenic Love'—that's a neat title," he says, looking over her shoulder. "What are these?" He picks up one of her rejects: " 'Of Intimate Love.' " He grabs another: " 'Love Twist.' " Another: " 'Love Triangles.' " And another: " 'Three in Love with She.' Hmmm." He reads a stanza, then says, "More confessions? This is about Wyatt Puck and his pals, right?"

She doesn't answer. She stabs her cigarette out in the ashtray. She hasn't made up her mind if she will make him pay for coming home so late or not.

"Whew, this is hot stuff, Didi," he says. "Whoa, 'creaming her at both ends'? 'Spraying his libation on her face'? And what's this mean, 'Transmitters of their caustic culture / they invade the glory of her woes'? What's that mean? I don't get it. 'Glory of her woes'?"

His string of questions annoy her. "I write them, I don't explain them?" she says, mocking him, making her answer into a question.

Jasper leans over to chuck Lummox under the chin. "I get the gist," he tells her. "Especially where it says it's the only 'ultimate climax' she's ever known. But they made her skim? Is that, like, multiple orgasms? Skimming?"

"Can you be a little more dense?" she says.

Looking up from the typewriter, she sees his eyes glittering. Dewdrops of sweat cling to his forehead. Are we horny? Yes, something has made him horny. She smells smoke and stale perfume on his shirt. He's been to a topless bar and those dancers have made him horny. But this time at least it isn't like the sit-on-my-face time, at least this time he isn't drunk and stinking. She decides to tease him some more.

"It is like a stone skipping over a pond," she says, "and every time it hits the water there is a little tweak. You climax. You go eep, eep, eep, just like the stone."

His eyebrows go quizzical, then he says, "Hey, you'll never guess what I seen. I seen this woman hanging on a hook. Going in circles on a hook. She had these tattoos all over her body. She did these contortions. It was incredible. She was as limber as a python."

"I'm limber like that," says Didi.

"I know."

He touches her breast. His mouth covers hers. She decides not to punish him just yet. "What's this?" she says, touching him.

Later, when they are lying in bed, holding hands, his leg over her leg, she says, "Your Mary Quick is something else."

"What did she do?" he asks.

"She was at least an hour in that closet tonight. Maybe she fell asleep, I don't know, but she didn't come out till eleven. What do you think is in there, Jasper?"

"I don't know. I've never seen. Henry says it's her conscience."

"That's interesting," she says. She thinks it over. "You know what just occurred to me? You remember how Mary Shelley kept Shelley's heart in a little box? You remember that?"

"Was it his heart?" says Jasper. "Yeah, I guess it was, uh-huh."

"It was. Well, I'll bet our Mary has something like that in there. I'll bet you anything she has her son's heart in a box or a jar or something. I heard her say one time in there, 'Sacred heart.' I heard it plain as day. What if she has his heart, Jasper? Wouldn't that be something?"

"How would she get his heart?"

"The mortician might give it to her, or . . . I know, she snuck into the graveyard and dug him up and cut his heart out. She and Henry, I'll bet they did it together."

"No way."

"It's possible. Anything is possible when it comes to mothers and sons."

Jasper tries to explain that Mary might be crazy, but not that crazy. "She wouldn't do something that sick, cut her own son's heart out and keep it, nawww. The closet probably has mementos and religious things. They bring her comfort. She wants to keep them private, for herself alone. What's wrong with that?"

"Well, let her. Who's stopping her?" says Didi. She turns on her side, adjusts herself, puts her leg over his hips. He feels her bush pressing against him. She tells him how living with Mary is giving her writer's block. She's been trying to work on "Schizophrenic Love," her breakthrough narrative poem, and nothing is happening with it. "It's because of Mary. It's because of this creepy house. This whole place smells sick, like there's something dead in the basement."

"There's no basement," says Jasper.

"I want to get away," she says. She goes into this long Walden-type fantasy about living in the mountains, in a cabin near a pond, sur-rounded by woods, where she can commune with nature, where she can get inspired again and have the solitude and peace of mind to write. No true artist can get anything done when she is surrounded by distractions like Mary Quick.

"But then what happens?" says Jasper. "I can't just forsake her like that. You can't depend on Henry. I mean, she could die here and rot for two, three days while he's off on a toot, and nobody would know it. Poor Mary."

"Aren't you just the nicest?" she says, miffed at him. "Poor Mary, uh-huh," she says. "What about Didi Godunov, Jasper John? Do we love her? Do we care about what she needs? Hmmm?"

He scratches his beard. He sucks at his lower lip. "Yeah, I guess," he says. "You need to be doing your work, I know."

"She's had her life," says Didi. "Now she's reaping what she sowed. Listen, what would you have as a legacy if you could choose, that you sacrificed your talent to nurse a half-wit or that you wrote 'Ode to the West Wind'?"

"Or *War and Peace*," he adds.

"Exactly. Where would those works be now if Shelley or Tolstoy had to spend their best years nursing their old mothers or something? You see what I'm saying? Listen, I've got to see the proper values in you, Jasper. Or you're not the man I thought you were."

Jasper sees what she is saying. He puts his hands behind his head and stares at the ceiling, at the little oblong disk of light thrown there by the reading lamp. The light is small. Outside its corona the ceiling goes grayish, the corners are dark. All the corners look like they could be hiding creepy-crawly things. He hears the hum of the typewriter. Shifting his eyes, he can see the piece of paper sticking out of the roller, little chicken tracks across its facing—Didi's "Schizophrenic Love." He sees Lummox's tail rising and falling behind the typewriter.

"It's sort of like that question, what would you save in a fire, a priceless Picasso, say, or a crippled old man? What's a human life worth? What's an old man's life worth?"

"What would you save?" she asks.

Jasper is uncertain. He knows, or thinks he knows, most people would save the old man. But then again, the old man is *old*, and he may not live very much longer, and there goes a one-of-a-kind Picasso, a piece of art that could live forever, that could be enjoyed by people a thousand years from now when the old man is long since turned to dust. Is a man's life worth an original Picasso?

"It's a quandary, isn't it?" he says.

"Not for me," she says. "I'd save the Picasso, absolutely. Anybody who has her ducks in a row would save the Picasso."

"You think?"

"I know. Listen, most people, old or not, aren't worth Picasso's little finger. Nobody wants to admit it, but everybody knows it's true."

Jasper sits up. He stretches out his arms. He turns his palms up as if he is holding something in each one. "Human being," he says, and shakes his right hand. "Work of consummate art," he says, and shakes his left hand. "Death and destruction," he says, indicating the area between his legs. He waits for an answer to come.

"You're disappointing me," says Didi. "I thought you were more of a visionary."

"All right then, what if this person in my right hand is Didi Godunov?"

She starts to say something, then stops, her mouth open. She studies his hand. Finally she says he isn't being fair because Didi Godunov could easily be the future Picasso of poetry. Either way would be destroying art.

"Yeah, but just say you had to pick," he says.

"Do you love me or not?" she says.

"I love you."

"Then you pick."

He turns his left hand over. "Bye-bye, Picasso."

She tickles him. She calls him a brat. She says he hasn't given her a straight answer about moving out of the house. Now what's he going to do about her problem? What? Pulling him down next to her, she wraps herself around him and says she won't let him go till he gives her a straight answer. Her voice gets very serious. "Do you *really* love me?" she says. "If you do, you'll see how important this is to me."

"Yeah, I know it's important," he says. "I know it means everything." It is at that moment he decides to go along with Henry's plan for fame and fortune. Henry is right, nothing can happen if they don't have money. They will start with robbing Calvin Cleans. It's the least he can do for her.

"I know where we can get maybe five, six grand," he tells her. "Henry and I have been talking about it. This guy, he owns a cleaners.

Henry says he's loaded. We'd have to knock him over first. That would give us the money to start on the movie. Then the movie would open everything else for us. I could buy you that cabin in the woods. I can make it happen for you, Didi. I *will* make it happen for you."

"You would rob a dude . . . for me?"

"Yeah, I would."

"With a gun?"

"Yeah. Well, Henry's got the gun, not me."

"But would you shoot him if you had to? Like if he fought back and wouldn't give you his money, would you kill him, Jasper? Jasper, can you kill?"

Jasper is eye to eye with her. She kisses him. Her hand is down below rousing him again. "Tell me the truth," she says.

"He better not try anything or he'll be dead," he tells her.

She gets aggressive. She pushes him onto his back and straddles him, eases him into her, starts slip-sliding like she's in a hurry to go somewhere. "An outlaw, a man who would kill for me," she says. "That's so goddamn sexy I could just eat you. Just something about it. You have a *dark* side, hmmm. You have a deep dark side I didn't know about." Her motions increase. He clutches her breasts, hangs on to them as if they are a pair of reins. Her eyes are closed. There is this look of sweet pain on her face. "I could just eat you, I could just eat you!" she cries.

He really believes he might do it for her, that he might kill for her. He knows for certain he will rob Calvin Cleans for her. He loves her, does he ever! Above him, she becomes a stone skipping over a pond. She makes eep-eep noises. She skitters, she squirms.

♡

On Friday, Jasper and Henry take the motorcycle and go to Calvin Cleans. They case the joint. Calvin's back door lets out on an alley. Jasper and Henry pace the width of it. It is twenty giant steps from Calvin's back door to a tall wire fence that runs the length of the alley.

Beyond the fence is a row of apartments. Beside the cleaners is a café. Behind the café is a Dumpster with a sign on it that says CAPON ENTERPRISES KEEPING SAN DIEGO CLEAN. All this is satisfactory with Henry.

Next, they pace the number of steps to the bank. They take large steps down the alley until they come to the back of the bank. It is a hundred yards, give or take a foot or two. Henry says that it is important to know how many yards Calvin will have to traverse to make his deposit. Jasper doesn't know why this is important, but he defers to Henry's wide experience in crime. Henry tilts his head and does some calculations. He keeps looking from the bank to the back door of the cleaners. Finally he has it all worked out.

On the west side of the alley there are no openings for Calvin to dash into the street. It is all brick walls and back doors and trash cans and the Dumpster. On the east side of the alley is the fence, too tall for Calvin to scamper over in a hurry. What Calvin must do when he comes out his door with his receipts is walk down the alley and turn onto the sidewalk at the end and go out on El Cajon Boulevard to the front entrance of the bank. So the plan is for Jasper to park his bike behind the café, to jump inside the Dumpster and hide. Henry will take up a position at the other end of the alley in the Dumpster behind the bank. When Calvin comes out, Jasper will climb out of his Dumpster, hop on the bike, wait for the signal. The signal will be when Henry, waiting like a tiger to pounce, leaps out of his Dumpster and knocks Calvin Cleans upside the head and grabs his money. When Jasper sees the tiger leap, he will come down the alley fast as he can. Henry will jump on the back of the bike, and that's it, finished, over.

Jasper listens to this plan, then he says, "Why can't I just hide behind the Dumpster? Why do I have to get in that stinky thing?"

Henry snorts in disgust. "Because, Jim, somebody could see youz lookin suspicious back here. Nobody can see youz *inside,* can they? Look here, who's the professional here, me or youz, Jim?"

They go back to the starting point. They pause to look down the long alley, at the natural snare it provides with its high walls and its high fencing. Henry decides they should try a dry run. He has Jasper hide the bike behind the Dumpster, then climb in and count to one hundred, while he goes to the Dumpster in back of the bank. Jasper holds his nose, breathes through his mouth, counts a quick one hundred by fives, then leaps out of his hiding place, jumps on his motorcycle, kicks the starter over, and roars to where Henry waits. Jasper slides to a stop. Henry hops on the back and tells him to go like a rocket from hell. Jasper gives the gas and lets the clutch in, but the clutch doesn't catch against the flywheel. The clutch makes a noise like it is having a nervous breakdown.

"Throw-out bearing," says Jasper.

He works the lever as the bike eases forward. Jasper cusses. Henry puts his feet down and gives them a push. Finally the clutch spins, chatters, catches, and they are off. "Gotta get that fixed," says Jasper.

They stop at Sears and buy ski masks. Jasper gets a green one with red eyeholes, Henry takes an all-black one to match his outfit. They go have coffee and hamburgers at the café next door to the cleaners, where they wait until it is time for Calvin to make his deposit. Jasper finds that he is very nervous, so nervous he can hardly swallow his hamburger. He eats only half of it. Henry eats the rest. Jasper wonders if the lump in his throat could be cancer from being around Helga. His palms are sweaty. He has spots in front of his eyes. He sits sipping coffee and smoking cigarette after cigarette, waiting for the time to pass.

Henry finishes his meal, finishes his coffee, finishes his cigarette, then slumps in the booth, his arms crossed, his chin on his chest, eyes closed, he takes a nap. Jasper wakes him when it's time to go.

Henry pays for the meal, meets Jasper outside, and they take up their positions in the alley. Jasper parks the Harley behind the Dumpster, then he climbs inside. Henry strolls to the other end of the alley and climbs into the Dumpster there.

Inside Jasper's Dumpster, the smell is making him ill. He knew this would happen, smells always get to him, he has a very sensitive nose. Streaks of light come through around the rim of the lid and he can make out brown bananas lying like turds on top of other garbage. He is so nauseated he thinks he will pass out. Putting on the ski mask, he tries to filter the smell, but the mask only makes him warmer, more nauseous. He burps and breaks wind several times, but finds no relief. Finally he cannot stand it anymore. Pushing the lid up, he sucks air. He leans half out the opening and moans.

"What the fuck you doing?" he says to himself. He reminds himself that this is for Didi, for love of Didi, so she can become a great poet.

Suddenly he doesn't care if she becomes a great poet. Suddenly he feels really stupid here with his stupid ski mask on and his stupid stomach on the verge of upchuck and his stupid friend Henry making him get in this stupid Dumpster when he could just as easily have waited outside for Calvin. The whole thing is just too stupid. He doesn't want any part of it. He is about to climb out of the Dumpster when he hears a door shut nearby. He looks to his left and sees a man wearing rimless glasses and a Hawaiian shirt testing the doorknob to make sure it is locked. It is Calvin Cleans and he has a canvas wallet under his arm. While Calvin is testing the door, Jasper hears a car turn into the alley. It is a police car. Jasper ducks down as the car moves slowly along and stops near the Dumpster. The radio squawks. There is the sound of the motor idling.

Jasper doesn't know what to do. He considers tossing the lid back and making a run for it; but that's no good, the cop is too close, so he considers lying down and acting like a homeless person sleeping in a Dumpster. They do it all the time, old throwaways huddled in trash bins all over San Diego, it's nothing unusual anymore. This seems best. If the cop opens the Dumpster that's what Jasper will do, pretend he is a throwaway. Quietly, he inches the lid up to see what is going on. The car has stopped a few feet past him in back of the cleaners. Jasper glances down the alley and sees Henry Hank scooting out of there, making his getaway *now*. Henry is looking over his shoulder at the police car. When he reaches the corner of the bank, he slips behind it, he's gone. Jasper wishes he had had the far Dumpster. He lies down on the garbage and waits for the cop to find him.

"This damn door," he hears someone say.

"Won't lock?" says someone else.

"See if you can do it, George."

Jasper hears the car door open. He hears footsteps. He hears something rattling. "There," says a voice. "Better get that fixed, Calvin."

"It's been giving me fits since the earthquake. Everything gets warped a little, you know."

"Tell me about it. I got a crack this wide runs the length of my patio."

"Someday we'll fall into the sea, George."

"That's what they say, that's what they say."

Jasper hears the footsteps returning, the car door slams.

"Thanks, George."

"See you later, Calvin."

Inching the lid up again, Jasper watches with a light heart as the police car pulls away. It goes to the end of the alley and turns. At this point, Calvin happens to look up and right at Jasper wearing his ski mask and peeking from under the lid. Calvin's face bleaches white. He looks toward the door, then toward the end of the alley, then back to Jasper. Calvin's eyes are magnified behind his glasses.

"Aw, shoot!" says Jasper. He stands up, pushing the lid with his head so hard it flies back and bangs like a gun going off. Calvin jumps a foot.

"Don't shoot!" he cries. "I'm a human being!"

"Say what?" says Jasper.

"Jesus keep me," says Calvin. "I've got a wife and children," he says. "I support my mother. Don't kill me. No senseless killing of me now. I'm no trouble." He holds the canvas wallet out toward Jasper. The wallet is shivering. The whole man is shivering. Calvin Cleans watches too much TV, Jasper thinks. He has never seen anyone so scared. I'm like his worst nightmare, Jasper tells himself. He wants to calm the guy down.

"Hey, it's okay," he says.

Calvin goes rigid at the sound of Jasper's voice, then he comes alive all-business, tosses the wallet against the Dumpster and runs the hundred-yard dash up the alley, legs churning up dust storms. He disappears in the direction the squad car took. Jasper watches him go, then jumps out, picks up the wallet, and looks around. He can't believe how easy it was. He can't believe his luck. He clutches the wallet. It feels full of money. He stuffs it into his waistband and beneath his shirt. Ripping the ski mask off, he tosses it into the Dumpster.

He takes a minute to cruise the block on his bike looking for Henry but doesn't find him. Finally, he turns down El Cajon Boulevard and drives along slowly east, trying his best to look like some tired fellow heading home from work. He feels like whistling. He can hardly keep from howling.

At home, he sits on the back steps to wait for Henry. Inside he can hear the TV. Lummox comes from under the porch and jumps into Jasper's lap. He strokes Lummox. Lummox purrs, offers his chin to be scratched. They wait for Henry.

A few minutes later he shows up. He is a mess. His shirt is open and black sweat drips down his chest. There is blood on his lip, a little tearing of the skin as if someone has taken a nip out of it. "Sufferin sonsabitches!" he says when he sees Jasper and Lummox. "Sufferin sonsabitches!"

"What happened to you?" says Jasper.

"Sufferin sonsabitches! Dog mange! Pickled pig's feet!"

"What's the matter?" says Jasper.

Shoe polish is melting from his overheated hair. There are black streaks that look like war paint on his forehead. A droplet runs between his eyes and follows the rim of his nostril to the top of his lip, where it curves downward into his beard and disappears. He shakes his head and black droplets rain on the lawn.

"Some buddy," he says. "Some pal."

"Me?" says Jasper.

"Youz popcorn fart whozit! Tell me this, Jim. Are youz a coward? Are youz a coward, Jim?"

"What did I do?"

" 'What did I do?' " mimics Henry. "Like he's so innocent. Youz pickled onion!" Henry kicks the apple tree, a parched apple falls and rolls to a stop in the garden.

"Hey, I looked for you," says Jasper.

"Youz looked for me," says Henry flatly.

"I did! I drove around the block and didn't see you, so I figured you were probably heading for home, so I came here. I saw you take off when the cop came, Henry."

"Youz saw me? The Hank took off?"

"Didn't you?"

"Hell no, Jim!"

"Well then, where were you?"

Henry looks offended. His eyes are haughty, his beard juts forward aggressively. "It's a miracle I'm here after what I've been through," he says. "A miracle. Sons of darkness. Whozits and whores. What's the world comin to? I slipped in the bank, then I went back to the Dumpster and waited for Calvin, that's what I did. I jumped him when he come by. I ain't lyin. Slice me for bacon. Use my sausage with eggs if I'm lyin. Bad company. Bad company is keepin me from success. That crafty noodle had bodyguards. When I put the move on him, they come out from everywhere, three of em, or maybe six of em, I lost count at nine. The Hank had to fight like bloody hell to stay alive. It was my Viking blood. My Viking blood kicks in and gives me the strength of ten men when I'm in trouble. I laid all them sonsabitches out. Not even death will take away their shame."

"You're kidding," says Jasper.

"Do I look like I'm kiddin? Look at my shirt. Look at my lip. My body is a mass of bruises and contooses. It was a war, Jim, a war."

"Did you get the money, Henry?"

Henry looks exasperated. "How could I? Tell me how I was to get the money when I'm fightin like a lion for my life? I tell youz, Jim, it's a miracle I'm alive, and that's no bullshit."

Jasper looks at his own shoes and thinks maybe he could use some hip boots, some waders right now. "Lookee here, Henry," he says, pulling the canvas wallet from under his shirt. "What do you think this is?"

Henry's mouth drops open, his eyes blink. "What's that youz got there?" he says.

"The money. I got the money. I robbed Calvin myself. I don't know who youz were fighting down at your end of the alley, but believe me it wasn't Calvin and his bodyguards. He took off like a bunny when I popped out of that Dumpster, and as far as I could tell he didn't have no guards, not one nowhere nohow, far as I could tell."

"Street scum!" shouts Henry without missing a beat. "Muggers. California riffraff. A man can't take a walk around the block without muggers pullin some shit." Henry's eyes are glittering with mischief. He and Jasper laugh. Jasper unties the wallet and shows him a thick wad of bills inside and some rolled change.

"Awww, by gawd, Jim, youz sure do got the money! Awww, haw, haw, haw, look at that!" He pats Jasper on the back, gives him a playful shake, almost knocking Lummox off his lap. Lummox gives a tiny tiger roar and jumps on Henry's leg, sinks his claws in, and receives a pair of slaps upside the face for his trouble. The cat lets go and Henry drop-kicks him across the grass, tumbles him like a ball of wool. He comes up shaking his head, looking around as if to see if anyone else wants some action.

"Crazy humpin cat," says Henry. "If I wasn't in such a good mood I'd kill that whozit." Henry rubs his leg, shows Jasper the tear in his pants Lummox made.

"*Youz* can buy new ones," says Jasper.

They go into the house and Jasper throws the wallet on the table. "Hah!" he shouts. He pulls the money out and starts counting. Didi comes over, puts her hand on his shoulder, watches him peel those bills. He can hear her breathing next to his ear. Mary stays in the living room, watching the credits roll for the *CBS Evening News*.

"How much, how much?" says Henry.

Jasper adds it up. "A thousand bucks and change," he says.

"That's all?" says Didi. "How much do we get?"

Henry tells her five hundred.

"That's not enough," she says. Didi looks betrayed. "You said six thousand, Jasper." Her lower lip puffs.

"It's what Henry told me."

"Must've been a bad week for Calvin," says Henry. "But hey, this is enough for film. I'll rent a camera and lights, and whatever extras is needed. That can't cost much. And Deadeye is throwing in his thousand too. It's enough if we pitch in together. We gonna pitch in together, ain't we?"

"I was counting on some real money," says Didi.

Henry promises her it will be real money before very long. He says things are full speed ahead now, just stick with him a bit. "Yes sir, just stick with the Hank and hang on, cuz there's a hell of a ride comin up."

In the living room a voice says, "Welcome to TV-Eight local news." Music follows, then the voice says, "For our lead story tonight, we suggest that children and the squeamish leave the room. We have some graphic scenes to show you, not suitable for children."

A woman's voice says, "You might call this story X-rated, Mel."

"Yes, Catherine, you might." Mel clears his throat and begins. "A religious studies professor at San Diego State University threatened to maim himself in front of hundreds of students and faculty members today gathered on the steps of the administration building. A Professor Godot, said to be a longtime veteran adjunct instructor, took over the entrance to the administration building at two o'clock this afternoon and held police at bay with a straight razor, holding it over his own, excuse the term, his own penis and threatening to cut it off if he wasn't allowed to make a speech in front of cameras."

As Mel narrates the story, pictures of the barefoot professor in his white suit come on-screen. Behind him, propped against the glass doors of the admin building, is a sign on a stick. The sign says CHAOS IS COMING. There are bushes on either side of the sign, then a spacious cement terrace. The windows of the building are tinted black. The wide double doors are black. The building itself curls upward like a tombstone and is of a white so pure it dazzles the eyes to look at it.

Jasper, Henry, Didi, and Mary watch as the camera zooms in on Godot's face. His beard and lips are trembling. His lemur eyes stare wildly at the crowd. Godot is speaking to the crowd, but his words are not being relayed over the air. The camera pans the crowd. Hundreds of students and faculty stand in the courtyard below the steps watching Godot, some with amusement, some with curiosity, some with fear.

The camera eye shifts from the crowd to Godot's face again. The eye travels downward across his chest and stomach to his groin area, where it focuses on a straight razor in his right hand, poised above Godot's penis. The penis area is caught in a fragmented dot, so that all the television viewers can see clearly is Godot's left fist. They can see the razor above and the fist below, and a bit of wrist. Jasper notices stitches peeking from the cuff of Godot's white jacket. They look like tiny ants biting him.

"Look at the stitches," says Jasper.

"Poor Godot," says Mary. "Oh, the poor man."

"He won't do it," says Henry. "It would be a sacreligion."

"Look at the size of that thing," says Didi. "Look how far away his hand is. Can that be real?"

The announcer is explaining that Godot is a disgruntled employee, who is protesting his recent dismissal by the university after many years of loyal service.

"We have not been able to verify any of this," says Mel the announcer. "But the professor said that what he was doing was making a symbolic protest for himself and for all Caucasian males who have been made the scapegoats for everything that's going wrong in society. Those are his words. The professor also said that what he was doing was symbolically removing the source of what created the Western legacy. The professor quoted the head of his department, Dr. Bertha Tatem, as saying that he and his brothers are going to pay for the sins of their fathers, and that he, personally, was ready to give her what she wanted."

241.

Mel goes on to apologize again for what he is transmitting. He says it is obviously the incoherent product of a disturbed mind. He says that Godot also talked about pentameters and trimeters and dimeters and slithy toves and a number of things nonsensical, things that have been edited from this broadcast.

As Mel talks, the TV shows Godot's mouth moving. At one point he is laughing and rolling his eyes, at another he is baring his teeth like a werewolf, then he is saying something in what appears to be the voice of reason. Mel tells the TV audience that Godot went on for thirty minutes. He talked about the *im*patient sufferings of Job, about Messalina at the stews of Rome representing the hidden truths of the female heart, about Abélard castrated for loving Héloïse, about the death of merit, and the rejection and impotence of men like himself, whose minds and wills created the Western standard of living. Mel explains that Godot was recently committed for erratic and dangerous behavior, having threatened his colleagues with bodily harm, and having slashed his own wrists, and that he escaped from the hospital just this morning, and that he had phoned all the news stations, telling them what he was going to do on campus at two o'clock.

The exposition and edited shots last for no more than five minutes as Mel gives them the rundown and the camera moves back and forth from Godot to the crowd, until at last it comes to the point where he is about to do the deed, and then the on-scene sound comes on and they can hear Godot's voice. He is saying, "Portents in the heavens and on earth—blood and fire and columns of smoke. The sun shall turn to darkness, the moon to blood—and the terrible day will come!"

Amid cries and screams, the razor slashes downward. To everyone it looks as if it has passed through Godot's penis. Blood shoots out, the razor falls clattering over the steps. Students leap away from the razor as if from a scorpion. Godot's hands fly to his cheeks. He is looking down. He shrieks, then he wilts like a parched flower. He sinks to his knees, he drifts sideways and rolls over onto his back. Staring upward, his eyes blink slowly. His mouth is open in a wide, crooked grin.

"I punked out," he says into the camera. "Bleeping punked."

242.

With every beat of his heart a tiny fountain of blood spurts from his penis onto his pants. Now that there is blood to see, the fragmented dot disappears and the audience beholds Godot's blood-soaked penis shrunk to the size of a petite finger. There is a wound in its side, but it is still attached to his body. The blood pumps steadily, it soaks his thighs, his crotch, the cement beneath him.

"Did he cut it off? Did he cut it off?" someone is heard saying.

Someone else can be heard crying out, "For God's sake, he's bleeding to death! Do something!"

There is pandemonium, people scurrying, some frozen in place, a blathering of voices. A campus policeman bends down and removes a shoelace from one of his shoes. He forms a loop in the shoelace. Then, careful not to get any blood on himself, he works the loop over the penis and cinches it tight. The blood flow stops. The camera eye moves over the crowd once more. Students are seen weeping, there are close-ups on tears and anguished faces, close-ups on girls hugging each other. Boys stand shaking their heads. Some are seen smirking. A girl lies faint with her head in the lap of a boy who is stroking her hair and saying something. Faculty members stand in mute shock.

The scene shifts back to Mel at the news studio. Mel looks very sad. He tells them that the professor was taken back to the hospital, where he is listed in critical condition.

The mad professor's story is on the national news the next morning. Jasper sits through the whole thing again. He can't help himself. He has to watch it over and over as each station picks it up. In the San Diego *Union,* under the headline PROFESSOR ATTEMPTS DEPHALLICIZING SELF, there is a story that claims Godot is a lapsed priest who, according to unconfirmed sources, was thrown out of the priesthood for molesting little boys, and his act may have been, according to a noted psychologist, a symbolic form of self-punishment. A famous Darwinian says that Godot is a victim of natural selection: when changes came to the university, he was unable to adapt to them. The paper quotes a Mensa source who says that Godot was not a deep thinker, nor a systematic one. A professor from the political science department says Godot was a fascist at heart. He is called a racist antifeminist by another colleague. The point is made that he is a caricature of the intellectual right, but another point is made that he is a dupe of the intellectual left. One source says that once upon a time Godot was considered an excellent teacher.

Below the article on Godot is one about a fourteen-year-old girl who jumped off the Coronado Bridge because her boyfriend told her he couldn't stand her fat ass. There was a note in her pocket, it said, *Yes, I like your new hairdo but I still can't stand your fat ass.* She hit the water with such force her head was torn from her body.

10. TRANSFIGURED

Fat Stanley has kept the diner closed for three days staying home with the kids. They are waiting for Helga to die. Earlier in the day, he took the kids to Helga's bedside and listened as Nancy gave her mother permission to die. Nancy whispered in Helga's ear that it was okay to go now, it was okay to die. Kathy and Mikey stood on the opposite side of the bed brooding, not saying anything.

Fat Stanley has taken the children to the hospital every day since Helga's collapse. The visits are wearing him out. The children are worn out too. No one says it aloud, but it is time for Helga to go away. She is suffering. Her fever is 105. Her heart is spongy, her lungs are filling with fluid, and there is little science can do. She is *not* dying of cancer, strictly speaking. Rather, she is dying of an unknown infection, which has sent her temperature soaring. To keep her cooler, the nurses pack ice bags around her legs. They drip saline into her veins. She is getting a combination of antibiotics around the clock. None of it matters very much.

Helga's breathing is ragged. She makes grunting noises. She lies in bed with a grimace on her face. When anyone tries to touch her or caress her, she pulls away and whines as if her skin hurts. Fat Stanley has noted that her skull is prominent around her eyes, her cheekbones and jaw. The flesh is tight over her nose. Her cheeks and ears are flushed. Thin blue veins in her forehead show through the skin. At her temple, he can see a tiny pulse ticking off the remaining minutes of her life.

He knows she is going to die, but he doesn't know when. He is surprised to see how much the human organism can take, how it wants to keep living, how it should die to ease its pain, but won't. Helga's endurance fills him with awe, but he wishes she could give up now, go to sleep for good. He wants to help her die. He wants to put a pillow over her face and smother her. He constantly thinks of killing her, how it would be a mercy, how it would be an act of great kindness and humanity.

Once when the kids were outside the room, he put his hand on Helga's pillow, clutched its corner in his fist, and willed himself to smother her. Anxiety pricked him like a needle in his soul. His mouth turned to cotton, his lips shivered, his heart beat so hard he could feel it in the tips of his fingers. He could feel the sweat beading on his forehead. His breath came and went in gasps. His legs turned watery. He thought about Helga taking forty years to reach these final stages of the end. Forty years flying by so fast—you rise up, you shimmer a moment like a butterfly, you fade, you fall. He thought about how she must have been as a little girl, so full of life, so happy to be *alive*. And she ate food with gusto, and she got growing pains, and her legs grew long, and her breasts grew, and she went from a child to a young lady to a woman in full bloom, and she did her best to experience what life had to offer. And all of that nourishing and gathering and putting together one woman over the course of time came to this final process of decline. All that trouble to create the thing that is Helga, and what for? Try as he might, Fat Stanley couldn't make sense of it that day or any day since. Its purpose and meaning escape him completely.

At home, the two girls slump on the couch. Mikey sits in the big chair turning a football over and over in his hands. He frowns at everyone. He has an angry what-are-you-doing-to-me? look on his face. He is taking his mother's dying as a personal betrayal. She is abandoning him. He hates her. He hates his dead father too. He hates everybody.

Fat Stanley sits at the piano and plays extemporaneously. His hands move, melody follows, but he has no name for what he creates.

For the moment, no one is crying, which is a small blessing. Fat Stanley is not sure how many more tears he can take, nor how many more he can shed himself before he just collapses. The room smells of exhaustion. The children look like people who are suddenly, prematurely old. Their brows are furrowed like warped washboards, their mouths are pinched, their eyes are angry, puzzled, fearful. For the ten thousandth time he wishes he had something to say to comfort them, some words of wisdom to give them strength, some simple bit of Scripture they might cling to, but nothing, not even a platitude, comes to mind. He is a hopeless dolt. He plays piano for them, he sings for them —it's all he can do.

Over the past few days Nancy has often sat beside him on the bench and he has taught her some simple chords. They have played "Heart and Soul" together. She has done well and he has told her she has natural talent. He would be glad to teach her piano if she wants him to. He likes to have her sit close to him, their arms touching, and now and then their hands touching as he places her fingers just so on the keyboard. Fat Stanley knows he could love her deeply and forever if only it were allowed.

He watches her secretly as she sits on the couch, her legs crossed, her foot swinging. He loves it when she stands at the window in the light and he can see the graceful lines of her body in jeans and a tank top, or in a long, limp dress, or when he looks in on her at night and sees the serenity of an angel on her face. In such moments his heart nearly breaks with love for her, and he wishes he had the right to hold her adorable body and be exactly the boy she wants. She reminds him over and over that life has passed him by, that he will never be an opera soloist tenor, that he will never know fame or financial success, that he will never have someone like her to love him. He is old. It is all over for him. It is too late.

Turning the football in his hands Mikey says, "We should'na have told her to die, goddammit." He looks at Nancy.

Her eyes are benevolent. "I read this thing," she says. "It is about dying people and how they will hang on and suffer if you don't give them permission to go. Mothers and fathers *will* themselves to live, husbands and wives do it, and they suffer because they need permission to die. Mama is doing that now, I think. We don't want her to suffer, do we, Mikey?"

His voice is hostile. "Shit noooo. But I don't want her to die. I don't want her to."

"Me neither," says Kathy. "Why can't she just get well?"

Nancy looks at Fat Stanley. He smiles helplessly. He wishes none of this was happening. He wishes the children would go away, so that he wouldn't have to know over and over again how inept he is.

"We'll see what God wants," says Nancy. Her voice is feeble. Mikey cusses some more. Kathy whines.

When Fat Stanley starts playing again, Nancy comes to sit by him and watch his hands. She says, "Do you believe in God, Uncle Stan?"

God. He doesn't think about God very often. There was no religion except music in his uncle's home, and God was a vague presence, an uncertain something that made the heavens and the earth and who might help you out in times of trouble—if he was in the mood. *God.* A being whose existence is questionable, to say the least. There is no proof of his, her, its existence, but Fat Stanley would like to believe there is *something*. A universe of pure mathematics is a concept his mind can't grasp. *Let us be true to one another, for this world—*

"I don't know exactly," he tells her. "I don't think it's an old man with a white beard, you know. Someone who looks like Godot, I mean. But I feel like there must be some calculating presence out there somewhere." He waves his hand. "Up there somewhere working things

248.

out. Otherwise, I don't know, it's just too bloody hollow, the whole thing. People need to feel spiritual, don't they? In the meantime . . . I mean till the cosmic plan is done, I think he means for us to look out for one another. It's like the test is if you can do that."

She takes a deep breath. Her breath shudders as she exhales. She sits tall, composes herself. "I've prayed hard," she says.

"Yeah . . . yes indeed," he says. He takes her hand. He pats her hand, looks at it. Her hand is a delicate thing, smooth, slender, with tiny veins and tendons running beneath the skin. He thinks of Helga's hands, how they have turned into warped talons. He doesn't want that to happen to Nancy, but he knows he is powerless to prevent it. Time is going to get her. Time is coming.

" 'But at my back I always hear / Time's winged chariot hurrying near.' "

"Another poem?" she says.

"Another poem," he says. "This boy is telling this girl to live in the present tense. He is telling her that the present tense is all they have. He is telling her to make the most of the moment. He says, 'And yonder all before us lie / Deserts of vast eternity.' In effect, he tells her that the greatest wisdom is to enjoy this moment. Live in the present tense. It's what he's saying deep down."

Nancy says, "Right now. Sure, it's true."

"But we forget, don't we? We always forget that."

She leans her head on his shoulder. "Play," she tells him. "Play something nice."

"Let's do it together," he says.

They put their hands on the keys, but before they can begin, before he can show her what moves to make, the phone rings. It is the hospital. They'd better come *now*.

When they arrive, he knows by the expression on the nurse's face that Helga is dead. The nurse looks at the children and asks Fat Stanley to step aside. "Please, I'm sorry," she says. "But, well"—her voice gets lower—"it's over now, she's gone." The nurse tells him his wife passed away just a few minutes ago and he shouldn't let his children see her just yet, not until they've had some time to fix her up a little.

Fat Stanley imagines the look on Helga's face. The grimace, the agony, the terror. What is it? Is the mouth open, silently screaming? "We'll wait out here," he says.

She touches his arm. Her face is full of compassion. She is a short woman, with slanted eyes and a look that makes him think of Egyptian beauty. "We'll prepare her," she tells him. And then she says, "Your wife is at peace now. Try to think of that. Her suffering is over."

"Yes," he says. "At peace. Yes."

He watches the nurse walk away. He goes to the children and parrots the nurse, tells them that their mother is at peace now, her suffering is over.

Nancy says, "What's the date today? This is the twenty-seventh, isn't it?"

Fat Stanley thinks it is the twenty-seventh, yes.

"You know what?" says Nancy. "We forgot her birthday. It's her birthday today, it's her forty-first birthday."

They wait in an alcove furnished with benches padded in a rough blue cloth. There are some magazines in a rack, and a tall potted plant in one corner. The children say nothing. They sit together on a bench, Nancy in the middle. They stare at the floor. Fat Stanley keeps wiping his palms on his pants. His chest feels full. There is a constriction in his throat. He wishes he could run away. He wishes he could put his head back and bellow. He wonders how he got in the middle of this thing. It is hardly his business, any of it. He and Helga were never *that* close. The whole thing is a damn imposition, that's what it is. The kids are orphans now. All he need do is tell the nurse they are orphans. She thinks he is the father and that Helga is his wife. Now, whatever gave her that idea? This is how people get burdened with luggage they don't want.

"I'm just a friend. I'm just being kind," that's what he'll tell the nurse. And she will understand what he means. She will get hold of the proper authorities.

Sometime later, when the nurse beckons them to follow, he lags behind, not wanting to see Helga if she still has her roadkill face, the grimace he remembers, the teeth, or if it is screaming, or if there is anything about it that looks bad. He wants to ask the nurse if they were able to fix Helga's face. He wants her to look serene. His uncle in his coffin had looked serene. No agony, no goddamn agony. He won't be able to stand it if he has to see agony.

When they enter the room, the nurse pulls the curtain back and there is Helga and it isn't so bad. She is beneath a white blanket, legs stretched out, arms at her sides on top of the covers. Her face is relaxed. Wrinkles and furrows are gone. She looks smooth and shiny. Someone has put makeup over her nose and chin, covering up what were a number of blotches and enlarged pores. Her hair is brushed out, strands of it lie strategically over the thin, balding spots dotting her scalp. Her lips are fuller. She looks almost young. She looks amazingly like Nancy. Fat Stanley takes comfort in the thought that as long as Nancy is alive, Helga can be seen as not truly dead.

"Oh, Mom," says Nancy.

"Goddammit, goddammit," whispers Mikey. His mouth is meager, his chin is hidden inside his collar.

Kathy touches her mother's hand. "It's warm," she says.

"My God, it's really happened," says Nancy. Her voice breaks. She leans on her mother's body and sobs, "Mommy . . . Mommy."

Mikey kicks the bed. He punches the curtain, he hammers the edge of the mattress with his fist. He cries, "No, no, no . . ."

There is much crying, much loud sobbing, much deep grief as the children hang over their mother, touching her, caressing her, telling her how much it hurts—"*It hurts, it hurts*"—and at the same time convincing themselves that her death is real. Four or five minutes pass. Then, as if of one mind, all three kids suddenly turn toward Fat Stanley. He doesn't trust himself to speak. He feels his great bulk will be indestructible as long as he doesn't speak. His hands open, his arms open, and the children come to him. They embrace him. They sob on his chest, they sob on his huge belly. They cling to him as if they are clinging to a raft in the middle of an ocean. He holds them and he looks at Helga Martin all pacified now, as tranquil as someone floating on a cloud. It may be his imagination, but he thinks he has seen her lips turn up at the corners. She is smiling, he tells himself, because she knows she has won.

That night Helga appears in Fat Stanley's dreams. She is in the diner and he is serving her at a table. When he puts down her food, she takes his hand and asks him to sing for her. His voice flows effortlessly and with such power that the walls give way, they burst outward and disintegrate, and behind the walls he sees an ocean of candles and honey-colored faces flickering in the lights. Multitudes are gathered to hear him. Helga stands beside him. Together they bow while the audience applauds. He looks at her and sees that she is Nancy. He walks Nancy to the edge of a shoreline. He waves his arm over an unpredictable sea.

In the morning at the breakfast table, he tells the children he dreamt of their mother. Mikey says, "Me too! I had this dream she came to my bed and tucked the covers around me. I saw her plain. I really did."

"Me too," adds Kathy. "She tucked me in too. She had on this white pretty gown and she looked like in the picture on the dresser when she was really young." Kathy looks at her sister. "Did you dream of Mama too, Nancy?"

Nancy says, "It was a bad night for me. I don't think I slept much."

"Well, I saw her," says Kathy.

"Me too," says Mikey.

The two children compare their stories and run through them again and again. Each time they tell the story, they remember more details. They both agree Helga had wings and a halo and she flew over their beds and she blew kisses. They both agree that she is watching over them. Kathy says that God has appointed her mother as her personal guardian angel.

"Mine too!" says Mikey.

It is an exciting idea. The children agree that their mother is now in the realm of the angels and is someone they can pray to. Nancy asks Fat Stanley what he thinks of such a notion. He says, "Oh, why not? Whatever works, you know. I mean, Albert Einstein believed in an afterlife, and if *he* could believe, why not us? No one was smarter than Einstein."

He takes his coffee into the living room to get away from all the chatter. Sitting at the piano again, he looks at the portrait on the wall, the cliffs of Dover "Glimmering and vast, out in the tranquil bay." He imagines the cliffs calling to him, telling him to come home. The children's voices filter through from the kitchen. The cliffs, the children, both seem overwhelming at the moment.

Rising from the bench, he goes into his bedroom and closes the door. He lies down in his robe and pajamas, his head propped on pillows. Looking down, he notices with distaste how long his toenails have gotten. He wishes he wasn't so fat, so he could bend down and cut them. He wonders what he should do about Helga's funeral arrangements. There should be a service. Helga was Irish. Maybe there should be an Irish wake of some kind. He doesn't know much about Irish wakes except that there is a lot of food and a lot of booze. He thinks of *Finnegans Wake,* a book he was never able to get through; but he remembers a man named Finnegan who fell off a ladder and died, and they had a wake for him, but he wouldn't stay dead in his coffin. He kept sitting up and they kept pushing him down. He wanted to join the party, but they wouldn't let him. A party for Helga, that's what it should be. A celebration of her life with her there in her coffin with the lid off, the center around which life revolves for one last day. Some speeches, some songs. People dancing at her wake. A wake should be about life, it should be about taking the sting out of death.

Fat Stanley yawns. He closes his eyes and takes a deep breath, sighs, thinks about how much work a party for Helga will be. If only he can work up some enthusiasm. If only he can get some energy. He thinks he has never been more tired in his life and that he would sleep a thousand years now if they will let him.

Henry Hank strides into the living room and the three grays scatter. They go to the dining room and sit under the table, next to Mary's bare feet. Lummox is in her lap. Lummox reaches down and tries to bat the ears of the grays, but they stay out of reach. Henry tips his dark glasses up, his movie-mogul shades, and hangs them on his forehead. Surveying the room with a director's eyes, he puts his hands out, thumbs touching, and makes a frame to sight through, and he says, "We can make a tomb out of this. Put the lights here. Use the coffee table with a sheet over it for the slab. JuleeTit's feet will hang off the end, but that's okay. We'll work around that. Flamin legs, this is gonna be fine!"

Looking at Mary, Pirate, and Didi at the table, he says, "Youz three can be the dead bodies in the tomb with JuleeTit. We'll cover youz with gauze and get a long shot and a medium shot, usin the zoom lens and the freeze frame. It'll be good, trust me. I'm on top of things now, I'm in my element." He taps his chest. "This is what the Hank was meant to do," he says with great satisfaction.

On the table is a book called *Auteur: A Guide to the Filmmaker's Art*. Henry comes back to the table and turns the pages of the book to a section called "Visual Rhythm." He reads a few lines and says, "Right, I'll use the zoom lens. I'll zoom in. I'll filter the lens and make youz guys look like models outta *Playboy*. Lemme tell youz, filters can make a kangaroo look like Marilyn Monroe. Can't have flaws in a fuck film, no bruises or none of that stuff. I'll use the filter and the zoom and the freeze frame with dramatic effect." He grins at them proudly. "The zoom and the freeze frame supplies stress to the *auteur*'s canvas." He jabs his thumb at himself. *"I'm the auteur."*

His actors nod. Everyone looks deferential. "Now, let's see here," he says. He reads a few more lines in the book, then tells them, "We're going to produce integral beauty by using cha . . . cha . . . by using— What's this word, Ruby?"

Ruby looks at the word. She spells it out: "c-h-i-a-r-o-s-c-u-r-o. What's that mean?"

Didi looks at the word. "It's from painters," she says. "It's an art word. Chiaroscuro, it's the use of light and dark, the use of shading."

Henry says, "That's what we're going to use, light and shadow in strong opposition to give us the raw detail and artistic realization."

"Wow," says Pirate.

"That's nice," says Ruby.

"Yeah, right," says Didi. There is a wisp of irony in her tone, but she is smiling, she looks very cheerful.

All of them are smiling. They look pleased at Henry's verbal prowess. He keeps glancing at the book, and telling them that the *auteur* is constantly aware of light like a painter is aware of light, and he and the painter are one in using light on the canvas to ". . . excite optical responses and stir psychological processes in the viewer. Heh! Flamin legs, I'm good."

"Whoa, you're smooth, baby," says Pirate.

"Yeah, baby," says Henry.

The phone rings in the kitchen. Mary tucks Lummox under her arm and goes in to answer the phone. Henry frowns at the interruption. Then he says that what they need to get is plenty of the concrete details with the zoom and the freeze frame, but especially the zoom. His voice caresses the word "zoom" as if it tastes like champagne. He tells them they are going to zoom and symbolize and make the images bear the complex associations and convey the beauty of fucking like it's never been conveyed in the history of mankind. They are going to make a fucking film that Godot would be proud of. They will make him famous in absentia. Due to Godot "fuck" will no longer be a dirty word. The movie they make will force people to associate fucking with art. With the freeze frame, the zoom lens, the use of light and dark, and purifying filters and symbols in every nook and cranny, porno filmmaking will become the *literature* of tomorrow, expressing the forthcoming new age of American culture.

"Yo, Hen baby!" Pirate cheers.

Those assembled at the table clap. Henry puts the *auteur* book down and bows. Mary returns. She is holding a fat, oddly shaped potato. There is a stricken look on her face. "Doesn't this look like a heart?" she says. "Like Christ's cracking heart? Look at it. Don't it remind you?"

"Oh, Jesus," says Didi.

"What's that she's saying?" says Pirate.

"It's another of her little fits," Didi whispers to him.

Mary says, "It's another sign. I tell you, the signs I've been getting. My picture of the Madonna cries real tears. I have to keep wiping them off. Tears . . . real. That was Fat Stanley on the phone. I don't know. It's . . . he says Helga Martin is dead, she died last night. She was in horrible pain to the end, horrible, horrible pain."

There are a few seconds of stunned silence.

"Poor Helga," says Jasper.

"Her three kids too," says Ruby. "Think how they must feel."

"That's a tough one," says Henry.

Mary tells them the funeral plans. She says Fat Stanley is going to be at the diner at four and he wants Ruby and Jasper to come help get the place ready for a wake. He's going to have Helga in her coffin there. He's going to invite all her friends and have a real party. Mary caresses the potato that looks like Christ's cracking heart, and she says, "They chose a nice coffin this morning. She looks real good in it, he said. There's gonna be lots of food and booze. We're all invited, of course."

"At his restaurant? That's weird," says Didi.

"Don't you think this looks like Christ's heart? Look at this crack here."

"Who ever would put a dead body in a restaurant?" says Didi.

"Nothin wrong with that, sweet stuff," says Henry. "Let's raise hell for that fox. Who cares where, baby, who cares where?"

"I'm going to paint this here," says Mary. She runs her finger down the crack in the potato. "Blood red," she says, "blood red. Signs. That's what's important now. The world is going to end in the year two thousand, January first at midnight. The apocalypse. The judgment of Babylon. Just read the signs and you'll know. I think we should say a prayer for Helga. Let me get my Bible."

Henry tries to stop her. He tells her there's no time for that. He says if Jasper and Ruby have to go to the diner at four, then there's no time for prayers. "We got an important movie to make here. We got to get rollin," he says.

Mary brings the Bible. "Just a short one," she says. "Let us pray," she says. She turns the pages of the Bible with her eyes closed, then she stabs her finger at the verses. "Okay, this is it," she tells them. "Bow your heads."

They do as they're told, they bow their heads.

" 'Pure religion is this, To visit the fatherless and widows in their affliction, and to keep unspotted from the world. Resist the devil and he will flee from you. For what is your life? It is a vapor that appeareth for a little time, and then vanisheth away.' Amen. Isn't that appropriate? It's like another sign. I'm telling you, things are happening."

"Amen," says Ruby.

The rest of them mutter "amen" after Ruby.

"Helga's dead," says Jasper. "Geez, I didn't even visit her in the hospital. Some friend."

"None of us visited her," says Mary.

"I sent her a card," says Pirate.

"Big deal," says Jasper.

Mary takes her transmogrified potato and her Bible and goes to the living room. She lies on the couch, no longer interested in the movie doings. The three grays swirl around her, like protective angels. From the kitchen doorway, Lummox watches over everything, his cyclopian eye blinking from time to time, creating and destroying worlds.

"Okay," says Henry. "Let's get to work. First thing youz do, Jim, is shave off the beard. Can't have a hairy ReemHerHole, hell no."

"I don't feel like playing ReemHerHole right now," says Jasper.

"Now c'mon, Jim. If youz get busy, youz'll feel better. She wouldn't want youz to miss this opportunity. Do it for her, Jim."

Jasper doesn't argue. He goes into the bathroom and runs the hot water and lathers up. Over a bottle of Incorrigible Ike, the others wait for him. They discuss the script. He can hear them talking as spidery bits of his beard fall into the sink. It wasn't much of a beard anyway. Too sparse. Too slow to grow. Water spatters his pants. He bends away from it and closer to the sink. He can smell the methane stench coming from the drain. He imagines there are diseases in the fumes, bad things like cancer.

Hurrying to finish, he is soon a pink, beardless boy again. He looks at his chin and feels slightly repelled at its paleness. He doesn't like how exposed his mouth seems. He doesn't like the space between his nose and his upper lip, it is too large. Who would want to kiss such disgusting monkey lips? he wonders.

When he comes back to the table he thinks he detects criticism in Didi's eye. "You liked me better with a beard, didn't you?" he says.

"I sure did *not*," she says. "You look much better now. You look clean-cut."

"Oh God, no," he says. "I'm done for."

"ReemHerHole to a T!" says Henry. His gums glisten. "We was just sayin how we're gonna choke *Deep Throat*." Henry laughs boisterously.

Pirate says, "No doubt about it. So what if she could swallow a peeper whole? Man, we've got Shakespeare on our side."

"That itty-bit talent of hers is gonna look like nothin next to what Ruby here will do. Right, sweet stuff?" says Henry.

"I *can't* swallow a whole one," says Ruby. "It makes me gag."

"You've got to try harder," Pirate tells her. "It's just the gagging reflex. You can overcome that. It's what people expect to see now, a girl who can go to the nub. You want to be a star, don't you, Ruby?"

Ruby shrugs.

"What an attitude," says Pirate. "Try to make a person a star and they don't even appreciate it."

"Will youz at least give one for the gipper, baby?" says Henry. He pats her hand. He looks at her with hopeful expectation that she will try to be good at oral sex, for him, her *auteur*.

"I don't mind," she says, shrugging. Her mouth barely moves when she talks. To Jasper it seems she has a mouth too inadequate for what they are asking her to do. All of her looks either too small for the role or too old.

As if reading his mind, Henry leans over and whispers in Jasper's ear, "The Hank has it figured, Jim. Trust me. Movie stars can be anythin youz want em to be. None of what youz see is for real, Jim. It's all a delusional. Youz understand my philosophics? Nobody would pay to see actors being real. Waagh! Flamin legs!" He leers at Ruby. "Almost sixty years of smarts in this brain, Jim, youz stick with me and youz learn somethin valuable."

Pirate is worried about the balcony scene. He doesn't know how they will hold a balcony scene with no balcony. He is holding Godot's script and smacking it with the back of his hand and saying they've got to find a balcony, it's crucial, it's the centerpiece of the play.

Henry fires back, "Aw, fuck that, we don't need no balcony scene."

"Do too!" says Pirate. "Everybody will be expecting a balcony scene, Henry!"

Tempers flare. They get face to face and shout. Jasper wonders if they are going to start beating on each other again. He looks at Ruby. She at him. She smiles and her face breaks into fissures. Juliet, my ass, he tells himself.

"What do you think?" Pirate says to Didi.

"Got to have a balcony scene," she answers.

"See, Henry?" says Pirate triumphant.

Henry turns away. He stares out the window. His brow is red with anger. He whips his unicorn tooth with his tongue. He snorts. "Who's the *auteur* here?" he says. "Flamin fuckin legs! I'm the flamin fuckin *auteur* here!" Turning back, he stares at them with cold killer eyes.

"All right then, fuck the balcony scene," says Pirate. "Go ahead, ruin the whole movie, Henry. See if I care."

"We could use the back porch," offers Jasper. "She could stand on the top step and lean over the rail and you could get a tight shot on her. That ought to work. We can put up screens so the neighbors can't see, some four-by-eight plywood will do it."

"The zoom lens," says Henry. "A medium shot and then the zoom lens on her whim-whams. Jim's right. That'd work. We'll do the balcony scene on the back porch. Satisfied, Deadeye?"

Pirate raises a cryptic eyebrow at Jasper. "Ferment the cider," he says.

Jasper has no idea what he means, but he nods as though Pirate makes perfect sense.

"Look, we've got to go over the script, that's the first thing," says Didi, her voice impatient. "You've got to start with the words and see if they mean anything. If our Romeo and Juliet can't speak Godot's verse, the play will bomb, believe me it will."

Pirate slaps the script on the table. They gather around it and stare at the title page all in carefully lettered capital letters: REEMHERHOLE AND JULEETIT—AN ORIGINAL SCREENPLAY BY WILLSUCK SNAKESHIT.

Henry turns the pages. "I'll pick the part," he says.

Didi tells Jasper he must read in a natural voice, as if he is reading prose.

"It's all rhythm," says Pirate.

"I don't like this," says Jasper.

Henry growls. He says, "I don't want it singsong. I hate singsong."

"Blank verse is our gimmick," says Pirate. "It's what will set us apart and make *ReemHerHole and JuleeTit* a unique theatrical event."

"This stuff sounds like tots in toyland," says Henry, pointing at a page of verse. "Even Sam-bam couldn't make it sound good that night he read to us."

"That's cuz he was drunk," says Pirate.

"We've got to at least try it," says Didi.

Henry regards her with suspicious eyes. "How come youz always agreein with Deadeye?" he says. "Youz two conspirin?"

Didi laughs. "We just think alike, dear. Artists, you know, they tend to be that way."

"Bullshit," says Henry. "If there's any real artist round here, it's me, and I don't think like none of youz." He puts a hand on Jasper's shoulder. "Can youz read this stuff, Jim? Are youz willin, or should we break it into real talk?"

"I can read it," says Jasper.

He reads a line. He reads it badly. His heart isn't in it. Henry has a fit and says it sounds like ReemHerHole with a speech impediment. It sounds like he's pounding pickles. It's no fucking good.

"Say it like this," says Didi. She eases into the line. " 'But soft, what breast through silken fabric breaks?' You see what I'm saying? Just like reading prose. It's not 'But SOFT, what BREAST through SILken FABric BREAKS? Smooth it out. Do it trippingly from the tongue. It's iambic pentameter, but you don't have to stress it, you know."

Trippingly from the tongue, he knows she's stolen that line from somewhere, some Shakespeare thing. "I know how to read poetry," he tells her. "Who read Shelley to you?" he says. He hates this side of Didi, this pompous intellectual side she shows off now and then. She is doing it for Pirate. The two of them are *changing eyes.*

Jasper pulls himself together, bears down, concentrates. He eases into the lines just like Didi said to. And he does a decent job of it. Ruby joins in on her half, and she's not bad either.

Reem: But soft, what breast through silken fabric breaks?
        These are the titties of my only love.
        Arise, fair cock, and show your worth to she,
        Who is so supple smooth, so pale, and sweet
        Enough to eat; my tongue doth drool to taste
        The nectar of her leaking nether lips.

261.

	This flimsy gown doth show her sexy curves;
	O, be thou slut, my dove, and ope your thighs
	That I might gaze upon your luscious cunt.
Jule:	O me, O my, O me, O my, O me.
Reem:	My fair bird speaks! O, speak again, sweet suds
Jule:	ReemHerHole, ReemHerHole, why don't you answer,
	ReemHerHole?
Reem:	What would you have, my cherry
	Nipple love?

"Hmm, that's better," says Henry. "Not half bad a'tall." He looks at them through his enframed hands.

"It's the balcony scene," says Didi. "She's hanging over the balcony staring into the dark—"

"With her wham-whams hanging out," says Henry. "I got it."

"And Reem below is getting horny," says Pirate. "Shit, man, the audience will eat it up."

"They're bound to," says Didi. She presses Pirate's arm. He smiles at her. "They'll laugh, they'll really enjoy it," she says.

He says, "That's what we want, that's what Godot says to do. Get them laughing, get them horny at the same time. Godot knew what he was talking about. He told us this play fulfills a law of second thermodynamics of people wanting to laugh and fuck as the whirlpool pulls them down. If somebody can make them laugh and fuck, they'll make him a millionaire, guaranteed. Isn't that what he said, Henry?"

"A wise man, Godot," says Henry. "Read some more," he tells Ruby and Jasper.

Jule:	(*Gazes upon Reem passionately, gripping her breasts, tongue flicking at him*)
	O ho, big boy, I see you brought your boom.

(Tight shot on Reem's erection swinging back and forth as he comes toward her)

"The zoom lens and the freeze frame, that's what I'll use in this scene," says Henry.

> O, fly to me, you fiery-headed thing.
> O, bring that bird within my sopping nest!
> *(Reem enters with alarums.*
> EXTEMPORIZE)

Reem: My love goes deep, as boundless as the sea:
O wee! O wee! I love to bang your bush
And doubt it not that I can make it whoop.

Jule: Ooo whoopee do, my ReemHerHole, my stud,
I feel the rush of your internal flood.
> *(Sexual moans and groans. Lute music drifts into hard rock guitar and drums. Rising crescendo. Break into opera, soprano rising toward high C. Show pot of spaghetti sauce bubbling. Show fat Italian sucking up a noodle. Show Reem's cock being sucked by Jule's cunt. Go to major climax scene, cum shooting over her face)*

END FIRST SCENE.

"Waagh, flamin legs!"

"Yummy," says Didi.

"Yummy, yummy yes," says Pirate.

From the living room, they hear Mary quoting loudly from the Bible, " 'Touch not; taste not; handle not' Epistle of Paul to the Colossians."

"Aw, *shut up!*" Henry and Pirate and Didi shout in unison.

"Let's do a wet rehearsal," says Pirate. He licks his lips.

"Let's have the ménage à trois scene I saw in there," says Didi. "The one with the Nurse. I'll read her part if you want."

"Hey, you gonna be Nurse?" Pirate asks. "That's great!"

"I might," says Didi. "Let's read it through first, then we'll see how I feel."

"Flamin legs, it's gettin better and better," says Henry. "Read, noodles, read!"

> (*Enter Nurse, who tells Jule that Reem has fucked her cousin Two-Tittie Sue to death*)

Jule: O, serpent dong, within its poison cave
    Did ever dragon keep so fair a prick?
    O, monster angel! Damn ram! Hated lover!
    O, mouth of semen dribbling nectar sweet,
    As from a flower pure. I must forgive,
    And get within my burning cunt, his gluey
    Aquavit!

Nurse: Will you still ope your thighs to him
    What split Two-Tittie Sue in half?

Jule: You bet.

    ENTER REEM, GIANT COCK IN HAND.

Reem: Look round, big boy, see if you missed someone.

> (*Nurse screams and faints. Reem strips her:*
> *EXTEMPORIZE THREESOME*)
> *ENTER MEN WITH SWORDS. REEM BATTLES THEM—SEE*
> *HEADS FLY OFF, SEE FOUNTAINS OF BLOOD BURSTING, SEE*
> *EYEBALLS PLUCKED OUT, SEE EVISCERATED SWORDSMAN*
> *SCREAMING AS HE TRIES TO TUCK HIS GUTS BACK IN—REEM*
> *DOES HIS WORK AND ESCAPES OVER THE BALCONY AS MORE*
> *MEN ENTER ROOM, SEE JULE AND NAKED NURSE—*
> *GANGBANG AMID THE CARNAGE.*

"So, can we count on you for the threesome?" says Pirate, winking his one eye at Didi.

"I just might," says Didi.

Henry pats her bottom. "One for the gipper," he says.

"Let's do the ending," she says.

They skip to the final scene in the tomb. They put their hearts into it.

Reem: My love, my fuck of all fucks past and gone,
            Death hath not power upon thy pair of prongs.
                (Reem kisses her breasts, massages them, moves his lips
                to her mouth)
            Her lips are warm, her mouth as sweet as gum!
            Let's see what else this death hath failed to cool.
                (Reem gropes beneath her gown, finger-fucks her,
                holds up glistening fingers, licks her juices off)
            O sweet, the doors of death have not closed yet
            Upon the heat of your enchanting cum
                (He mounts her)
            Here's to my love, O true womb of mine own—

"Whoa!" says Henry. " 'O true *womb*'? 'Womb'? Flamin legs, that don't work. 'Womb' don't work."

Didi agrees. She says "womb" breaks the tone.

"That's true," says Pirate. "Godot uses 'cunt,' 'twat,' and 'quim,' all through the script. 'Womb' don't sound right."

They all agree that "womb" is wrong. They scratch "womb" out, replace it with the tried-and-true "cunt."

Reem: Here's to my love. O true cunt of mine own
            Thy grip is tight and quick. Thus with a thrust—
                (Jule's eyes open)
 Jule: Ho boy! Don't be so brief in me—plunge on!
            O happy prick so long, so fat, so sleek,
            Here lies thy quiver slim and sugar sweet;
            Thy strokes of love have rescued me from death
            So lay on, Reem, and hump me to the max!

The last instructions read:

> *(They suck, they fuck, she dies, he dies, she dies again.*
> *EXTEMPORIZE—VOICE-OVER AS CAMERA GAZES*
> *LOVINGLY AT THEIR NAKED BODIES:*
>
> For never was a story of more moans
> And groans than JuleeTit who sank the wick
> And broke the prick of her sweet ReemHerHole.)

Immediately Pirate calls for a wet rehearsal again. Henry gives the orders. He tells Didi to handle the boom for the sound. Pirate will run the camera since he rented it. Punkin will—

"Punkin will stay out of it!" she shouts from the sofa.

"Stay out of it?" says Henry. "Flamin legs, Pun*king*, how can youz stand to stay out of it? This stuff is right up your alley. Come on! Youz can be Two-Tittie Sue!"

"Go to hell, Henry."

A vein throbs in Henry's forehead. He clenches his jaws and his fists. He looks like he might beat Mary. "Talk to youz later," he tells her.

"The answer will still be no."

"We'll see," he says. He turns his attention to Jasper and Ruby, tells them since everybody is so hot about the balcony scene, it's best to see if Ruby has the whim-whams for it. He has Ruby take off her shirt and show her breasts.

"Won't do," says Henry, shaking his head. "Too small. Won't hang over the rail." Again he looks toward Mary. "Yours would hang," he says. "Youz're lettin the Hank down, Punkin."

"A higher power is calling me, Henry," she says.

"What higher power?" he says. "Ain't no higher power than the Hank."

"That's what you think."

Henry growls. Didi steps in and offers her breasts. "Forget Mary," she says. "Let her be that way, who needs her? Mine'll hang over."

"Here's a trouper!" says Henry. He pats her butt again.

"How can she be my boobs?" says Ruby. "What's happening?"

Henry taps his head. "Slicing and editing, the zoom lens," he explains. "We make illusions here." He picks up the book on filmmaking, flips through it. "Read page a hundred sixty-six here," he says. "Tells youz all about it."

At this point Pirate asks why Didi doesn't just go ahead and be JuleeTit all the way. Didi says she doesn't want to. She says she'll do the Nurse part and be Ruby's breasts, but that's it. They all watch Didi take off her blouse. She makes little half turns with her torso, showing them what she's got. Henry and Pirate are appreciative.

"Love the tattoo," says Pirate.

"It's a pansy," says Didi.

"People will like that touch, huzza-huzza," says Henry.

Jasper feels his ears get hot. He had heard her say more than once that only trash bitches would do porno. When she had first heard about the movie, she told him not to even *think* about asking her to be in it. He was glad she didn't want to be in it. To him, she was a cut above that sort of thing. But now . . . she's caught up in the excitement, he can tell, and when she gets excited, there's no telling what she'll do.

"Put your blouse on," he says. He takes her arm and pulls her aside. "I thought you said this was all shit."

She gets a hard face. She is panting. He smells Incorrigible Ike on her breath. "I changed my mind. It looks like fun. A poet has to have experiences, Jasper. I'm going to make a narrative poem out of all this."

"You're just showing off for Pirate."

"Don't be stupid."

"I see how you look at him."

She denies it. She says he is paranoid. She says he will be screwing Ruby right in front of God and everybody, so what's his problem?

"You're not even jealous. That's the problem," he says.

"It's a movie. It's an illusion like Henry says. It's just all an act, honey."

"Bullshit. You know it's all bullshit, Didi."

"Oh, dry up." She turns away, then turns back. "You're getting too possessive, Jasper John. I don't like that. I don't see a wedding ring on my finger."

"I'll marry you," he whines.

Her lips curl scornfully. "On with the show," she says.

In the bedroom, Henry has them try various positions with their clothes on first. He moves them this way and that, having Pirate take notes about what are star positions and what are just so-so. Didi stands next to Pirate making suggestions. Pirate keeps whispering things to her, and she keeps giggling. At one point she brushes her fingers down Pirate's beard and tells him he looks like Gawain and the Green Knight except he isn't green. She asks him if she can peek under his eye patch. Pirate lifts the patch and bats his eyes at her.

"Clever faker," she says.

"Youz takin notes there, Deadeye, or playin grab-ass?" says Henry. "We got some bisness here."

"I'm taking notes," says Pirate.

Jasper is positioned upside down, sideways, round and round, on top and under Ruby, while Henry tests the couple with his framing hands and light meter and says things like ". . . running metaphors achieved by repetition of image, I'll unify the themes with the repetition of shots in different contexts and hold the image with the zoom lens and the freeze frame, when youz do it I'll freeze frame and zoom in and zoom out, that's my distinctive *auteur* touch, the mark that this is a Henry Hank film. Move over Scorchezee, step aside Spulberg, you're through Frankie Ford Capella. Here comes the Hank, here comes the Hank."

It takes them two hours to go through the script scene by scene and outline exactly what they'll be doing on each page. By then it is three o'clock and Jasper reminds Henry that Fat Stanley is opening the diner at four.

"Then let's get wet," says Pirate.

"One scene," says Henry. "So youz can get used to each other. Get into costume." He claps his hands briskly. "Let's go chop-chop!"

Pirate hands out the costumes, a sheer nightgown for Ruby, tights and a codpiece for Jasper.

"This is my costume?" says Jasper. "This stupid thing?"

"What more youz need?" says Henry.

"We want you naked, naked," says Pirate.

Didi laughs and punches Pirate on the arm. He pinches her earlobe. They put their heads close and talk. Jasper takes the codpiece into the bedroom and changes. When he comes back, he has to sit and wait for Ruby.

Thirty minutes later she and Didi come out of the bathroom. Ruby has slipped into the diaphanous gown. She and Didi have piled heavy makeup on her, filling in the dent in her cheek, plastering over the wrinkles, making her lips larger with glossy red lipstick. They make her eyes bigger with false lashes and eye shadow and by shaving off her eyebrows and penciling liner above the original brow line. Jasper is amazed at the change. She looks like a sixteen-year-old prostitute.

"Do you like me?" she says, grinning boldly at him.

Jasper sees wrinkles cracking her makeup.

"Keep your face still," Henry tells her. "Just be big-eyed, that's all. No squintin. No grinnin."

Jasper leans near her ear and tells her she looks just fine. "But I look stupid," he adds. "Look at this thing." He flicks the codpiece.

"Quiet on the set!" says Henry. "Players in position!"

They stare at him.

"Where youz think, noodles?" He points to the bed.

"I thought we were doing the balcony scene," says Jasper.

Henry says no, it's the hark-the-lark scene.

They get on the bed. It squeaks and creaks, the mattress plunges in the middle and rides up on the sides. Ruby lies down and opens her legs. Jasper opens the codpiece and gets on top of her. He can feel her belly heaving with giggles.

"No, no," says Henry. "Gimme the script. Can't youz remember nothin what I said?" He stabs his finger at the script. "Right here, right here. What's the margin say?"

"Doggy position," says Jasper.

"And I'm doing the zoom lens and the freeze frame on her pussy, and what do youz say, Jim?"

"I say, 'O, turn to me those pale globes of thine / Deliver up your luscious heart-shaped tush.' "

"And there my zoom is on her luscious heart-shaped tush, see?" Jasper nods.

"Wants to fuck her so bad, he won't let me get my shot," grumbles Henry.

"I don't want to fuck her," Jasper says. "I don't want none of this shit. No offense, Ruby."

A quick guffaw suddenly bursts from her. She puts her hand over her mouth.

"Temperamental goddamn artists," says Henry. "Bend over there, Ruby. Pull up that gown and let's see how your tokus looks through the viewfinder."

Rising on all fours, Ruby cinches up her gown, shows them her ass. Pirate and Henry look through the viewfinder and make some focus adjustments and lower the legs of the tripod so there is more of an upward, rather than a downward, angle.

"How's it look?" says Ruby. "Is it bad?"

"Looks like a valentine with a little beard at the bottom," says Pirate.

"It's cute," Didi tells her.

"Are you sure?"

Everybody assures her her ass is cute. She settles down at the edge of the mattress, feet hanging over. The bottom of her feet are dirty. Henry orders her feet washed. Didi gets a wet hand cloth and gets the worst of the dirt off. Ruby looks toward the wall and waits. A little trill of laughter breaks from her at intervals, like a bird warbling on a fence.

Henry gives the orders. "Now, youz come behind her on the floor,

270.

on your knees, nose to anal asshole level, Reem, and youz *extemporize*."

"Get out!"

"Say what? Look here, Reem, it's in the script. It's written down. There's the words. Read the words, Reem. Am I lyin? I ain't lyin. Hope to catch the clap if I'm lyin."

Jasper is shaking his head. "I don't care what the words say," he says. "I'm not coming up behind her and put my nose up her butt. I don't even know her that well."

"No trouper," says Pirate.

"No trouper," says Didi. Her eyes are bright. There is mischief on her face.

"Enjoying yourself?" says Jasper.

"Uh-huh."

"Youz won't follow the word, Reem?" says Henry, slapping the manuscript. "The word, Reem. If youz won't follow the word, what the hell will youz follow?"

"Fuck them words there, fuck them goddamn words." To his chagrin and embarrassment, Jasper feels as though he might cry. There is weakness in his eyes, a trembling in his chin, his mouth is all wet, his nose is dribbling. He doesn't know how he got here. He doesn't know what he is doing. To keep from shaming himself he shouts, "Fuck them motherfucking words of yours, Henry!" He knocks the script from Henry's hands. He puts his fists up, ready to fight. He stands before them sniffing and daring.

"Flamin legs, what I got here?" says Henry. "Temperamental artist. That's what we *auteurs* have to deal with, temperamental artists. Put them dukes down, Jim. Take it easy now. We're all friends here."

With a great effort, Jasper manages to control himself. He points to the clock on the nightstand and tells them he has to get to work. Pirate says there is time for a quickie. "C'mon, get it in her. You'll be fine once you get it in her, Jas baby."

Jasper looks at the camera, then to where it is pointing. He looks at Henry and Pirate and sees how loose their mouths are, how glittery their eyes. Both men have semi-erections making mole motions inside their trousers. Didi keeps rubbing a thumb over one breast. He knows what's happening here.

Pirate pleads with him. "We're almost there," he says. "Break the ice, man. I mean, Jas baby, look at that *ass.*"

Henry puts his arm around Jasper and pats his cheek. "Listen to Pa*pe,*" he says. "Don't be shy about this shit. It's natural action, that's all. Right this second fifty million men are greasin the goose in southern California alone. Nothin to be ashamed of, Jim. We're makin a movie here, a little artsy-fartsy wham-bam movie. What's the harm?"

"I can't believe Godot really meant this," says Jasper.

"Course he meant it."

"It'll be a cult film," says Didi.

"Shut up," he tells her.

"You shut up," she fires back.

He hates her. "Cult film, my ass," he says.

Bottom up, Ruby looks over her shoulder and says, "It's okay, Jasper. Let's just pretend it's only us." She puts her head down, looks at him from between her legs, and giggles wildly.

"Listen to this, she's getting hysterical," says Jasper. Reaching out, he yanks Ruby's gown over her butt. "We gotta stop this shit," he says. "They're making fools of us, Ruby. They just want to watch us fuck, so they can get their rocks off. It's all a bunch of crap. Jesus Christ, look at us. I mean, look! Mary's in there stroking a potato, poor Helga's dead of cancer, Godot's locked up insane for trying to cut his prick off, and here we are . . . I mean, how the hell can we . . . I mean, what the hell are we . . ."

He realizes he doesn't know what he means. He wants to tell them the truth with a capital T, but it comes to him like ice slipping down his spine that the truth is he doesn't know the truth. "Reduced to this," he says weakly, making a sweep with his hand. "I don't know what I thought we were going to do, but this stuff isn't for me, no way."

"Sonofabitch!" says Henry. "Temperamental artist shit. I ain't puttin up with it, Jim."

"Fuck you, man."

"You're no trouper," says Pirate.

Jasper leaves the room. They call him names. He tells them to go fuck themselves. In the bedroom, he peels his costume off and flings it at Shakespeare's bust. The bust topples from the bookshelf. When the bust hits the floor, the head breaks away and goes shooting past Jasper's feet. He puts his clothes on. He hears the filmmakers mumbling and cussing at him as he walks through the dining room and kitchen and goes outside. The screen door bangs behind him. He leaps over the railing and hits the grass running.

✛

Fat Stanley puts the finishing touches on his new love ad and slips it in an envelope. It's been a long, emotionally exhausting day and there is still lots to do. But this is good. Staying busy is very good. They went to the funeral home, he and the kids, and picked out a coffin, a nice one, guaranteed waterproof forever, with the patented diamond silicate coating and the maxifit seal, done in pale green exterior, with kelly green inside, all satin, and a satin pillow too. After lunch, they went back and visited Helga lying in the new coffin. She looked content. Her dark red hair made a nice contrast with the green interior.

He chose the coffin for security and aesthetic effect, not price. The coffin cost thirty-eight hundred dollars, plus state and federal taxes. There was another fifteen hundred for the plot under the palm tree. The funeral director praised his choices and said he was a man who obviously loved his spouse and wanted her to have a restful afterlife. The coffin he chose was designed for lasting comfort. There will be other charges for preparations and burial and all. Fat Stanley didn't even ask about them. He just said to send the bill. He knows he is being ripped off, but he doesn't care, he wants to give Helga a good send-off in a coffin that looks like a piece of art, like a Renaissance painting. It is the least he can do, the least a real friend would do. He hopes someone will do as much for him when he dies. He hopes someone will say that the world is a poorer place without him, which is what it feels like now without Helga Martin in it.

After seeing Helga in her coffin, they went to her old apartment and met a man there who bought the furniture and kitchenware. He paid five hundred dollars for everything. All the kids took were the rest of their clothes and some mementos. They've been holding up well enough. The two youngest ones keep matching dreams of their angel-mother, each trying to top the other. Nancy is quiet, subdued. She has confided her guilt to Fat Stanley about not being a good daughter, about actually hating her mother, hating her tough, motorcycle mama ways, her boozing, the barflies she brought home, and hating her cancer too, which seemed almost a deliberate thing she did in order to make Nancy suffer. Nancy admits to being nasty to her mother, and self-pitying, and saying once to her, "Why don't you just die and get it over with!" But that's the thing about *dying,* Nancy says, she didn't really believe it would happen. You see all these things on TV about miracle cures and how science can practically create life itself, and you don't believe in death anymore. People with horrible diseases go on and on. Nancy thought Helga would. There was this sense of having time yet to straighten everything out.

Fat Stanley leaves the three kids at home, while he walks to the corner and mails his ad to the *Union.* Then he walks to the diner and goes in the back way. It smells kitcheny and quiet inside. He opens the vents in the kitchen. He turns the overhead fan on in the dining area. He dampens a rag and starts wiping down the counter and the tables. As he moves from table to table, he looks around and realizes that the restaurant isn't really his anymore, it belongs to Capon Enterprises and they will probably tear it down and put up a parking lot. The area is growing. More parking spaces are needed every day. He is aware of Capon's reputation, a man who pulled himself up by his bootstraps the American way, a man who put together enough money to buy a trash truck and went into business and became so big and rich in twenty years that his trucks and his parking lots were all over California, and he was being talked of for State Treasurer. From there he might go to

Congress, maybe even the White House. Fat Stanley knows how important money is. He knows if he had Capon's money, he and Helga's orphans would never know want, would never fear ending up on the streets like the two men, those two bums over there, who have become a permanent fixture in front of Texas Style.

He broods over this. He broods over a feeling of guilt he has for selling the diner to a Capon and shagging off to England, to what he thinks is the remnants of civilization. But now there is this responsibility he didn't want and he's not sure what to do about it. Take them with him? Get the authorities to take them over? Foster homes? An orphanage? He doesn't see how he can go for any of those things. He feels trapped. He *is* trapped. It is in his mind now that he has made a mistake in selling the diner, that he is a victim of middle-age crisis, a man trying to renew himself by running away, that he knows, or should know, better. New sights and sounds soon become old sights and sounds, and the whole *trapped* business starts over again no matter where you are. Truth is, everybody is trapped in one way or another, and there is no renewal. There is only delusion and a temporary energizing of the adrenals and then you're right back with *you* again and the problems of aging and earning a living and your fat gut getting fatter and your thinning hair getting thinner and your nagging health problems, the pains in your lower back, your knees, your feet, and the feeling that your organs are disintegrating in unison, that they know the time of your death down to the millisecond, but they won't tell. You'll find out soon enough, they seem to say.

Fat Stanley sits at one of the tables. He puts the rag under his elbow on the table and leans his head on his palm. Never in his life can he remember being so depressed. Just the least thing, a stray thought or a whispered word could make him cry right now. A fly lands on the table and walks around a damp smear left by the rag. The fly's proboscis touches the smear daintily. Why should a fly have life and not Helga? Fat Stanley lifts the rag slowly, then flicks it at the fly, catapulting it off the table and to the floor. He checks to see if the fly is dead. It has disappeared.

The door opens in back and he hears Jasper coming through the kitchen, his long, loping walk. He comes through the double doors, sees Fat Stanley, says, "What's up, boss?"

"Jasper."

Jasper has shaved his beard. His hair is slicked back. He wears jeans, tennis shoes, an undershirt. Fat Stanley thinks he is a fine-looking boy, but booze and bad company will probably ruin him before long. "So what have you been doing today?" says Fat Stanley. "Have you seen Ruby?"

"Ruby? Yeah. She's up at Mary Quick's. They're making the movie. Ruby is JuleeTit."

Fat Stanley says, "So they're using Godot's takeoff on Shakespeare. I was hoping they wouldn't. It's not him, it's not the Godot I've known for what? Thirteen, fourteen years."

"Did you read the papers?" says Jasper. "What they say about him?"

Fat Stanley shakes his head sadly. "None of it's the truth. He's a better man than they say. He just finally couldn't cope. There's a lot of that going around. I find it hard to hang on myself. Some days I think I'll bust."

"I hear you," Jasper says.

They look at each other. Fat Stanley thinks if Jasper knew what was coming in later years, he wouldn't want to stick around. It never gets better, not really. Life is ninety-nine percent the mallet.

"You sure look tired and gloomy," says Jasper.

"I'm that and more," says Fat Stanley. "But what can you do? Nothing to do but keep on keeping on. So, anyway, do you think Ruby's coming, or is she going to stay up there and do the movie? I called Beehive too. She said she'd come."

"Ruby'll be by in a bit, I think. She wasn't all that hot for what they were doing either." He takes a stool and leans his elbows back on the counter. "It's all over, I hear. Mary told us when you called today, and we said a prayer for Helga, all of us. Mary stopped production so we could pray. I wish I had gone to see ole Helga, you know? I never got to say goodbye. I feel pretty rotten about it, boss. Helga was a friend. I feel like I let her down, you know?"

At the mention of Helga's name Fat Stanley's eyes abruptly become wet. He doesn't understand why he cries so easily over her death. He thinks maybe it's because he's fifty and when you're fifty you start losing control. Your nerves have had it by the time you're fifty. He wipes his eyes on the rag in his hand and tells Jasper how it was with Helga, how she suffered, but then how peaceful she looked when it was over. Death has its compensations.

"And now we're going to have a party for her, in her honor, I've decided," he says. Waving his hand at the room, he explains how he wants it decorated. He wants green and red balloons and crepe paper and a sign saying BON VOYAGE HELGA MARTIN. He wants her picture on the wall. The coffin will be open so she can be part of the celebration. None of that depressive stuff. He wants to laugh her out of this world.

Not long after Jasper leaves to buy the party supplies, Ruby comes in. She enters the dining room and looks at Fat Stanley, gives him a big smile. She is wearing a black skirt and a white blouse, her usual uniform, but her face looks different. She has pulled her hair back and tied it with a bow as usual, but there is lots of makeup on her face, arching brows, dark eye shadow, creamy lipstick. She looks agitated. She keeps picking at her skirt and sort of squirming.

"I didn't know if I was gonna make it," she says. "We got so busy over at Mary's. You should've been there, Stanley." Looking down at her skirt, picking something off it, a thread which she rolls between her fingers, she pauses, then adds. "Or maybe not, actually."

"You're Juliet? Jasper tells me that you're Juliet," says Fat Stanley.

Ruby giggles. "JuleeTit, they call her. I *was*. But I just got fired. Jasper's girlfriend is taking over the role. Pirate's ReemHerHole now. You should see them." She laughs shrilly. She puts her hand over her mouth, then takes it away. Her words are punctuated with irrepressible titters and snorts as she says, "I'm sorry. It's just so . . . ridiculous. They don't know . . . oh Christ . . . what the hell they're doing, none of them. Henry is giving orders and doing the camera, and Mary's locked herself in the closet . . . and, oh shit . . . and those two are going at it like a pair of minks and they're not even listening to Henry and he's so goddamn mad he's practically having a stroke . . . oh holy Christ, it would make a funny movie itself if someone would just . . . just film the three of them trying to make a film! Christ, what a scream! Weee! Oh God!" She breaks down, has a little fit. Then she tells him, "I'm sorry. I'm really sorry. I just needed to let it out. I haven't laughed so good since the day I left my husband. I think I'm a little hysterical, Stanley. I think I better sit down." She puts her hands on her knees and goes all hysterical for a few seconds again.

Fat Stanley has been chuckling himself, imagining the scene with the three of them and Mary in the closet. He's glad Ruby has told the story. For a few seconds Helga and death and his downer of a life was off his mind and he is grateful. "Bunch of real dreamers," he says, "if they think they're going to make the big time that way."

Ruby has taken a chair at the table with Fat Stanley. She is wiping her eyes with a napkin. Every second or two, she breaks into another giggle and has to wipe her eyes again. Her eye shadow is smeared. Fat Stanley reaches over, he takes a fresh napkin and dabs at the black splotches.

"I'm making a mess of myself, aren't I?" Ruby says. "I can't help it. Jesus, I've seen some things in my life, but this takes the cake."

She allows Fat Stanley to clean her up a little. Finally he rises and goes to the cooler, grabs a couple of beers. He brings them back and sits down, twists the caps off the bottles.

After a calm interval in which they sip their beers and get composed, Ruby says, "I was so sorry to hear about Helga, so very, very sorry."

"A better world," he says. "She's in a better world."

"Yes," says Ruby.

Fat Stanley tells her that Jasper is on his way to Kmart for party favors. He tells her the plans for the wake. As he finishes his little speech his lips start to quiver again, his eyes get wet again.

"I don't know what's wrong with me," he says, smiling. "This is so stupid. I just can't seem to help it. As soon as I think about her, I start to bawl. So stupid, a grown man like me, who would think?"

"No, no, it's not stupid," says Ruby. She tells him she knows what it's like, she remembers her father's death and how she couldn't stop crying for a month. "It's grief," she says. "It takes a long time."

For about half an hour, they sit and drink some beers and talk about it. He tells her how Helga looked dying, how you couldn't even touch her, how she whined and grimaced. Ruby tells him about how her father threw up dead blood cells that looked like coffee grounds, how his liver shut down and his body bloated and how he slipped into a coma and died. How she fainted when she realized he was actually gone. She loved her father very much.

"There are men, and there are men," she says, touching her cheek, the dent.

Ah yes, there are men. All the while he and Ruby have talked, he has noticed an odor eddying from her, slightly acrid but not awful. It is a mixture of perspiration and perfume and something else, something vaguely like an odor of tuna clinging to a man's fingers, but not so pungent as that, more spicy maybe. Somewhat involuntarily he finds himself leaning toward her, breathing her in, imagining her doing the movie.

"Life goes on. We live and learn," he says. He is feeling impulses he didn't expect to feel this particular day. He wants very much to touch her leg, the bare knee below the hem of her skirt.

"Time heals," she says.

They look at each other. She puts her hand on top of his hand resting on the table. "Those kids are lucky to have you," she says.

Again the tears start up in his eyes. "God, what's wrong with me?" he says. "I'm a mass of contradictions. Maybe I'm having a nervous breakdown."

"It's okay—it's okay, you just let it go. There's nothing wrong with it."

"I'm such a baby," he says.

279.

"No you're not. You're a good man. You've got a big heart." She pauses while he grabs another napkin and wipes his eyes, blows his nose, then she says, "Maybe this is the time to tell you this. I've been wanting to tell you what I think. People don't know it, but I have thoughts too. I'm quiet, but I have my thoughts, and let me tell you, I think you're the best man around here, Stanley Lipton. Listen, I don't care who knows it, I've been half in love with you since the first time I heard you sing. You were in the kitchen and your voice just took me over, and I said, 'There is a beautiful man, there is someone I want to know.' That's what I said to myself. And now I know you, and you're just what I thought you were."

"Really?"

"Really." She gives him a kiss on the cheek.

He looks at her, his neck stretching.

"Actually, you probably need a better kiss than that," she says, and she kisses his mouth. The kiss lingers. Her lips are very sweet.

"Oh, Ruby," he whispers, when she pulls away.

"I really like you," she says.

"Jasper said you liked me."

"Jasper knows."

He finds it hard to believe, and he remembers once when he was little and a girl on a playground taking his hand and saying that she liked him and that she wanted to be his girlfriend. He remembers rejecting her because her hand felt rough. She had a sort of dishpan hand. But then he grew up and grew fat, grew repulsive, and was in turn rejected by others. He sees a sort of justice in it, and he wonders if the system is set up that way: if we pay for the life we live by the life we live.

"What about Pirate?" he says.

"The faster I get away from that guy, the better off I'll be," she says. "Pirate is just another user. Pirate loves only Pirate. You're not like him. You, you're a sweetie."

Fat Stanley almost laughs in her face. Instead, he just smiles. "I'm a sweetie, huh?" he says.

"When you've been through what I've been through, you start looking beyond the surface," says Ruby. "You start looking for what's inside."

He wonders what she would think if she could have seen him a week ago laying a hundred bucks down for ten minutes with a tattooed hooker. Over the years he has slept with probably three hundred prostitutes. What would Ruby think of that? What would Ruby think if she knew of his desire for Nancy Martin? What would she think if she could read all his evil thoughts, if she knew, in fact, that her aroma has aroused him in the midst of his grief, that he is sitting with an erection right now and wishing he could get her over the table?

"I'm not a sweetie," he says. "I'm really not, Ruby. Don't get the wrong ideas about me."

"I don't have the wrong ideas," she says. "I didn't say you were a saint, I said you were a sweetie."

The sound of the overhead fan and the vents mix with the sounds of traffic outside, a backdrop of life. He is glad to be himself at this moment, to be Stanley Lipton, fat as a pig, frisky as a colt, and so blessedly *alive*. He inhales deeply, expanding his lungs to their fullest. He smells Ruby. He wonders what she would do if he ran his hand up her skirt. She would allow it, he thinks. After all, she was just bareass in a porno movie. What a strange life it is, he tells himself. Out of the blue, when you least expect it, in the midst of despair comes this. This is what a woman can do for a man.

"God bless you," he says. He touches the dent in her cheek.

Reaching across, he curls his fingers around the back of her neck, beneath her hair, his fingers rubbing lightly. "So what happens now?" he says.

"What do you want to happen?" she says.

A minute later, Beehive arrives. She walks in on them standing up, holding each other. "Bad timing," she says, and starts to leave.

"We were just comforting each other," says Ruby.

"Uh-huh. Yeah, geez, I'm sorry about your friend," Beehive says. "I hope she went easy."

Fat Stanley explains that she went hard, but it's over now. Then he tells Beehive the plan for the wake. Beehive says it's the nicest thing he could do for Helga, a sign of real respect and love, and she hopes someday someone will do as much for her.

"We'll make this place spic and span," she says.

She and Ruby get mops and buckets and start cleaning the diner. Jasper returns with crepe paper and balloons. He starts blowing up the balloons. Fat Stanley puts three tables together in the middle of the floor. He covers the tables with blankets of the green crepe paper. The coffin will go on top, sort of center stage. He hauls the two remaining tables to the storeroom in back, making space for the chairs and for people to mingle, for them to drink and dance and make speechs about Helga. It's going to be a great party, he thinks. He's going to give a big, important eulogy for Helga. Pull out all the stops for her. And she'll be there in her aesthetically correct Renaissance coffin listening to herself get commemorated. There will be food and drink, plenty of friends to give her a proper send-off. He's going to make sure of that, and make sure too that they put some spirit into it, make enough noise, by golly, to raise her from the dead.

11.   O MY ENEMY

For the wake Jasper John splurges on a white shirt and a green tie. He would wear a suit to show Helga respect, but he doesn't have a suit. He wears his best pair of jeans and his Nikes. He shaves. He combs his hair back into a short ponytail and ties it with a rubber band.

As he walks toward the Narcissus with Mary beside him, he sees the marquee has only half its title in lights. The large letters say ISSUS. The other half buzzes NARC as they walk beneath it. People are lined up for the matinee to see the film entitled *The Best of XXX-Rated Animation.* The heat wave has broken and it is a cloud-covered day. A few people in line look up as if they are expecting rain. Jasper feels a little spritz dotting his face now and then. The clouds are low. They are dark gray, gloomy things stretching from horizon to horizon; they match Jasper's mood. He doesn't believe Helga's wake can be a celebration as Fat Stanley says. Jasper feels awful down today. He feels bummed out and betrayed and lonely and mortal.

Part of his problem is Mary herself and her weird notions about

283.

supernatural things happening to her. Mary is wearing a blue dress with black pumps. The Celtic cross dangles from her neck. Gold upon a blue background, it makes clumsy fluttering motions as she walks. Sister Augustine's Bible is in her hand. In her pocket is her nitroglycerin, and before they pass by the two derelicts leaning on the carcass of the Ford, she slips another pill under her tongue. She has told Jasper of her anxiety over the oracle she received from Sister Augustine about Helga. In her anxiety Mary has taken three pills already, and it is only four o'clock. She has made Jasper promise not to stray too far from her side. He has tried to reassure her. He has given her Fat Stanley's speech about celebrating Helga's life and not mooning over her death, but he can tell that Mary feels fragile and is just hanging on by a thread.

When they enter the restaurant there is nothing of the party atmosphere. The place is gloomy. It is crowded. The people are jammed in the booths or sitting on stools and chairs, or milling around quietly, talking in whispers. Some are filing by the coffin. Jasper sees a few women wiping their eyes. One short, wide woman in severe black seems to be having a good time displaying her grief. As she looks into the coffin and sobs into a hanky, a man pats her on the back.

Jasper wants to tell her there is no crying at this wake, but he doesn't do it. Many of the people, including the sobbing woman, are strangers to him. Maybe some are employees or customers from her other job at the pancake house. Maybe some are neighbors or relatives. He doesn't know. He recognizes only her regulars from Fat Stanley's, the ones she teased, the ones she made feel at home.

At the entrance, he and Mary stand for a few moments taking it all in. Mary's breath quickens. She grips his hand so tightly it hurts. Her hand is cold. It is bony. BON VOYAGE HELGA MARTIN, says the huge sign on the wall.

"Do you want to go home?" he whispers. He imagines her dropping dead from the strain. Two dead ladies. Wouldn't that be something? Put them together in the coffin, have a double wake. Jasper presses his lips together in a grim smile.

Mary whispers back that she doesn't want to leave, she wants to complete her mission first. She lets go of his hand and starts to make her way through the mourners, toward the coffin at the back of the restaurant. The coffin is centered beneath the aperture where Helga used to stick her orders on the carousel. There is room to walk all the way around it. Bouquets of flowers line the edges of the coffin. Above it the overhead fan slowly whirls, stirring a number of balloons and curls of crepe paper that Jasper, Ruby, and Beehive hung the night before. Jasper follows behind, keeping his eyes on the bull's-eye Mary's braid makes on the back of her head.

They arrive at the coffin together and peek in. The lid has been completely removed and set aside, which gives the effect of Helga lying in a narrow boat floating on flowers and crepe green water. Even though they know Helga is dead, and even though they have both imagined what she will look like in her coffin, they are still shocked to see her actually there, wearing a falsely painted face, manipulated hair, the fake tweak of a smile on her lips. Her head looks small lying on the pillow. She wears a white dress, with a gauze frill at the waist imprinted with tiny velvet white roses. The dress is something a bride might not scorn.

Mary gives Jasper a stricken look. Her lips are tight, formed into a severe line. The bags beneath her Irish setter eyes sag like pockets full of loose change. He puts his arm around her. He holds her tightly to him, supporting her and supporting himself too. He thinks he knows what she is thinking, that she who very nearly died could die any second, even now, standing in front of the coffin—there, but for the grace of God, that sort of thing. She reaches trembling fingers toward Helga and touches her shoulder.

"Goodbye, my dear," she says. She pats Helga's folded hands, then slips the Bible underneath them and murmurs a little prayer that Sister Augustine told her the night before, " 'For me to live is Christ, and to die is gain.' "

There, the deed is done, and Jasper wonders if Mary will be satisfied now, or is all this just a preface for the nut farm? According to Sister Augustine, Mary's luck will change, the filthy bad luck that has pursued her all these years, caused by her whoring and what she did to J.J. and compounded by stealing the purse and Bible from the suicidal sister, will be expiated by this one holy act, this giving of the tainted Bible to departed Helga, followed by the short prayer—all forgiveness contingent on leading an exemplary life hereafter, of course.

According to Mary, she has had all the signs she needs. She has seen a pillar of clouds form into an image of Jesus, arms reaching out, white robe flowing; she has seen the shadow of the cross streaking across her bed, the word BELIEVE in the Scrabble letters adding up to 33, the picture of the Madonna weeping oily tears, bloody water in a vase of red roses, a potato shaped like a cracking heart; and many mighty visions of hell shown to her by the sister: whirlwinds attacking sinners, driving them like darting crows up and down and around end-lessly; sinners roasted in coffins, torn by dogs, boiled in water, drowned in rivers of blood, buried upside down while fire licked their feet, heads turned backwards and tears streaming down between the cleft in their buttocks, bellies ripped open, guts dragging on the ground, bodies buried in ice: all the torments of the damned have been shown to her with a wave of Sister Augustine's hand, whose own soul was barely saved from torment an instant before dying by a final murmur of the Act of Contrition: so merciful is the Lord!

In giving the Bible to Helga to take with her into eternity, Mary has told Jasper that, in effect, she will be burying her past. Jasper hopes so. He wishes she would stop torturing herself with visions of hell. Her monstrous visions are terrifying her. They are so . . . cruel, so *medieval*. He hopes she can get some rest from them, but he has huge doubts. He watches as she turns away. She straightens her shoulders and gives them a shake as if ridding herself of a burden. He tries to imagine her heart now as light as the balloons floating at the corners of the coffin. He tries to imagine her all well.

At the front of the restaurant the door opens, the bell chimes, and Jasper turns to see Henry Hank enter. He is wearing his usual black cowboy outfit. Behind him is Pirate with his guitar and Didi. Jasper stares at Didi, willing her to look at him, but she won't. Her eyes search the ceiling, the balloons, as if they are the most interesting sights in the room. Nervously, he sucks his lip.

He doesn't know what to say to them, especially to Didi. He sees Didi naked again, there in the yellow lamplights, sprawled across the bed. He sees Pirate in the easy chair, his mouth open, snoring, his eye patch shoved high on his brow, creating the illusion of a hole in his head, his beard covering his naked chest, his penis hiding in the thick thatch of pubic hair. He sees Henry's hairy body curled like a fetus beneath the tripod wearing nothing but chrome-toed boots. Henry, his beard rubbed clean of shoe polish from mouth to point of chin, the hairs there as white as foam. Between Didi's thighs is an empty bottle of Incorrigible Ike. On its tripod at the foot of the bed, the eye of the camera gazes at her. The camera's motor is still running, making a soft ticking sound, the expended film slapping inside the canister as the gears turn. The pages of Godot's script are all over the floor and the furniture, as if the three of them had used it for confetti.

Jasper had not been shocked to see what he saw. In fact, he had expected it, even though a part of him had hoped she would fool him, that she would be in his room as usual waiting for him to come home. But a poet had to have experiences, a poet had to know all sides of the human condition, and he told himself he did not blame or hate Didi for disappointing him. In his heart, he had always known she was woman-as-betrayer, or poet-as-betrayer, a kind of ur-poet-woman. In the large scheme of things (that began and ended for the moment in Helga's death), Didi's betrayal did not seem that important. He was able to look at her à la Mary Quick lying in a similar fashion only a few weeks before, and Didi looked uncannily like a worn version of Mary—used, abused, and yet somehow desirable too. The mouth of Incorrigible Ike was only inches from her vagina and looked gluey, as if they had been using it on her, or she had used it on herself for the camera. The lips of her vagina sagged tiredly. Her breasts also sagged, leaning outward as Mary's breasts had done, looking vaguely like eggs sunny-side up. Her slack mouth whistled with air that smelled sharply of sex.

When he left the room, he found Mary on the couch sleeping, hugging her knees, her Bible beneath her head, the three grays draped around her. He got a blanket and covered her. He went to bed with Lummox and lay awake most of the night wondering what to do. When he got up in the morning, Didi and the two men were gone, and so there was nothing he needed to do, until now, seeing her there at the entrance, clutching Pirate's hand and refusing to look in Jasper's direction.

There is a pumped-up keg of beer on the counter, and next to it bottles of Incorrigible Ike, vodka, scotch, bourbon, gin, crème de menthe, and anisette. For the first hour or so, the mourners line up with cups to pour themselves something to drink. As they drink, they get noisier. Whispers and murmurs, sad mouths, eyes full of tears metamorphose as if one mask is replaced by another. There is even laughter bubbling up here and there after a while, and the room fills with the buzz of voices. Mourner after mourner comes to both sides of the coffin, clutching its edges, peeking at the dead, speaking to the dead as if somewhere deep down the ear hole is still an ember that lives. Some call her a good ole girl, a sweetheart, a pistol. They give her kisses and pats. They say, "Remember the time . . . ?"

Pirate sits on the counter, his feet on a stool, and plays his guitar. He and Didi sing Simon and Garfunkel tunes, nice placid, melancholy stuff for the occasion. People hum with them. A few couples stand in front swaying, their arms around each other. At the end of "Sound of Silence," Fat Stanley, wearing a dark green suit and a red tie, gets up from the booth in the corner, where he and the three children and Ruby have been sitting watching and quietly talking, and he raises his hands and he says that this is what he wanted, a real send-off party for Helga, and that she is probably enjoying watching them right now.

"Here's to Helga!" he shouts, his defiant fist in the air.

A roar bursts from the crowd, glasses go up, and a great shout of "Helga!"

Fat Stanley takes out his handkerchief and blows his nose. He looks at Ruby and the children wet-eyed. He nods his head. They nod back.

"All right," he says to the happy mourners, "let me just say a few words about our girl here"—he pats Helga's stiff red hair—"and then I want to sing something for her, and then Nancy wants to say something, and we'll just do whatever feels natural after that. We'll dance for her, how's that? We'll act just like Helga would act if she was running this show."

The mourners clap.

From his pocket he takes out some sheets of paper and unfolds them. He reads the words he has written there, and he gives an eloquent speech, a little testament about beloved Helga. He says that Helga Martin was born May 27, 1949, in Phoenix, Arizona. She died on her birthday, May 27, 1990. She came to San Diego eighteen years ago with her husband, Mike Martin, who, a few years later, was killed in a motorcycle accident and left her with three small children to raise, Nancy, Katherine, and Michael Junior. She worked two jobs, waitressing in the mornings at the International House of Pancakes, and in the afternoon and evenings at Fat Stanley's Steak and Chops. Helga was a fun-loving, party-all-night woman who lived fast and loved hard. She knew how to live life to the hilt, and she also knew how to be a devoted wife and mother.

Fat Stanley says it was a bitter and tragic experience to watch what was happening to her, and not be able to do anything about it. Such experiences make us all very humble, and make us appreciate all the more the blessings we have, he says. When Helga died, she did so without fuss or bother. Like a candle which had used up all its wax, the light fizzled out and she was gone. The world is poorer without her. The world needs her energy, her toughness, her humor, her goodness, her honesty.

He clears his throat and continues. He says: "I'm going to miss Helga Martin, and I know you are too. But it is the way of things that we must die, that each of us will have to step up and take our turn, and what will *matter then* is what we've left behind. Ten thousand years ago, people just like you and me knew what it was to grieve over the loss of a loved one, and ten thousand years from now, people will still know what it is to grieve over the loss of a loved one. Grieving is eternal. All life and love ends in loss. All things break away and fall into the sea and leave us diminished. This is what John Donne meant when he told us that no man is an island entire of itself; every man is a piece of the continent, a part of the main. We grieve because a piece of the continent has been washed away from us, and we are the less for it. Each man's or woman's death diminishes us, says Donne, because we are involved in mankind."

Fat Stanley's words and his trained voice hold them mesmerized. No one whispers to another, no one moves. He is onstage. He is at the Met. He has his audience and he makes the most of it. "We are all one and the same being. This oneness applies especially to Helga's children sitting here trying to cope with the loss of their mother. But it may help a tiny bit to remember that as long as they are alive, she is alive within them. And if they have children, Helga will be in those children also, and so on and so forth forever, or until the ending of the world. This is no small immortality to be kept alive in the cells of your descendants.

"In others sitting here, she is alive in memory. Every time you think of her, every time you mention her name or recite an anecdote about her, you honor her, you bless her, you keep her alive. Perhaps the worst thing we can do to the dead is to destroy them utterly by refusing to remember them. If Helga's spirit is standing here with us today looking on, she need not fear we will forget her." He pauses. He looks up at the bobbing heads of the balloons and the slowly swishing fans. The mourners look up with him.

Fat Stanley puts his notes back in his pocket, takes a deep breath and lets it out. Again, he clears his throat. The mourners wait, anticipating more. "Let me share with you a dream I had just last night. I've dreamt of Helga two nights running, but the one I had last night is the most meaningful, I think. I dreamt I stood on the porch of a house. The porch went over the waters of a vast lake, a lake so wide I couldn't see the other side, and there were steps leading from the porch into the water. A boat came to the steps and a man got out. The man was my uncle, the uncle who kept me here in America after my parents were killed in the war. My uncle took Helga by the arm and led her down the steps and into the boat. Helga was submissive and looked contented. She didn't say anything. I followed after and was about to enter the boat too, when my uncle held up his hand and said, 'I'll be back for you later.' He rowed away with Helga and they disappeared over the horizon. I am reminded of a poem that says 'even the weariest river winds somewhere safe to sea.' I hope it is true that my uncle met my friend Helga Martin and transported her somewhere safe to sea. It would be a great comfort to believe it, and if anyone deserved such an honor for being a courageous, dignified, uncomplaining celebrator and acceptor of life with all its ups and downs, Helga Martin was such a one. At least, that's the way I see it."

Fat Stanley pauses once more. He looks at the mourners with benevolence as if he is saying, "Don't worry about a thing, I love you all." Then his mouth opens and he sings "Ave Maria" to them in a voice filled with rich emotion. His words flow over the audience like a caress. The words are warm. They are the color of Indian summer. The words tell them of grief and hope, of fear and belief, of faith and melancholy. Fat Stanley is singing not so much for Helga now as for these living listeners waiting their turn. A few are moved to get on their knees. Others bow their heads. Jasper folds his hands in front of him. He watches the growth of spirituality as it evolves in the room in the wake of the song, and he experiences a mild epiphany that seems to come from the fountainhead of all things pious, and he understands the pull of religion and he wants to *be* religious, and for the duration of "Ave Maria" he is.

When the song is over, Fat Stanley stands for a moment in silence, then turns toward his right and motions to Nancy and he says, "Now, let me step aside here and introduce Nancy Martin, Helga's oldest daughter, who has something more to say."

Jasper feels like clapping for him, for his testament to Helga, but he doesn't. He puts his hands into his back pockets and focuses on Nancy, who speaks ad lib, her fingers fidgeting over and over with the collar and the sleeves of her dress.

Looking at the floor, her voice a flat, almost indifferent monotone, her lips barely moving, she says she wants to tell them what her mother taught her, especially in the last year as she wasted away to almost nothing, her flesh melting, but her spirit seeming to grow stronger and stronger, and by her example teaching her children how to handle bad things in their lives. How to handle sickness. How to handle death.

Nancy says, "Older people, they're always telling young people how to live, what to do, how to do it. Mom once said that she was a hard-head and no one could tell her a thing, she had to find it out for herself, what was good, what was bad. But older people, they want to run your life even though it seems they don't much run their own that well. But that's okay. I'm sure I'll be like that too. It's natural. But the thing is, I hope I'm like Mom and can show my kids how to handle the awful breaks that come with living, I mean handle them with courage and dignity, that's the most important thing, I've learned . . . the example . . . it's what I've learned most. Courage and how not to whine and feel picked on all the time like I was doing to her, being a . . . a whiny brat, which I hope she'll forgive me for. And that's the thing, you never know. I mean, I didn't know how fast people could go. I was too young to remember much of it with my dad. I was like eight years old then, and Kathy was five, and Mike was just a baby. But now I know how fast people can go out of your life. It's amazing. I didn't think she would ever really die. It just didn't seem possible for someone like her, someone so full of fight, someone so fiery about everything. It just didn't seem like it could happen. But it did. Here she is." Nancy's voice breaks for an instant, her lower lip trembles. She clears her throat several times, she coughs, she looks up and takes a deep breath, she touches the coffin.

"But anyway, she taught me to spit in the eye of cancer and death and not go kicking and screaming and bawling and clinging to your kids like they've got the answer because they're young."

Nancy's eyes run over with tears as she scans the mourners, but her voice gets stronger, it is an angry, exasperated voice now. "That's the mistake everybody is making these days, thinking young people have answers. Young people don't know shit. Don't count on us. All we know is that you're drowning and we don't want you to take us down with you. That's what it was like sometimes; I mean before she got the cancer. She was a know-it-all, and when you come home drunk and barfing all over, you can't expect your kids to think much of you. That was her worst time, after Daddy died, that was bad, lots of men coming and going, lots of being drunk, lots of crying then and slapping us like it was all our fault, and I hated her so much! But I don't hate her now, I don't begrudge her nothing. What she did, I think I get it, I think I know why—when you love somebody that much, like she loved my dad, then when *they* go, your life is *over,* and even though she talked of the future, of us doing things for her to be proud of, I don't think she ever believed she would live to see it. I think she gave herself the cancer, she willed it to happen, so she could join him, so she could get the hell out of this stupid life! Oh God!"

Nancy weeps. Fat Stanley comes forward and puts his arm around her. He hands her a napkin. She blows her nose, she dabs at her eyes. Her eyes are puzzled. She glances at her mother silently smiling in the coffin. "I don't know where that came from," she says, as if to the corpse. "I don't know why I said it. I . . . sometimes I just wish a comet would come and smash this whole planet to pieces!" She turns to Fat Stanley, leans her cheek on his chest. "Can I go home, Uncle Stan?" she asks.

She and her sister and brother leave. Fat Stanley says he'll be right back, and he tells the mourners to stay and remember Helga. He and Ruby follow after the children. The bell tinkles, the door slams. There is a hush in the room, the mood is once again funereal. A minute passes in silence, then some people cough, some shuffle their feet. The short, wide woman is sobbing into her hands again. Everybody is looking at everybody else, wondering what to do. A few people are looking at the door.

"Well," says Henry Hank. "Well, flamin legs, youz noodles, are we going to party for the fem or not? Goddammit, Deadeye, make noise with that get-*tar.* Pass the booze! Let's go! Gimme some goddamn

Incorrigible Ike, somebody! Where's my horn? Shoulda brought my goddamn horn. *Saint Louie woman, wit youz di'mund ring!* Play, furface, play!"

Single-handed he breaks the ice. He gets Pirate playing the guitar again, gets him playing "Saint Louie Woman," gets the others to start drinking again, starts slapping butts and hollering and making eyes at all the pretty women. He grabs Beehive and makes her dance. They hop and bop as Pirate makes music and people clap and stomp their feet. The booze flows, the chatter returns. The short, wide woman turns into a linebacker and knocks people out of her way as she goes to the door shouting, "Disgraceful! Disgraceful!" She leaves and a few other sourpusses follow.

"Can't keep a good party down!" somebody shouts.

Someone gets to the stereo in the kitchen and turns it on, tunes it to a hard-rock station. Everybody who can starts dancing around the coffin, jostling it, making it shimmy as though Helga inside is feeling the rhythm and wants out. Pirate puts down his guitar and dances with Didi. They do a lot of groin bumping and leg twining, which makes Jasper more jealous the more he drinks. He knows he is drinking too much and that it will make him aggressive, but he doesn't care. He wants to dance too. He pulls Mary after him and makes fancy things happen with his legs, while she stands slightly swaying, not daring to get too rambunctious.

Fat Stanley and Ruby return. They get into the act, dancing round the coffin with everybody else. There is noise enough to wake Helga from her long sleep. Jasper half expects her to sit up and ask for a beer. He wonders what would happen if she did. Would they all run off screaming? Would they take her out and dance with her?

Later on, Henry Hank takes Jasper aside, into the kitchen, and talks to him about how bad the movie is going without him as ReemHerHole, and what does the Hank have to do to make things right again? Jasper tells him there's nothing he can do, there is no way Jasper John is going to play the role. No way.

Henry whines. He says that Deadeye ain't no ReemHerHole, the stupid sonofabitch can't speak verse and won't even shave off his beard, can you imagine ReemHerHole with that motherfucker's beard? Everything that's happened is all his fault, he started it, he brought out the Incorrigible Ike and they all got so drunk they didn't know what they were doing. The Hank would never betray his best pal in the world, not for a million bucks, but when the booze talks, what are you going to do? Flaming legs, once Didi gets wound up she really knows how to use it! She's the new JuleeTit, don't Jim want to ReemHerHole once more, please, oh please please!

"Nuts," says Jasper.

Henry squeezes him and coaxes him into taking another drink. Henry spins dreams of endless sex and bathtubs full of money, fast cars, houses with swimming pools, and he's trying to take Reem-HerHole there but ReemHerHole keeps backing up like a stubborn mule. He offers up Beehive as the Nurse in the threesome and hasn't ReemHerHole ever wanted to have two women at the same time? What red-blooded American male heterosexual don't want that, one to sit on his cock and one to sit on his face? "Is youz normal or not?" Henry puts on a stern look, eyebrows low, eyes focused and full of fire as if he is matching his will against Jasper's.

"Nuts," says Jasper.

"Look here, son, I'll drop Deadeye like a ton of turds, youz juss give the word, I'll send him packin, he's no good for us, he's no good for our future, youz and me, youz and me." Henry hangs on to his arm, keeps kissing him, hugging him, patting his butt. At one point he reaches between Jasper's legs and wants to know right now should he send Didi or Beehive back to take care of it?

Jasper's head is becoming light as dust. Henry is confusing him, making him want to be two people, the one who plays ReemHerHole and the one who is above all that. "I want to be better," he says softly. "I don't want to live that way no more."

"Say what?" says a tearful Henry, hugging him, practically slobbering on him. "Oh, Jim, youz is the best motherfuckin child this sonofabitch has ever known. The Hank done never love nobody like he loves youz, Jim. Now, goddammit, do what I say! Youz fuckhead, come here. Let me show youz somethin. Jesus Christ, the things I have to do to spread a little lightment."

Henry drags Jasper out of the kitchen and shows him Pirate and Didi clasped together like Siamese twins dancing on the floor. "Look at that goddamn Deadeye, look at that sonofabitch practically boppin your broad standin up on the floor. Ain't he got no shame? If that was my pussy I'd kick his ass. Youz understand my philosophics, Jim? Youz gonna let that happen? Youz gonna let him be the ReemHer-Hole?"

"The dirty bastard," says Jasper, his soul flooding with hot jealousy.

"Amen."

Jasper watches Didi and Pirate. They are crushed against each other and grinding. Jasper is sick with covetousness. She is Pirate's girl now, but he can't get used to the idea. Pirate has a hand on her ass, she has a hand on his ass. Very possessive.

Henry says, "That whozit can't speak the words trippingly. He ain't a true artist like youz."

"She's my girl, she's my girl," says Jasper.

"Amen, Jim, hallelujah."

"Mine," says Jasper.

"If youz a man, youz will," whispers Henry in his ear. "Woman needs to know who's boss. They respect that."

The gauntlet is down. *If you're a man, you will.* He has heard it before, an echo from the past, from a place that put high premiums on manhood, the warrior gone to fight for his country, the blessed savior of Mom and apple pie.

"I'll straighten out his IQ," says Jasper.

"That's my Reem," says Henry.

When Didi puts Pirate's finger into her mouth and bites it, Jasper can't stand *no more.* He shrieks, "Dog of the hair that bit you, you bassard!" A stream of cussing explodes from his mouth. He rushes toward Pirate, leaps at him, finds himself knocked sideways and slithering over the floor, banging into legs, people falling over him. He hears screaming. He hears the bellowing of a bull.

Looking out from between a pair of thrashing legs draped over his head, he sees Henry and Pirate slamming into each other, fists flying, head-jarring blows landing, blood flying from Pirate's nose. Their arms are churning like windmills. Huge, clubby fists drum away, keeping the beat to the stereo playing Stevie Ray Vaughan's "Testify." The mourners have backed up to give them room. They wail away, their faces full of fire and hatred. Both men are panting. Pirate is spitting blood. Henry is winning, but he is tired, both are tired, neither will go down. Pirate connects with an uppercut that snaps Henry's head back. Henry returns with a sweeping right to the head. He kicks Pirate in the knee. Pirate lunges forward, butting Henry in the chest and knocking him against the coffin. They wrestle. Legs and arms entwining, they look for a moment like lovers about to kiss. Both men coiled together smash into the coffin again. The end table collapses, the coffin drifts toward the end, then pitches sideways and falls over, ejecting Helga. Women scream as the coffin makes a complete roll, depositing Helga on the floor and landing right side up with a profound thud. Helga is beside the coffin, face down, her nose pressed against the tile, the split in her dress showing up the middle, the Bible peeking out from under her ribs. Fat Stanley muscles his way between Henry and Pirate and breaks them apart. Henry gets in a last kick at Pirate, Pirate kicks air in return. Someone shouts, "Turn off that goddamn music!"

The music is turned off.

"Jesus Christ, look at this!" says Fat Stanley. "Jesus Christ, will you look at this! What the hell is the matter with you blighters? Look what you've done, look at it!" His beard, his whole head is shivering with indignation. Ruby stands in a corner looking glumly at the scene. Mary is sitting in a booth with her head in her hands. Didi is behind the counter, her eyes just above the rim looking drastic.

Fat Stanley shakes his finger at Pirate and Henry, who are regarding the damage they've done. "Nobody has any respect for anything, that's the trouble, not even for the dead! Look at poor Helga!"

Dutifully all eyes turn toward Helga, who is showing them her hard ass as if it is her last statement on things. Her nose is still pressed to the tile. Her elbows too. Henry gets down on all fours and crawls over to her, turns her over. Pats her chest, straightens her dress. He picks her up. Jasper reaches to help, takes her cold ankles, and together they deposit her back in the coffin. They tuck her skirt underneath once more and put the Bible beneath her hands. Henry smooths her tufts of hair back. "She looks none the worse for wear," he says.

"What the hell happened?" says Fat Stanley.

Henry points at Pirate. "Playin with her ass," he says.

"So what?" says Pirate. He is sitting on a stool wiping his face with a wad of napkins.

"I'll drive your nuts into your nose!" threatens Henry. "Rubbin it in there, right in front of my ReemHerHole. This fur-face sonofabitch is fuckin up my movie." He shakes his fist at Pirate.

"It's my movie as much as yours," says Pirate.

"Give the fem back to the kid," commands Henry.

"Kiss my ass," answers Pirate, showing Henry the finger.

"Lousy verse reader."

"Stupid director."

Henry turns to Jasper and tells him to sock the whozit and take Didi back. "Women respect that," he reminds him.

Spotting Didi behind the counter, Jasper snorts disdainfully. "Slut," he says.

"Drunken bum," says Didi. "Loser!"

Mary is beside Jasper. She takes his hand and tugs at him. "We're going home," she says. "Take me home. I don't feel good." Jasper notices the bluish ring around Mary's mouth again. Her skin looks clammy. He no longer feels drunk. He no longer feels anything for Didi. He turns his back on her. Gratefully he allows Mary Quick to lead him away, outside into the drizzle.

"This is just what I needed," she says, putting her face up to catch the rain.

Pit, pitter, pat—cool, moist it falls, knocking down the sewer stench, turning the dusty streets and sidewalks into ringlets of thin mud swirling around their feet. They cross the street and go by the derelict car and the two men still sitting at the curb, slump-shouldered, their heads down now, looking as if they are just too tired to move. One holds out his hand, says, "Change?"

The other says, "Vets."

"They look so tired," says Mary, regarding them with melancholy eyes.

"Who isn't?" says Jasper. He feels not only sober but deeply depressed again. Stopping for a moment, he clears his pockets of change, drops the change into the outstretched hand. Mary fishes for some coins in her pocket, drops them into the open palm. "God bless you," she says.

"Have a nice day," says the man.

Bluegrass sounds drift from Texas Style. Someone laughs. Someone says, "I told her, here eat this!" and there is more laughter. Under the buzzing Narcissus sign, the triangular marquee, it is dry and they pause a moment at the entrance, looking toward the ticket booth, where a young man with buzzed hair, an earring in his left ear, and a tiny tuft of chin beard sits behind the glass reading a comic book. The entrance exhales an odor of popcorn. They pass on and go by the video store and the bookstore and the corner drugstore, where they turn for home.

When they get inside, Jasper asks if he should phone the doctor, but Mary says no, she just wants him to stay with her a while and see if anything happens. She takes another pill, slips it under her tongue. She unwraps her braid, gets a towel, and dries her hair.

In the bedroom she undresses and puts on a robe and lies on the bed, propped on the pillows. Jasper sits at the edge. He removes his tie. He wipes his face with his shirttail. He apologizes for starting the fight, but she waves him off. She says she's seen a thousand brawls in her day. She says that most men are too stupid to live.

After a pause she says, "And most women too. A plague on both their houses."

She looks at the weeping Madonna portrait. She says, "I want to tell the truth now."

"What truth?" Jasper says.

"I am an old lady," she says, her smile quivering.

"You're not old," he tells her. He knows that fifty-two is called "middle age," which is not supposed to be *old;* but it does seem old to him, and she looks every day of it, definitely. She looks older, much older, her eyes especially.

"Open that drawer," she says, pointing to the nightstand next to the bed. Inside the drawer, he finds a shoebox, which he hands to her. She opens it, she shows him her keepsakes. He sees: a dried horny toad, a silver horse, a lock of blond hair, a red kidney bean, a miniature plastic 1964 Corvette, a hairbrush, and a newspaper article yellowed with age. One by one she picks up each memento and explains it. The horny toad was J.J.'s pet, which he kept even after it died, letting it mummify in the sun, the silver horse used to sit in the window and J.J. would turn it to divert sunbeams into the room, the lock of hair was from his first haircut, he had once shoved the kidney bean up his nose, and it took three men holding him down and a pair of tweezers to get the bean out, the Corvette was from a collection of dream cars he had put together, the hairbrush was the one he used to brush his mother's hair at night, he would do a hundred strokes, he would make her hair crackle and shine.

Unfolding the article, she hands it to Jasper. The article is short and to the point:

SAILBOAT CAPSIZES, BOY MISSING

Ten-year-old Jimmy Jack Quick is presumed drowned after his sailboat capsized in high winds on Long Lake. His mother, Mary Quick, was with him. She managed to swim to shore in the freezing waters. Mary Quick says her son was right behind her. She does not know where he went down. Searchers continued to drag the water throughout the day, but no body has been recovered yet. The search will resume tomorrow.

Mary tells Jasper that the searchers never found the body. She says that everyone blamed her for what happened, said bad things to her, said that she should have stayed by J.J. and hung on to the boat until rescue came. It was a rented boat and someone would have come for them after their two hours were up. But those who said she should have stayed with him at the boat didn't know what they were asking. The water was freezing cold, she was freezing to death, her son was freezing to death. The water was *cold*.

She presses her temples. "Nobody knows nothing," she says. She puts the mementos away. Then she tells him that she is the world's biggest coward. Jasper tells her that drowning is a quick death, once you've taken that first breath—or so he's heard. She grunts as if she is in pain. She calls herself a coward again.

"Why do you say that?" he asks. "What could you have done?"

"Because I killed him," she says.

"No," he says. "It was an accident."

She says, "You don't know."

And she proceeds to tell him the story. As she tells him the story, this is what Jasper sees—he sees a gray lake brittle with cold, he sees the two of them on the lake, skimming over the water in full sail, J.J. at the tiller, bold J.J., ten years old and a daredevil sailor, experienced in the ways of water and sail, finessing the rudder so that the wind blows full against the sheet, stretches it to capacity and sends the little boat flying across the water at a crazy angle, practically lying on its side, until somewhere, somehow, *it is* on its side and going over, and the sail hits the water, the mast snaps, the bow digs in and the stern swings round, then crashes into the water and settles low. J.J. and Mary are thrown clear. They go under, fight for air and light, come up gasping, horrified, not believing that what has happened *has happened*. Both swim to the overturned boat and cling to its side. They look around, they look at the

301.

serrated line of trees, dark as ink blots and far away, trees and shore an impossible distance. No one is out on the gray lake but them. Mary tells him to hang on to the boat and someone will come, someone at the rental office will miss them eventually. They tread water and hold to the side of the boat, and she keeps saying it will be all right, someone will come, don't be afraid, J.J. Mommy is here. Her teeth are chattering, her feet are numb. Her hands have little feeling. J.J. is blue with cold. He hunches into her and she puts her arm around him, feels him trembling, hears him complaining of the cold, hears him asking, *Where are they? Where are they?* Waves lap against the hull, lap against their faces, air and water mixing in their mouths, getting sucked into their lungs, forcing them to cough and cough, the weight of the water tries to drag them down, their muscles are already tired, nerves are screaming, panic is rising, water keeps slopping into J.J.'s mouth, he keeps spitting and coughing, and when he can speak he keeps saying, *Mama, Mama.* She pulls his leg up and unlaces his shoe, does the other shoe, pulls his pants down and struggles to get them off, gets him out of his jacket, then gets *her* out of *her* shoes and pants and jacket, gets the waterlogged weight off and thinks for a moment in her new freedom that she could make it to shore if it wasn't for him. *I'm freezing,* he says. He grabs her round the neck and presses against her, wraps his legs round her waist, he clings, he clings like a panicky kitten. She grips the boat with weary hands. *It's my fault,* he tells her. *No,* she tells him, *it was an accident, nobody's fault.* He whispers, *My fault.* This clinging state lasts for a long, long time, until her numb hands finally slip from the boat and they both go under, and then she goes insane, then she bullies him off her, pushing at his ribs, unpeeling his arms, his legs as he tries all the harder to cling, scratching her neck, her shoulders, her arms, as they go down, way down, down to where the water is even colder, darker, more terrifying. Hysterically she beats him away from her, shoves at him, kicks at him, claws her way upward. Breaking the surface she gasps, her lungs fill with air, her arms and legs flail. She coughs up water. The wind blows over her face again. Greedily she sucks at the wind. She lies on her back breathing through her mouth.

She looks for the boat. It is already far away. She looks for J.J. There is no J.J. She understands what she's done. She calls his name. She rolls over and stares into the water, sees nothing but murky darkness. She imagines his shoes still falling into the depths. For a few minutes she floats on her back, saying his name, telling him to answer her this minute or else, but she knows he can't answer, she knows she has kicked him into the deep, she knows she is a weakling and a coward, she knows a *real mother* would have saved her child or gone down with him. In great gulps she swallows the air, she can't help but be grateful for the air, she can't help feeling horrible about herself and grateful to be breathing. Something nudges her hand. There is a wild moment of hope. She draws her hand away, turns over in the water, half expecting to see her son, but it is the broken mast instead. She grabs it. And this is how she lives, she kicks her legs, she hangs on to the mast, and little by little she moves toward the shore, until at last her feet touch mud and she can crawl away, she can stagger to the road and walk toward the boathouse miles away, she in her bra and panties and the wind freezing her, until a man comes in a pickup who takes her in, a man who wraps his jacket around her and turns the heater on full blast as he races to the boathouse to spread the word.

Jasper digests the story. He looks at her, at her mouth moving, twisting like a snail eating salt. He remembers reading about a man who was dying of AIDS. He had lost control of his bladder and bowels. He had to take food through a tube. He reeked of rotting flesh. As the signs of death drew close, his friend asked him if he was reconciled to dying, and the man said no. The man wanted to live, even if it meant living in his own shit and stench, even if it meant living in his own shit naked on a ledge on a mountain somewhere miles above civilization all alone and always in pain—even then it would be enough just to be alive and not be forced into nothingness. Jasper understands him and understands Mary Quick. Jasper hopes that he will be brave when his turn comes, but he doesn't know for sure. He looks at Mary hiding her face and he wonders: If it was my kid pulling me down to drown, would I panic too,

303.

would I do *anything* to save my skin? Would I take life at *any* price, wallowing in my own shit on a narrow ledge?

"Damn these things that happen," he says.

Mary nods. She won't look at him.

"Moments of truth," he says. "That's the hard thing about it, to live with it. People say they'll be brave, but they don't know. Probably anybody would have done the same thing, Mary."

She shakes her head. She slides down and curls onto her side. He doesn't know what more to say. He doesn't even know how he really feels about it. He thinks he understands well enough, but he feels revulsion too. He doesn't want to touch her, but he touches her, he strokes her arm, her hip. He stays at the edge of the bed until she falls asleep.

Taking her keys from the dresser, he goes to the green door. When he opens it, he sees what he half expected to see, but still, like the sight of Helga in her coffin, it is a shock. It is a holy icon he sees, a relic, the lord himself, little J.J. Jimmy Jack dressed in a white robe and squatting on the floor like a Buddha.

Heart pounding so hard he can feel it in his ears, Jasper backs away and circles the table and takes deep breaths and glares wildly at the cubist painting, the fragmented woman on the dining-room wall. He is still circling the table when Henry Hank comes in, a bottle of Incorrigible Ike in hand. "Beehive wants to ride the Harley, Jim! I said I'd take her out! Gimme a key!"

Jasper tells him the key is in the ignition.

"She's got a plum ass, ain't she? Candy cherry nipples on her whim-whams, I sucked em in the storeroom," says Henry, cackling and leering. "Sucked em and put my finger up her snatch. Smell this!"

He holds his finger in front of Jasper's nose. Jasper smells Beehive's pussy. "Go ahead, youz can have a lick," says Henry.

Turning away, Jasper goes to the window and stares out at the gray clouds and the sheen of water over the eugenia berry bushes. "What's up?" says Henry. He starts forward, goes sideways, bounces into the

304.

wall and begs its pardon sincerely. Then he notices the closet door is open. "Ah, youz done seen the hank of hair, the piece of bone. Oh boopy doo, boopy doo, that's Oswald!"

Taking giant floppy steps, Henry goes to the door saying he wants to see the little booger in his finery, the little whozit noodle. "Flamin legs, ain't he ugly!"

Jasper crosses the room and looks too, picks up details he hadn't noticed before. There it is, all of it tucked into the recess of the closet, cross-legged on a huge red satin pillow. In front is a makeshift altar, a white board set on a pair of bricks. On the altar are two brass candleholders, with the stumps of burnt candles in them, and an image of a Celtic cross, the eternal ring going round and round its hub, done in Magic Marker on the board itself. J.J.'s blackened, noseless face is painted: white over the cracked eyelids, reddish orange over the lipless mouth, its yellowed teeth exposed, flesh tones over the leathery forehead and over the cheekbones. Some of J.J.'s hair is still there, a fine, dusty blond mop. Around his neck is a leather collar, which has been nailed to the wall to keep his head high. The walnut-colored face smirks at something only it knows.

"This is what she prays to," says Jasper.

Henry says, "To him, at him, up him, in him, over him. I seen her squat here for hours." He nudges Jasper with his elbow. "Can youz imagine how he smelled till his juices dried up, Jack? Pah! Pew! Dog mange and rotten eggs!"

"You were there, Henry?"

"I was there. I'll tell youz what, I fished this little bastard outta the lake. I'm the one that brought him up when none of them noodles could find him. Every fuckin day she has me go out in the boat with her and we search the lake, till finally I spots the whozit starin at us from under a drowned tree. I had to dive down and get him. Freezin fish farts, it damn near give me a heart attack." Henry crosses both hands over his heart. "Kids are such trouble," he adds.

He tells Jasper that they brought the corpse home and put it in the attic because Mary wouldn't hear of giving him to an undertaker. They were going to bury him, but she couldn't bring herself to do that either, and so for months they kept him wrapped in potash alum with a coat of lime on top, but he still stunk up the house. Finally when he was tolerable, Henry cleaned him up, broke his joints and screwed gate hinges into him, dressed him in a robe, gave him some makeup and a splash of perfume, and they took him with them wherever they went. He became a sort of mascot to Henry, a sort of holy presence to Mary.

"Look, he's just like a puppet," says Henry. And he shows how J.J.'s limbs can move, and where the hinges are on the inside of his elbows and his hips and his knees.

"She's crazy," says Jasper. "You're crazy too."

"Whole fuckin world's crazy," Henry says. "And so fuckin what? Whatever it takes to get youz from point A to point XYZ, I'm sayin whatever it takes is your goddamn bisness. What was I spose to do, force her to bury the little pecker? She was three-fifths candidate for the freak farm already. Takin him away would've been like takin a poodle from an old lady who calls it Fifi. It's all some of em have to live for, you know."

"I would have."

"Youz don't know Punkin, buddy."

"I'd have just done it and to hell with it."

"Youz would, huh? People always know so goddamn much about how other people should live their lives."

"I would, man. I mean, no wonder she's having heart attacks at fifty-two. I don't know what you've been thinking, Henry, but this whole thing is just too sick for words. I mean, look at him, he looks like a mummy, an Egypt mummy, man. If you're not crazy already, staring at him, praying *to* him is bound to make you so. The freak farm, man, is right here." He indicates the corpse. He indicates the house.

Henry shoves Jasper into the door and yells at him, says, "It weren't my idea! Given my druthers he be six feet under twenty-two years ago! Little buggery bastard, I never liked him no way!"

Jasper is disgusted with Henry and with the gnarled thing in the closet. He wonders if there are any people left in the world who aren't freaks. Some way or another there is no longer any such thing as normal—everyone is freakish. Was it the way the world was going, or was it just natural, something you found out as you got older? He doesn't know. No doubt everybody thinks he, Jasper John, is a freak too.

"We ought to bury him," he tells Henry.

"Is that your bisness? Who're youz to say what's right? Flamin fuckin legs, Jim, ain't he valid?"

"He's dead, Henry."

"So's Jesus fuckin Christ, so's Buddha and Mohammed, so's the mother of God, but people still pray to them whozits, and to the teeth of saints . . . and people still make miracles with splinters of the cross and bones of this guy and that guy . . . so why not this hand-me-down?"

"Sick. *Sick.*"

"Aw, crap, nothin is sick but thinkin it so, Jim. Ain't youz learned it's the comfort that counts? Here, have a slug of Ike, and the little bastard will look better to youz."

"Leave me alone," Jasper tells him. He goes outside, out behind the garage, where the shovel is, where he buried Lummox's headless rat.

He is about to dig a hole in the soft mud of the garden to bury J.J. when suddenly he hears Henry bellowing like a man sliding down a razor. Jasper throws down the shovel and races inside. He finds Henry at the table jabbing his forehead with a dinner fork. He is hitting himself hard enough to make droplets of blood appear. Jasper grabs his arm and jerks the fork away.

"What the hell, Henry?"

"Don't gimme no shit!" says Henry.

He stands up. He takes a swing at Jasper, misses him, whirls side over, and slams to the floor. From there he looks up at the ceiling, toward heaven, shakes his fist and shouts, "I fucked yer mother! I fucked yer mother! Youz flamin faggot ecclesiastical mutt! I fucked yer mother!" He looks at Jasper. "Put it in my neck, Jim. Right here, get the jugular, be a pal."

"What, what, what!"

"Go on see." He points toward the bedroom. "My Punkin is dead. That's my signal. Good enough, good enough, I say. I'm comin, Pun-*king*. I told her I would. Lived long enough, I'm comin!"

Jasper finds Mary still on her side, her head resting on her arm, face slack, peaceful. She looks dead. He kneels down and listens for air coming through her nose . . . and it does come. He puts his ear on her back and hears her heart beating.

"She ain't dead," he says. "What the hell you talkin about? Jesus fuck, Henry, you scared the shit outta me."

"She ain't?" Henry comes in and puts his ear where Jasper indicates. He listens. He grins sheepishly. "Ain't I the noodle?" he says. "But I shook her, man, I shook her and yelled and tried to get her to wake up and she don't do nothin but look dead as a doornail."

"Yeah, well, she's alive, Henry. It's the sleep of exhaustion you're looking at."

"Well, that's good, that's better. One corpse a day is enough." He jumps off the bed and heads toward the back door. He tells Jasper the poontang won't keep. Jasper tries to stop him, but Henry says, "Smell my finger, and then youz tell me youz wouldn't follow it up."

"Not on my motorcycle," says Jasper. "It's wet outside and you're drunk."

Henry taps the side of his head and says he has special talents, radar kind of talents that make it okay to drive when he's drunk. Jasper pushes at him and says no, but Henry isn't listening. "Youz would keep me from that pussy?" he growls.

"Come on, Henry."

"Double-crosser!" Henry slams his fist into Jasper's belly, knocks the wind out of him. Jasper backs away, leans against the kitchen sink, fighting for that first breath of air, and by the time he gets it, Henry is out the door, on the motorcycle, and spinning across the lawn. Jasper hurries after him, his heart hammering like the wings of a humming-bird. He climbs into Agnes and takes off after Henry. They race around the back streets and up alleys, Henry looking over his shoulder and grinning, making Jasper gnash his teeth in rage. They fly past Fat Stanley's and see Beehive beneath the awning, waiting for Henry, but him not stopping, going left instead at the corner and hanging a knee-dragging right round the cloverleaf entrance to the freeway, where he cranks the Harley open and weaves in and out of the cars as he changes lanes. Jasper can't catch up. He sees Henry far in front of him, gliding along like a skater on ice.

Henry toys with Jasper, letting him come up alongside, the rain pattering Henry's face while he laughs and hollers something that Jasper can't hear, then pulls away, then eases up again, grins his unicorn grin, hollers "Flamin legs!" followed by more words Jasper doesn't understand, and Jasper is snarling, growling, cussing under his breath, and wondering what he's doing chasing this fucking old man on this fucking freeway full of fucking cars and fucking rain spattering every fucking thing, fucking water rising like a mist behind the tires of cars and trucks and all over the windshield and the limping wipers hardly keeping up, leaving streaks behind as they whip from side to side, and it's getting dark too, and aw, fuck it, let the stupid old fart go, who cares. *Who cares, you stupid old fart!*

Jasper can't stand no more. Old Agnes, valves banging like tin sticks, smoke pouring from the exhaust, the front wheels shimmying so hard he can barely hang on to the steering wheel, is no match for the motorcycle. He lets up on the gas a bit and the shimmying stops. He turns on his lights. He sees Henry not too far in front of him, still weaving in and out of traffic, looking back, taunting the drivers.

Up ahead some few yards is this Ford Pinto with the passenger-side window down and a pair of bare feet sticking out in the rain, the rain washing the feet and the feet rubbing against each other. Pretty feet, girl's feet, Jasper decides immediately. He watches Henry glide by a car behind the Ford and come into Agnes's lane, up beside the wiggling feet, in close enough to reach out and give them a tickle. His fingers reach out and touch the toes. The girl jerks back, the Ford rocks a bit, rocks just enough to lean on the Harley and make it wobble. Henry is cracking the throttle, trying to steady out the bike, but the motor is roaring and the clutch isn't clutching, and in the instant that the bike needs to leap away, it doesn't. The wobble worsens, sending Henry into the side of the Ford, sending Henry up and into the air. It is just bam-bam how the whole thing happens, and there he is upside down, flying in front of Jasper, in the headlamps, like a big bat, his face looking toward the car, the unicorn tooth, the wide mouth, the dark dots forked across his brow, the jug ears flapping—all of it frozen for a split second of time-stop, then *whoosh,* he is gone, he and the Harley are tumbling along the concrete, skittering like a Frisbee, until they hit the edge of the freeway and tumble into mud.

Several cars pull over and people leap out, people run to help. Jasper gets there first. Henry looks like a pile of rags. Jasper yells into his face, "Henry! Henry!" and the old man looks up at him, eyes blinking like he's waking from a long sleep.

"Flamin legs," he whispers. "That fuckin flamin clutch. What youz do now, Jim?"

Jasper tells him not to talk, tells him everything is going to be all right, tells him he is sorry about the clutch. "Don't die, Henry!" he shouts when Henry closes his eyes.

The eyes snap open and a look of scorn crosses his face. "I ain't dyin, youz whozit. Take more than a goddamn Pinto and a swim across concrete to kill the Hank. Get my lawyer. I'm gonna sue that flamin jackass of a driver. Youz saw what he done to me."

The driver, standing behind Jasper, says, "You seen what he did? He grabbed Debbie's feet, and when she pulled away, she hit my arm, that's why I hit him! I didn't mean to! It just happened!" He is a thin, gawky kid with a wispy mustache, and he looks scared to death.

The barefoot girl stands beside him, wearing cutoffs and a man's undershirt, little wet breasts poking against the material. She looks no more than twelve or thirteen years old. She says, "He tickled my feet, he tickled my feet, did you see that? He tickled my feet." She looks down at her feet as if they might confirm her story.

"That's the dumbest thing I ever saw," says a man who is leaning over, hands on knees, staring into Henry's face.

Henry's voice is even more raspy than usual. He says, "Who asst youz? Fuck off, noodle. Let a man die in peace."

"Is he drunk?" asks someone in the gathering crowd.

"Got to be," says the man looking into Henry's face. The man sniffs, says he smells alcohol.

"Fuck off," croaks Henry.

"Was it a joke?" asks the boy with the wispy mustache.

Blood is seeping from beneath Henry's hips and legs. His legs are twisted at odd angles. One foot is on backwards. A pointed piece of thigh bone sticks through his pants. His hips look shifted like a fullback trying to avoid a tackle. The rain has washed most of the dye from his beard and hair, creating black rivulets running into the ground. His shirt is shredded over his arms and shoulders, pieces of it trail from beneath his back, it is ripped open over his chest. Amid the tatters, Jasper can see the blurred tattoo over his heart that says MOTHER, and the panther, the naked woman, the BORN TO WIN, the dice rolled seven on his left arm. On his right biceps is another fading tattoo that says SEMPER FI. His white belly rises like a snow cone in the air, his belly button and the chips in his skin are filled with water.

"Somethin's startin to hurt," he whispers. "My back don't feel good."

Jasper asks him if he can feel his legs, and he says no, he feels nothing below the waist. Jasper asks him if he can move his legs, and he says no. His back feels like a cat's been at it, trying to flay the skin off, he says. Some ribs feel broken, the ribs are making it hard to breathe, he says.

Somebody brings a blanket and covers Henry. A few of the people mumble in groups and point to the motorcycle forming a triangle of parts on the side of the hill. Jasper stays by Henry, while Henry closes his eyes and goes to sleep and makes faces, makes throaty, mewing sounds and little grunts and groans. It crosses Jasper's mind that he should drive off and disappear. Go back to Colorado and hang out. Or join the exodus of Californians going north. Go to Seattle. Or north to

Alaska. Or maybe join the Marines, who need a few good men. This California experiment hasn't worked out so well, he thinks.

Sirens wail in the distance. Red lights flash.

He doesn't commit himself when the police and the ambulance arrive. While they are taking down names of witnesses, he slips away and watches from the car as the medics attend to Henry. They ease him onto a stretcher, strap him down, take him away. The Harley sits leaking gas and oil on the side of the hill. A cop goes over to it and writes something down, which Jasper assumes is the license plate number. Jasper doesn't think they can trace the Harley to him. He never registered it, and it still has the ancient 1968 Colorado tag on it. Another cop is talking to the boy with the wispy mustache and to her-of-the-feet, Debbie. He is writing down what they say. The boy keeps gesturing how Debbie hit his arm. Debbie keeps looking at her feet, lifting them, showing the bottoms one by one, pointing to the exact spot.

When Jasper gets back to the house, he goes inside and tears loose the collar holding Jimmy Jack to the closet wall, carries him airy as a basketball to the garden. The porch light illuminates his efforts as he digs a hole beneath the apple tree, its gnarled apple and a gathering of blossoms looking on. He makes a hole about three feet deep, into which he tumbles the body, hastily covers it up, hastily stomps the muddy earth in and piles more on and stomps that in too. When he is satisfied, he replants the flowers. As an afterthought, he grabs the last old apple from the tree and fires it into the mud, grinds it with his heel. Then he stands for a moment, head bowed, letting the rain wash over him, not praying but feeling like he should either shake his fist and curse God or fall on his knees and beg for mercy. He does neither.

Afterwards he goes inside, strips and takes a scalding shower, puts on fresh underwear, and climbs into bed with Mary and the three grays. He lies there staring at the ceiling, his eyes hot, his mind hovering over the irony of lying beside the one with the Liberty Bell heart, who gave all kinds of signals this day about dying, was thought dead by

312.

Henry, but didn't die, and the other one who seemed so indestructible, so fiery, so immortal that nothing disabling could ever happen to him, but who is now either dead or crippled forever, those twisted legs, the warped hips, the paralysis—Henry Hank the pretzel, the *kontortionist*. Who would have thought it up, that kind of ending to a wake? Not Jasper John. If there is one thing he's learned, it is that nothing in life turns out the way you think it will, not in its essential details. Upside down, Jasper sees him, his face gaudy as a cartoon, the Hank taking his outrageous individuality to its ultimate glory. Jasper closes his eyes against that final prank, those fingers tickling the soles of Debbie's feet, and he calls Henry a whozit, a noodle, and a damn flamin old fool.

"Them's *my* philosophics, oh urban mystery," he says.

Outside, Lummox calls, and scrapes his claws against the screen. Jasper gets up, lets him in, dries him with a towel, carries him back to bed. Lummox doesn't bother to run the three grays off. They declare a truce and all settle together against the cold, rainy weather.

The rain falls outside, coming down harder with the night, drumming heavier and heavier against the roof and the window. The Harley-Davidson is no more. Henry Hank is no longer a temptation. Fat Stanley and Ruby have paired off, as has Pirate and Didi. Helga has been to her last party. Nobody stays still, nobody can be counted on to be the same from one day to the next. They scatter their notes as they please, playing the tune that tickles their fancy. And yet all their music, all their frenzy, seems to boil down to one thing, and that is their need to find somebody with enough voodoo to get this suffocating world off their backs, make some room at least to live. That's all we're asking here, a little time and a little room to breathe and a bit of loving mixed in. Seems simple enough, seems like we're not asking too much. So why is it so hard to do? He answers himself lamely: Life, he says, it's just life. He doesn't know when he's ever felt more dissatisfied and he wonders if all life really has to offer is hooks and jabs, and now and then a swift ecstasy, a swift happiness, *a day of gold out of an age of iron.* If that's all there is, then a fellow might as well be dead, might as well just kill himself, circumvent the jokester. No wonder people drop their reason like a bad habit in order to believe in something in the sky that knows when sparrows fall. Anything else is ludicrous.

Above him, upside down, Henry's bat-winged soul beckons, and he takes a moment to appraise the meaning of the man, tells himself that at least the old fool did it his way, lived life giving and taking no quarter, shaking his fist at authority, going all out, hell-bent, and damn the consequences. Jasper wonders if he has that kind of moxie. He touches his genitals, weighs them in his fingers, tells himself that probably Freud was right and it all begins and ends there, and everything else is pretense, a mask, a mere fiction. He remembers what Godot said about women expecting men to pay for the sins of their fathers. Godot had taken it to heart, had wounded the offending appendage that causes all the world's women's woes. Godot had tried to sacrifice himself for mankind. What he didn't understand was that mankind needed no sacrifice. Never would. And that women were creating fairy tales if they ever thought men would let themselves be punished for what they or their fathers had done to mothers and wives and sisters and daughters and girlfriends and— Maybe a few Godots would fall. But not the vast majority, not the Henry Hanks of this world, not the Jasper Johns and the Pirates and—

Rain rushes against the window, beats against the walls and roof. Lummox purrs beneath his hand. Mary snores softly. He can see the outline of the weeping Madonna on the wall. All around him there are no compromises. There is nothing left to do—nothing left but to *play out the play.*

12. TENDER MERCIES

Sensitive, down-to-earth young man looking for love and longtime relationship with woman whose feelings are compatible. If you've asked the
questions raw and sown your wild oats and are tired of guessing who's
who and are ready for a mate who believes that one is known by action,
not words, and that the point of life is life itself, and the hope of life is to
find something of value worth struggling for, write J.J. in care of Adam
and Eve Possibilities. All races, creeds, colors will be considered.

More than a year has gone by since Helga's wake. Jasper is still in San
Diego. He thinks he will do Seattle *someday*, or join the Marines
maybe, but right now he is content to stay with Mary Quick. She needs
him. And oddly enough, he thinks he needs her. He doesn't know why
exactly, why he should need a semi-invalid, decaying old lady with a
parchment-paper heart. It has nothing to do with reason—reason tells
him to get a degree, find a career, get money in his purse, invest,
consume. Jasper realizes that sticking with Mary is a result of following
his feelings. He's been around long enough to know that following
one's feelings is a surefire way of ruining one's life. But there it is, he's
only *human*.

Today has all the signs of being one of Mary's good days. She has
more and more of them as the months roll on. She never mentions
what happened to Henry or her dead son. She no longer talks about
her unfortunate past. It is enough that she has Jesus and a spanking
new Bible and a Church of the Resuscitated within walking distance of

home. She no longer lies listening to her heart beat and wondering if she will catch the moment it quits on her. She is down to an average of one nitroglycerin pill a day, and sometimes she doesn't even need that. Her life has settled into a routine of prayer and soap operas and cooking for Jasper when he's home.

On Saturday afternoons she and Jasper usually go to the Narcissus to see a film, then he goes to work, and at ten o'clock she will join him at Fat Stanley's Steak and Chops for a late meal. On Sundays she attends church, she sings, she talks to the nicely scrubbed people about the Lord, and she comes home to baseball on TV and preparing a nice dinner for herself and Jasper. Afterwards she might read more of his manuscript if he wants her to. Jasper has stumbled onto an *ambition* at last. Didi left her typewriter behind when she vanished, and Jasper has taught himself to type with two fingers. Now he thinks he might want to tell the world about Henry and Godot and Helga et al. Mary thinks he might have promise as a writer, though she often urges him to cut back on the descriptions of sex in his book. Really his words are far too earthy, far too graphic. They make her very uncomfortable, words like pussy, cock, cunt, fuck, prick, suck, anal, asshole, semen, and so on. She tells him it is painful for the newly purified of soul to read such words. She is now the pure of soul. He says they are only words, not fangs to bite people. She wishes Godot would talk to the boy about this preoccupation with sex and its hard-core descriptions, but Godot mostly keeps to himself in the room in the garage, keeps to his quest, and rarely talks to anybody. He has rejected those outside the pearly gates who have rejected him.

Jasper found him one day last fall in the park. Long since released from the hospital, he was idling on the grass, looking thinner than ever, and very soiled, but essentially the same. He greeted Jasper as if they had parted only moments before, saying, "You've seen how they beat me, how I'm reviled and rejected everywhere. It's a vicious, silly lot of morons we've created, son."

Jasper nodded in agreement.

Godot said, "Well, as you age, you begin to care less and less about them. When you're young you care. When you're old you don't care so much. I don't understand where the caring capacity goes. Do you know?"

"It wears out," said Jasper.

"It wears out. Yes, it turns into bits of paper whirled by the cold wind. Who said that?"

"I don't know."

"Do you know how I pee now? I sit down like a girl. How poetically appropriate, don't you think?"

"I guess so."

"Justice."

"Yes."

"My penis is fine, a tiny scar on the side is all, but my prostate is bad. If I sit on the toilet, it relaxes my prostate a bit and I pee better. I tell you, son, a cock and its equipment have always been more trouble than they're worth."

Godot was homeless, so Jasper brought him back to the house and the old man went straight to the garage and has stayed there ever since. He spends his mornings tending the garden, the lawn, the hedges, the apple tree. He was somehow able to nurse the few walnut-sized apples of summer into respectable shape, and in November some were as plump as a fist. In January he pruned the tree back, and now it is full of blossoms and emotional bees. The garden itself is a mass of flowers and roaming insects. Godot has the farmer's touch, the green thumb.

When he isn't tending the grounds, he is inside the garage writing with a fine-point pen on the unpainted drywall. Under the heading in huge letters I AM THAT I AM, Godot writes tiny words on the drywall. He says he is looking for *the* word, the *kinetic* word, the *tactile* word, the *combustible* word, and when he finds it he is going to use it to undo all he has done, going to deconstruct and reconstruct, going to dissolve and resolve. He will use this ultimate Word to cease being and begin over again, from scratch. He is certain he can do a better job next time. He has learned from his mistakes.

During the week, Mary and Jasper have a morning routine. She

317.

gets up and makes him breakfast. He eats, then he sits a while after-wards, drinks coffee, reads the morning paper. Then he goes to work. Jasper works two jobs now. From seven to three-thirty he works for the hospital, in the warehouse, filling supply orders for the nurses and receiving shipments.

When things are slow at midafternoon, he sits at his desk and reads novels and tries to figure out how writers do it. Some, he notes, are *stylists*. Some of the stylists are very good. He knows he can never match them, not in a million years, but that's okay. He'll take whatever comes. He just hopes it means something now and then, all the words he puts in rows. He hopes it communicates a piece of truth now and then. He likes open-eyed writers, the kind who find humor in the follies of this world. He likes detail and spice and sometimes a certain amount of *ambiguity,* vaguely untidy bows that need straightening. He doesn't read Shelley anymore. Shelley is too demanding, too philo-sophic, too much like a fanatical preacher beating the twin drums of social decay and immorality. And besides, Shelley reminds him of lost love, of Didi.

In poetry his tastes run to plainspeakers. Those who write about their *real* lives in plain language and with no apology, which is what he wants to do. He realizes the irony of this, that it has made him into the thing he disliked about Didi. It has made him a *confessionist*. He doesn't care. In the process of learning to write, he has also learned that everything written, even "true" confession, is fiction, is, ultimately, a *lie*. But at least lying confessions are fun, are full of blood and bones and bodily fluids. And besides, his life, filtered as it is through his own sluggish understanding, is all he really knows. He understands now what Didi was doing, and he wishes he had paid more attention to what her poems were saying. Maybe it was something important. Maybe. Maybe.

Jasper is too busy for college, which he thinks is probably a waste of time for a writer anyway. He thinks Didi Godunov was probably right, that a writer needs to have experiences and to read and write, that's all. He is trying to get everything down before he forgets the relevant details. It isn't easy to find the time. After his hospital hours, he works at Fat Stanley's from six to ten, with only Sundays off now. Fat Stanley had to go to a six-day workweek and cut expenses to deal with the rising costs of his new family, Ruby and the three Helga orphans, and with a lawsuit from Capon Enterprises, which is asking damages for nonperformance of a contract. When Fat Stanley decided he was staying put, he called the realtor and told him the deal with Capon was off. The realtor told him there would be penalties, that one did not do this sort of thing to a man as important as Capon.

Beehive and Ruby have stayed with Fat Stanley. Beehive has taken a cut in wages. Ruby works for tips. Helga's three kids come in and help out after school and on Saturdays too. Things are going as well as can be expected. Fat Stanley doesn't make any promises or predictions about tomorrow. Today, now, the present tense, is enough, he keeps saying.

Jasper often visits Henry in the Veterans Home. Henry is a paraplegic, but he can get by with leg braces and wrist crutches. Shuffling himself over the grounds in a twisty orangutanian sort of way, he gets around the sprawling complex well enough to drive some of the staff crazy.

He has his horn, and he has put together a jazz band. There is a tenor sax and an alto sax and a piano player. This little group of musicians monopolizes the recreation room. They call themselves the Second Coming. Henry says a few more practice sessions and he's going to get them a gig. Jasper has heard them play and he thinks they're pretty good, especially the fellow on tenor sax, who says he learned his style from Charlie Parker. Henry calls himself the Louie Armstrong of honkies. He says he's got a Cannonball Adderley on alto sax and an Oscar Peterson on piano. He says his band is pure nigger-cat groove beyond bebop in seventh-heaven-ebony jazz, and all it lacks is a drummer and a bass fiddle and Ella Fitzgerald's pipes. In due time it will all come, it will all happen, he says, because the Hank lives a charmed life —born to win, that's him.

The last time Jasper visited the home, Henry took him aside and showed him a screenplay. Over the past few weeks, Henry has been writing a porno film about prostitution inside the Veterans Home. Henry claims that some of the female staff are ready and willing to make extra income by pleasuring the old soldiers, and all they need is an organizer like himself. He says he can smell sexual frustration in the air and it's time somebody does something about it. Henry says he's going to get things hopping, put together a film crew and make a porno movie that will make every other porno movie look tame. The gimps that couldn't get laid before will get laid now because of his tender mercies toward them. He will fix up the gimps himself, and let some of them have it free, if they allow themselves to be filmed with naked secretaries in *flagrante delicto*. He says he has a large following in the home, ambulatory vets who want to be his film crew. He is known as the *auteur*. He has named his new film V *Spot*. He will use zoom lens and freeze frames as his *auteur* signature technique. He says he has "aesthetic authority." He talks about aesthetic authority, zoom lens and freeze frame, caressing the words with his voice as if they added up to something gigantic and mystical. He tells Jasper he is really into letting his actors emote. He wants emotion, primitive emotion. He wants the naturalism of extemporization. He says that V *Spot* is a breakthrough movie with a new twist—porno documentary. His advertisement will read THESE ARE NOT ACTORS—THIS IS REAL LIFE. He says real life is what people want; they want to be reminded of their common humanity, their solidarity—their crotch connection with their own species. Why else would they watch all these talk shows like *Donahue* and *Geraldo?* Henry asks.

Henry wants Jasper to pressure Godot into helping with the script, help fix it up a little. He wants Godot to come visit and talk it over. Henry knows that together he and Godot would make an unstoppable team. Flamin legs, they would rule the celluloid world!

And Henry has one extra scheme on the back burner. He talks to Jasper about a place in El Cajon, a jewelry store that would be a cinch to knock off, ten grand guaranteed! He hopes to catch the clap if he's lying. When Henry first told him of the vast possibilities for lucrative crime, Jasper laughed silently at the idea of a man with leg braces and crutches busting in on a jeweler and saying, "Stick em up!" But he didn't say no to Henry. He could see how happy it made him to believe in his limitless options. He allowed him to think his protégé would consider it. Rob a jewelry store? Get the big bucks? Why, maybe so, maybe so, Henry Hank.

The last time Jasper saw Pirate Pomegranate was nearly a year ago, at the Del Mar Fair. Pirate was walking past the booths hand in hand with some red-haired strutter femme fatale. When he saw Jasper, he made a gesture toward her, flinging his hand in front of her face and walking by crabwise, his back to Jasper, his hair providing a curtain behind which he hid his woman. It was as if he thought Jasper might try to steal her the way he, friend Pirate, had stolen Didi, but Jasper doesn't hold any grudges. None of that stuff matters now.

And as for Didi, it was mere coincidence that he saw her on television the first week of June. She was at a rock concert in Massachusetts being televised on MTV. It was raining and the crowd was getting soaked while the band played on. The camera did a close-up of Didi and some other girls standing beneath a giant piece of cardboard. There was no mistaking her. She wore one of those never-never-land dresses that make one think of gypsies wandering over the earth telling fortunes. On her head was a bright red bandanna, beneath which the tips of her ears showed dressings of golden bangles. On her finger, curling over the edge of the cardboard, was the silver roadrunner ring he gave her the night she wouldn't sit on his face. To Jasper she still looked like the hottest thing since Marilyn Monroe or Sophia Loren. A *woman all woman.* He told himself that no doubt she was out there gathering those experiences she needed to write verse which will devastate the world and win her the Pulitzer Prize and create her the third member of the coveted trinity—Plath and Sexton and Godunov.

Jasper stands behind Mary this morning as she sits at the table, and he brushes out and braids her hair, which is what he always does on Sundays before she goes to church. She says Jasper will acquire the church habit when he gets old and understands what a wisp of dust he is, but he doubts it. He's not sure where the spirit is, but he doesn't think the handbook atmosphere of the church is where you find it. He finds more of it in just doing her hair. He has learned the French braid, the under-and-under weave that looks dairy-maidish in the bright beams that come through the window and wash over her head. She has the most beautiful hair he has ever seen, strong as manila rope, glistening, healthy, and he loves the contact of his hands on it, how it crackles beneath the brush, how he can mold it into a cap of art.

She is reading his scribblings aloud as he does her hair, and it sounds to him like something all unique and full of biblical harmonies and hard knuckles of truth. He wonders if all writers feel like prophets. He can feel his ears munching on his own words as she reads them. He can hear himself roaring and saying things he didn't know he knew. Mary stops now and then to comment, to tell him if he is capturing the color and the form and the movement and the truth and, above all, the *passion* of what occurred. She gripes at him again for the gutter terms he uses to describe sex, and she says he exaggerates some events too much and others not enough, and sometimes he's not as honest as he could be; but all in all she believes he is getting the essence of the way things were, and maybe that's the best any writer can do, capture the essence and trust the reader to fill it out. Just don't give them no wacky writer's code, she tells him. One thing Jasper has found out about Mary, now that she isn't so sick anymore, is that she is a sensitive critic. Though about her complaints he tells her proudly that he must be true to himself, that he chooses his words with care, that he loathes euphemisms and so he strives to make his words say what he means them to say, and this is how he maintains a purity of spirit all writers should have, all writers who are not just diddlers, that is. He wishes sometimes that she would just tell him how wonderful he is and not be so picky and smart.

After Mary leaves for church, he will shower and shave, he will splash his face with Old Spice and put on tight jeans and a white undershirt. He is going over to Fat Stanley's for barbecue. Fat Stanley has introduced him to Nancy Martin. Jasper knows it is too soon to tell, but he has a feeling about this Nancy, that maybe she is the one. She has this small crimp in her brow that makes him feel she is the thoughtful type, like maybe she has important things to say and she's just waiting to see if he is worthy of hearing them.

Love, oh love.

And if Nancy's not the one? Jasper has a backup plan. He has put his own ad in the paper and he expects to get some letters any day now. He is keeping his eye on the other ads too, and there is this one that sounds promising. He may even date her in any case, just to see what's what:

Multicultural brunettish, 24, built to last, wants to meet 20-something, 6-footer, slim-bottom, 30-inch-waist man who is not inclined to moralize about the media's responsibility in creating an uncouth world. Bohemian tendencies a plus. So is a face that won't give me indigestion. I am pro-Beethoven & Rousseau; pro-love & experienced in ways of same, but don't sleep around unless I'm in Paris. Let's meet for green tea & confessional talk about ourselves & poetry. If you can discuss the Holocaust images of Anselm Kiefer, & emblematics in *Jude the Obscure, Invisible Man,* & *Apocalypse Now,* I'll love you forever. Deep physical significance is promised & perhaps film rights if things take off. Bonus points given to neo-Romantics. No numbing *normalcy types* need apply. Write O.O., c/o Adam and Eve Possibilities.

About the Author

Duff Brenna's first novel, *The Book of Mamie*, won the Associated Writing Programs Award for Best Novel in 1988. He is also the recipient of an NEA grant and *Milwaukee Magazine*'s Fiction Award. A onetime Wisconsin dairy farmer, Duff Brenna teaches courses in Shakespeare, the Renaissance, and nineteenth-century Romanticism at California State University in San Marcos. He lives in Poway, California.